PERFECT

BEAUTY

ALSO BY PETER PITZELE

•◆•

Our Fathers' Wells: A Personal Encounter with the Myths of Genesis

Scripture Windows: Towards a Practice of Bibliodrama

PERFECT

BEAUTY

a NOVEL

PETER PITZELE

EPIGRAPH BOOKS

RHINEBECK, NEW YORK

Book design by Colin Rolfe.
Cover art by Susan and Peter Pitzele.
Cover design by Jeffrey Philips, All About Images.

Paperback ISBN: 978-1-948796-04-0
Hardcover ISBN: 978-1-948796-05-7
eBook ISBN: 978-1-948796-06-4

Library of Congress Control Number: 2018936541

Epigraph Books
22 East Market Street, Suite 304
Rhinebeck, NY 12572
(845) 876-4861
EpigraphPS.com

For Sam Klagsbrun, my Dean.

The felon is memory, which takes a face
and slices up what was once very simple.

—Mr.X
Mary Jo Salter

•♦•

At last I am bored with the Louvre Museum.
One gets fed up with boredom very soon.
I am fed up with my boredom.
And from the ruin inside me
I drew this lesson:
To visit
A museum is fine,
To be a museum piece is terrible!

—Giaconda and Si-Ya-U
Nazim Hikmet

•♦•

In my opinion, in the next century so many physical problems will have
been surmounted that a woman's beauty will be a dream that will be
completely obtainable...The future holds a golden world.

—Vogue, 1967
Diane Vreeland

PART I

Claire Alexander closed the front door behind her, felt her unseeing way through the foyer, and sat down at her Queen Anne's desk in the library, resting her forehead on her palm. She was afraid she was going to be sick. Truly, she thought, this is more than a body can bear. She would call Claus for Valium.

The world wavered before her eyes like a mirage, and she had a disorienting series of flashbacks: the savaged Guest House, the white form in the twisted sheet, the gashes to that priceless face. She had no recollection of calling 911, but suddenly an ambulance had appeared, white-jacketed men pushed her aside, then refused to answer her frantic questions. She had one last look at that swathed, motionless form on the metal stretcher, and then she was gone. The dust settled on the driveway, and the roaring in her ears finally ceased. Now what, for God's sake?

With a shaking hand she slid a cigarette from the glass box on the desk, snapped the gold lighter, and drew the smoke down into her lungs as if nicotine were oxygen and she was at the bottom of the sea.

She stared for a long time at the leather secretary on her desk as if it too had the power to betray her. Then, because she had no alternative, she opened it and paged slowly through the alphabet, growing increasingly concerned at how many names called up no face at all. She'd had this address book for years. How many? A decade? And now it seemed to be a book of strangers, of vanished associations, of momentary and lost connections. It might as well belong to another person for all the good it was doing her. Even those "old friends" were absolutely wrong for her present need. Or rather she could feel that they belonged to that social circle that had willingly taken her and her husband at face value and whose intimacy they had neither sought nor needed. It was unimaginable to reveal this present anguish to any of them. Was there no one beside Ruth to whom she could confide?

It was not until she was halfway through the tabbed pages that she sighed in momentary relief. Of course. Why hadn't she thought of him sooner?

She tapped in the numbers on the handset, replaced a fallen strand of hair behind her ear, and exhaled blue smoke. Pick up, damnit, she thought as she heard the call deliver its metallic ring. She began counting and found some small comfort in the steady, unvarying sound. She would let it ring and ring and ring.

She had reached sixteen when a familiar and sleep-slurred voice broke the trance, " Who th' hell's this?"

She gripped the receiver to her ear, "Biron, it's me. I know it's early, but I..."

"Claire? What time is it?"

She looked at the jeweled clock in its crystal case. Ten fifteen. She reported the time.

"You oughta know better than to call me at this hour. 'Sfucking Saturday for Chrissake."

Now that she had him on the line, her wobbling world seemed to right itself, and her urgency waned. "What were you up to last night?" she asked as if the call was merely casual. "You're hung over, aren't you?"

"Till three or four."

"Not 'till,' I asked what were you up *to?*"

"None of your business." Biron Lord rolled over in bed and reached for his cigarettes, "I'm going back to sleep." He put a cigarette between his lips and found some matches.

"Biron, don't you dare." In a flash her anxiety returned. "I need you."

"It's too early for phone sex, Claire." He folded over the matchbook cover, struck a match, inhaled.

"That's crude and unkind. You have no idea what I've been through." Then she stung him with the truth. "Parthia's in an ambulance on the way to Good Samaritan."

He snapped his wrist and the match went out. "What happened?"

"She went fucking berserk, that's what."

"Where are you?"

"I'm about to get dressed. I went out to the Guest House this morning to bring Parthia some breakfast. We had a fight last night, and I prepared a peace offering."

He sat up in bed "Go on."

As she supplied details, his mind, the mind of a photographer, produced an image: Parthia at the door of his studio, turning half away, giving him the profile he had shot a thousand times, the dancer's neck, the rounded chin, the long straight nose, the eyes with those heavy lids that were always distant, always intriguing. It was a face that said Italy and the Levant, that said secrets, ice, lava. Three days ago.

"I thought the place had been vandalized," Claire was saying. "Then I saw Parthia lying on the couch. And her face, my God, I thought someone had taken a razor to it. That face…ruined. I couldn't even tell if she was breathing."

He had watched her breathing as she turned over the prints, one after another. They were going to be spectacular when printed full size. Big folio. Leather bound. Even with her extraordinary skill of self-possession, she had registered surprise, eyes widening, breath caught as she gazed at one picture, then the next. He watched that incredible face with its perfect features as it flinched and blinked, witnessing. "Wait till you see them finished," he had said. "Her face," did Claire say? Genuine alarm seized him for the first time.

"They wouldn't tell me anything, but they looked worried. I was terrified. I still am. I called 911. I told them not to have any kind of siren on. Willi didn't need to know. But what will I tell him? God knows what's going to happen."

He'd tried to warn Parthia. But it was always like this when any of his subjects first saw the stills, laid out as a whole, telling their story, the assembled fragments far more powerful than any single part. It was like waking into a nightmare. This is me? The face no one ever saw, utterly private, alien.

"Are you there, Biron?"

"Yeah, I'm here."

"The ambulance just left. I have no one to talk to. You've got to come be with me when I go to the hospital." He had won her trust. In the end she had wanted to do this. He had tried to warn her about that, too. Claire was going on. "I asked about visiting hours. I can go anytime. They couldn't reassure me that she would live. She may die, Biron. Then what? How do I tell that to Willi? Tell me that, will you?"

He had captured the poses, the shattered mirror, the bandages, the hooded executioner who became the man in the white surgical mask, the scalpel, the stethoscope, the metal gurney with its manacles, that terrible bright light.

"Biron, are you there? Talk to me goddamnit."

"I'm here, Claire." But he wasn't. He was seeing her turning over the last photograph, face down with the others on the table. She had seemed remarkably calm. She was OK, right? She had placed them back in the big manila folder, her hands steady. They smoked a little and had a drink. They had talked about shooting for Revlon the following week. Once again he saw the face the world knew, Parthia Alexander. Her iconic face, smooth as polished stone. Then she was at the door. Then gone.

"So will you come? Will you? Biron!" Claire's hoarse voice yanked him back. "Did you hear what I said? I want you to meet me at the hospital."

Jesus! Who would he get for the Revlon ad? Sasha? Nadine? Fuck all. "You want me to meet you at Good Sam?" He knew he could not say no.

"Yes, I will be there within the hour."

Within the hour. How Claire, he thought. He had to dress, get himself to the Long Island Railroad, then to Babylon. Hours. But it was on the way to Fire Island, and that offered him an unplanned junket to the beach. Why not? He wasn't doing anything in the city. Adin was manning the gallery. Two birds. One stone. "I have to look at a train schedule."

"Well, come as soon as you can."

Biron stubbed out the cigarette and ran a hand through his long hair. On the night table beside the bed sat his little Leica. Criminals slept with guns under their pillows. He had a camera by his bed. He would bring it with him to the hospital. How could he not? "Sure, Claire. I'll be there." Fucking Claire. He was starting to hang up the phone.

"I know what you've been doing with her."

He brought the receiver back to his ear. "And what is that?"

"She couldn't handle that kind of work, Biron. You knew it was risky. You did this, Biron, you pushed her too far. I'm not sure we'll ever get her back."

CHAPTER ONE

The referral had come to the Admissions department at North Forks midday on Friday. Ellen Redy took down the particulars and called Dr. Farmer to inform him of a Monday admission to his unit: A female, Caucasian, 25, mandated for psych evaluation and a treatment plan. Length of stay undetermined. Attempted suicide. Long Island Life. Good policy, but tough reviewers. Alexander comma Parthia. Currently at Good Sam. Would Doctor Farmer please let her know to whom he would be assigning the case?

That same afternoon a second call came in pertinent to this particular admission. This one was fielded by the hospital operator, bounced upstairs to the desk of Dean Venables, co-founder and Medical Director of North Forks. A Mrs. Claire Alexander needed to speak with him and no one but him on a matter of the utmost importance. As a result of that call---the hysterical rant of an entitled woman---Dean had scheduled a meeting in his office for half past four that afternoon.

Dean's office was longer than it was wide, with windows on one side that overlooked the front lawn of the Administration Building. One end of the office was dominated by a desk and its comfortable swivel chair. On the wall behind the desk medical certificates hung beside a large black and white photo of Dean Venables, grinning and windblown, holding hard to the tiller of a sailboat heeling to its gunwale.

At the other end of the office, a leather couch and matching aluminum-framed chairs surrounded a glass-topped coffee table. It was here that Dean convened a meeting with his senior partner, Serge Lucore, with Ben

Farmer, the psychiatrist for the young adult unit, and with Pamela Rivers, his Director of Social Services.

Serge had arrived first, and he and Dean spoke of the construction of a conference center for which ground had been broken. The two men had been in business together for a decade, Dean as Chief Medical Officer "tinkered with the nuts," as Serge liked to put it, while he took care of "the bolts." Their success as partners depended on keeping one another informed and respecting one other's turf. Vigilant about anything that would effect the hospital's reputation or incur liability, Serge came as a matter of course to every admissions conference that was out of the ordinary. When the others arrived, greetings were exchanged and seats taken. Dean came quickly to the point.

"We have an admission scheduled for Monday," he began, a single faxed sheet of paper in front of him on the glass topped table. "Her name is Parthia Alexander, and from what her mother tells me she is a 'pinstriper.'" The coinage--- *a person in need of special treatment*---was Dean's, and it reflected the fact that in ten years North Forks had become a hospital of choice for a special class of people in need of psychiatric care. The buildings and grounds looked far more like a resort than a sanitarium and inhabited forty rolling acres of woods, old orchards, and manicured lawns ninety minutes from New York City on Long Island's North Shore. It possessed an excellent staff, and Dean, as its media-appealing co-founder, had become a natural emblem of the hospital's public reputation and values. In a relatively short period of time North Forks had become a preferred refuge for high paid executives, celebrities, and, as in this case, a very successful New York fashion model who did not need her face in the papers. "And the question is: Who do we assign her to?" Dean looked up. "Ben? She's 25; she'll be on your unit. "

"Evelyn Messenger discharged a patient today. She would be due in the natural rotation for our next admission."

"But this is not a matter for our 'natural rotation,'" said Serge Lucore.

"I think we all know that Evelyn Messenger is not ready for a celebrity admit," Pamela Rivers said.

"Why is that?" Dean asked. "She's been here...what? Five months?"

"Two and a half," Pamela corrected. "She's not half way through her probationary period. Anita should get this one."

"That won't work, Pam," said Dr. Farmer. "Anita has the last two weeks of June off. In fact the summer vacation schedule makes this a little difficult."

"What's the problem with Evelyn Messenger?" Dean asked Pamela. He knew her to be demanding, highly professional, and sometimes a little hard on his recruits. Evelyn Messenger had been one of his.

Pamela took her time to compose her answer. She met with Evelyn weekly for supervision with the eight other social workers on the adult units, and she reviewed her cases as a matter of course. "Evelyn---she prefers to be called 'Vale'--- is still very new to this work, and I think she lacks confidence. Perhaps even commitment."

"Really?" Dean said. "What have you seen that makes you think this?" Then, before Pamela could respond, he went on, "Confidence is a matter of time and experience after all. We are her first job. She had good recommendations from her internship I recall."

"Dean, you pay me because of my judgment, and all I can tell you is that she seems tentative and..." Pamela paused, searching for the right word--- 'uninspired.' She's like someone who... No, never mind. It's just my sense, that's all. I know you are fond of her. I know you are, too, Ben. But I..." Pamela seemed to change her mind and let her sentence hang half-finished.

"What were you going to say, Pam?" Ben Farmer asked.

"She seems a little depressed to me, if you want a term for it. I know she has come to us from having failed at her previous career. I know in the interview she impressed us with her intelligence. She's a bright woman, but I can't escape the concern that being a social worker is a real second choice for her, that she's making the best of it, but that her heart is elsewhere."

"That's a lot to get in two and a half months," Dean said. He was disappointed, for he remembered the interview with Evelyn Messenger, and there had been something about her he had liked enormously.

"Something happened this week," Ben Farmer put in. "She had a patient, Leah Kayin, who needed ECT. Vale, had never seen it before. I was struck at how the procedure seemed to affect her. I think she may be a very good therapist, but I am not sure how ready she really is to deal with the chemical and biological aspects of mental illness. She's pretty green, as Pam says. But..." And here Ben Farmer let his voice trail off.

"But given the vacation schedule and the current status of case assignments, she is the best candidate." Serge Lucore was frowning.

"I'm afraid she is," Farmer said to him.

"Well, I am not saying for a moment that she's incompetent," Pamela put in. "With continuing supervision, I am sure she will develop. It's just that it sounds like we are going to have a very narcissistic young woman on our hands who has tried to kill herself and who is definitely an involuntary admission. In addition she will be on special status which always makes patients angry, and her insurance coverage means whoever has her will have to argue to keep her here."

Dean spoke into the silence. "I spoke to the mother today, and she strikes me as a woman who is used to being in control." Dean turned to Ben Farmer, "It's your call, Ben. What should we do?"

"Let's assign her to Vale," he said. "We'll just do a bit more close supervision than usual."

Everyone cut their eyes briefly to Serge Lucore's face, but nothing could be read in his look, and they took his silence as consent. And so the meeting ended.

Dean, back at his desk, re-opened the manila envelope Mrs. Alexander had sent to his attention by courier that afternoon. It contained a single photograph that he had stared at for some time. He had refrained from sharing it with his colleagues, and he wasn't quite sure why. Messenger would see it in due time.

CHAPTER TWO

All the other passengers had vacated the Fire Island ferry's upper deck that Friday when the June squall broke. Perched on a metal bench in the lee of the wheelhouse, Vale Messenger took a certain pleasure in her solitude, in the surge of wind and wet, the scouring air, the raking gulls. She could use a storm of her own.

As the ferry skirted the breakwater, she saw a bearded angler, slickered and determined, casting his line in the wind. Black pilings rose beside him, and a gull was diving for his bait. Vale drew her Pentax from under her poncho and caught the moment in its bleak chiaroscuro.

The empty deck gleamed with a watery sheen. Raindrops hung from the silver rails in luminous beads. Long Island behind them, the bridges and cause-ways ahead, everything was vapored in mist. The horizon was shrinking to this boat, to this slick deck with its empty steel benches, to her five senses coming keen as the vessel ploughed into the soup. A gust of wind spanked her face with spray.

Suddenly a girl darted up on deck and dashed down the aisle between the empty rows, a flash of yellow rain-gear, black curls flying around a flushed face. Vale's first thought---*My God, she's going to jump!*---brought her to her feet.

"Elizabeth!" A voice cried from below. "Elizabeth!" The voice acquired a body; a woman in a red anorak reached the top of the stairs and was now look-ing Vale's way for the fleeing child. Vale raised her arm, pointing, and saw the girl skid on a wet patch of deck, grasp for something to stay her fall, then hit the deck with one knee. At the same moment mother's head was turning, but

Elizabeth was already rebounding to her feet. "Just for a little while, Mom?" the voice pleaded.

"Elizabeth, you'll get soaked and there's no one here to ..."

"I'll keep an eye on her," Vale called to the mother. Their eyes met. The woman shrugged and ducked back down the stairs. Elizabeth gave Vale a glance, then favoring one leg, walked to the far end of the deck, where she slid down the last row and pressed herself against the rail, peering into the ferry's wake.

Vale sat back down and uncapped the camera lens. She saw how blue benches marched in empty rows all the way back to the small yellow figure at the stern, a comma of color against the arc of a distant causeway whose ends were swallowed in fog.

• ◆ •

By the time the ferry tied up in Ocean Beach the storm had passed. The sidewalks held small puddles that sparkled like little windows of sky. Sunlight glistened on bamboo leaves and winked in the dune grasses in front yards. Summer was coming to Fire Island like a blustery, occupying force. Vale knocked at her sister's front door, and getting no answer walked down the deck to the back gate.

"Yo, No-No!" she called, swinging open the gate, then saw her, pulling window screens from the shed.

Naomi brushed a gray forelock back from her face, wiped her hands on her jeans, and grinned. "Hail, Messenger, what news of the world?"

"*I have not loved the world...*"

"*Nor the world me.*"

They beamed at one another over their familiar greeting, and Vale stepped into Naomi's welcoming arms.

"Come on in," Naomi said when they drew apart, "I've got some coffee ready, and I baked some muffins this morning. This chore can wait."

They settled themselves at the kitchen counter, Naomi pouring two cups of coffee, brought two muffins out from her little electric oven. "Bit wet coming over?

"I had the upper deck to myself. Like a dog with her nose in the wind." Vale slathered butter on her muffin. "There was a little girl up there and me. In the rain."

"You get some pictures? I see you brought your camera."

"I can't remember the last time I took pictures. Last fall. Out here, I suppose."

"The butterflies," Naomi reminded her. "How long can you stay?"

"I have to take a mid-afternoon ferry Sunday. Robert's bringing Meli back at five."

"And how is my curly girlie?"

"Busy as only a ten year old can be. She's reading, writing 'plays' for her beanie babies, and wants to be in a dozen places at once: with me, with her Dad, with you out here, with her friends after school, and she can't wait to get to camp. Starts in a week." Naomi frowned. "I know. I know," Vale said. "We both feel so homesick for this place. This time of year..." she did not finish her sentence.

"But you'll have July all to yourself? Any plans?"

"Baby, I'm a working stiff. No vacation time. No personal days, and sick days are docked from my pay. Until September."

"Ah, that's when your probationary period is up."

"If I survive it." Vale leaned her chin on her palm, suddenly glum.

"But we'll have July Fourth weekend at least," said Naomi.

"Definitely."

Naomi was staring at Vale with a sister's love and an artist's detachment. She had put on some weight, she could see, the face a little fuller, a thickening around the middle. Vale's eyes lacked their usual animation, and tight lines around the mouth suggested a trace of bitterness, as if she were permanently out of sorts. Here and there a strand of gray showed in the thicket of her dark hair. Naomi could see the tension in Vale's hunched shoulders. Middle age was beginning to measure her sister. And care.

"I've missed you, Evie," Naomi said, a name from childhood, used only in her most maternal moments. "Evie," the late blossom from an aging couple, and "Evie" a child as much hers as their mother's. "Evelyn" had been her name through high school and college, "Vale" after the divorce, when she had taken back her maiden name. "I don't know why we don't see each other more often over there." She nodded her head in the direction of Long Island.

"Because you're a hermit."

"I'm a crone; there's a difference."

"Whatever you call it, you won't even leave here when they declare a hurricane evacuation."

"Too true," Naomi laughed. But the fact was that the telephone linked them, and they were at their best on short visits or when Meli brought out all the sunshine in her aunt, whose "No-No" was Meli's "Yes-Yes" in the family naming game.

"Later I want to hear all about North Forks." Vale only sighed, and Naomi came and stood behind Vale, resting her hands on her sister's shoulders. She gently kneaded bunched muscles. Vale rested her forearms on the counter so Naomi could bear down. Touch, she thought; a single woman could go without it for months. Years, she feared.

"It's been a shitty week," Vale said.

"Because...?"

"Well, among other things, one of my patients had ECT."

"Electro Convulsive Therapy?"

"Yeah. Shades of Frankenstein. Actually the procedure is pretty simple, but something about it scared me. Gave me a bad dream." Vale leaned back against Naomi, smelled her sweat and shampoo and a hint of turpentine. "God, I'm glad to be here."

Naomi's hands finished their work and rested again on her sister's shoulders. They had time. " Listen, you go settle in. I've got to wash the screens; the mosquitoes have arrived, and I'm a month late., Rest a bit. Then we'll get some sand between our toes. You can tell me about Frankenstein later."

Vale sighed, rose, took up her overnight bag, and headed for the stairs. The deep quiet of this island refuge, like Naomi's hands, soothed her, but the echoes of her week---voices of patients, medical urgencies, the constant plague of second-guesses, a testy call with Robert and his alarming news, Melanie's inexplicable crankiness--- irritated her inner ear like news from a badly tuned in radio station.

Upstairs in the guest room under the sloping eaves, the bed was dappled with sunshine. Just for a minute, she thought, and kicking off her shoes, she stretched out like a cat. Through the open window she could hear the sputter of the hose, and then Naomi singing softly, "Oh we ain't got a barrel of money..." A breeze stirred the curtains and brought in the smell of the sea and the distant, irregular percussion of the waves.

• ◆ •

The shouts of children coming down the walk from the beach woke her. The bedside clock told her she had been asleep for half an hour. Her gaze scanned

Soap
and 2-Prong
file folder

the familiar room and came to rest on Naomi's self-portrait that hung at the foot of the bed, the weathered crone with the naked scarred chest and the stare: *I have not loved the world, nor the world me.* Vale had been with Naomi through her mastectomy and with her as she deliberately set out to do those self-portraits, her "salvages," as she called them.

Vale got up, changed out of her jeans into shorts and a tank top. She stowed her few things in the armoire, used the bathroom, and found Naomi on the closed-in porch that served her as a studio. She was gazing at a work on her easel. "You napped."

"I did." Vale stared at the black tangle of lines on white paper. She felt she could be looking in a mirror.

"You ready for a walk on the beach?"

"Am I ever!"

"Well, let's hit it then."

Naomi pulled on a faded windbreaker. Vale slung over her shoulders a blue sweatshirt with "Brooklyn" written across its front and followed her big sister out the door.

They walked up the street to the stairs that bridged the dunes. On the top step the sea blazed before them, frothy, frolicking, incandescent, vast. A dizziness came over Vale as that vista of blues smote her heart. She gripped the rail, then sat on a wooden bench. Her gaze traveled to the horizon. "Oh God, I have missed you," she said to the sea, and she could feel a sob--- why, a veritable tantrum---rising in her breast. No, she would not revisit those places, thank you very much, and she shut down something inside her as one might close the lid of a box. She found a piece of tissue in her pocket and blew her nose. Then, her composure back, she turned to Naomi with a sardonic smile on her lips. "When I die, bury me at sea. Take me out in a boat and feed me to the fishes."

"You always say that."

"Yes, I do."

"Anyway I expect you will outlive me."

"Oh stop. Let's walk," and they took off their sandals, placing them underneath the bench, and then, as if the wind itself had blown the years off of them, they pounded down the stairs, and like girls on a dare raced towards the water's edge.

Twenty minutes later they were seated at the end of a breakwater where the sea slapped against the boulders, and gulls veered near. "So, want to tell me about the ECT thing?"

"I guess"

"And the dream?"

The sea gurgled in the crevices between the rocks. By water's edge couples strolled and children romped. A kite held steady above, its dragon's tail lazy in the wind. Vale picked up a seashell from the rocks, fingering it absent-mindedly. Leah. Leah Kayin. She told Naomi the story.

Leah was twenty-three, the late-born and only child of Holocaust survivors. She had dropped out of graduate school and retreated to her childhood bedroom in her parents' apartment. She refused to eat more than a single meal a day. In desperation her parents had brought her to a psychologist who recommended hospitalization. A month ago Leah had been admitted to North Forks.

"From the beginning, she resisted me. Didn't talk in our sessions beyond monosyllables. It was like she was in mourning or on strike."

Dr. Farmer, the unit psychiatrist, had prescribed anti-depressants, but Leah either threw them up or cheeked them. Was this the onset of clinical depression in all its inexplicable, debilitating ferocity? Was her return to her parents a recoil against growing up? The sign of some buried rage? Was her withdrawal from life the first sign of adult schizophrenia? Or was history itself implicated in Leah's condition, some trauma that passed to her from her parents out of their terrible ordeal?

"I didn't know," she confessed to Naomi. "Clueless. I couldn't find out."

With her thirty-day coverage running out, Dr. Farmer had recommended the ECT. Leah was led to the treatment room. They removed her shoes, put her on a rubber mattress, and applied a tourniquet to her right leg just below the knee. "It's to isolate a part of the body, so they can see the response," Vale explained. Then the anesthesiologist inserted a catheter into Leah's arm. A drip was started, and Leah was counted down. The eyes fluttered once under closed lids, and then she was still.

The nurse had fit a breathing bag over Leah's mouth, attached electrodes to the head- band. A dial was turned, a button pressed, and electricity buzzed in the room like a bottled fly. Vale saw the right foot straighten, the heel jut out as if it were hitting the brakes, and the foot vibrate like a soundless tuning fork. Then, a moment and an eternity later, the buzzing stopped with a sharp click. The foot tilted outward to its normal angle of repose.

"That's it. That's all. I know we were trying to help her, but it was de-humanizing, medieval." Vale returned to examining the shell in her hand. "I thought Leah might be better, but when she left, she seemed as listless, as depressed as when she came." Vale paused; Naomi was quiet. "'Treatment averse' is what I wrote in her summary," she said. "It means she didn't respond well to therapy. But was it therapy she didn't respond to or me? Maybe she was just 'Messenger averse.' Shouldn't she have had a more experienced therapist? Someone else might have been able help her. I have to hand in my notes to my supervisor on Monday. I hate to think what she'll say."

Above them the kite caught a sudden downdraft and went spiraling towards the beach, its long tail whipping in circles. "And what was the dream?"

Vale looked out to sea as if her dream might be written on the few white clouds that floated over the water. "I dreamed it was winter, a bleak barren landscape. In the distance there were low sheds, a smokestack with grey smoke rising. I was running away from there, but then I looked back, and far behind me I saw that there was a figure, a girl, caught in the white beam of a searchlight." Vale's eyes searched Naomi's face. "That's all."

"Who was the girl behind you?"

"Leah."

"But if she is in your dream, she is an aspect of you, yes? You were the one running and the one being run from. One figure wishes to escape; the other is caught and wishes...what? What does the one caught in the searchlight want?"

"For the running girl to escape."

"And also?"

"For her to come back." Somewhere inside her Vale felt the pull and push of contraries. "It was a... a camp," Vale said. "That place in the dream." She paused. "Leah's history."

"But we have our own connection to that history, don't we, love? Poppa. "

"Yes," Vale said, "Poppa." Her fingers worried the whorls of the shell in her hand. "I'm in over my head, No-No. This therapy work gets inside you in all kinds of ways you can't predict. I don't know what I'm doing. I miss my teaching life."

"This time of year especially, I'd think."

"Yeah. My hormones or something. I want to be here. I want to read. I want time with Meli. Instead I feel as if I'm captive in the funny farm. I mean at least my patients get to leave." Vale tossed the shell into the water where a gull dove quickly as if for a scrap of food, then sheered off with a derisive caw.

Later in the long shadows of the afternoon, they walked to the market and bought scallops and fresh asparagus for their dinner. They bought a bottle of

Prosecco and put it into the freezer to chill. The sun was tangled in the trees when Naomi rolled a joint, lit it, and passed it to her sister. Vale drew on it and passed it back. Naomi put rice on to boil and some music on the stereo. Van Morrison's gravelly voice filled the little house.

I'll be waiting
I'll be waiting on that shore
To hear the cry for home.
You won't have to worry anymore
When you hear the cry for home.

Vale felt her throat constrict. "I am not sure I'm cut out for this work, Naomi."

"You're boring me, sister. Go set the table," and gave her sister a playful slap on her behind.

Vale set out the plates, napkins, and silver on the little table on the deck, then meandered into the tiny garden to pick some flowers. She arranged them in a vase, late irises and early roses.

With the rice done, Naomi simmered the scallops in butter and garlic and steamed the asparagus. Then she brought their meal to the table. Vale uncorked the bubbly, filled their flutes and paused for a moment. "Courage, my sister," they chimed.

They ate and talked of this and that, a book read, a gallery visited, a movie seen, a movie missed, of the fact that neither woman had a man in her life, and neither professed to miss one, And so it went until the mauve darkness enfolded them, and mosquitoes drove them inside.

Later, the last of the Prosecco in their glasses, and a small fire in the fireplace taking the nighttime chill out of the air, Vale lay on the couch, all but purring as Naomi rubbed her bare feet with oil. Dyed in the wool Grant- Hepburn fans, they were watching the video of *The Philadelphia Story*, periodically reciting lines together, when the phone rang. Naomi lifted Vale's feet and went to answer it. Vale reached for the pause button on the remote.

"Hello." And then a moment later, "Yes, she is."

Vale got up, feeling the cold floor on her bare feet.

"Robert," Naomi mouthed.

"What?" she said into the mouthpiece. "Yes?"

"Vale, it's Robert."

"What's happened?" Why else would he call?

"It's no big deal. Melanie cut her hand ..."

"How?" No, that wasn't what she wanted to know. "How bad?"

"Not bad, I mean she bled some, but we stopped it. She was scared at all the blood, but she's fine now."

"Where are you?"

"We're, umm, we're at the ER. Don't get all alarmed, Vale. She needed a few stitches, that's all. I wouldn't have called, but Meli wanted to talk to you."

"You wouldn't have called? Why in God's name not?"

"We have it handled, that's all. She's with me and Elaine.

"Put her on," Vale said.

A receiver changed hands. "Mommy," a small voice spoke, sounding five rather than ten.

"Yes, sweetie, Mommy's here."

"Mommy, I want you *here*."

"I'll come as soon as I can, sugar. Tell me what happened," but even as Melanie started to talk, Vale could hear Robert's voice in the background, telling his daughter not to ask Mommy to come. Everything would be fine. "Say that again, sugar. What happened at the birthday party?"

Slowly Vale got the story straight. Cutting the cake, a squabble over the knife at a moment when no one was watching, a serrated edge had sliced the meaty part of Melanie's palm, too deep for a bandage to stop the bleeding completely. With a towel pressed hard against the cut, Daddy and Elaine had driven her to the Emergency Room. "It hurts, Mommy." Melanie had never been in a hospital before. The thought of Melanie quarrelling over a knife seemed out of character.

Vale pulled the ferry schedule off the wall, inadvertently ripping it in half. Her hand shook so much she could not put the pieces together. Naomi stepped in to help, then shook her head. "Too late," she whispered.

Vale had missed the last ferry. A water taxi was the only way off the island, and that cost a fortune. She would have to borrow some money from Naomi. She was frantic to be with her baby. But she could hear that Melanie was calmer as she finished her story. "It doesn't really hurt so much, Mommy. They gave me some stiches and some pills."

Vale knew she could never get to the hospital in time. The crossing, the drive, it would be an hour and a half at the least. More likely two. Past midnight.

Too late. "You are being so brave." Doubly so, brave with the cut, brave with the divorce which cut them all at this moment like a randomly slung blade.

"Daddy wants to talk to you."

"Wait, sweetie…" but Melanie was gone.

"She's fine, Vale, really. Don't make a big deal out of it."

"Don't tell me what to do and what not to do."

"You don't have to interrupt your weekend. I know how important it is for you to have time with your sister."

"Spare me your generosity, Robert."

"Really, Vale; Daddy's can be good Mommy's, too, can't they, Meli? Vale, don't take…" but something distracted him, and he did not finish the sentence.

"I can't get there," Vale said, defeated.

"Everything's under control. Melanie is fine. Elaine is here." Vale heard Melanie laugh in the background. "She's doing a finger puppet show for her."

Instantly, jealousy replaced concern. In the end there would be a scar and a story and a link to Robert and Elaine.

She was aware of Naomi standing beside her, felt the comforting hand on her shoulder. She fetched a deep breath. "Let me talk to Melanie again."

She heard her daughter's voice come back on the line, "Mommy, I'll still be able to go to sleep-away camp, won't I?"

"I'm sure you can, honey." Only a week away. "But maybe not Y camp on Monday. We'll have to see." Melanie was silent. "You can call me any time you need to, sugar. I'll be home tomorrow, and I can come get you early if…" She felt Naomi's hand squeeze her shoulder. She emended her words; "Daddy will be bringing you home at five, honey. I'll see you real soon." Vale's heart was rending. The misery of this distance poured in. "You'll be fine, honey," she said again. "Call me before you go to bed, OK?"

"OK, Mommy. I'll talk to you later."

"Or tomorrow," Vale heard Robert's voice coaching.

"Or tomorrow," Melanie said. "Bye, Mom."

Vale hung up the phone and walked back into the living room. The black and white image of a frozen scene jittered on the screen. Naomi shut off the television. Vale sat, her mouth a hard line, her hands gripping one another in her lap.

"Talk," Naomi said.

Vale opened her mouth, but nothing would come. The events of the past week knotted her throat. Naomi sat beside her on the couch.

"Robert has been offered a job," Vale began. "The Frick wants him to be their new Assistant Curator of Painting. That's been in the works for a while. It's a dream job for him. He's going to move. He and Elaine are looking for a place of their own. In the city. Apparently she's got money."

Naomi took this in. Robert Abrams and Vale had been divorced for almost three years. Vale had taken their old apartment, and Robert had found a place within the school district so that he and Vale could hold together some part of Melanie's. Neither had had to make any hard choices. Until now. "And Robert wants Melanie to do what?"

"He wants to take Melanie with him to New York."

"To live?"

"He's not saying that. To help him find a place. You know, to be part of looking around."

"When?"

"This week, before camp. After camp is over, if they haven't found a place by then."

"Sounds enticing."

"But he's talking about opening up the whole custody agreement. He says Melanie is left alone too much, that I can't really mother her and work full time."

"Bullshit."

"Yeah, well, Elaine works from home. He might make the case." Vale could hardly bring herself to look at this possibility.

"What will you do?"

"She's only ten. Living with those two in New York is not a life I want for her." Vale felt a tremor begin in her breast. "I need her, Naomi, and she needs me."

CHAPTER THREE

From under the shaded portico of Good Samaritan Hospital in Babylon, New York, an ambulance slid into the mid-morning sun. The driver flipped on his sunglasses and cranked up the AC. The man next to him popped a cassette into dashboard player. The Highwaymen throbbed into the cab. "Perfect," they said. The man made sure the speakers in the rear were on as well. Give her something to listen to.

"There's a girl in 307 coming down from Thorazine...."

They spared the flashing lights in the village, but once out of town the driver leaned on the siren to startle slow drivers from his path. He suspected the sound startled the arrogant mannequin strapped in the wheelchair behind the front seats.

"...Coming down from Thorazine..." the two men crooned with Johnny Cash.

• ◆ •

That same morning Vale was at her desk, struggling to summarize her case notes on Leah Kayin, but she could not concentrate, her mind looping fragments of Meli's homecoming.

"She was a very brave girl," Robert had said, leaving their daughter at her door the evening before. The hand, neatly bandaged after five stitches, had throbbed a little that evening. There would be no New York trip or Y Camp that week. Vale called Rosy to arrange for her to babysit---an expense she could hardly afford.

Mother and daughter spent Sunday night watching the new video of *The Last Unicorn* and indulging in orange sherbet. By the time she closed her eyes Melanie was cranky with the soreness, the stress, and the lack of sleep from the night before. "I wish you had been there, Mommy" were her daughter's last words to her before she fell asleep. Not exactly the recipe for a sound night sleep for a mother.

The plaintive call of a bird outside her window dialed Vale back to her desk. She felt no interest in the young woman who had left on Friday with a limp handshake and a shrug of her shoulders. The phone at her elbow rang. "Hello," she said, "this is Vale Messenger."

"Ms. Messenger, Ellen Redy here from Admissions. My chart says that you have a patient, Kayin, Leah who was discharged Friday."

"Yes, I was just finishing the case notes."

"Good. You have a new admit on her way. She's a single Caucasian female 25 years of age---name Alexander comma Parthia---that's P-a-r-t-h-i-a---unusual name, don't you think? She was admitted to Good Samaritan Hospital on 18 June for attempted suicide. The mother signed the patient in. Claire---that's with an 'e'---Alexander. Two physicians are mandating residential treatment. ETA here around eleven. Long Island Life is the carrier. She has one hundred and twenty days full, and a year of outpatient twice a week. But they are a tough outfit; you'll have you to document her treatment. I have a fax of the discharge notes. The patient had been started on twenty five milligrams of Tofranil and..."

"Mrs. Redy," Vale broke in, "let me read the record when it arrives. Thank you." She heard the curtness in her voice, but she hated the thumb-nail caricatures from Admissions, the business-like voice that belied the fact that this "new admit" was a person and not a case arriving with its list of broken parts and attempted repairs. She needed a face to go with the data.

Not to be stopped entirely, however, Mrs. Redy managed to remind Vale that someone admitted for an attempted suicide needed immediate and continuing supervision until she could be assessed by the treatment team.

"I know," Vale said.

"Well, then," Vale heard an answering pique coming down the line, "I will expect you in Admissions shortly before eleven." Ellen Redy broke the connection without a good-bye.

Vale finished her notes, took them to the Xerox machine in the Administration Building, made a copy for Medical Records, and slipped another into

Pamela Rivers' mailbox. In her own she found a manila folder with "Attention Vale Messenger" on its cover. She tucked it away in her bag and promptly forgot that it was there.

• ◆ •

Later, waiting for her "new admit" in the lobby of the Admissions Building, Vale distracted herself with an article in Vogue about Mariel Hemingway. Shown bare-breasted in a photo that rather surprised her---more in the Playboy line she would have thought--- Ernest Hemingway's granddaughter was being hailed as a "machine-tooled Venus" because those breasts of hers were plumped to their perfect shape with silicone gel. She was, in the author's words, a "renovated beauty," which made her sound like a New York brownstone. Silly stuff, she thought. Then, reaching into her bag for her compact and lipstick, her hand found the manila folder. She opened the clasp and withdrew a single 10x12 photograph. A note, clipped to the photo, read "your new admit" and was signed "Dean Venables".

A ripple of queasiness ran through her as she studied the photograph. It was a "head-shot," the face revealed in a three-quarter turn to its left, the light striking one side of the face, but leaving the other side in shadow. Heavy-lidded eyes looked out at the viewer, something vulnerable and remote in their expression. The mouth seemed as if it might be about to speak. Wisps of fine gold curls spilled along the brow.

In its stark, intimate style, the photograph immediately reminded her of the work of Robert Mapplethorpe. She had seen his series, "Lady Lisa," at the Castelli Gallery the year before, and she had been stunned at his mixing of classical portraiture and something quite close to pornography. The photograph she held in her hands had the same vivid clarity, the same lurking drama, the same sense of mischief and collusion. And there was something vaguely familiar in that image as if... But the sound of a car door slamming shut brought her to her feet.

She slid the photograph back into its manila envelope, the envelope back into her bag, and watched through the window as two men, white jackets unbuttoned in the summer heat, opened an ambulette's rear doors, positioned a ramp, and trundled out a figure in a wheelchair whose head and shoulders were covered in a maroon shawl; face downcast, hidden.

One of the attendants picked up two alligator-skinned suitcases; the other pushed the chair towards the doors of the Admissions Building. Vale came into the foyer as her patient was borne into the cool pastel interior of the hospital and, for better or worse, into her care.

They assembled in the lobby. The one carrying the suitcases set them down while the other handed Vale a clipboard. She scrawled her signature on the transfer sheet and returned it. "She's all yours," the man said. Then he leaned over the young woman in the wheelchair. "Excuse me, Miss," he said to her. The seated figure might have been carved in stone for all the response it gave. He looked up at Vale for her assistance. "The wheelchair, Doc," the man said to her; "we gotta take it back with us."

"Miss Alexander?" Vale leaned over and spoke to her patient. She caught an antiseptic scent and the odor of dried sweat unsuccessfully masked by perfume. She waited until the head tilted up, and as it did so, light fell onto what had been concealed.

The eyes that met hers in the briefest glance were a Nordic blue; they seemed listless, unseeing. Crudely applied make-up covered dark smudges under them, but could not conceal the welts that ran in parallel lines down the pale cheeks all the way to the jaw. The face clearly resembled the photograph she had been studying, but it was worn, haunted, and seemed much older. "Miss Alexander," Vale said, "could you stand up, please? They need the wheelchair."

Miss Alexander stood, and as she did the shawl slipped from her head to her shoulders. Vale now saw the hair, chopped in odd lengths as if someone had taken a shears to it in the dark. The hair was a dull, dyed, artificial gold---like the hair on the head of a doll---but unlike a doll's hair, it was streaked with blood-red accents.

"Thank you, Miss," the man said, drawing the chair aside. Vale saw his gaze feed on the face, detected, she thought, a slight curl of the lip---scorn or lust? Then both men were turning away. One held open the door while the other wheeled the empty chair through it. They disappeared into the glare of sun.

Alone with her patient, Vale looked again at the strange visage that refused to look at her. *De-faced* was the word that came to Vale's mind: *a defaced face.* Like a mustache painted on the Mona Lisa. She could see it had been, it was still, a beautiful face despite its markings. Were these self-inflicted wounds?

"My name is Vale Messenger," she said, stepping away. "I'll be your thera-pist here." The eyes did not look up. "I'll call the unit," she went on, "they will send a cart and a mental health worker. You and your bags will be taken to Gables. You'll be assigned a room, and the nurse on duty will walk through the schedule and the rules." No flicker of response. "You will have some time to un-pack---to shower if you want to---before lunch at twelve thirty. I will meet you in my office at two; the nurse will tell you where that is." Nothing. "I hope that the time you spend here will make a difference to you." Now a passing glance met her gaze.

Vale went to the wall phone, dialed the proper extension, made her re-quests, and looked at her patient out of the corner of her eye. Under the shawl, this Parthia wore a long-sleeved dress, high-waisted, a paisley print on mid-night blue. A ruffle traced the throat and wrists. On her feet, incongruously, she wore high black leather boots trimmed in yellow thread and laces. Taken all in all---boots, girlish dress with the delicate lace, maroon shawl in a glossy chenille, the waxy face with the gashed lines and the blood-spiked two-color hair---her patient had a *look*, casual and studied, elegant and throw-away, girl-ish and gothic. Punk. Wasn't that what they called it these days?

Presently the cart arrived. But instead of a mental health worker, a man in faded jeans and a sweat-stained work shirt came through the door. "Some idiot forgot to charge the golf cart up at Gables," he said. "They called me to do the fetching. This the patient?" he asked with a short nod to Parthia.

"This is Miss Alexander," Vale said. "Thank you for going out of your way to help."

The man only grunted and turned to look at his charge for the first time. Vale registered the look on his face, the glance that became, in spite of itself, a stare. "You look like Halloween," he said. Vale was shocked. That was no way to speak to a...

"Boo," Parthia said in a voice barely above a whisper.

"Come on," he said, "I've got work to do."

CHAPTER FOUR

Parthia rode beside the man who smelled of sweat and dirt. "What is this place?" she asked.

"North Forks." He did not turn. "You want a look around?"

"Why not?" She lifted her feet to the dashboard and allowed her skirt to slide above her knees.

He turned the cart up the curving driveway. They passed behind a long, two story building in a mock Tudor design. "That's the back of Gables," he told her. "That's where you'll be staying, the young adult unit."

At the top of the driveway the road forked. To her left she saw several two-story buildings painted blue-gray with decks and garden plots. "And those?" she asked. As if she cared.

"Patient residences. They're called 'units' here. Overlook One and Overlook Two."

"What do they overlook?"

"A meadow. A baseball field. An old orchard." He turned right and drove the cart past the side of Gables.

"This place doesn't look like a hospital."

"It used to be a private estate. Belonged to a son of John Ringling North."

"The circus guy?"

"He's the one."

Parthia could see outbuildings in stone with slate gray shingles. Old trees spread immense shade over well-cut lawns. Gardens, hedges, fountains gave the place the feel of a college campus or a European resort.

"You ever been in a hospital before?" the man beside her asked.

"A nut house, you mean? No."

"Well, you could have done worse."

"You an expert?"

"On this place? Yes."

"You a serf?"

Ignoring her slur, he slowed the cart under a row of trees; their shade dappled and cooled her. "Over there," he said, pointing to his left "is a unit called The Glen. It's for kids."

At the foot of the hill, the road forked again. He put his foot on the brake. "Down there," pointing to his left, "is the unit for the old folks. It's called Forest."

"Sounds like Disneyland. Where's the main road?"

"There," he pointed to his left where the driveway curved downhill through a stand of birch trees. "You came here on 25A."

"Which goes where?"

"You really don't know where you are?"

"I was in the back of an ambulance. They didn't give me a map."

"You're on the north shore of Long Island, east of Port Jefferson." They were heading uphill now. "That's Manor House on the right," he was saying, "the dual diagnosis unit."

"Dual diagnosis?" She pictured doctors with foils.

"People who have both an addiction and a psychiatric problem."

"Depressed drunks, for example?" she said.

"That's the dining pavilion on the left. That's the main quadrangle straight ahead," and presently they were crossing it. Cars were parked in appointed spaces. They passed through a broad opening in a stone wall. He stopped the cart again. "Down the road that way," pointing to his left "are the adolescent units, the gym, the tennis courts, and the Educational Center. Over there," he pointed almost straight ahead, "are the maintenance buildings. And up here," he swung the cart to the right and headed up the hill, "is the Admission Building where you arrived. We've basically driven in a circle."

Her driver steered around the side of Gables and onto its broad front lawn. Parthia saw deck chairs and tilted green canvass umbrellas. Beside the arched front door that looked like it should have a turnkey standing at attention rose a round stone tower that gave Gables a faintly medieval look. Her driver pulled the hand brake and dismounted.

"Where is everybody?" she asked.

"At group, in sessions. I don't know."

He lifted her bags from the back of the cart, and they went inside. "Willa," the man said, "special delivery."

"Thanks, Win." A big woman was coming towards them. "Welcome to Gables," the woman said to Parthia. "My name is Willa Maynard. I'm the head nurse on the unit." Parthia heard the screen door slam. The serf was gone. "Your room is on the second floor, number twenty eight. Your roommate's name is Julia Kessler."

"Big fucking deal."

• ◆ •

Back in her office Vale found a message on her answering machine: "It's Arlene Keniston, Mrs. Rivers' secretary. She would like to see you *at your earliest convenience*." Vale heard the italics in the voice and hurried down the hill to the Administration Building.

Where Dr.'s Lucore and Dean Venables were the money and the vision of North Forks, Pamela Rivers, everyone knew, was the guiding hand. The social workers, among whom Vale was the new kid on the block, lived for Pamela's approval and died from her opprobrium. Accused by some of micro-management, she took the fullest responsibility for everything at North Forks: the conduct of mental health workers, the well-being of the nursing staff, the design of programs, the hiring of teachers for the school. She even reviewed the menus for the staff dining room. She possessed an aristocratic dignity and had a career as a social worker at Bellevue before earning a Ph.D. in Social Work at Fordham. She was the iron fist in the velvet glove, and Vale was in awe of her.

Vale took the stairs to the second floor, and approached Arlene's desk. "Mrs. Rivers wants to see me?" She could hear the quaver in her voice.

Arlene picked up the phone, punched in a three-digit extension. "Vale Messenger is here." She gave a nod and hung up. "Go on in," and then in a stage whisper added, "she had her claws filed today." Vale smiled weakly and knocked.

"Sit down, Vale," Pamela said, motioning her to a seat at the round table in the center of her office. Several fine prints hung on her wall, and a vase of cut flowers gave her office a feminine air.

"Let me come right to the point. I got a call from Ellen Redy just after she spoke to you this morning. Apparently she felt cut off when she tried to give you some information about your new admit." Vale started to speak, but Pamela held up her hand. "I am sure there are good reasons for being somewhat brusque with her; she can be officious, and no doubt you were rushed, but the fact of the matter is she is part of a team and has been with us since the beginning."

"I understand," Vale said. "I will make sure I remember that."

"Anyway, that's not the only reason I asked you to come in. Ellen Redy told me a little about this girl Parthia Alexander. I want to make sure you understand hospital policy. Your patient has been placed on SA, Special Awareness. This status is routine for anyone who is here for an attempted suicide, especially a patient who is here against her will. Until you and the clinical team at Gables assess her differently, SA means she is always to be within sight of staff. I don't believe you've had a patient on that status yet, have you?" Vale shook her head. "Well, no one likes it, so be prepared." Vale nodded. "I would particularly like you to keep me up to date. Any questions about treatment feel free to consult with me." Vale nodded again. "Now, how did Leah Kayin leave us?"

"Not much changed that I could tell."

"I have your notes. We can talk about it at our next supervision meeting." This was not a reassuring thought for Vale. "I will see you then," and with that Rivers dismissed her.

With less than an hour before she was to see Parthia Alexander, Vale returned to her office to read her patient's case history. Her office was the thing she liked best about her job. The silo-like building that sat to the right of Gables' front door was called the Tower, and it had a single room at its top where a Princess might gaze through the mullioned windows for her prince to come. Meli would love it.

Because the Tower lacked amenities, like central heating or air conditioning, it was, until proper office space became available, temporarily assigned to whoever was new to the Gables' therapeutic staff. But Vale loved the Tower, and she was sure she would love it in any season. It even came with a stone staircase.

North Forks had furnished her with a desk and two blue upholstered chairs. Between them lay a faux Persian rug. Along the far wall stood her bookcase in which her literary past and her clinical present leaned against one another on two sagging shelves. Atop the bookshelf sat a wooden clock, noisy as a metronome; it had belonged to her poppa, the only thing of his she owned.

On her desk she had two pictures of Melanie in a double frame. In one mother and daughter are dashing shoreward, out-running a wave. In the other, taken after last summer's camp play, Melanie is wearing a green Robin Hood tunic and showing a wide, gap-toothed grin. Also on her desk sat *The Diagnostic and Statistical Manual of Mental Disorders*, Third Edition, already well-thumbed.

Before Vale could turn to the file on her new patient, a door slammed below her window. She got up and looking down, she saw Parthia's blond hair in which the red glints, dull as rust, showed among the platinum highlights. She had changed her clothes and was wearing black jeans and a black tee shirt. On her feet black, silver-buckled sandals. Vale watched as Parthia sauntered onto the grass past Amanda, Jane, and Phyllis, three eating-disorder patients, who kept their own company at a picnic table under the beech tree. Vale saw Ed Paley, one of the mental workers, come out from Gables and stand beside the door, doing his SA duty.

Parthia crossed the lawn without haste or a sideways glance. She was walking towards a small out-building that crouched under the spruce trees at the far end of the upper lawn. This was the "Glass House," so called for it had once been a small greenhouse. Long ago it had been converted to an all-season refuge to which only loners seemed drawn.

As Parthia crossed the lawn, all talk and movement on the greensward stopped. Raymond---one of Vale's patients---gazed at Parthia while the Frisbee Catherine had just sent his way sailed past his ear. Frank Jessup and Earl Andrews, playing cards at the picnic table, froze with their mouths open. Liza-Jane, another of Vale's patients and ever the isolate, stood all but camouflaged in the shade of a tree and followed Parthia's movement with a predatory stillness. The banter of Amanda and her minions died on the air, and Amanda's hand, with a cigarette burning between her fingers, stopped on its way to her lips. All three heads swiveled slowly as Parthia made her casual transit. Where was Julia? Vale wondered; then she caught sight of a solitary dark form through the windowed wall of the Glass House. From her overhead view, Vale could not see Parthia's face, but she was sure beauty and mutilation made a stunning mask, just right to ignite the minds of these fragile souls.

If Parthia was aware of the attention that eddied towards her, she did not acknowledge it. She reached the door of the Glass House, opened it and stood for a moment at the threshold, then disappeared inside. Vale saw Ed Paley stroll down the lawn, doing his best not to appear to be shadowing the new patient, but keeping an eye on her as he was charged to do. Raymond retrieved the Frisbee from the flowerbed. Earl and Frank looked back at the cards in their hands. The girls put their heads together, nodding and pointing.

Vale brought the patient notes to her desk, withdrew the photograph from its envelope, and looked at it again. Then she sat and began to read.

CHAPTER FIVE

Julia, seated alone in the Glass House, did not hear the door open. She was hearing her own voice treading the rhythm she had just set down:

> *When Sycorax stewed her brew of desire,*
> *And Caliban reared his brutish head,*
> *The two of them, rude by a smoky fire,*
> *Smoldered in lust on their terrible bed.*
> *There among the broken things*
> *Ariel was bent to their poisoned wills.*
> *They bound his feet and stripped his wings*
>   *And...*

Something, something, something, "quills". Julia heard the rhyme word in her mind, the end of the line quivered with it, prickled her skin. "Quills," she said aloud

Suddenly she became aware of a presence in the room. She looked up, squinting. "Go on," said the person whose shadow now fell across her page.

"That's...that's all I've written," Julia stammered.

"It's terrible. How about, 'Then Ariel downed too many pills?' Or 'Shot a bunch of porno stills?'" Julia was speechless. "Do you have a light?" the intruder asked. Poison dripped from her tongue.

"What?"

"L-i-g-h-t. For this?" The person drew a pack of cigarettes out of her pocket.

"Uh, no, I don't smoke. There's a lighter…" but the figure at the door had already turned and was striding back into the dazzling sunshine and up the lawn. She left behind the odor of musk and crushed flowers.

Julia saw the ice-wraith walk towards Amanda, saw her reach down without a word and take the burning cigarette from witchy fingers and put its smoldering tip to hers, saw smoke plume into the air, the disdaining return of cigarette to owner. Julia watched the apparition turn on silver-buckled feet and walk to a shaded bench at the edge of the lawn where the Princess of Quills sat, ankles crossed, arms folded, and smoked, oblivious to glances, whispers, stares.

Julia's notebook slid from sweaty hands to the floor. O God, she thought, not my new roommate.

• ◆ •

There was a knock on Vale's door, and Parthia came in before Vale could welcome her. The cold blue eyes gave a dismissive glance at the office, passed over Vale's expectant face, lingered for a moment on the bookshelves, registering titles, then sought the partially open window where she went to stand, her back to Vale.

Vale came out from behind her desk. "Welcome to my office," she said and sat in one of the blue chairs, notebook on her lap.

Parthia remained at the window. She took a cigarette from her dress pocket. "You have a light?" Still she did not turn to face Vale.

"Actually, I'd prefer that you didn't smoke," she said.

"And why is that?"

"Cigarette smoking, gum chewing, they're distractions." It was something they had taught in school.

"*Defense à fumer?*"

"I beg your pardon," though Vale knew what it meant.

"The fuming defense," said the girl.

"Ah, I see," Vale said. "Would you sit down please?"

Parthia did not oblige, holding the unlit cigarette between her fingers. "So you're my shrink?"

"While you're here, yes. I notice from the report that you had been seeing a therapist on the outside, Mark Warren?"

"Not recently; he got poor marks with me."

"Still, he has known you."

"Not in the biblical sense. Not in any sense."

"I see he visited you at Good Samaritan." No response. "I'd like to consult him about you." Nothing. "At some point you will be discharged from here. It will be helpful to you to have someone apprised of your progress. Do you have any problems with my conferring with him?"

"I haven't seen him in more than a year. He's worthless."

"Still, I would like..."

"Do I have a choice?" Parthia turned sharply from the window to give Vale a frigid stare. "Are you asking permission or telling me what you're going to do?"

"I can't do anything without your consent. You're in charge." Vale immediately regretted declaring this half-truth.

"But I can't smoke or chew gum in your office, and I am being hounded by the little people."

"Little people?"

"The nurse people, the mental health people. They never let me out of their sight."

"You're on status. You're considered 'at risk,' and we need to protect you. Didn't Willa Maynard make that clear to you in her orientation?"

"Maynard moos." Vale restrained a smile; Willa, the head nurse on the unit, was a big, corn-fed woman from Nebraska.

"I think you'll come to feel differently about her," Vale said. "Did she explain to you what the levels system is?"

"Yeah. Each week the staff votes on whether you can go up a level or down. Higher the level the more freedom you get." Parthia's voice had become singsong, "Gee whiz, if I get up to level three, I will be able to go home and play with my friends. Do I get stars beside my name?" The cold eyes seem to dare her, "What kind of place are you running here?"

"It's the way things..."

"This is bullshit."

"We need to see how much freedom you can handle."

"You sound like a school teacher. Besides, I won't be here long enough for you to find out anything. And if you want to protect me, protect me from that horror I'm rooming with. The place smells like a pig pen." Vale knew there was some truth in what Parthia said; Julia's self-care could be somewhat primitive.

Parthia glanced at the empty blue chair, then went on, "So what am I being protected from?"

"From yourself."

Parthia turned from the window. "Who writes your script?" She pointed the cigarette at Vale. "Protect yourselves, you mean. What would happen to your reputation if a patient did away with herself while in your care?" No answer came. "Well?"

"You're right, of course," Vale said. "We are legally responsible. But whether you want to be here or not, you are here, and what brought you here is an act which we are bound to take seriously." While she rattled on in this way, she was again registering the face that looked at her. The welts on each cheek ran from under the eyes down almost to the jawbone. They were scabbed, and Parthia had made an attempt to mask them with make-up. In some way the face was made more arresting by these strident lines---totemic, primitive, hinting some rite of sacrifice. Despite its disfigurement, Vale had the oddest sense of déjà vu.

"So do I have any say at all in what happens to me?" Under the anger there was the trace of a whine.

"You have a say up to a point, and the more responsible you are---the more you respond to treatment, take part in it, care about yourself---the more you will be given choices and options." Vale was getting impatient with looking up to the girl. "Please sit down," she said.

Parthia ignored the request, but came around the side of Vale's desk to look at the photograph. "Where did you get this?" she demanded.

"Dean Venables included it in your file."

"Who's Dean Venables? Sounds like a church warden in a Victorian novel."

"He's the Medical Director of the hospital."

"Ah," said Parthia, "Claire."

"Claire?"

"Claire. She will have made sure I get special treatment. She will have made it clear just how precious a cargo has landed on your shore." Sarcasm vinegared Parthia's words. Then, her tone shifting to something like sincere interest, "What do you think?"

"Of this?" Parthia nodded. "I'm no expert, but I assume it's a head shot for work."

"My face is insured for a million dollars. My breasts are half a million apiece. My hands..." and here Parthia held out her hands with their coral nails and cuticles ragged from picking, "another half million. I'm worth a fortune in body parts." Vale felt overmatched by this odd mixture of candor, irony, and information. Parthia went on, "And this status? This surveillance?"

"It will not inconvenience you too much. Let us get a chance to get to know you."

"I hate this shit," Parthia said, and she tilted her head to read the spine of the book on Vale's desk.

Again Vale had the impression of something familiar in the face. "Meaning what?" she asked.

"Meaning this place with its sanitized insanity. Meaning you, Doctor, and this tit-a-tit we are having, this little pap de deux, mamo a mamo."

"You are making it difficult," Vale said, though inwardly she marveled at the wit.

"And why should I trust you?"

Why indeed? "Because you can," Vale said, surprised at her own words.

"And how do *I* know that?"

"Find out. Some part of you is already testing, probing, trying to understand who you've ended up with."

Parthia looked at the empty chair and then sat down. "What kind of a name is Vale?"

"And what kind of a name is Parthia?"

"I asked you first. A 'Vale' of tears? How about v-e-i-l? The veiled Vale. Behind the veil. Can anyone see you?"

"Names can be revealing, or simply names."

"Aren't we pedantic. By any other name, you would still smell..." and here Parthia sniffed the air, "cheap. Tea Rose at $3.99 an ounce. Oh, rosy Vale."

Vale caught her breath. "You have quite a way with words," she managed to say.

"And you do not." Parthia stood up and stepped towards the door.

"We have more time," Vale said, a little desperate now.

"'More time.' And what does that mean? Am I free to go? Or must I stay here for the full half hour? That's how long Willa the Holstein said the sessions last here. A half hour? Time for such a deep exchange, for such lengthy therapeutic explorations."

"It's up to you." Their eyes met; then Parthia looked away. Vale waited, heard the tick and tock of her clock in the room.

"*Valé,*" Parthia said, giving the name a Latin pronunciation. "It means farewell, doesn't it? Vale-diction, Good-Bye-words." She sat back down at the very edge of the chair.

Suddenly Vale wondered if Parthia had left a suicide note, "Good-Bye words". She hadn't seen any reference to it in the report.

"Did you leave a note, when you tried to...?" She let the sentence hang unfinished.

"I didn't try to kill myself."

"From what I read in the report, you..."

"What report?"

Vale pointed to the file on her desk. Parthia rose to look at it. Vale intercepted her, putting her hand on top of it. The two women looked across the short space between them. Close up, Vale saw that Parthia's face was strained with exhaustion and, something else, perhaps fear.

"What does it say? I have a right to know."

"Sit down. I'll summarize it for you."

Parthia sat. Vale picked up the file from her desk, sat back down in her chair, and opened it. "It tells me that you took an overdose of barbiturates and some other pills. It was serious enough to knock you out. It could have killed you." Vale looked up. "You say you did not mean to end your life, but no one knows beforehand how they will react to..." Parthia held up her hand, palm out. Vale stopped.

"Tell me what else it says."

Vale scanned the page. "Your mother found you and..."

"Step-mother, two steps removed, loony éclaire"

Vale made a note. "And your biological mother is...?"

"Closed subject."

"Is she...?"

"I said closed subject."

Vale saw the set of Parthia's jaw. She returned to her notes. "Claire Alexander, your step-mother, found you. According to her you have no record of previous hospitalizations. Mark Warren was called in and was unable to shed any light on why you had done what you had done. There's mention of a family physician, Claus Adenauer, apparently he was called in by your step-mother." Vale tried to read Parthia's face for a sign of response. The face gave nothing away. "It might be helpful if I could speak to him. Would you mind if I did?"

Parthia shrugged.

Vale took that for a Yes, withdrew a consent form from her desk drawer, quickly filled in Adenauer's name, and sent it across the desk for Parthia's signature. The girl scrawled her name. "He doesn't know a thing."

Vale folded the paper. Later she would fax it to the physician. She resumed her account. "The psychiatrist who saw you at Good Sam notes the medications he prescribed. They started you on Tofranil and gave you some Haldol the last day you were there."

"And some for the little trip here," she said. "Disgusting stuff."

Vale went on. "The doctor's notes say you refused to talk about what you had done." Parthia snorted. "There is basic information: your age is 25; you graduated from Sarah Lawrence College with a Bachelors in Theater Arts; you earn your living as a model; you live in Manhattan. When you took the overdose, you were staying in the Guest House of your parents' home in Babylon. The internist at the hospital reports that your health is basically excellent. You have no siblings." Vale looked up. Parthia feigned a yawn.

"There are notes from an interview Dr. Venables had with Mrs. Alexander," Vale continued. "She said you had come home two days earlier. She believes you had just finished a strenuous piece of work. The report says she found you in the Guest House of their home. When she was asked why she thought you tried to…do whatever it is you did, she said she could not imagine the reason." Vale glanced up again at Parthia's face. She detected a faint condescending smile, the barest shake of the head. "She visited you every day while you were at Good Samaritan, went to your apartment in the city and packed your bags when the transfer to North Forks was arranged. There is no mention of your father coming while you were in the hospital." She looked up again. "Is this all accurate, as far as you wish to tell me?"

"I do not like to think of Claire as my step-mother," Parthia said. "It never seemed right that just because your father marries someone, you have to regard that person as related to you. Claire is my father's wife. She is nothing to me."

"But she has been in your life a long time."

"Too long."

"How long exactly?"

"Exactly sixteen years, four months, sixteen days, eight minutes and thirty two seconds too long."

"Parthia, I need your co-operation to learn something about your history. I need your permission to talk to Mark Warren, even though he does not score well with you; I need permission also to speak to your step…to Claire, and also to your father."

Parthia stiffened. "Under no circumstances whatsoever are you to speak to or to contact my father," she said.

"And why is that?"

"Because I say so, and if you want to preserve the pathetic illusion that I have some freedom to make choices while I am here, then you will take this as an absolute."

"And Claire?"

Parthia gave a derisive sniff, "You are welcome to Claire. I'd like to be a fly on the wall."

Vale passed over another release form for Parthia's careless signature. "Would you be willing to meet with Claire and me if and when she comes?"

"No."

Vale sighed and leaned back in her chair. "And Mark Warren?"

"Mark Warren is an ass."

"But he knows something about you?" She slid a form across her desk.

"Claire called him in. Claire meddles; it's her middle name." Parthia signed the form. "She used to be Claire Summers. Does that name mean anything to you?" Vale shook her head. "Well, too bad. She likes people to know who she was."

"Who was she?"

"Oh, she will tell you. You can do *her* history; it's a doozie. Just make sure you have plenty of tissues and more than a thirty minute session. She'd just be getting started."

"And you?" Vale asked, "Can you tell me something about what brought you to your father's house?" Vale needed to get an in-take written. She felt Pamela Rivers looking over her shoulder.

Parthia now eyed Vale, a smile playing about her mouth. Then in the voice of someone reciting a fairy tale she began, "Once upon a time, there was a little girl…"

"No, Parthia, please. I need the facts, just the simple…" but she saw the mouth clamp shut, and instantly she knew she had blundered.

Parthia began again, her voice cold now. "Once upon a time there was a woman who had been locked in a tower and was forced to wear a veil. It hid her deformities. She dreamed someday that a prince would come riding over the hill to take her away. But it was to no *avail*." Parthia's voice sneered. "No prince ever came. She grew old in her tower, old, and, bitter, and lonely." Parthia looked at Vale. "The end," she said and got up.

"Parthia, I..." but Parthia was already through the door, slamming it behind her.

•◆•

"What do you think?"

"She's a bitch."

"You see the way Paley was looking at her?"

"He's got to; he's doing SA on her."

"He's wants to be doing L-A-Y on her."

"Jealous?"

"Fuck you."

"Well are you?"

"I'll tear her eyes out she fucks with me again."

"The look on your face when she waltzed over and took your cigarette."

"She's got some nerve. Who does she think she is anyway?"

"I heard she tried to kill herself."

"Too bad she didn't make it."

"Jealous?"

"Will you lay off that shit!"

"She's rooming with Julia."

"The Beast."

"Makes them Beauty and the Beast."

"You call that beautiful?"

"Yeah, I'd have to say so. She must be a model or something."

"What about that hair?"

"What about those scratches?"

"Her tits are too big."

"Her ass is, too."

"Well, we like thin remember."

"Very thin."

"Still, how could you have any problems if you looked like that?"

"Yeah, I know what you mean. I'd die for a face like that."

CHAPTER SIX

"Parthia says she does not want to come to session." Willa Maynard was calling from the nurse's station after lunch on Friday. "She says she's called her lawyer, and he's told her not to comply with anything. I think she's bluffing, for what it's worth. What do you want us to do?"

"Is she still going to groups?"

"Yes, but sits still and says absolutely nothing. Of course, the boys are transfixed and the girls fit to be tied."

"Where is she?"

"In her room."

"I'll be right down," Vale said.

A few moments later she was climbing the stairs to the second floor of Gables. Jean Newcombe was sitting status by the partially opened door of the room that Julia and Parthia shared. Vale knocked lightly. When there was no answer, she called out Parthia's name; when there was no reply, she pushed the door open.

Parthia was seated cross-legged on the bed under the window, headphones over her ears, deaf to all intrusions. Vale stepped into the girl's line of sight. Blue eyes took her in for an indifferent moment, then closed to the trance of whatever throbbed between her ears. On the bed beside her lay several cassette cases, one with a picture of children dancing in flames with the title *Hell's Lovesongs*. Vale picked the case up, waited a moment, then carried it across the room, where, sitting down on the chair in front of Julia's desk and ignoring as best she could the disarray and the odor---acne medication, dirty socks, and the antiseptic pine from the bathroom cleanser--- she drew out the cover notes.

Before she had read a word, Parthia snapped, "What are you doing here?"

Vale closed the little booklet. "It's our time to have a session."

"Go fuck yourself. I want my privacy."

"You give up a few things when you come to a place like this."

"I don't belong here. I'm here against my will."

"You feel trapped."

"Duhh, yeah. Claire has engineered this. She's punishing me."

"Why would Claire punish you?"

"Because I wouldn't play along."

"With...?"

"With her little homecoming scene. I don't want to talk about it." Parthia lifted the headphones to her ears. Vale waited, then turned her eyes back to booklet of lyrics in her hand. A moment later Parthia's voice interrupted her again. "Maynard says that if I don't show some cooperation, I can be transferred. She mentioned someplace, Pilgrims Progress or something. She made it sound horrible. Can they do that?"

"Pilgrim State," Vale corrected. "I haven't had to deal with a situation like this, Parthia, but I think legally they can. This is an 'open' hospital as you know. Pilgrim State is not. If you can't co-operate in your treatment, then your insurance company will cease to pay for re-imbursement."

"This isn't treatment; it's coercion."

"Or put it another way. The choice is yours how you use your time here."

"So what am I supposed to do? You can't force me into therapy. You can't force me to take medications."

"No we can't."

"So?"

"So. Here we are."

"It's unendurable," Parthia said, but there was no heat in her voice.

"You sound tired."

"Can I talk to you, but not have it written down somewhere? Like just between us?"

"*Mamo a mamo?*" Vale offered. Parthia stiffened. "No, that was brilliant," Vale said.

"You weren't offended?"

"Actually I was sorry I cut you off when you started your fairy tale. I'd give a lot to be able to turn back the clock. I'm sorry."

"So, is there such a thing as 'off the record'"?

"You're afraid something you tell me will be used against you." It was not a question.

"I don't want to give anyone any reason to keep me here."

"I can't make that promise. I am part of a ..." Vale stopped herself. "OK," she said, "just between us."

"I don't believe you."

"Parthia," Vale said, "something difficult and frightening has happened to you. I don't know whether you tried to take your life or simply took too many pills. I don't know whether Claire has designs on you or whether she is trying to help. But for the moment you are here and you have a choice."

"And every choice has its consequences," she said as if reading a lesson.

"Yes, that's true. And we never know beforehand what they will be."

"Whatever." Parthia said and pulled the headphones back over her ears. "Maybe tomorrow." Tomorrow was Saturday. Their next contact would be Monday afternoon. Vale sat for a while, wondering what to do, as her patient nodded to the inaudible beat of her music. She glanced briefly at one set of lyrics---*Les Enfants de l'Enfer*---then rose and placed the case and cover notes on Parthia's bed. She left, returning her patient to Jean, who kept watch at the door.

CHAPTER SEVEN

That night a summer storm broke.

In its wild current, Julia lay awake, terror pinning her arms at her sides. The red numerals on the bedside clock said one forty. Click flick. One forty one. Click flick. One forty two. Lightning made the room dance. Thunder made the room throb.

It seemed to Julia as if the storm's source and subject was the tormented soul on the bed across the room, as if the snicking lightning sought the sleep-gripped maiden like a viper's tongue, as if the thunder boomed to accompany invisible detonations within her. Between fusillades Julia listened to the sound of labored breathing, ragged rasps, the animal pant of desperation. The figure across the room thrashed, as if in trying to break free of an invisible grip, but did not, could not, wake.

Dragging the weight of her panic, Julia sat up. Another stab of lightning, and the room flashed into eye-stunning neon. In the dazzled after-dim the sleeping form across from her raised a hand, pawed the air, as if to ward off a blow. The head shook back and forth as if trying to evade a smothering hand.

Julia got out of bed on pale fish feet. Wake her, she thought, but it frightened her to touch that perfect skin, to risk the sting of those electric eyes. She crossed the floor. Parthia now seemed in the grips of a seizure, head rocking back and forth, lips flattened against her teeth in a kind of snarl.

Julia reached over and put the barest hand on Parthia's shoulder, half expecting raw voltage to run up her arm. She heard the rapid gasps, saw eyes squeezed closed as if blinded by a light. Julia pressed down on the shoulder, shook Parthia gently. Nothing. She was about to remove her hand when suddenly a claw gripped her arm. The white face with wide, unseeing eyes rose from the pillow, and Parthia's mouth opened as if in a cry, but no sound came, yet a soundless shriek reverberated inside Julia's skull. Julia recoiled, but could not escape the grip of the hand on her arm, the nails that dug into her flesh. In the wavy mirror of her mind, Julia saw the perfect reflection of her own terror: she is twelve years old, and he is in the room with her, gripping her by the wrist. Her heart is pounding like mad. Her breath swells in her lungs. Lightning rakes across the window pane and lights up the face before her. Thunder breaks as if it is in the room with them. In the room. In the room. Boom Boom Doom. Julia's gathered breath unleashes a scream.

• ◆ •

Vale awoke. Fragments of a vanishing dream teased her. The setting was some old University town, spires, cobbled streets, and she is hastening somewhere, wearing a black gown, her hand holding a black cap to her head. She has a lecture to give, but cannot find her way to her classroom among the maze of streets with their close-built houses. All the doors are of different colors.

Where was she? England. There was more, but for the moment out of reach. Vale did what Naomi had taught her to do, counted her breaths while recall gently lifted another scene.

Yes, she had arrived at the lecture hall. But she was there to hear a lecture not to deliver one. An important lecture. But the immense cathedral-like door of the lecture hall was closing. Booming shut. Too late. She is too late. The sound of the closing door reverberates in the hall, as if many huge doors are closing. She feels frustrated and ashamed at once. In the suddenly silent corridor she presses her ear against the keyhole. A great man is saying something. All she can hear is a single syllable: "pire." *Empire?* Another great door slams somewhere, and now she is jolted fully awake to the sound of thunder. And the sound of the rain. A summer storm.

Gathering her wits, she remembered that the windows were open. She closed the one by her bed and went and looked in on Melanie, who was fast asleep. Like her father she could sleep through anything. Vale reached across her and pulled the window down. Rain had dampened the sill. She saw the half-packed duffle bag that lay on the floor by the closet. The two of them had been up late, she ironing labels into clothes, Melanie pulling out one thing and then another to pack, jabbering about her last year camp friends and the play. The bandage was off her hand and the stitches had come out. She had a scabby scar. It would fade, Vale reassured her.

Finally they had curled up with *Alice In Wonderland*. Not five sentences down the rabbit hole Meli's eyes had closed. Vale had slipped the sheet over her and then sat beside her, the familiar, tender wonder coming over her as she watched her daughter sleep.

Vale was heading back to bed when the phone rang. "Hello," she said, sure it was a wrong number.

"Is this Dr. A?" It was a man's voice, a plushy, unfamiliar baritone.

She was not sure she heard the name correctly. "Who?"

"Dr. A."

"No," she said, "you have the wrong number."

"Is this..." and the voice at the other end of the line read out the numbers of her exchange.

"Yes," she said, "you have the right number, but there is no Dr. A here."

"But I must speak to him. This is important."

"Well, I can't help you. Please check the number again."

"I have lost my face," the voice said.

"You've what?"

"I've lost my face. I need Dr. A." Losing face... a pun?

"Good-bye," she said, setting down the receiver. She got back into bed and stared at the ceiling. She replayed the curious phone call. Finally her mind shrugged and she slept.

CHAPTER EIGHT

Saturday morning, and the last minute mayhem of getting Melanie break-fasted, her stuffed animals crammed into her duffle bag, her bee-sting kit and the medical forms packaged separately, and all of it stowed in the trunk of her car. Robert would be arriving by ten, and together they were going to drive to the debarkation point in Manhattan. From there a bus would transport the kids to Camp Brightwater in Vermont.

Somewhat guiltily Vale found she was looking forward to this spell of solitude when she could read the paper in the morning and go into the city at night after work: Shakespeare in the Park, concerts under the stars, the Fourth of July weekend on Fire Island with Naomi. She'd have her hair done, maybe get it cut for the summer. Do a little shopping. Maybe there'd be a man somewhere.

Melanie did non-stop babble as they drove into the city. In her voice Vale could hear the mixture of excitement and anxiety. At the rendezvous she was all squeals as she met up with last year's best friend, Pia Moreno. Once re-united, they were instantly inseparable.

Vale listened as a counselor, wearing a green Brightwater tee shirt, read out campers' names. Bags were tagged and loaded into the bellies of the buses. "All aboard!"

Melanie broke away from Pia and ran to her parents, throwing an arm around each of their necks as they stooped to embrace her. "Now, listen, Mom and Dad," she said, "you have to come to the play. Promise you'll come." The first camp session always climaxed in a play.

"Yes," Vale said, "we'll be there if you get the part."

"*If,* question mark, exclamation point." Meli had recently discovered the power of punctuation.

"*When,*" Vale said.

"You better," Melanie said. "And Mom, please send me a surprise box, like you did last summer. Please." Then wringing their necks in the crooks of each arm, she kissed their cheeks and whirled off.

They returned to Vale's car, and she made their way out of the city. The ride was silent for a time, the unspoken between them like a third person. Sometimes it was Meli, sometimes Elaine, sometimes it was the past itself, twelve years, four thousand days and nights.

Then Robert shifted in his seat to look at Vale. "We need to talk, Vale," he said.

"So talk." Her hands clenched the wheel, and she stared straight ahead.

"Elaine and I are going forward with our plans. We found a place." She refused to ask a question. "It's in Brooklyn Heights. Near the river. You can see the Bridge from the rooftop garden."

Vale kept her face a mask of automotive concentration; traffic was heavy as the city folks headed East to the beaches.

"There's a room for Meli. With her own bath."

Vale knew there was nothing mean in Robert. His comment about the room and the bath was not meant to remind Vale of her small two bedroom apartment with its shared bathroom. Nor did he wish, she knew, to wound her heart with the suggestion that he was now in a position to provide for their daughter in ways that would increase her comfort and her culture. Brooklyn was close to the heart of a world both Vale and Robert loved and to which he had now ascended, while she, far from the center of things, watched a girl receive electro-convulsive therapy and dealt with young men and women with whom she had so little patience.

"And I have reserved a place for her at Brooklyn Friends School." Vale was so shocked at this that her old Pinto veered out of its lane and brought a sharp honk from a passing Mercedes. "Reserved, Vale, that's all. We have to have a long talk about Meli's future and this next phase of our lives as a family."

"You know I have legal custody, and you have visitation and weekend rights. I am not giving her up."

"Evelyn, I...we ..." and he stopped at the impasse between them.

57

For this silence Vale was grateful. At this moment she was having a hard time breathing. Some part of her knew that life in Brooklyn would lift her daughter beyond Long Island, and their tacky suburban town, its neighborhood on the edge of a slum. Public school failed to challenge her; it burdened her with ugly bus rides, vulgar kids, and overcrowded classes in which the dysfunctions of broken homes played out in constant fights. Vale knew she could not provide for her daughter as Robert could, even with her alimony. But that truth was a tiny island in a sea of need and love, attachment and joy. A grief like bereavement seized her at the prospect of living without her daughter.

Vale turned on the radio, a Mozart piano concerto with its airy arabesques mocked her heavy heart.

At last she pulled up at the curb in front of her house where Robert had left his car that morning. He opened the door and got out, standing for a moment bearing his own distress. Then, turning, he said, "I guess we'll see you in Vermont."

"We?"

"Yes, of course, Elaine will certainly go."

"Does Meli know you are bringing her?"

"She asked her to come."

"Did she now?" Vale got out of her car and slammed the door, hard. She faced him over the hood.

"Nothing has changed, you know, Evelyn. I am still prepared to go to court."

"You think the courts are going to award her to you and Elaine?"

"Evelyn, Melanie spent five days this week with Rosy while you worked. I know they have a great time together, but she could have been with Elaine and me. Meli needs a family. I don't want her to be a latch-key kid." Robert opened the door of his car and got in.

"You and Elaine are not her family," she said to his back.

He started the car and rolled down his window. "Evelyn, don't..." but she was turning away and climbed the steps to her front porch. His voice carried to her, "I'll fight you on this, Evelyn. Besides, she wants to live with us." And then he was gone.

She entered the apartment to see the remains of her daughter's departure everywhere: a pair of jeans and the two tee shirts she needed to return to Marshalls, the teddy bear too threadbare to travel, the stickers that did not make the cut, the bed a-tousel, the drawers agape, the cup of cocoa half drunk on the bureau, the smell of shampoo and bubblegum, the pictures of elephants pasted to the refrigerator, her house key with its sequinned clasp hanging by the door, the box of Rice Crispies on the table, the wet towel on the toilet seat: all these things seemed to call out her daughter's name and grieve her disappearance, and for a moment Vale was seized by a dread so fierce that it was all she could do to grope her way to the phone and call Naomi.

CHAPTER NINE

When Vale came in to work on Monday morning, she found a message on her machine.

"Yes, hello, this is Claire Alexander. I am Parthia's step-mother. No doubt you know that. Could I have the courtesy of a phone call please? I know you are her therapist. Here is my number."

Vale dialed the number.

"Hello?" A mannered voice lengthened the final vowel

"Yes, hello, my name is Vale Messenger. I am..."

"Thank God!"

"I beg your pardon."

"I thought you would never call. You have no idea how worried I am. How is Parthia? Why will she not return my calls? I am at my wit's end." Vale thought she heard the snapping of a lighter and then a long indrawn breath.

"Parthia has signed a release..."

"You are releasing her? I'm so glad. Her father..."

"No, you misunderstand; she signed a form saying that I could talk to you."

"How is it that she needs to sign a form so that you can talk to the one person in the world who knows her? Aside from her father, that is."

"I was hoping to..."

"Doctor, you have no idea what a bundle of nerves I am, an absolute jangle."

"Mrs. Alexander, I was wondering if I might see you in my office here at North Forks."

"Absolutely, darling, nothing is more important than my daughter. Just say when."

"Is later today possible for you?"

"No. I am having my nails done, and then there's an Arts Council cocktail party Sag Harbor... It's been on the calendar for months. I can't."

"Tomorrow?"

"I would have to rearrange some things. I have a fitting at Bonwitts. There's an opening in the evening."

"Then when might be convenient for you, Mrs. Alexander?"

"Call me Claire, please, doctor."

"I am not a..."

"Wednesday would work. Yes. Late morning. Say eleven?"

"I will see you then."

"I can't tell you how relieved I am."

"I'm sure you are," Vale said. "Do you know where we are?"

"I'll find it. Have no fear."

•◆•

"What was your weekend like?" Vale asked Parthia that Monday afternoon.

"In-fucking-terminable." She had brought an emery board and nail polish to her session and was doing her nails. "I watched television until my eyes crossed. The boys are assholes. The girls are immature bitches. The unit's like a badly run summer camp. A drama group not fit for high school. Tennis with spastics. Boring. Art workshop. Boring. Old movies on the VCR on Saturday night. Boring. As for Julia, she is a total disaster, a fucking creep show. She woke me up on Friday night screaming. Standing right beside my bed. She said she was trying to wake me from a bad dream. Excuse me. Who wouldn't have nightmares locked up in this nut house?"

Vale had heard about that part of Parthia's weekend in morning report. "Were you having a bad dream?"

"I don't remember." Parthia concentrated on her nails.

"What color is that?" Vale asked after a long silence.

"Incarnadine," Parthia read off the label. "Just a red."

"Yes and no," Vale said. "Incarnadine comes from the Latin word for flesh, same word in 'carnivore'. It is the red of blood: red meat."

"I'm so impressed, Miss Schoolmarm. So what?"

"You've changed the color of your nails. Last week it was coral if I recall."

"You a shrink or a beautician?" She began her left hand. "It's a color Biron liked."

"Byron?"

"Just a friend."

"Tell me about him."

"No." Parthia deliberately overloaded the little brush with polish, then held it above the white napkin on the desk until a single heavy drop fell and was absorbed into a fuzzy pea-sized dot on the cotton.

"What kind of music were you listening to last week?"

"I listen to it all the time, not just last week." During the long silence Parthia finished her last nail.

"Is it punk?"

"Names don't matter. My nails are dry." And before she could stop her, Parthia got up and left.

When Vale regained her equilibrium, she picked up the phone and dialed Rebecca Waters, the drama therapist at North Forks. She got her on the second ring.

"Rebecca, this is Vale Messenger; I'm a new social..."

"Yes, I know who you are. You're Parthia's therapist. She was in drama group this weekend."

"What was she like?"

"Powerful. We did improvs. She clearly had some training."

"Yes, BA in Theater Arts. Then modeling."

"What's with the face?"

"I don't know. She hasn't let me in that far."

"Yeah. She's a cold one. What can I do for you?"

"You know anything about the music these kids are listening to? Did you ever hear of a song called *Les Enfants de l'Enfer*?"

"Yeah, sure. That's the lead song on an album called *Hells Lovesongs*, by a group that's at the top of the charts around here, *Primal Rage*. The first track is *Les Enfants de l'Enfer*. I bet you can't get through it. Frightful stuff, but it seems to match the feelings they have inside and can't express. Cleans out their heads."

Vale was making some notes. "I'll give it a try. Thanks, Rebecca."

"Any time."

Vale found herself gazing at the white tissue with its tell-tale mark: *incarnadine*, and then, without any effort on her part, she remembered her Oxford dream, the slamming door, the half-heard word "...pire." And she knew now what had eluded her. The lecturer behind the door was Walter Pater, the mandarin Oxford don, who had written about art and literature at the end of the 19th century. She knew that the half-heard word had not been *empire* but *vampire*. And she knew the source.

That afternoon on the way home from work she bought *Hell's Lovesongs,* and that night found Pater's book *The Renaissance* on her shelves at home. While making dinner she listened as long as she could to the wails and the electronic shriek. Nails on a blackboard. She shut off the music. Rebecca was right; if hell had a soundtrack this was it, and if this was what the kids were using to clean out their brains, it made steel wool look like cotton. She read the lyrics of *Les Enfants de l'Enfer.*

> *Vous etes les enfants de l'enfer*
> *Dance in the flames*
> *Burn up your names*
> *Fire in the eyes, blood red hair*
> *Les enfants de l'enfer beware*
> *Their tricky ways, their wicked games.*

Later she pored through Pater and found the paragraph she was looking for. It was one of the most famous passages of nineteenth century prose. Pater was writing about the Mona Lisa:

> She is older than the rocks among which she sits; like the vampire she has been dead many times, and learned the secrets of the grave; and has been a diver in deep seas and keeps their fallen day about her; and trafficked for strange webs with Eastern merchants; and, as Leda, was the mother of Helen of Troy, and, as Saint Ann, the mother of Mary; and all this has been to her but as the sounds of

lyres and flutes, and lives only in the delicacy with which
it has moulded her changing lineaments, and tinged the
eyelids and the hands.

Vale stared into space, recalling her first impressions of Parthia, the
red spikes in the hair, the scored cheeks, the hint of some rite the girl had
suffered. She would not have been surprised to see teeth marks on her long
pale neck.

CHAPTER TEN

Tuesday morning Parthia again failed to come for her session. Vale called the unit and spoke to Willa. "She said she was sick to her stomach. Jean Newcombe heard her vomiting after breakfast."

"Purging?" Vale asked.

"It's a possibility. Something is upsetting her. She won't talk about it. Maybe she's bulimic; many models are."

At three she had her monthly supervision conference with Pamela Rivers, and after they were done with the depressing task of dissecting Vale's work with Leah---- "My sense is that you might have pushed a bit harder" was Rivers' conclusion---she asked her about Parthia, her failure to come to her latest session, and where Vale stood with putting together a history.

"Make sure there are consequences if she does not come to sessions," Rivers said. "Do you have trouble with that?"

"I...I don't think so. What kinds of consequences?"

"It is more in your manner than actions. We don't punish patients. But you may withhold yourself from her. Don't pursue her too much. Believe that she actually needs help, but she must come to know that for herself, and to seek help from you, from all of us." Vale listened as if to wisdom itself.

"One of the hardest things about this business is walking the fine line between taking a patient to your heart and detachment. There must be some kind of bond between therapist and patient, and yet there must be distance. You are not here to be liked, but perhaps in the end to be loved. You represent the reality principle."

Back in her office she reviewed Parthia's file as a preparation for her talk with Dr. Mark Warren. She hoped he could give her some perspective on Parthia as one clinician to the other.

"What diagnosis have you made?" he began abruptly after she introduced herself.

"What was your assessment?" she asked, buying time, but little anticipating his mind-numbing analysis of the differential diagnoses of personality disorders, the variations among primary and associated features, cyclothymic versus dysthymnic depressive patterns, atypical bi-polar symptoms, and the clinically demanding task of teasing out the factitious from the real. "In the end," he said, "I decided she was 301.20. Now that may surprise you, but after careful consideration that was my judgment."

Warren was referring to the number codes in the Diagnostic and Statistical Manual of Mental Disorders, Third Edition, known as DSM Three. The book was the procrustean bed on which every patient was laid and measured.

Vale opened her desk-copy and found his reference: Schizoid Personality Disorder.

"What made you think that was the right diagnosis for her?" Vale asked.

"Well, as you know I am sure, the key characteristic in 301:20 has to do with the incapacity to form social relationships. In all the time I treated her, off and on for two years, I never heard Parthia Alexander talk about anyone in her life, no friends, no lovers."

"What did she..."

"She's a classic loner," he continued, "and you can't have missed her coldness, the arrogance, and she often seemed ahedonic to me."

"But usually the Schizoid type has problems expressing anger. I've already seen some of her aggressiveness, both verbal in a clever, intellectualized way, and more directly in her feelings about her step-mother."

"Yes, Claire. When Parthia wasn't talking about her work, she was talking about her relationship wit her step-mother. Very ambivalent."

"Can you tell me more?"

"Actually not."

"Are you currently treating Claire Alexander?"

"Mrs. Messenger, you surprise me. I would have thought you understood the nature of professional confidentiality. One never asks a physician about his patients."

"I'm sorry. It's just that I can't get a handle on Parthia. She won't give me an inch."

"301.20," he said. "I rest my case."

"Did you ever learn anything about her biological mother?"

"No, nothing. Only that she died of a heart condition when Parthia was seven or eight. I always sensed that her entanglement with Claire was a kind of defense against other feelings, but she never showed me what those feelings might be. She often skipped appointments, and when she came, she took charge of the session or terminated them prematurely."

"And her father?"

"About him I can tell you nothing, and this is not from a sense of professional ethics. She rarely spoke of him, and it is not my style to probe. He had cared for her as a child, doted on her. I know this reliably and in terms of her current arrangement. I believe in..."

"What current arrangement are you referring to?"

"Her trust fund, the co-op her father bought her in So-Ho. He has taken very good care of her."

"I see. I'm sorry, I interrupted you."

"Yes, I was saying, I believe, in the gradual evolution of the therapeutic relationship. I am a psychoanalyst, after all. But given her spasmodic treatment pattern, I was never able to analyze the transference."

"Did you have reason to believe that she was or had ever been bulimic or anorectic?"

"Oh, everyone in that profession has their issues with food and weight. But in a pathological sense? No. I had thought for a while that she might be 310.83---" Vale quickly turned the pages: Borderline Personality Disorder--- "but frankly I didn't see the impulsiveness or the dependency/self-assertion dynamic that is usually the key transferential feature of the diagnosis. Parthia never formed an attachment to me, and that seemed to me to be a decisive element. And remember, borderlines tend to run through relationships with a certain desperateness."

"How did she look to you when you saw her in the hospital?"

"She was unwilling to see me."

"Really? Somehow I had the impression that you spent some time with her."

"No. I looked at her chart. They were starting her on a tricyclic, and frankly that made no sense to me since they take forever to metabolize, and she was clearly going to be transferred."

"Was her attempted suicide a surprise to you?"

"As you know suicidal ideation is part of the depressive phase of the Schizoid Personality type. I was surprised, yes, since Parthia never had the histrionic quality one associates with the hysteric. It seemed more a gesture than a true attempt."

"Any thoughts on why?"

"Clearly something triggered it. Never in the time I worked with her had I seen her disturbed enough to consider taking her life. Perhaps that was due to the steadying effect our therapy had on her. She was, in her own way---and this again is true to type---very fastidious about her health and dress. Modeling was a perfect career choice for her. I think Claire was right about that." There was a pause. "What is your diagnosis of your patient, Mrs. Messenger?"

"I really am not sure yet," she said.

"Is she co-operative?"

Vale looked back on her sessions with her patient. "Not yet," she said, "but I have hopes."

"Well, a therapist should always have hopes for his client. But personality disorders, I need hardly tell you, are rarely susceptible to change." A silence followed. "Is there anything else?" he asked. "I have a patient to see."

"No," she said. "I was just wondering whether I should keep you updated on her treatment here. Parthia may need you when she leaves." It was not a comforting thought.

"I hardly think that's necessary," he said. "Parthia terminated with me. It has been at least a year since I last saw her with any regularity"

"And when was this exactly?" she asked.

"Let me see." There was the sound of riffled pages. "That missed appointment was scheduled for the 28th of May. I spoke to her on the phone on the seventh of June." Again there was a silence.

"Thank you, Doctor Warren." And they made perfunctory good-byes. Vale added Warren's comment to her case notes. She could really grow to hate this work.

Later, having successfully tracked down a number for Dr. Claus Adenauer, she placed a call.

She introduced herself and asked whether Dr. Adenauer had received the release form she had faxed him. Yes, he had. And could he supply her with any information about her patient, Parthia Alexander? No, the voice said, noticeably accented, he could not. Vale waited, hoping the doctor might wish to fill the silence, but he outlasted her. "Nothing at all?" she asked in the end. He was not the young woman's physician, he told her. A friend of the family.

Vale thanked him for his time. "You are welcome, I am sure," and the conversation, if such it might be described, ended without even the faintest light having been cast on her patient and her history. A dead end.

⬩◆⬩

Before dinner on Tuesday afternoon, Willa Maynard sent Ed Paley to take his turn sitting SA on the Alexander girl. "Make it clear that she will not get dinner unless she has it in the dining room," Willa said.

"Anything doing?" Ed asked Jean Newcombe, his young colleague, who, with a book on her lap, was seated on a folding chair in the hall outside Julia and Parthia's room.

"No, she's sitting by the window, listening to her Discman."

"Talking?"

"Not to me. Parthia's been on her bed all afternoon. Julia's in the Glass House. Every now and then she gives me a dirty look. I hate doing SA; it feels so intrusive."

"I heard she was throwing up this morning."

Jean nodded. "She's been all right since then, though. We brought her lunch."

"Willa wants her to go to the dining room for dinner."

"Good luck." Jean looked at her watch, "That's fifteen minutes." She leaned into the doorway and passed the information on to Parthia, who gave no indication that she heard. "Parthia? Did you get that?" Jean asked again, loud enough to cut through the headphones. A monosyllable was all the assurance she got. "She's all yours," Jean said and left Ed her chair.

Parthia kept her back turned three quarters away from the door, nodding to the music, apparently oblivious to him. She was not oblivious. And she was hungry. Five minutes later, she pulled off the headphones and went to the bathroom. She came out humming to herself and went to her closet. Didn't give Paley the time of day. Invisible as far as she was concerned. But she felt the flicker of his glance. Ed Paley with his button down white shirt, his creased chinos, his freshly shaved face. Where did they find these preppies? Her bored pulse quickened. Playtime.

"Is it very warm this evening?" A touch of Blanche DuBois in *Streetcar*.

"No," he replied, "not particularly, but it will cool off later."

"Is that right?" She could hardly resist a slight southern drawl. "Why, then I just might need something with sleeves."

She reached into the closet as she spoke and pulled out the lavender silk shirt with mother of pearl buttons. She held it up in front of her and then turned towards him. "What do you think?" For a moment she looked directly into his eyes. "It's called planting the hook," said Biron, who had taught her everything she knew about the camera's eye. God, what would Biron make of this nuthouse?

"That works, I guess," he said.

She hung the shirt on the knob of a bureau drawer, freeing her hands. Swiftly she pulled her black tee shirt over her head, pivoting away from Paley's eyes at the same time. It was a practiced gesture. She'd done a sequence for Jordache fifty times before Biron got what he wanted. "Innocent and coy," he kept saying as he moved around her with the camera, the shirt coming up over her head, the head half turned, the eyes darting to see if she was seen. "Innocent and coy. You're like a young teenage girl who is getting ready to show off a new outfit for your Daddy." It worked, but then Biron always knew what worked.

And she knew to a millimeter what Paley's eyes could see and what he would have to imagine, a glimpse of her breasts in a pale blue bra before she turned her back. If she could hold his eyes, she could school his mind.

She knew how the thin blue bra strap showed against her bare back. She folded the tee shirt and pulled open the second drawer of her dresser. She leaned forward slightly to place the shirt inside the drawer, measuring her angles. Count one, count two, count three, and reach for the fastener in the center of the bra strap. And four, the bra came down. Rest. Pause as if enjoying the air on your naked skin. Now fold the bra, slowly. Reach out to the lavender shirt on the door knob. Are you looking Eddy? How can you not? The line between them was tight as a noose. No hurry. Her head clear. She was her old self.

She slipped the right arm into the sleeve of the shirt and settled it over her shoulder. She reached her left hand back to find the empty sleeve; she let it paw the air as if in helplessness. Not finding what it looked for, the back-reaching arm naturally turned her torso so that the side of her breast swung into his line of sight. Her hand groped again. Wouldn't you like to help, Eddy? He would not dare. She reached back again, the arm crooked like a swimmer's. Again the glimpse offered. Now her left hand found the sleeve's hollow and disappeared.

She turned towards him, but kept her eyes down as if preoccupied with her own thoughts. Before she drew the sides of the shirt closed, she let him see, clearly, the shadow between her breasts down to her navel. Do you know how hard that is to do, Eddy Paley, that teasey, tempting timing? Still her eyes did not look for his. She made some little movement as if settling her body in the clothes. Her nipples, brushed by silk, stiffened. It was all she could do not to run her palms over them. But she was all business. Head down, beyond reproach, she deftly, demurely fastened up the buttons. She turned away, undid her belt, let her pants slip to her hips---you like the color of my underwear, Eddy?--- then with a free hand she smoothed the shirttails down under her pants. Back still turned, she cinched her belt, reached for her perfume, applied a drop of scent to the nape of her neck, to the hollow of her throat and, like a girl looking for approval, turned, raised her eyes to his: "Shall we?" she said.

CHAPTER ELEVEN

On Wednesday morning, Vale stood waiting in the lobby of the Administration Building for Claire ("Nothing-is-more-important-than-my-daughter") Alexander to arrive. She was already twenty minutes late.

Finally a car drew up, and a liveried chauffeur stepped with alacrity to the passenger door and handed out a striking blond in a tailored suit of cream-colored linen. Sunlight sparkled the diamonds at her ears, flashed off the ring on her finger. Stylish fifties, Vale guessed, stepping outside to meet her. Ten years younger in the right light.

"You must be Dr. Messenger," Claire said, extending a manicured hand. "I'm sorry we are late. Arthur went right instead of left when we came off the Expressway. Why I don't know. Can we get out of this blazing sun?"

Vale led Claire up the stone steps to the Gables' lawn. "I have an appointment with a patient in thirty minutes," she said over her shoulder, "I had hoped we would have more time."

"I can always come back," Claire said, "now that Arthur knows the way." They climbed the stairs to the Tower.

"How very quaint," Claire said on her way up, "I half expect to see Olivier behind the door. You know, Heathcliff." At the entrance to her office, Claire paused. "What you could do with this room, darling," she said, "it's made for a little Spanish mahogany and some sconces."

Vale sat behind the desk, leaving Claire her choice of the blue chairs. Claire went to look out the window. "My goodness, this place is a country club. I had no idea. How idyllic. And those," she said, pointing a finger, "those are patients?

They look so...normal." Then she swung around. "How is Parthia? Tell me. I haven't had a word from her since...since she was admitted here." To Vale's surprise, tears started in Claire Alexander's well mascaraed eyes. Her hand darted into the beaded clutch she carried and withdrew a linen handkerchief. Deftly she dabbed her eyes. "It was shocking, her trying to take her life like that. And there, and then. My God. I've had no one to talk to since it happened. I mean there's Ruth, but no one who..."

"Ruth?"

"Ruth Adenauer, my closest friend, but no one who can understand the way a psychoanalyst can understand. I used to see someone, but I haven't in a while. Perhaps I should start up again. I just don't know." Claire turned from the window. "May I smoke?" she asked withdrawing a gold cigarette case from her bag, opening it with one hand, and putting a cigarette to her lips. Without waiting for a reply she lit it from a gold lighter.

Vale brushed aside the cloud of smoke that drifted towards her. "I am not a psychoanalyst," Vale said, "I'm a..."

"Do you have an ashtray, darling?" Vale pointed to the saucer in the bookshelf. "Yes, that will do," Claire said, waiting.

Vale rose and fetched it, and Claire sat down in a blue chair, the saucer on the table beside it. "These past few weeks have been hell. I have been trying to get someone to repair the damage she did. It's in shambles. She trashed the place."

"What place is that?"

"The Guest House, of course."

"What had she done to it?"

"Didn't she tell you?" Vale shook her head. "Well, at first I thought it had been attacked by vandals. To be honest, when I saw her lying across the bed that way--- the walls smeared in red--- it was nail polish we found out later, but at first I thought it was blood--- and the pillows gashed open---good goose-down pillows from Bloomingdales, mind you---a hundred and ninety dollars apiece---and that's without the satin covers---which were specially ordered---there were feathers everywhere---my God, Dr. Messenger, it looked like the scene of a violent crime--- I thought Parthia had been murdered."

Questions flooded Vale's mind. "I'm not..."

"Then I saw the pills on the floor by the bed, and I knew the violence was hers."

"Mrs. Alexander..."

"Such violence. Where did it come from? Why? Has she told you anything about it? God, it's good to be talking to someone. I am sure you can help me."

"You must have talked to her father, your husband?"

"To Wilhelm? You must be out of your mind. Why would I tell him something that would so completely upset him at a time like this?"

"At a time like this?"

"Surely Parthia has told you."

"Told me what?"

"You mean you don't know about her father? What have you been doing here? It seems like the girl's been here forever. You must know about her father and why she must be released as soon as possible."

"Mrs. Alexander, I..."

"Please call me Claire. I will call you Dale. We are allies. We must work together." Claire turned the ash from her cigarettes onto the saucer. "I could use a drink," she said. "Did I just call you Dale? I 'm sorry. It's Vale, isn't it?" Vale nodded. "Is that short for something? I am at sixes and sevens. I've never been to a mental hospital before, and this so different than what I had imagined, so sunny and lovely. I could use a place like this. My God, could I ever. I almost envy Parthia."

"Mrs. Alexander...Claire...I am...we don't have much time. I..."

"I have time, darling. Nothing is more important than this."

"No," Vale said, "I have a patient coming..."

"That's right you mentioned that. Well, perhaps they could re-schedule. I mean they're here all the time. No? Well, then, where would you like to begin?"

"I'd just like to reconstruct things. You found Parthia in the Guest House?"

"The man who came in last week estimated repairs and new furniture would cost about ten thousand dollars. She'd actually stabbed lines in the walls with a knife from the kitchen. We need to re-plaster, paint---the upholstery needs complete repair---I'm not even sure we can find the pattern. We will have to redo everything. Wine stains on the rugs. Of course, it's not the money---it's been more than fifteen years since we decorated the old carriage house----that's what it used to be---I mean, of course, we can afford it--- that's not the point--- probably could do with a make-over, though why we'd do it now I don't know. We'll never..." Claire stopped herself.

"Never?"

"Nothing."

"You said that your husband did not know about Parthia's suicide attempt."

"Do you really think she meant to take her life? That's the question I've been dying to ask. I mean they took it very seriously at Good Sam, pumping her stomach and all, they kept such a close watch on her. But really isn't it possible that...you know she was exhausted. I am sure she was very upset. I mean she and her father are so close." Claire jabbed her cigarette into the saucer, extinguishing it.

Vale looked at the clock in some desperation.

"Claire, why did you not tell your husband about Parthia's attempt, about this hospitalization?"

"He has quite enough on his mind right now without worrying about her. What mind he has left." Claire's tone was shifting; it was like a cloud darkening the sun.

"And what is he worrying about?"

"About dying, of course." Claire looked at Vale. "You really don't know do you? Somehow I assumed the whole world knew. And no one does. Ruth knows, Claus knows, of course, Parthia knows, I know, Biron knows, the servants know, and you."

Vale flagged a name heard for a second time: Byron. "Your husband is dying?"

"My husband is dying, dying awfully and dying fast. Which is why Parthia must get out of here. He needs to see her; it was why I asked her to come home."

"Parthia's father is dying, and you summoned her home."

"I didn't need to 'summon her'. What an odd word. No, she came, she came as soon as she could."

"What is your husband dying of?"

"Do you have to be so clinical? This is my husband we're talking about here. Seventeen years of marriage. He saved my life, and now there is absolutely nothing I can do for him. Nothing." Again the handkerchief was in her hand, dabbing at the eyes. "My husband has cancer, Dr. Messenger, cancer of the pancreas. Do you know anything about pancreatic cancer?" Claire withdrew another cigarette, lit it, and filled her lungs; the words that followed were all but written on the air in smoke. "Pancreatic cancer is fast, and it is lethal, and it is very painful." Vale made a quick note on the pad in front of her, one word: "Time?"

"We went to Europe for the last two weeks in April. We spent three days in Florence, three days in London; the weekend in Paris and the last five days in Spain. He was sick on the plane coming home. Wilhelm has the stomach of a soldier. When he came back to the seat---we always fly first class---he was pale, and I was suddenly very alarmed. I looked at him, really looked at him. His eyes---those beautiful blue eyes---the whites of his eyes seemed a little green. It was a shocking sight."

"It must have been," Vale said.

"Have you ever lost anyone you loved, Dale?" She said nothing. "I see," Claire said, "you are not here to take *me* into *your* confidences." She stood and went to the window, turning away from Vale.

"I am here for Parthia. You and I both are."

Claire turned. "Yes, of course, for Parthia. Everything is for Parthia." The words plumed on the exhale. "But this is the problem. There has been entirely too much *for* Parthia, and not enough expected *from* her, not enough coming back. You would think that she would come home and give her father her company. A few days. Of course, she is busy, a hard working young woman---though if the truth be told, she wouldn't be where she is if I hadn't taken a hand, hadn't introduced her around. Who called Biron? Me. Who arranged for classes for her? Me. All in a day's work. I don't suppose you are a mother, but the things a woman will do for her daughter. And she isn't even my daughter, of course. But I love her as if she were. I love that girl to death. And she? Grateful? Is she appreciative? I don't ask for that. I don't. I'd do it all again. In a heartbeat. But he...he's her father. He deserves more. And she walks into the house looking like she just came from a masquerade, and the next morning I go to find her out in the Guest House, and she's got these scratches on her face. And I asked her what she was doing, taking all the attention for herself when it's her father that needs it. We had a fight. Then she sulks and refuses to see him. The next morning I go out again to find her---he is asking for her--- and the place looks like a tornado had gone through it. And she's lying there, her face a mess, and I can't wake her up. I can't wake her up. My God, I thought she was dead. Imagine that. Can you? Can you? It was as if she had plunged a dagger in my heart." Claire's hand trembled as she took a last drag on her cigarette. "But it was just self-indulgence, acting out you call it, these pills she took. I mean, my God, Dr. Messenger, what's a woman to do? I've got a husband on my hands who is in pain, who is dying, and a child on my hands, a spoiled little child, who comes home and turns me into a nervous wreck. What am I to do?"

And whether it was theatrics or grief, or a mixture of both, Claire Alexander's shoulders shook, and she made no attempt to staunch her tears. Mascara ran down her cheeks in inky lines.

•◆•

"You see that limousine drive up here today?"

"Yeah, Parthia's mother or something."

"Really. Can you believe it? Money as well as looks."

"But no brains."

"Maybe brains. Who knows, she never opens her mouth."

"I saw the woman come out of Messenger's office just after noon."

"Yeah? What'd you see?"

"She looked pretty shaky."

"I wish my mother would come up here."

"Not me, keep that bitch out of here. Curcio keeps trying to set up family meetings for me. No thanks."

"Looked like a movie star."

"Just a rich bitch, probably had a thousand face lifts."

"Would you ever have one?"

"I had a nose job when I was thirteen."

"No kidding?"

"No kidding."

"Lemme see."

"No way you can tell."

"Did it hurt?"

"No, you're out, and then you wake up, and your face has a bandage over it, and you get to take some drugs. You just stay out of circulation for a while."

"Everybody's doing it."

"I'd like to have smaller tits."

"Bigger tits, smaller tits, they can do anything now."

"Expensive though."

"Big time."

"What are the limits? I mean, what can they do? How much can they change you?"

"I don't know."

"Still you have to have something to start with."

"Fuck you."

"I was only kidding."

"Look, here she comes."

"Look at Paley."

"I told you he has his eye on her."

"What a stuck up bitch she is."

"On three let's turn our backs. One, two, three."

CHAPTER TWELVE

Friday Morning.

The phone rang while Vale was standing in front of her closet debating whether to wear red or blue to work that day. Her mind was only partially on her wardrobe. She was going to Fire Island for the July 4th weekend, and what she wanted to do this minute was pack her bag and head for the ferry. "Hello," she said with the phone crooked to her neck as she pawed through her hangers.

"You have a collect call from Strawberry Finn," an operator said. "Will you accept the charges?"

It only took Vale a moment for the question in her mind---*Who?*--- to dissolve into a smile. "Of course," she said and waited the half beat while the operator cleared the line.

"Mommmeeee!" Melanie's voice was like a bird call at the window sill, a head-turning, heart-lifting surprise.

"Melanie," Vale squealed.

"Mom, listen, I got in the play!"

"You did?"

"We are doing The Adventures of Tomasina Sawyer, and I get to play Tomasina's best friend Strawberry Finn."

"Good girl. Is it a big part?"

"I have one song, one dance, and one scene where Tomasina and I...but I don't want to tell you. You'll see it. It's in two weeks."

"Of course, I will."

"Daddy and Elaine are coming on Friday and staying over."

Vale felt her stomach roll over. Melanie had called her father first. It rolled again at the thought that he and Elaine were free to make a weekend of it together. "That's nice," Vale said, keeping cheer in her voice. Then, "Who's playing Tomasina?"

And Melanie babbled on about Pia Moreno, who lived in Brooklyn and whose Daddy illustrated children's stories. "And he's divorced, Mom, just like you." Vale could imagine the whispered schemes in the bunkhouse after dark. And how was the food? And did she pass her swimming test?

And after these answers, Meli went on the offensive, telling Vale how bad the mosquitoes were; how the little kids were a pain in the neck; how there was this drama counselor named Alexis, who was the most beautiful girl they had ever seen with long blond hair and "you know, Mom, a really good figure and all the guy counselors are in love with her;" and on and on until Vale felt the tug of time and found a way to ease away from her daughter's happy babble.

"Honey, I've got to get to work but before I go I've got a fashion question. Red or blue?" she asked. "Should I wear red or blue today?"

"Oh blue," said Melanie immediately, "it's a blue day."

"Beautifully?"

"Terrifically. Sensationally."

"Scrumptiously. Enough, pumpkin. Gotta run."

"Bye, Mommy."

"Kiss."

"Kiss. Kiss."

"Kiss."

Driving to work she saw hardly anything, the memory-movie was running in her mind: Meli, her honey pot, her pumpkin pie, her red-pepper-hot-cakes-cuddle girl. The nick names, the laughter, the hugs. The adverb game. The feel of the body in her lap when she read her a story; the sight of Meli on her little trampoline, hair flying, Meli asleep, Meli in the kitchen making waffles, Meli leaning over a book her lips moving as she read her homework to herself. Meli, her melody.

Which brought her to the entrance of North Forks Hospital, where she was met by spectral figures lining the driveway, the sneering Parthia; Julia, hollow-eyed; Raymond with his addiction; and Liza-Jane in her smoldering remoteness, her great losses all unmourned. There was Rivers, vigilant as a gatekeeper; Venables, the genial figurehead; and the whole supporting cast. She felt like a waif in need of adoption. She felt like a drone reporting to the factory where mismatched parts were sorted, where human puzzles were assembled or discarded.

She was late to the Unit meeting and stayed afterwards to read the nursing notes about her patients. Once again there had been a great deal of agitation in the sleep patterns of both Parthia and Julia. So little during the day, so much at night. When, she wondered, would some of those night demons make their appearance in her sessions?

Just at that moment Julia came to the nurse's station and asked Vale if she might speak to her. Vale read the signs of her agitation. "Sure," she said. "Let's go sit outside."

"Maybe the Glass House?" Julia suggested.

Once seated there, Vale asked if anything had interfered with Julia's plans to have lunch with her grandmother on Saturday. "That's still on, isn't it?" In the past Myrna Kessler, Julia's hypochondriacal and unreliable grandmother, had often promised Julia a date only to call at the last minute with some change of plans, some sudden attack of emphysema or a migraine. Julia dangled precariously at the end of Myrna's caprice; she had fallen often; it always hurt.

"No, Myrna's plans are pretty much set, I guess," Julia said, her voice flat. "I'm not feeling safe, Ms. Messenger. I wonder if you could increase my meds for the weekend. I'm pretty agitated, and I'm having a hard time sleeping."

"Are you feeling panicky right now?" Vale asked, to which Julia nodded her head, sweat beading on her upper lip, her breathing shallow and rapid. They had developed strategies over the past seven weeks to meet these squalls of anxiety, and Vale walked Julia through a breathing exercise. "Now," Vale said when Julia seemed more composed, "what did you want to talk to me about?"

"Did you ever see a painting called 'The Scream'? At least I think that's its name. There's a figure on a bridge with its hands on either side of its head. You can't tell whether it's a male or female, kind of a head like a skull..."

"I know the painting. It's very powerful." Vale reached over and took her clammy, trembling hand. "Breathe, Julia, breathe."

"And the mouth is open, and you can't tell whether the figure is screaming or the world is screaming and the figure is trying to cover its ears..."

"Yes, I know. Breathe."

Julia inhaled and exhaled with a hissing sound like someone breathing through a straw. After several breaths her hand steadied, then she spoke again, "This may not be my place. I mean it's probably none of my business, but you know Parthia is..."

"Is this about Parthia's nightmares?"

"So you know about them?" Julia seemed relieved.

"It's in the reports."

"It's pretty much every night, Ms. Messenger. It's like she's possessed or something. I feel I am living with someone who is, yes, silently screaming all night long." Julia withdrew her hand from under her therapist's hand; Vale resisted the urge to wipe her own hand against her skirt. "Ms. Messenger, I want to change roommates. Can you arrange that?" Julia's agitation resumed.

Vale knew it had been hard for Julia---ever the accommodator---to ask for this. Leah had been a trial; now Parthia even more so. Not that Julia was anyone's first choice. Room-mating in North Forks was hardly collegiate. Vale was particularly struck by the words, "It's like she's possessed." Julia had sometimes seemed that way as well.

But this was not the time nor place to explore this image or the sources of Julia's agitation. There was no time in her day to arrange an appointment, and she was not going to delay her holiday weekend. "See how it goes this weekend, Julia. You have the day with Myrna on Saturday, and I'll leave an order for Valium and an increase in sleeping meds. It's supposed to be a beautiful weekend. We'll evaluate everything on Monday. OK?"

"All right, Ms. Messenger."

She closed the door of the Glass House behind her. Parthia wasn't dangerous, just very unpleasant.

•◆•

Vale moved briskly through her day, saw patients, wrote her end of the week report, and finished the June summary notes on Liza-Jane and Raymond. One last appointment, Parthia, then the pre-weekend staff meeting, and finally she would be free.

Parthia came in snarling. "This SA status shit is driving me crazy. You've got to get me off it; I've got no privacy. That Paley guy. Christ I can't even get dressed without being watched."

"I can't take you off status unless I feel you are engaged in therapy in some way. So far all you are doing is holding me off at arm's length. Your group therapists say the same thing."

"Why should I let you or them in?" Parthia once again refused to begin their session sitting down, but walked to the window and stood beside it looking out.

"You don't have to let me in. All I am saying is that until you are engaged in therapy in some way, I can't take you off status." Vale was seated in her usual place, the blue chair farthest from the window.

"So what do you need?"

"For starters, I need to know why you tried to take your own life."

"What did Claire say?"

Vale debated. "Parthia, Claire is irrelevant at this moment."

Parthia snorted. "You got that right." Then she turned and looked at Vale. "I can tell you I did not intend to kill myself. If I had wanted to, I would have taken what I needed."

"So you calculated that?"

Parthia came and sat on the edge of the blue chair opposite Vale. "I wasn't thinking too clearly. I had pills, a bunch of them, diet pills, pills to get me started in the morning; pills to slow me down at night. All of us are a bunch of pill heads. I took some. But I didn't take anything that could have killed me. I just wanted to knock myself out for a while."

"The ER doctor isn't so sure. You were lucky Claire came in when she did."

Parthia didn't say anything for a moment; her hands in her lap were restless; she began to pick at the cuticle of her thumbnail.

"And the vandalism? Claire says the place looked pretty torn up."

Parthia was silent, her gaze on her hands. "I'd had a very hard spring," she began. "I'd..." and she stopped. "This is very difficult," she said, then looked up, staring hard at Messenger. "I don't want you to tell Claire anything I say here."

"I most certainly will not." The face before her was intent, eyes searching hers.

Parthia looked down. The picking finger had raised a tiny edge of skin. "I did some free-lance work as a model. Almost everybody does. A way to make some extra money."

"Did you need extra money?"

"Well, to be honest, no. I have enough money. I needed to feel... I needed to feel I was more than just a pretty face. Oh God, there's so much you don't know."

"We have time."

"But I want to get out of this nut house."

"There is no shortcut, Parthia." Vale said gently. She saw the eyes search her face again. "One step at a time," she said; "one thing leads to another."

"Can I be a little vague for now, please?"

"You can be vague for now," Vale said. "You wanted to be more than a pretty face. What did you want to be?"

"I wanted to be…" Parthia stopped. "I don't know, exactly. I was tired of being a face for Revlon, a neck for Cartier, tits for Ce Soir." Vale nodded, remembering Mariel Hemingway's public breasts. "A photographer I knew proposed that I do a series of pictures of myself, for myself, pictures that were not dictated by an ad man but by my own… my own…" Parthia let the sentence go unfinished. "I felt like I was…" her eyes fell. "He made me feel I was an artist." She looked up as if fearing scorn.

Vale nodded. "Would this be Byron?"

Parthia nodded. "It's his alias; I don't now his real name. He spells it with an 'i' by the way. The pictures were not pornographic, but they were not pictures you'd see in Cosmo either." Vale waited. "This," and here Parthia gestured to her hair, "I did this for those pictures."

"And your face? The scratches on your face? Were they for the pictures, too?"

"Uh. Yes and no. I mean for the pictures I did with Biron, we painted the lines on my face. But afterwards, at my father's, I guess I scratched myself."

"Why?"

Parthia went on as if she had not heard the question. "Just before Claire called me about my father, I had seen the contact sheets of the series. They told a story. It was…" The cuticle was now bleeding a little and Parthia put her finger in her mouth. "I need a smoke. Will you let me smoke here?"

"I don't have any matches."

"I have some," said Parthia, and she drew a book of matches out of her pocket.

"Parthia, you are putting me in an untenable position. You know that patients are not allowed to carry matches. If I have to play the rule enforcer with you, I'm afraid I'll lose my chance to connect with you in another way." She looked at the unreadable face before her. "Do you understand what I am trying to say?"

Parthia hardened for a moment, then mutely held the book of matches out to Vale. "Did you ever smoke?" she asked.

"No."

"It's a bad habit, I know, but I'm hooked. I'm not sure I can handle these sessions without a crutch."

Vale weighed the words. "OK," she said, "I'll keep matches for you. You can smoke during our sessions. Use this saucer as an ashtray, please." Vale took it from the bookshelf and set it on the table by Parthia's chair.

"Thank you," and taking the offered light, she got up and stood by the window, blowing the smoke out. Calmed by the cigarette, she was quiet there for some time.

"What are you thinking about?" Vale asked.

"I like this room."

"And why is that?" Vale asked.

"It's not like an office."

"I like it, too," Vale said. "You were telling me about the series of pictures."

Parthia sat down again. "I saw the pictures, and what I saw upset me. I was surprised. Then Biron left town. I wanted to talk to him about them. I didn't want anyone to see them. I was afraid…I was afraid he might blackmail me. I was afraid somehow that Claire would see them. I suppose I was kind of paranoid. I was disturbed by them, like I didn't recognize myself in them at all. But I did. It was very strange, like I was dividing in half or something, or that I had another self I'd never seen or shown. I guess I was ashamed of them." Parthia's color changed as she talked, blushing and pale by turns; the finger nail was picking again at the bloody cuticle. Vale handed her a Kleenex. She put down her cigarette and took it, and looking suddenly like a guilty little girl, wrapped her thumb in it. "I came home to my father's house feeling…in pieces, I guess."

"And you knew he was very ill, that he was dying?" She kept her voice as kind and mild as she could. This was not to be an inquisition.

"I couldn't face him. I couldn't face him looking the way I did."

"So you took these pills. Why?"

"I wanted to make myself sick, so I wouldn't have to deal with him. I wasn't thinking very clearly. I didn't know how else to get out of being there. I couldn't say no to Claire, and I couldn't say yes either." She stubbed out the cigarette. "And also, I didn't want to deal with the fact that he might be dying. It all felt like too much. I was trying to escape. And then I had a fight with Claire."

"A fight?"

"Yes, the night I came home, she ranted at me. Told me I looked like a freak, that my father would be disgusted. After all he had done to me, for me, 'his beautiful girl. His 'princess'. She kept repeating that, 'his beautiful girl.' After Claire left me, I just lost it. I didn't try to kill myself, really, but I did some very crazy shit. I admit it. I don't remember a lot of it. I was high and boozed. I got a knife from the kitchenette. Then nail polish. Then..." she stopped.

"Your face?"

"I honestly don't remember that part. I felt so cold, so numb." Parthia was sweating now. "I felt...anaesthetized."

Parthia got up suddenly and went back to the window. "I gotta get out of here," she said. "I can't breathe here. Will you let me get off status?" The voice trembled.

"I will talk with staff at our four o'clock meeting. We can perhaps ease restrictions a little. Hourly check-in's with a definite plan of where you will be if anyone wants to find you." Parthia scowled. "It may not be what you want, but these things proceed in slow stages."

"I hate being treated as a child," Parthia said, yanking open the door, slamming it behind her.

The hell with her, Vale thought. I'm going to Naomi's for the Fourth of July.

CHAPTER THIRTEEN

Sitting on the front steps of the Administration Building that Saturday morning, Julia watches cars arrive and depart, watches the false gaiety of meetings, the "Looking good!" that resounds over the gleaming hoods of well-polished sedans, the sibling high-fives, the squeals from younger sisters calling to their older brothers who slouch down the paths with low slung army surplus pants and weird hair styles, trying to pretend North Forks is summer camp. They give Mom an obligatory peck, shake Dad's hand, rumple their sisters' hair and say, "Wassup?"

Wives, coiffed and scented, wait for their de-toxified hubbies who, shaven and shame-faced, emerge from their units for a kiss, a hug, and a chance to get behind the wheel again.

Little kids, scrubbed waifs, hop from foot to foot under the eye of a mental health worker, then all but wet their pants when foster mom and dad come in the old station wagon.

Julia envies every one of them.

She waits on the steps of the Administration Building for an hour before going in to the switchboard to learn whether a call has come in for her. Yes, there is a message: Myrna Kessler missed the train. She was sorry and would call Julia on Monday.

Julia is not surprised; she feels her disappointment as an emptiness of hope. They have nothing between them really, or at least nothing to talk about. It is mechanical. Mostly she listens to Myrna's complaints about life alone, a widowed life, about the cost of things at the stores, about how hard it is to get around now that she can no longer drive, about how she misses Arnold, and how just the other day she had seen a show on TV she knows he would have liked. Always "Arnold," never "Grandpa," never "Your grandfather," always "Arnold," her husband, as if he belonged to no one else. Myrna would talk about her recent trip to the doctor and her symptoms and their remedies; or her appointment with the dentist and the bridgework; or the check-up with the eye doctor and the new glasses she has to have---"Everything costs so much"; or the batteries she needs to get for her hearing aid, her "ears." Julia hates how the hearing aid squeals when she put her cheek to Myrna's for the kiss hello and the kiss goodbye.

During these duty-driven encounters with her grandmother, Julia would give an edited inventory of her life at North Forks---the trip to the Aquarium that she had taken with some of the members of her unit; the patients' "Olympics" for which they were all in training; the reading group on Thursday evenings; the puppet show last weekend and how the little kids had laughed. These topics Julia held in her fist to offer Myrna like a bunch of picked and wilted dandelions, as if keeping her side of the bargain neither had ever defined.

Then they would be at a diner, each trying to have something to say to the other, each chatting to stave off the unsaid that lurked in the silences between them and looked for entry. "Making normal," Julia called it to Vale. It is the mechanical duet she and Myrna do, so that they don't have to acknowledge the doom that threatens their trivial chatter. But no matter how hard she tries to find some last piece of inconsequence to tell her grandmother, or wishes for some last driveling complaint from Myrna's lips, the silence comes at last, eating like acid into the flimsy vessel of their connection until there are only bubbles of after-thoughts leaking from a sunken vessel, or a body expiring its last breaths. Until, at last, *Death* and *Insanity* sound off one another like Tic and Toc, like heartbeats in her chest, and Julia cannot breathe. Panic would steal towards her then like a predator. She hopes no one is in the lady's room when she bends over the toilet bowl to vomit up the lunch she has just eaten. Hell is fear.

Then, back at the table, Julia prepares for what was to come next. It always comes to fill this intolerable silence between Tic and Toc. As if reaching into the ashen urn of her deepest confidings, Myrna draws up her unanswerable questions. "Why did I have to lose Arnold?" Her eyes look past Julia as if into an open grave. "Why was it him to go, so healthy, so strong, and not me who was always the sickly one?" Then the eyes come up searching Julia's face, "Why, Julia, Why?" Naked. Pleading. And, of course, it isn't really Arnold, her husband, she is searching to resurrect, it is an earlier, far more terrible loss: Her son, Albert. Julia's father.

"Why is God punishing me?"

"No, Grandma, God is not punishing you. 'Bad Things Happen to Good People,'" she quotes the title of a book she has given her grandmother and which was still unread when Julia packed her small suitcase with her overalls and tee shirts, packed her books and papers in a second valise and left the apartment to go to North Forks when her therapist said she needed a hospital, medications, a chance to figure out some course of her life. By then Julia had stopped getting out of bed, and her room looked like a bag-lady's.

Julia had never read the book either. And Myrna would sigh as if that made sense, yes, bad things *did* happen to good people. But the very next time they sit together at the diner, the same "Why?" arrives like a letter posted years ago that has moved from one dead-letter box to another and is finally delivered. "Julia, why did Arnold have to go when he did?"

Lurking in the background, prowling at the edge of the small fire they build between them and feed with the dry twigs of their habitual patter, a beast prowls and waits for all these other lesser Why's to be consumed, waits for the final silence to come, as in the end it must, because these two, the mad girl and the piteous crone, are no match for it. Behind that silence, as behind a screen of trees, the Big Why is biding its time, its eyes glinting from the undergrowth, its breath on the air like carrion mixed with the rank odor of loam under the pads of its enormous feet. The beast of the Big Why. Sometimes it is a Tyger burning bright; sometimes it circles overhead like an immense shadowy bird, a vulture circling over the carcass of their past. The black-winged, razor-beaked bird of their past circling the rotted carcass of Myrna's "Why?" The unspoken, unspeakable Why of the charred automobile, the hardly identified bodies, of her son Prince Albert, of her lost daughter-in-law Allison, Julia's mother. That wailing why why why why why why of loss and desolation. That is the scab that would never scar. To out- live them all, Why? To be alone, Why? To stare at the urns of mingled ash in the china cabinet. Why? Why was a little girl pulled from the fire while Prince Albert was consumed? Why? Why not the ugly little girl instead of her handsome son? That is the truth of it. Behind the why: It should have been you.

And this unspeakable and ever repeated Why binds them together across the years, a grandmother and her granddaughter, reaching towards the ghosts between them, their fingers passing through the dry nothingness between them, their words avoiding the nothingness between them. Tic Toc. Bewilderment and loss, the bereaved mother and the orphan girl, this one with bifocals, the tremor, the hearing aid that squeals. And this other with dark eyes, unhealthy skin, the thick black hair, the nails bitten down to the quick. The pair of them: the younger one is Madness; and sitting across from her this other, withered, empty-eyed, is Death.

So Julia is relieved that Township Taxi service does not bring Myrna up the winding drive of North Forks that day.

She looks around at the now deserted grounds of the hospital, her way station between two nowhere's. Waiting for Myrna, she has missed lunch in the cafeteria. She hopes hunger will run its nails along the walls of her stomach and interrupt her thoughts which are veering like a car running the light on the village road on New Year's Eve.

She pulls her weight up the steps to the upper lawn, her shadow thrown before her like a stain on the stones. At the top of the steps she stops and looks out at the empty lounge chairs, the stage set from which the players have departed, though it seems to her the shrill sounds, the snide whispers remain behind. The tiles on the roof of Messenger's empty tower shimmer in the heat. Weariness weighs on Julia as if she walks on a denser planet. Soon she will plod to her room, read, sleep, wait. If Parthia is not already there, occupied with her music and mirrors. For now, though, she will go to her place of refuge, the Glass House, fragile as her own skin.

When Julia enters the Glass House, she is astonished to find Parthia there, smoking a cigarette and leafing through the pages of a glossy magazine.

"Sorry," Julia says, beginning to retreat.

"I thought you had a pass," Parthia says, looking up.

Julia pauses in the doorway, uncertain. "She didn't show up."

"She?"

"My grandmother."

"Nobody's going to show up for me," Parthia says, putting down her magazine. "I am bored out of my mind," exhaling her smoke with an exaggerated weariness. "There is absolutely nothing to do here."

"It gets slow on weekends. I think they're having a cook-out at five."

"Whoopty doo." Julia still stands at the door, waiting for Parthia to turn back to her magazine. "You want to go for a walk or something?" Parthia asks.

"Really?"

Parthia puts down her magazine and rises. Julia backs out the door. "This is the first day I've been off that fucking SA status. All dressed up with no place to go." Julia admires the lace-up boots with the bright yellow stitching, the sleeveless aqua sundress. Around her neck a tiny silver coin hangs on a silver chain. The gashed face is healing; beauty radiates through like light through thinning clouds. Julia has hardly dared regard that face for more than a passing glance. To be so near it terrifies her. Now it bestows a glance on her that is somewhere between a blessing and a spell. "Are there any interesting places to walk to around here?" Parthia asks.

"Yeah, sorta. There's the orchard. The hill top has a nice view."

"Yeah. Of what?"

"Well, the other side of the hill where it goes down to the stream over the property line. And the hill up on the other side. It's peaceful out there."

Parthia moves to the door. "Show me."

Surprised again. "Sure. I guess. Really you want to go? I could point you the way."

"No, take me," Parthia is stepping past Julia and out the door. "There's nothing else to do."

They walk across the lawn, Julia keeping her distance. "I've got to check in first and sign out," Parthia says. "They've got to know where I'm going every goddamn minute of the day. What do I say the place is we're going to?"

"Say the baseball field."

In a few minutes Parthia comes out of Gables, carrying two small plastic bottles of water. "Nurse Ratched says we should be careful to keep hydrated. Will you carry mine for me?" she asks, flashing Julia a smile. Julia obliges, shoving one in each of the side pockets of her overalls. "You got a watch? I've got to be back in an hour." Julia raises her naked wrist. "Can you keep track of the time?" Parthia asks.

"I guess."

"It's not far, is it?"

"No, just past Overlook Two. There's the ball field, and then at the end of it there's a path that goes to some woods and then the old orchard." They start walking. "I mean the orchard isn't really an orchard anymore. The trees are old and no one picks the..."

"It doesn't matter. It's some place to go for God's sake."

Julia leads the way around behind Gables and down steps to the Quad. She rummages in her head for something to talk about, but everything sounds stupid, or boring. Still, this is better than Myrna and better than no Myrna. So far. The faintest voice ---*I've got a friend*--- whispers inside her like a single candle in a vast dark hall.

They walk out the north end of the Quad and across the baseball diamond, through the outfield and then down a rutted path that enters a break in the tree line. Immediately it is cooler in their shade. "There are deer in here sometimes," Julia offers.

Parthia is quiet; she hardly looks around her, mostly keeping her eye on the heavy- footed Julia a pace or two ahead, Julia the troll.

"What got you into this place?" she asks to Julia's back. The girl stops and started to turn. "No," she said, "don't stop, but talk to me. Tell me, why are you here in this hospital?"

It feels strange, this way of going down the narrow path through the trees, but perhaps this is the way people make friends. Julia's mind skips ahead to a picture of Monday morning in the cafeteria: she will be walking in with Parthia, they are sitting together at a table. Together they will look over at Amanda and her mean minions. Julia is wearing a coin on a chain around her neck. "I..." *Where to start?* "I have panic attacks. I get very depressed." She stops and begins to turn around, a reflex.

"Julia, let's play a game."

"Uh, OK. What game?"

"We'll play twenty questions."

"What will you try to guess with your twenty questions?" The sunlight dapples the columns of the birch trees, the leaves tremble in the light breeze, the leaves tremble and flutter. Like anxiety. Anxiety is a tree in mid-summer whose leaves stir with an unexpected wind.

"Nothing," Parthia goes on. "I just want you to give me permission to ask you twenty questions, and you have to promise to answer; you can even make up an answer, but you have to speak." Julia considers this.

"Here, I'll tell you something about myself," Parthia offers. "I went to a therapist once, well more than once, and he had me lie on a couch, and he sat behind me where I couldn't see him. He said it was easier to talk if you did not see the expression on the person's face, if you did not try to figure out how the other person was feeling about what you were saying. Once I turned around and caught him with his hand in his pants. I think he was masturbating."

"Really?"

"He had a notebook on his lap, but when I turned around, he freaked. I used to dress for him. I would do things so he could, you know, see down the front of my dress. He was an ass."

"Gosh, that's..."

"So I will ask you questions, and you will not turn around. OK?"

Julia likes the idea. She does not want to see Parthia or be seen by her. She does not want to see the expression on her face. It will be like hiding, she thought. *Hide and Tell*: that could be the name of the game. "OK," she says. "Do you want to go to the orchard?"

"Well, that's part of the game," Parthia says. "It's like follow the leader. I follow in your footsteps, and you follow my questions."

"Let's call the game 'Hide and Tell,'" Julia says.

"'Hide and Tell'. That's good, Julia." Once again the sound of her name in Parthia's mouth.. "Go ahead," she says to Parthia. "Go ahead ... Parthia. You can ask your first question." Julia stumbles on an uneven patch of ground and rights herself.

"I'm thinking," Parthia says. "OK, question one: What's the worst thing that ever happened to you?"

The question stops Julia.

"No, no, no, you can't stop walking; you have to walk and talk; it's another name for our game."

Julia picks up her foot and puts it down, the other follows. She listens to the crack and mash of her footfall into the earth.

"Julia, you have to talk."

"I ...Can we start somewhere else?" I..."

"OK. Sure." The voice behind her cracks like a whip.

"Where were you born?"

"In Queens."

"What is your mother like? Don't stop."

"My mother's dead."

"Julia, you have to keep walking. You can walk around in circles. You can lead me anywhere you want, but you can't stop. That's the game." Julia resumes walking. In the orchard there are dead, fallen limbs. "How did she die?"

A crow flies overhead; its call claws the air. "In an automobile accident."

"Tell me about it."

"That's not a question." Julia feels the risk of contradiction.

"How did she die?"

"There's nothing to tell. There was an automobile accident."

"How old were you?"

"I was seven."

"Were you in the car?"

"Yes I was in the back seat." Julia is weary; she wants to sit under a tree. She is thirsty, but does not reach into her pocket for the water.

"Who was driving? Don't stop."

"My father was driving." The center of Julia's back is stinging as if darts were being thrown. Or quills. Julia feels little spots of blood appear through her tee shirt.

"How did the accident happen? Don't stop."

"I don't know."

"Julia, keep walking and talking. You have to. That's our game." Julia goes down the last row in the orchard of broken trees.

"My father was a...an alcoholic, I guess. We were coming back from his mother's on New Year's Eve. My father was angry about something. He and my mother were fighting. He ran a red light, and our car hit a car coming through the intersection. My mother and father were killed; the other car caught on fire. I was pulled out."

"There, that wasn't so hard was it?"

Julia's ears are filling with the sounds of sirens.

"Was that the worst thing that ever happened to you? Was it?"

Bright spots of blood are soaking through Julia's tee shirt. "Uh, yes that was..." but her voice betrays her.

"No it wasn't; I can tell. There is something worse than that. What was it? Tell me. No stopping."

Julia leaves the orchard and descends the hill along an overgrown path. The weeds are thick. Julia wades through them and steps on dried twigs that crack underfoot. She does not hear Parthia moving behind her now, hears only the sting of the questions. The game will never end because there is no end to the worst. It happens again and again.

"Answer," Julia flinches. "Julia, if I have to repeat a question again, then I get a bonus question." *Bonus... bonus...bone...bone.* "Tell me," the voice hisses behind her and the thongs of a cat o' nine tails bite into her shoulder.

"I can't..."

"Julia you have to. We can't be friends if I can't trust you to do what you said you'd do."

Julia walks aimlessly now on pitted ground, comes to the stone wall at the lower end of the orchard and can go no farther, for the woods are darkening, squaring into the small cold room. The sound of a voice---her voice?---is coming from far away. She can barely hear it; it is taking all her strength to hear the voice that sounds like her voice, to utter it.

"After my parents died, I lived with my grandmother and grandfather for a while. Then my grandfather got lung cancer, and Myrna couldn't take care of me and Arnold... and I was put into a foster family. I was nine... I had two foster placements. The first one didn't work out... I wet my bed... I was very home-sick. So they gave me back... and my grandmother became very angry... and so I had a second placement... and I stayed there until I was a Junior in high school."

She is there now in the dark apartment in Flatbush; her foster mother is working the night shift at the phone company. A twelve-year-old girl named Julia-not-Julia is watching the door of her room open at night, waiting, hardly breathing, divided between dread and vigilance, between nausea and appetite. What is coming is better than the fiery nightmares, though it is the cause of other nightmares.

The shadow is falling across the foot of her bed from the light at the far end of the hall. Julia-not-Julia wants to close her eyes and pretend she is asleep, but she cannot, does not dare, needs to see. She does not even blink. Ogre man is coming closer; he wears a nightshirt that falls to his thighs. He drags his leg. His dog, Whisky, low slung and black, comes down the hall with him. The man's bone sticks out straight from the front of him, making the nightshirt like a tent, a tee-pee, a pee-tree. He is lifting the shirt, and she sees the bone with its single eye, the eye that oozes. The bone is moving towards the stark awake girl on the bed. The man's hand reaches down and pulls aside the cover; Whisky watches, dog breath, panting. The hand reaches for the girl and pulls her to her knees. The hand grips her forearm; it leaves prints. Julia-not-Julia rises to her knees on the bed, asleep and not asleep, alert, so alert she can see every mark and hair, smell the night sweat of his body, smell the odor of dog. Her mouth is opening; it is full of saliva. Her mouth is watering. She is ashamed of that. Drooling for the bone. She is kneeling on the side of her bed; the covers tangle over her feet; the shadow of the man is thrown over her from the light in the hall. Julia-not-Julia is naked; she is always naked in this house at night, even in the winter, in this room she shares with her little foster brother Patrick--- *Paddy...paddy cake paddy cake baker's man...*he is asleep in the bed on the other side of the room. Always asleep. Innocently asleep in this house where mother works the night shift at the phone company. She must never wake him when the man is running his hand over the new breasts of Julia-not-Julia. Her mouth is open, and her eyes are open. He is touching the tips of her breasts with his rough hands. She is his machine. Julia-not-Julia is trembling. As if from a great cold distance the Julia-not-Julia automaton watches as the man's bone with its oozing eye enters the wide-open mouth of the girl, watches as the man's hand holds the head of the girl and reaches to touch the girl's breast tips, making the ice in them burn. Dirtiness is covering the girl now like an oily perspiration; the bone has become a rigid shaft that goes in and out of the mouth like a piston moving in and out of a socket, a bone machine going in and out of its bone hole. The girl's mouth is filled with saliva; there is a taste in the girl's mouth of saliva and something viscous that mixes with her saliva; it dribbles down her chin. It's the oil the bone exudes that makes it run smooth. The man is holding the back of the girl's head, his fingers grip in the girl's hair, guiding her, rocking. As he rocks, Julia-not-Julia starts to feel warm. Warmth starts in her mouth and then travels into her face, and into her head, and down her neck and spreads into her chest and into tips of her breasts, and then lower into her belly and the insides of her legs. Julia-not-Julia is not afraid anymore; she is part of the machine. Friction. Suction. Friction. Suction. It is the sound the bone-rod makes as it drives the warmth.

With one of her hands the Julia-not-Julia machine reaches up to hold the man's white bone and the man is whispering, "I love you, little Julia, I love you, little Julia; you're beautiful..." Julia-not-Julia hears the man whisper, "Don't stop, little Julia, don't stop. I love you, don't stop." And the girl hears the man who is so big above her starting to whimper. "Yes...please..." he whimpers, over and over. And Julia-not-Julia feels his hand release the catch at the back of her head. It is the signal. She pauses, stops, feeling him strain and quiver. "Don't stop," says the half-choked voice. Then Julia-not-Julia withdraws the rod from her mouth. She sees the loop of saliva sway from its tip. The bone bobs at her, quivers. She can make it do what she wants now. She has power. Julia-not-Julia has learned it; it has taken time, but she has learned.

Something crashes, snaps Julia-not-Julia back into sunlight. A deer is bounding to the verge of the broken apple trees. Then, stillness: a vacuum sucks up the phantoms; a black world disappears into dizziness. Stillness un-peels the sound of a stream. The stream is wide and washing over stones. A tree by the side of the stream, one limb reaching over a big flat rock, a long arm with splayed black fingers. From the branch elbow a rope. Hangs. Is stirring. Beckons. A finger of braided hemp scrawls her name on the face of the water.

•◆•

"What kind of a weekend you have?"

"I gained weight. I hate the Fourth of July. Everyone stuffing their faces."

"You hear the news?"

"What news?"

"Julia killed herself."

"No shit?"

"How'd it happen?"

"No one knows?"

"Where is she?"

"They took her to the hospital."

"She coming back?"

"I told you, stupid she's dead."

"I don't believe you."

"I don't care what you believe."

"No, it's true. I heard there was an ambulance here on Saturday afternoon."

"How'd she do it?"

"Hanged herself."

PART II

Serge Lucore paced his office on Monday morning with a phone clenched to his ear. He had already fired off messages to Austin Goldin, the hospital lawyer; to Emily Longstretch, the head of Quality Assurance; to Paul Davino in Purchasing. He was now barking orders to his Director of Building and Grounds. "Listen, Lawrence, get a crew down to the north perimeter of this hospital. I want a fence put up on our property line, barbed wire if necessary. I don't care what it costs, but I want it done as quickly as possible. You know why. We could have a lot of patients wondering what the place looks like where this Kessler girl hung herself. I've already left a message with Davino in Purchasing. Just tell him what you need, and hire an extra couple of men if you have to. I want this work done by the weekend."

Finally he saw Venables' red Jaguar with its top down come up the long driveway. Hardly able to control his ire and impatience, he watched as his partner lifted a royal hand to wave at someone who was walking up the road from one of the offices at the lower end of the campus. Then a beneficent nod to a groundskeeper. An I've- got-all all-the-time-in-the-world stop at a crosswalk while a flock of children passed. Smoothly the car slid into its appointed space. Up went the canvass top and down over the windshield. He watched Venables step out of the car, stretch, slip on his blazer, reach behind the front seat for his calfskin briefcase, then close the driver's door. A man without a care in the world, the master of all he surveys.

Lucore took the stairs down to the second floor, catching Dean as he came up from the first. "I need to talk to you immediately," he snapped and preceded Dean into his office. Arlene fielded her boss's questioning glance with a shrug. He had been sailing all weekend with his daughter and her family. He had told everyone he was going to be out of touch, and if they had learned one thing through the years, it was that when Venables said "out of touch," he meant it.

"Sergio!" Dean said cheerily, closing his office door behind him.

"Damnit to hell. I wish you would join the goddamn modern world. You could carry a pager---you are a doctor after all. And you certainly might spring for an answering machine at home. How the hell are we supposed to reach you in an emergency?"

"What's this about, Serge?" Dean stood beside his desk and read the fatigue as well as the anger in his partner's face.

"One of your patients came this close---" Lucore held up a hand with the thumb and first finger a quarter of an inch apart---"this close to killing herself."

"Who was it?" Dean asked and sat down in the swivel chair behind his desk.

"Kessler, Julia Kessler."

"What unit is she..."

"She's in Gables. Vale Messenger's her therapist. We haven't been able to get to the bottom of it yet, but it seems that she and another of this Messenger's patients---one who was two PC'd to us and was on hourly check-in's---went off grounds on Saturday. Off grounds, Dean. They weren't even on the property. They were AWOL."

"How did she...?

"Do you have any idea of what would happen if one of our patients eloped and killed herself within fifty feet of our property line?" Lucore leaned down on Dean's desk, knuckles to the wood.

"Serge, I am quite aware of..."

"Are you?" Lucore ploughed on. "I spent an hour on the phone with Austin Golden on Sunday morning---man's religion tells him not to pick up his phone on Saturday. We are going to have to file a report with the New York State Office of Mental Health. They can, if they want, send out their own investigator. This Kessler girl has the legal right to sue us for malpractice and for negligence. I went to North Shore Medical Center yesterday---in the middle of a family barbecue, mind you---to spend an hour with an overwrought grandmother. Thank God she's an ignorant old woman who feels guilty because she was supposed to visit on Saturday and didn't. It could have been a real mess. Still could be if the girl comes out of this with an injury, and some ambulance chaser gets to her. Not only couldn't I find you, but of course this Messenger was also out of reach."

"Who was the Doctor-on-call?" Dean asked.

"Farmer. It made containment a lot easier. Still, you are the Clinical Chief. This is your mess, not mine."

"Serge I'm sorry, but we have a competent…"

"Well, I have other things in my life, but I check in here, goddamnit. Routine weekend call to Security is all it takes, I have an answering machine. I have---" and here he snapped the pager from his belt---"this. It works. I can always be reached." He replaced it. "And this is to say nothing, of course, about the general sense of confusion and upset among the staff on the unit."

"I'll get over there immediately."

"I scheduled a staff meeting for ten. I will attend it with you. I expect some kind of report over your signature as soon as you can put it together. I need to be informed. Our insurance company needs to be informed, and OMH requires a review and a report of the incident.

"How…?"

"She tried to hang herself." Lucore saw with satisfaction the knit brows of his partner. "There may be lasting injury; that could cost us a shitload of money if our carrier decides to raise our rates. I want to know who's responsible and exactly what happened." With that Lucore stepped to the door. "I'll see you at ten in the unit conference room." He closed the door hard behind him.

•◆•

Vale had gotten home Sunday evening from Fire Island with a mild case of sunburn and the blues. Once entire summers had been spent on the island in the cottage she and Robert rented, where Meli had been conceived, where Elaine appeared, where the marriage ended in betrayal, confession, and in bitter recriminations that only slowly yielded to grief. And even though this holiday weekend with Naomi had had its parties, its flirtations, even a torrid, aborted encounter on the beach after the fireworks, Vale had come home to the empty apartment, pre-occupied with old objections, old fears. She hadn't seen the blinking light on her answering machine until she had taken a shower, opened a beer, and put her feet up on the kitchen counter.

"Vale, this is Edna White. It's Saturday 5:45 PM. Please call the unit as soon as you can. This is urgent." Vale's stomach rolled over. Oh, shit.

There was a beep from the machine; a second message began: "Vale, this is Pamela Rivers. It's Saturday at eight. Please call me when you get this message. I'll leave my home phone number. Call at any hour." Her number followed, and Vale had to repeat both messages to be sure she had transcribed Rivers' number correctly. She had a chance to hear in both voices an undertone of panic. Her own was rising; these messages were more than twenty-four hours old.

She called the hospital immediately and was put through to the unit. "Gables, Edna White here."

"Edna, it's Vale. What's happened?"

"Wait a moment," and Vale heard the phone put down and a door close. Edna came back on the line, "Julia Kessler made a serious suicide attempt on Saturday afternoon. She would have succeeded if Parthia hadn't found her."

"Jesus." Vale sat down on the edge of a kitchen chair. She thought of her last conversation with Julia on Friday afternoon; she'd been shaky but well enough, willing to go through the weekend with Parthia, more or less looking forward to Myrna…Ahh, Myrna. She had not come. Was that it? Was that enough? Vale didn't know. Had she missed something? Julia had asked for an increase in the dosage of her meds. Vale had persuaded her to tough it out.

"What did she…Is she all right?"

"She tried to hang herself."

"Good God, hang herself? Where? How?"

"There's a tree by the stream over the northern edge of the property. So they tell me anyway."

"That's way on the other side of the ball field?"

"Yes, that's right. Julia's grandmother didn't show up on Saturday. The log notes that Parthia came to the nurse's station and signed herself out for an hour walk with Julia about half past two. They were supposed to go to the ball field, but went on past it to the orchard."

"I've never been there."

"Who has? The next thing we know is that Parthia came rushing onto Quad 2. Apparently she was pretty incoherent. Security was called. The Building and Grounds guy was on duty over the weekend. He drove down there with a nurse. Quad 2 called an ambulance. Lawrence, that's his name, actually rode with her to North Shore Medical Center. We were totally short handed, it being July Fourth weekend."

"And Julia?"

"She's still at North Shore Medical. Dr. Lucore went to see her yesterday and Dr. Farmer. Apparently she has a mean rope burn, trauma to her vocal chords, but the rope broke before she choked to death. She fell and apparently hit her head on something."

Vale was numb. "And Parthia?"

"Parthia was beside herself when she came back to the unit. She had to be medicated last night. She's been totally withdrawn today."

"Thanks, Edna." Vale was beset with half-formed thoughts, questions, a sickening sense of failure and responsibility. Something terrible had happened. She saw in her mind's eye Julia's anxious, pleading face. I'm sorry, Julia, Vale said to that pale image. I'm so sorry.

"Oh, I almost forgot, there's a Gables' staff meeting at ten tomorrow morning."

"Tomorrow? Yes. I'll be there, of course." After a few last words, they rang off.

Vale sat staring at the phone, dreading the next call she had to make. Nothing had prepared her for this. Her training---well, she had always had supervision, her cases had been selected. Now she had stepped into chaos.

Vale placed the call to Rivers, and an answering machine asked her to leave a message. She spoke her name and said that she had talked to Edna White, knew what had happened on the unit, and would be at the ten o'clock meeting.

Vale looked at her half drunk beer on the kitchen counter and poured the remainder down the sink. She replayed in her mind her last sessions with Julia and Parthia, searching for clues. What had she missed? Or provoked? A panicky nausea gripped her. She dialed Naomi's number on the island and got her machine. Then she remembered her sister was on her way to stay with a friend in Brooklyn in order to be on time for a Monday morning doctor's appointment in the city.

Feeling caged in her apartment, Vale put on a polo shirt over her sunburned shoulders and went for a walk, ending up at a Chinese restaurant, eating alone. Her thoughts were full of the fragility of things: her patients' lives, her own precarious hold on her new career, of her lost marriage. Later walking home, seeing the lights in houses on the street, hearing music from open windows, she felt tears start in her eyes.

Her answering machine was blinking when she walked in the door. "Vale. It's Pamela Rivers. No need to call back tonight. I want to meet with you at half past eight tomorrow in my office."

•◆•

"I hardly know where to begin, Vale." They were seated across from one another at the round table in the middle of Rivers' office. "I grant you that it appears that this Kessler girl may owe her life to Parthia, but both those young women were out of bounds. What were they doing at the end of the orchard when they were signed out to the ball field? I expect you will seriously review this Alexander girl's status, and I hope you don't find that she was involved in what happened to the Kessler girl. A holiday weekend is a time for increased, not relaxed precaution. Changing her status to limited grounds appears, in retrospect, to have been a mistake in judgment. It could have turned out very badly indeed."

"Yes, Ma'm," Vale said.

"Now about Julia Kessler. Do you have any idea the significance of the date for Julia Kessler?" Vale confessed that she did not. "It was Julia Kessler's 23rd birthday." Vale blanched. "That's right, her birthday. She hadn't said anything about it to you?"

Vale shook her head, "No."

"And you did not have it in your notes?"

Vale shook her head again, "I hadn't made a particular note of it. Or perhaps it slipped my mind."

"It's there at the top of the intake." Vale knew it was. "Birthdays and anniversaries," Rivers spoke as if quoting holy writ, "birthdays and anniversaries. They are red letter days. Surely you remember that?"

"I missed it," she said. "It won't happen again."

"I'm sure it won't," Rivers said.

A question was nagging at Vale, but before she could ask it, Rivers began to read aloud from Vale's notes. Presently she stopped and looked at Vale over her half-glasses. "Vale, you are not writing character studies here. Your purpose is to document what is said in sessions and to make clear what your clinical strategy is and why you are pursuing it. Your notes should reflect the treatment plan that has been developed with the unit psychologist, or the psychiatrist, and with nursing staff. The treatment plan is the essence of clinical practice. I am not telling you anything you do not know, I trust?" Vale shook her head. "When we go to an insurance company and argue for re-imbursement or for an increased length of stay, we have to show them we have a plan and that we are documenting its progress." Rivers had taught social work before coming to work at North Forks. "Your notes make good reading, but they do not sufficiently link to a coordinated assessment."

"I understand," Vale said. Her nagging question returned, and she forced herself to ask it. "Mrs. Rivers, does it add up? Even with Myrna not coming and me not realizing how much might be riding on this weekend, does it add up? I mean, to do such a thing?"

"Well," said Rivers, looking at her watch, "often things don't add up. There are always missing pieces, things our patients don't tell us, or to which we do not give the proper weight. How much do you know about how she was treated by her parents when they were alive?"

"Almost nothing. The in-take history had a good deal of factual information about her parents and their deaths. Well, I guess you read that."

Rivers nodded. "And the foster placements?"

"Pretty complete records from Social Service. Lots of trouble in the first, bed wetting, night terrors. The second placement seemed to work out better. She was there until she was fifteen and then went back to live with her grandmother for a year and a half before City College."

Rivers considered this for a moment. "I don't know," she said. "No doubt there is something missing in this girl's story. I don't know where to look. Maybe in the placements, if you can get her to tell you about them. Sometimes in the aftermath of an event like this, patients will open up material they hadn't talked about before. Now," said Rivers rising and showing Vale to the door, "I will see you in the unit conference room at ten."

As Vale was leaving, Pamela added, "We all go through at least one of these, Vale. I had two patients take their own lives on my watch. It's a terrible business. We do the best we can. Learn, but don't beat yourself up."

Vale stammered something. Pamela patted her shoulder as she shut the door.

Back in her office, Vale was met with yet more outdated and urgent messages. She listened to them feeling the turmoil of the unit on Saturday night and Sunday. One message, however, made no sense at all. A woman's voice with something of an accent said without preamble, "Here is a clue and just for you. Don't believe the compliant look. A pretty face is not an open book." That was all. Vale played it a second time and was reminded of another voice and another strange message: "I have lost my face..." Where was this coming from and why? Vale felt dizzy with a sense of hidden things.

•◆•

The emergency unit meeting, attended by the entire clinical staff of Gables, was the first of its kind in Vale's experience. She was painfully aware of being the cause of it.

Dean, at the head of the table, flanked by Rivers and Lucore, made it clear that no blame was being directed against anyone. He informed them that they would be shifting some mental health workers to Gables for the week, so that patients would have more individual contact with staff. He reviewed what was known of Julia's current condition. "The good news," he said, "is that Julia Kessler is all right. This entire situation was handled with the utmost professionalism. We have every expectation of re-admitting her." Vale felt a mixture of relief and concern for how Julia's return would play out on the unit.

Vale studied Venables. He radiated calm and confidence, an altogether handsome man. "We have two tasks," he went on, "one, of course, is to get on with the therapeutic work of the hospital, and that means seeing our patients, running our groups, and listening with particular care to the aftershocks. Your task, our task, is to respond to their responses. Another ..."

Here the door opened and a man in came in. "Sorry, Dean," he said, "I had a crew to get oriented." He leaned against the wall by the door, then gave a nod to Dr. Lucore.

"Win, I'm glad you are here. For those of you who don't know, Win Lawrence was here on Saturday and acted with great dispatch to get Julia Kessler to the hospital. He's head of Building and Grounds." While Dean continued, Vale glanced from time to time at the rangy man who stood by the door, now recognizing him as the man who had picked up Parthia upon her admission and carted her to Gables. Here he was a blue collar among the white, broad-shouldered, brown hair bleached by the sun, jeans, work boots, dark glasses pushed up on his brow. She'd like a minute to talk with him.

Dean Venables was concluding. "The other thing we will be doing is taking a much closer look at hospital security. Dr. Lucore and I want the property policed. Are there other hazards we may have overlooked? That initiative will take place under your supervision, Win"---the big man simply nodded---"but we ask you all to look at things with fresh eyes and report to your supervisors anything you think we ought to re-assess. Thank you. That's all."

The meeting dissolved into a number of simultaneous conversations as people headed back to the unit. Vale tried to catch Win Lawrence's eye as he left, but Lucore had him by the elbow. Almost out the door herself, she felt a hand on her arm, detaining her. It was Dean Venables. She turned with him back to the room, and when the others had gone, he shut the door. "Sit down, Vale."

She did, feeling uncomfortable under Venables' steady, assessing gaze.

"Where were you when this happened?" he asked. There wasn't a trace of accusation in his voice.

In a few sentences she told him about her weekend.

"Well, I was on a sailboat. No one could reach me." Vale nodded, mute. "And, of course, you have been feeling guilty and responsible even though you may know on some level it is not your fault?" She nodded. "Vale," he said leaning towards her, the lemony fragrance of his cologne reaching her, "no one in this line of work---especially no one who works in an in-patient psychiatric facility---can hope to escape something like this. It's part of paying your dues, and you may pay them more than once." Dean got up and walked to the window, then turned to look at her.

"Let me tell you a story. I was doing a residency at Bellevue, a young idealistic newly-fledged doctor, working longer hours than I was required to. There was a young black man in the hospital for depression; he was a dancer. His name was Billy Dean. That's right. Same name. I had actually seen him on stage; he was part of the Dance Theater of Harlem. Anyway, he was bi-polar and was just bottoming out of a depression---or so I thought. Rachel, my wife, was pregnant. There were some complications. I had to take some time off. In the end we lost the child. It was a bad time. I was away for a week, and when I got back Billy Dean was gone. Just took off, and nobody knew where he went. Later I learned that he had showed up in the city morgue." Vale could see that even after all these years the story was not easy to tell.

"When my wife went into the hospital, I just called in to Bellevue and said I had to be away. Family emergency. I never spoke to any of my patients. Never got word to Billy Dean. Maybe if I had..." Here Venables' hands lifted, his hands palms upwards, a kind of shrug. "Who knows?"

He was quiet. She met his eyes and then looked down. "You always feel guilty," he went on. "You always feel responsible, but we aren't gods; we can't cover all the bases. No one is going to blame you for this. You shouldn't blame yourself."

"Dr. Venables, I don't know what to say." It was all she could do to maintain her composure in the face of his kindness.

"Vale, I know you took this girl Parthia Alexander off SA status on Friday. In the light of what happened, you could be inclined to reconsider that decision, but none of us has a crystal ball. Besides, if this Alexander girl were still on SA, perhaps Julia would not be here now. We can't know."

"I've got to get over to North Shore Hospital and see Julia," Vale said.

"I think you should," Venables said, "but not this morning. Your patients need you here. Something triggered this. You'll find out what it is. You have to believe that Julia has something to tell you, something perhaps she has never told anyone, something that reared up in her on Saturday afternoon. So, you do what you need to do for yourself so that you can be there for her, and for your other patients."

"It was her birthday," Vale said in a small voice.

"Ah, was it? " He paused for a moment, taking this in. "Well, who knows if this won't appear in retrospect to have been a remarkable gift. We don't know how the story comes out, Vale. Don't assume to know it." With that he patted her hand, got up, and closed the door softly behind him. He could see she needed a little time to gather herself.

•◆•

Serge Lucore still had a hand on Win Lawrence's elbow as he left the Administration Building. "So the fence will get handled this week." It was not a question.

"I've got contractors coming to look at the plans for the new conference center."

"Well, juggle. This fence is a priority."

"OK, I'm on it.

"I want a fence that clearly marks the property line so patients will know the boundary." They stopped on the sidewalk.

"Chain link?"

"That's good. Six feet high."

"You mean to enclose the entire property?" He knew Lucore's fence would keep the deer from the stream. He also knew such considerations would be utterly lost on his boss.

"Don't get funny with me, Lawrence. I just want to make sure we don't get sight-seers down there. I want to make a statement."

"I'll take care of it."

"Show me the plans before you execute. Better yet, bring me a survey. Also, I want you to comb the property and adjacent areas to see if there's anything else we should take care of."

"Every piece of broken glass?"

Lucore gave Lawrence a cold stare. "And the insurance company wants photos of the site."

"I'll take care of it."

Back in his office Win Lawrence went to the bin where the survey maps and blueprints stood on end in their cardboard cylinders. He drew out an aerial map of the North Forks property and spread it out on his desk, holding down one corner with a can of six penny nails, the other with the picture of his wife and daughter in their silver frame. He stared for a long moment at that photograph, then he picked up the phone and made a call.

•◆•

The light was blinking on her answering machine when Vale got back to her office. She had begun to dread their surprises and imperatives: "commanding machines," more like. She rewound the tape and listened. The first, from Emily Longstretch, advised her that she needed to submit a copy of her case notes to QA. "A Xerox of everything, please, plus a one page digest of strategies, interventions, medications, etc. etc. I need this by day's end."

The second message surprised her, "Mrs. Messenger, it's Win Lawrence. I imagine this is a hard day for you. I'm going to try to get over to see Julia after work. I wondered if you'd seen her yet and if you'd like to go over together. I expect you'll want to know some details. I can't get free before the end of the day." He left his three-digit extension.

She would like very much to hear his side of the story. And to see Julia.

The rest of the morning was consumed in filling out the QA report that was as long as a take-home examination. She had no appetite, but went over to the dining room and made up a takeout salad for herself.

At one thirty, Vale heard the lower door of the Tower open and a slow tread on the stairs.

The face she saw was pallid, the scratch lines only faint traces now, but reminders of a story Vale did not know. Parthia's eyes jittered in her head, roving and restless. There was a tremor in her hands. *A pretty face is not an open book.*

"Parthia," she began, coaxing the frightened eyes to look at hers, "I want to teach you something about breathing." And for the next ten minutes she taught Parthia what she had taught Julia, how to slow the breathing, bring the attention to the in-breath and the out-breath, how to use the breath as an anchor when her mind was overwhelmed. Perhaps it was her stage training, her discipline as a model, but Parthia caught on quickly and discovered how effective a tool this was for self-control.

"I can't believe no one ever taught me this before. You should learn this in grade school."

Vale was glad to see her color improve, her hands more steady and her eyes hold focus. "There," she said, "you look better."

"I feel less scattered. Less...scared," she said. "Thank you." The sincerity was evident, and her head was cocked a little to one side as if she were assessing her therapist anew.

"Has anyone given you an update about Julia?" Vale asked.

Parthia ran her tongue over her lips and nodded. "Ed did."

"So you know she's going to be all right?"

"Will she be coming back?" Vale couldn't tell quite what she heard in Parthia's voice, hope or fear. Probably both, she decided.

"I think so."

"I'm back on status. Why?"

"It's just a precaution. We need to keep a little better track of everyone for a while. Also, technically you broke your agreement. You were way off limited grounds." A sullen look crossed Parthia's face. "Still," Vale said, " if you hadn't been there, who knows what might have happened?"

Parthia did not brighten at this. "May I have a cigarette please?" Vale nodded and went around her desk to fetch the book of matches in her drawer. She handed them to Parthia.

"Can you tell me about that afternoon, Parthia?" She shoved the saucer towards her.

"There's not much to tell." Then seeing the look on her therapist's face, Parthia added, "Really there isn't."

"So tell me what you can."

Parthia took a long drag on her cigarette and began to speak at the end of her exhale. "I was bored. Everyone was away. There was nothing to do, and after lunch I went to the Glass House with some magazines and a book. I was reading *D.V.*". Vale gave her an inquiring look. "*D.V.* is Diane Vreeland. She's the editor of Vogue; it's her memoir. Anyway, I couldn't concentrate, and at some point, Julia showed up. She was looking...well, she looked depressed. I mean Julia always looks depressed; she looks like shit really. Anyway, I told Julia I was going nuts, and Julia proposed that we take a walk. Anything was better than the Glass House, so I said yes. I went to the unit signed out. They..."

"Where did you say you were going?"

"I said a walk to the ball field," Parthia admitted.

"So you knew you were overstepping the restriction when you went to the orchard?"

"I can see how it looks in retrospect, Ms. Messenger, but at the time I just wanted to feel a little more free."

"Go on."

"So we came to the orchard and walked around it, and then Julia climbed over the stone wall and went down to the stream. I knew I shouldn't go *there*. So I waited." Parthia drew on her cigarette, stood and went to the window, taking that familiar stance, looking down onto the lawn, her back partially turned to Vale.

Vale knew that Parthia was leaving out a great deal. What they had talked about? What was going on between them? She had no trouble imagining that Parthia was bored and that Julia was upset with her grandmother failing to show up---and it being her birthday---but she did not think the two young women walked for the better part of an hour without a word.

"The next thing I heard was a crashing splash. It was too loud a sound for a rock or even a tree branch. I called out Julia's name, and I didn't get a response." Parthia turned towards Vale now, "Before I knew it, I was over the wall and running down through the brush. I came down to the stream, and I saw Julia lying there with her face purple and a loop of rope around her neck. She was lying on her back in the water. It seemed to me she wasn't breathing."

"Speaking of breathing, Parthia, this might be a good time to try a little yourself." She saw the rigid shoulders rise, fall, rise again.

"Parthia," Vale said, "I think there's a little more to this." Parthia opened her mouth, closed it again. She took a last drag on her cigarette and then put it out in the saucer on the desk.

"You're going to lock me up and throw away the key."

"You make this sound like a prison. I am not a judge, and there is no jury here, Parthia." The figure before her appeared frozen. "Breathe, Parthia."

Again the shoulders rose and fell, and then Parthia, haltingly, began to speak: "I...we played a kind of game as we walked...I learned this game in acting class. I was terrible at it. It's called *Questions.*" Parthia's eyes stayed on Vale's face as if waiting to detect a judgment. "The group forms a circle, and the one who is going to be "it" gets in the middle. The teacher and the students can ask you any question they like, and you have to answer with no hesitation. You can lie, but the point is that you have to answer without appearing to take any time to compose your answer. You have to speak, and you can't stop until someone decides to fire the next question at you."

"A spontaneity exercise. And, of course, you get asked embarrassing questions." Parthia nodded. "Sounds grueling."

"It is. I hated it. We all did."

"And you played this game with Julia?"

"Sort of." Vale waited. "I told Julia I wanted to play this game, and she said all right. So I asked her questions. That's all."

"May I guess?" she asked. Parthia nodded, her eyes intent on her therapist's face. "I guess that you asked her about herself, about her history, and that Julia felt she could not stop you and went along. Maybe she talked about her grandmother...?" Vale saw Parthia's head give a slight side to side shake. "Maybe she talked about her father and her mother?" The head nodded up and down, "about their death, about the accident, about the fire?" The head nodded up and down again. Vale could see that Parthia was hardly breathing;

she was like someone hiding and hearing someone approach. Vale went on not wanting to break the connection. "But she talked about something else. I think she talked about something that she hasn't even talked to me about." There was a slight shrug. "And I think that whatever this was that she talked about, that it put her into a...a state of some kind. Maybe she looked funny to you."

"I couldn't see her. She had her back to me. That's how we set up the game. Julia could lead; she could go wherever she wanted to go, and I would have to follow in her footsteps. That's how we wandered off track. I followed her, and she wasn't paying attention to where she was going, and I asked her questions." Parthia was pale. "You have to believe me; I didn't see what was happening to her. I was only listening. And then she came to the stone wall, and she climbed over it, and I didn't. I knew I shouldn't. I said to her that the game was over. 'That's enough questions,' I said to her, but she was climbing over the wall and talking about a machine, about being part of a machine. I didn't know what she was talking about, Ms. Messenger. I said 'Julia, don't go down there. Julia stop', but she didn't hear me. And then she walked down through the brush, and I couldn't see her, and I didn't know what to do, so I sat down on the stone wall. Then I heard this strange laughing sound; it wasn't a human sound. It was spooky, and then there was this crashing. I called out. There was no answer. So I ran over the wall and down to the stream and found her, and I screamed and screamed, but she was...I thought she was dead. I ran back up the hill and through the orchard and the ball field, but there was no one around; the place was deserted. Then I went into the first unit I could find. I was screaming for help ..."

"Breathe, Parthia, breathe. I got it. I understand." Vale got up and stood beside the girl who was quivering in the blue chair. Gently she put her arm around Parthia's shoulders. The blond head tilted against her thigh and the girl just sobbed.

CHAPTER FIFTEEN

Win Lawrence spent all day with a two man crew by the stream. He cut off the offending tree limb with a chain saw and then, using the survey map, paced off the perimeter where the hospital property followed the old stone wall. There were almost two hundred feet of exposure at the crest of a little ravine through which the stream ran and pooled. A pretty little stream, and once, before the hospital sucked up so much of the water table, it must have been good for fishing and for fun. Win knew this fencing idea was a largely fruitless un-dertaking---God knows if a patient wanted to make an end, there are a thou-sand other ways to do it. He had scoped out more than one in his time. Still, he understood the hospital had to take some concrete action, however belated. At eleven, a pick-up truck made its way through the orchard and off-loaded metal posts and rolls of chain link fence. By two the posts were going into stony ground. Slow work.

Julia was on his mind. He remembered her in the ambulance, her terrified, disoriented eyes, the croak of her "Where am I?" He had told her who he was, what had happened, and where they were going. He had asked her if she'd ever been in an ambulance before; her eyes showed white around the pupils. She'd clung to him as they eased her from the ambulance onto a gurney, and he stayed with her all the way from the ER to her hospital room. He was there when her eyes closed under the sedative at nine pm on Saturday night. Before she slept, he had promised her he would see her on Monday. But not on Sunday; Sunday was out; he needed a day of sailing to lay his own demons to rest. He'd been in an ambulance before.

He called a halt to the work early enough so that he could get back to the office, take a shower, change his clothes, and drive over to see Julia on his way home.

A message on his machine surprised him: "Mr. Lawrence, it's Vale Messenger. It's just about three thirty. I do need to see Julia today. Why don't we meet there? I'll wait for you in the lobby, or vice-versa, If I..." A loud beep told him Vale Messenger had been timed out in mid-sentence.

He called her back. She picked up on the first ring. "Hi, it's Win, not Mr. Lawrence. I just..."

"I'm just finishing a session. Can I call you in ten minutes?"

"I'll call you in fifteen. I need to take a shower."

"Thanks." They broke the connection.

At twenty past five, Vale parked her car in the visitor's lot of North Shore Medical in Huntington. She saw the back of Win Lawrence as he pushed through the lobby doors ahead of her. She caught up to him in the gift shop.

"Hi," he said. "What do you think of this?" holding out a stuffed while owl.

"For Julia? I think it's perfect." He paid for it, and they walked to the bank of elevators. North Shore was a neat facility, three story buildings above parking lots on a woody knoll not far from the Sound. "Did you know Saturday was Julia's birthday?" she asked him.

"No," he said, "which one?"

"Twenty third." They stepped aside as an elevator disgorged its passengers, a wheel chair with an old man in it, two kids with balloons and tight-lipped parents. "I missed it," she said as they boarded; he pushed three.

"Missed what?"

"That Saturday was her birthday."

He looked at her, "Would you have done anything differently if you had remembered?"

She considered and realized that the answer was no. "Still," she said, "it may explain some part of it."

A few moments later they were standing at the open door of room 314. Win knocked on the frame. Something between a whisper and a croak invited them in. Julia's bed was closest to the door, and she broke into a big smile when she saw the two of them. Seated on the far side of the bed in a plastic covered hospital chair sat Myrna Kessler.

"Mr. Lawrence," Myrna said with a wan smile. "Mrs. Messenger," in a cooler tone.

"Myrna," Win said, and crossed to the other side of the bed, leaned over, and shook her hand. He was holding the stuffed owl in a plastic bag behind his back.

Vale in the meantime had come to take Julia's hand. "Julia," she said, "I'm so sorry."

"How's the girl?" Win asked.

Julia looked back and forth between them; a blush colored her olive complexion. "I'm all right," she whispered hoarsely. "Not much of a voice, as you can hear. My throat is sore, and my head still aches." Then she turned to Vale, "He was wonderful, Ms. Messenger."

"The whole thing was pretty traumatic for you," Vale offered. Julia nodded, her eyes lowered.

"I just learned it was your birthday on Saturday," Win said. "Here," and he held out the plastic bag, which Julia took and opened, then gave what might pass for squeal of delight. "I'll call her Athena," Julia said. "Thank you, Mr. Lawrence."

"You're welcome."

Julia was holding her owl out to Myrna, who took it briefly and then, like someone who does not know how to hold such a thing, handed it back quickly. But she sent a smile towards Win Lawrence.

"I used to have a German friend, " Vale said, making small talk; "he was doing a year in my university and was fascinated with slang. Once in his presence I used the phrase 'It's like bringing coals to Newcastle,' and he…" Vale broke off; Myrna was clearly confused. "Mrs. Kessler, 'coals to Newcastle' is a phrase that means bringing something to someone who already has more than enough of it already."

"Like bringing bagels to the rabbi?" Myrna said.

"Why, yes, I suppose so," Vale answered.

"Or salt to Siberia?" Win added.

"May I finish?" said Vale, smiling.

"Please." Win said.

"In German the phrase that's used is 'bringing owls to Athens.'"

"Really?" said Win.

"I love it," whispered Julia. "Grandma, the owl was the bird sacred to Athena. The city is named for Athena, the goddess of wisdom."

Myrna appeared not to be listening. "Well," she said, "I am going to make my way home." She leaned over and pecked her granddaughter on the cheek. "I'm so sorry I missed your birthday. I feel like this is all my fault."

"No, gramma, no," croaked Julia, tears coming to her eyes.

"I'll walk you to the elevator," Vale said. Out in the hall they went into a small visitors' lounge that for the moment was empty. "How are you, Myrna?" Vale asked.

"This whole thing has been terrible," she said, "just terrible. It's all my fault. Her birthday I should have…but I just couldn't…I…" Myrna's face was pinched with anguish.

"Lets sit down here, Mrs. Kessler," and Vale steered her to a chair.

"What will happen to her?"

"We will bring Julia back to North Forks in a couple of days, as soon as she has recovered her strength, and the doctors have made their final assessments. We'll take it from there. The important thing is that she's alive."

"But why?" asked Myrna, "why did she do this? Do you understand it? Why do these things happen, first her father, then my Arnold, now Julia?"

"It sounds like you feel cursed," Vale said.

"That's exactly how I feel. I've been trying to tell that to Julia for years. What did I do to deserve this?" reaching out to clutch Vale's wrist, "I feel Julia was attacking me by doing this. Just because I couldn't come on Saturday, she did this. Now what? Every time I can't make a date with Julia I have to be terrified she's going to kill herself?"

"Mrs. Kessler, I am Julia's therapist; we will work this out I promise you."

"I'm not so sure. Maybe it would be better if that Win Lawrence was her therapist. She seems to trust him very much."

"He is very good with her, but he's not a therapist."

"Sometimes people can be good therapists without being therapists," Myna said. She sighed and withdrew her hand. "I don't know," she said, "I don't know." Vale didn't either. "Well," Myrna said, getting to her feet, "I have to go." Vale walked her out into the hall and started towards the elevators with her. "No, you go visit with Julia. Maybe you can find out why she did this. If you do, tell me. Please. All I want to know is why." With that Myrna shuffled down the hall.

Vale came to the door and heard Win's voice. She listened for a moment. "…day putting in fence posts down by the stream. I'm thinking of naming the place 'Julia's Leap.' She heard a leathery croak that she took for a laugh. Vale was shocked at Win's lightness. And she envied it, a kind of freedom.

"I feel so ashamed," she heard Julia say.

"Don't be," he said. "Sometimes life just feels unbearable. For the Romans taking your own life was a legitimate choice." There was a silence then and Vale came into the room.

"How's my grandmother," Julia croaked. "No, don't tell me. She wonders why. I bet she asked you 'Why' six times."

"She doesn't understand."

"I'm not sure I do either," Julia said.

Just then a nurse appeared at the door. "Dinner time," she said, coming in with a foil-covered tray.

"I never thought I'd miss North Forks food," Julia said.

"Well, you'll be tasting it again soon enough," Vale said.

"I'll be coming back to North Forks?" Julia was unwrapping her plate, limp vegetables and a slab of meatloaf under a scum of gravy, purple Jell-O with a dollop of synthetic whipped cream.

"That's the plan," Vale replied.

"That looks awful," Win said, staring not entirely in mock alarm at her plate.

"My grandmother used to say hunger was the best cook; it can make anything look good."

"Well, I hope you're hungry," he said.

"Actually I am. I can't seem to get enough to eat."

"Julia, I'm going to be getting home," Vale said, getting to her feet.

"Me, too," said Win. "Happy birthday and many more."

"Thanks for this," she said, patting Athena on the head.

"We have a lot to talk about when you come back," Vale said, "but we have time. We'll make sense of it. The important thing is that you're alive."

"Yes," Julia said and gave Vale a look that rather surprised her; it was direct and her eyes were bright, "I am glad I am alive."

She and Win took the elevator to the ground floor and walked out into the low warm light of early evening.

"How about having a bite to eat with me?" Win said. "I can tell you my side of things."

"Dutch," she said.

"Dutch it is."

• ◆ •

She followed him into Huntington, and they parked in the municipal parking lot.

"You like sushi?" Lawrence asked.

"Who doesn't?"

"I know a good place."

The restaurant was tucked away on a side street and up a flight of stairs. There were aquaria along the walls, and a large tank divided the tables from the bar. "Wow!" Vale said gazing around; "I feel like I'll need a snorkel."

It was still early for the dinner crowd, and a waiter gave them their choice of where to sit. He put menus in front of them. "Something from the bar?"

"Sake," Vale said.

"Canadian Club on the rocks."

Presently the drinks arrived. Vale quickly emptied two small cups, sighed and leaned back on the banquette, listening to the sounds of water spilling into the tanks and mingling with the music of a flute coming over hidden speakers. The fish were dazzling in their glass worlds.

Win took a long swallow. "Do you snorkel?"

"I have. I went to Jamaica on my honeymoon. I loved it."

"The honeymoon or the snorkeling?"

"Both actually," she said. "I've been divorced awhile."

At a slightly slower pace Vale emptied two more thimbles of sake. They sat staring into the menus. Their waiter appeared. Win ordered a second drink and for dinner the mixed tempura. Vale ordered the sushi platter. Moments later two bowls of miso soup were set before them. Vale filled the ladle with soup. Win pushed his soup aside and nursed his second drink and appeared lost in his own thoughts.

"I have so many questions," she said tentatively, aware of his remoteness. She took another sip of her soup. "Do you feel like filling me in a little?"

He drew a long breath and let it out. "I really thought at first that she was dead. I got there first. Then a nurse pushed me aside and felt for a pulse and then very carefully felt under the head for the neck. Julia was alive, semi-conscious, disoriented. She was waterlogged and a dead weight beside, but we hefted her up and carried her to the cart. Then I went with her to the hospital. She was terrified when she discovered where she was."

"I've got a problem," Vale said, "I'd like to talk to you about Julia, but I feel a certain constraint."

"Patient confidentiality?"

"It's a little confusing. You aren't a therapist, but you're on the staff of the hospital. More to the point, you have a relationship with Julia, one which might do her some good."

"I think you can trust me to keep what you tell me to myself."

"I'd like you to know about her. I feel I'm in over my head, but then I have since the beginning."

"I believe you're new to North Forks."

"Yes. Three months."

"Second career?"

"Yes, I didn't get tenure. I was teaching English at Hofstra. Went for a Social Work degree. My sister thought I'd be good at this work, but..." she let her sentence dangle into silence.

"Probationary six months?"

"Un hunh. I'm still learning my way around DSMIII."

"What a pile of horseshit. Excuse my French." He caught Vale's quizzical look. "I think fitting people to a diagnosis for the purpose of getting an insurance company to give you money to treat them is... Well, it turns people into psychological accountants. Sorry."

"Sounds like you've argued this one many times."

"Yeah," he said, "mostly with myself. I was a... Never mind." He gathered himself, remembering her. "Was this the first time for you? The suicide attempt, I mean."

"Yes. Not that you don't know that patients in a hospital like North Forks are fragile. I have had several patients who'd made suicidal gestures before coming to North Forks. But this is the first time one of my patients has...tried it. I feel enormously responsible."

"Because you didn't remember that it was her birthday?"

"That and other things."

"Things you see in hindsight?" She nodded. He sipped his drink. "*If only*: now there's a pair of words that can drive a person crazy."

The waiter arrived with their food. They ate in hungry silence. Then she talked to him about Julia's history, about her being taken from a burning automobile at the age of seven on a frigid New Year's Eve and rushed in an ambulance to a hospital. Suddenly an orphan.

"That helps me understand what I was seeing in her face in the ambulance," he said. "It would have been scary enough without the memories."

"I think your being there must have mattered tremendously," she said.

"Perhaps."

Again she had the sense of his removing himself, going somewhere inside. Alone. She wanted to ask what it had been like for him, but she did not, only finished her meal and felt the fatigue of the day roll in like a fog.

Win called for their check, and they divided it when it came. They walked together to the parking lot. She stood for a moment while he took his key from his pocket and got into the cab of his pickup and rolled down the window. She watched him, a perfunctory thanks on the tip of her tongue, when she saw his big tanned hands gripping the steering wheel, the knuckles white. A stricken, indecipherable look on his face.

"I'm sorry," he said, looking out at her. "I kind of closed up. This whole thing with Julia has stirred up some of my own stuff. I've got some sorting out to do." Her eyes rested on his face. Gentle eyes, he thought.

She knew that had not been easy to say. "Sure," she said, "I understand," though she did not.

"Maybe you'd like to see the place where Julia went?" he offered.

She thought a moment. "Yes, that might be useful," she said.

"Maybe tomorrow?"

"I need to see what my day brings," she said, "but I'd like to."

"That's good." He reached for the ignition, then stopped. "You wouldn't have a camera by any chance. Lucore wants me to take pictures."

"I do. I'll bring it to work tomorrow."

Suddenly a smile broke over his features, boyish and winning; it gave her heart a lurch. What an odd man.

"Good night," she said, holding out her hand.

He took it in his, small as a bird in his leathery paw. "Thanks," he said, though she was not sure for what. Then he pulled away slowly, threading the parking lot, his tail lights winking red at each crossing.

CHAPTER SIXTEEN

The dreamer's cry, released from clenched jaws, flew out and battered against the window and the walls and echoed back into the dreamer's ears, while at the same time a distant voice was pulling the dreamer from sleep like a dead weight being winched up from a sunken wreck. "Parthia, Parthia, are you all right? Parthia!" The name made no sense. *Paula* was the girl in the dream, white-gowned and pinned to the table. "Help!" Paula was screaming under the examining lamp, bright as the sun. "Help me please!"

The dreamer's eyes opened and squinted against the light. "Parthia?" the voice said again. The dazzle resolve into a room, but this "Parthia" kept bouncing in and out of the body of Paula lying under a damp sheet on a gurney.

Then awakening, she looked towards the doorway: Ah, Ed Paley. She saw him leaning in; an air of concern twisting his features. His brown eyes skipped over her skin. "Are you all right?" he asked again.

"What day is it?" She lay back on her pillow. She knew his eyes were still on her face; she was grateful for his eyes.

"Wednesday."

"Ah, Wednesday. The day after Tuesday." She had no recollection of the day before.

"Yes," he said. "You've been pretty sedated. You were dreaming."

She felt his eyes leave her for a moment. It made her sit up. "What time is it?" The cotton sleeveless nightshirt was stuck to her. She lifted her arms to brush back her hair and felt the eyes come back. Eyes had a mind of their own; she pulled their strings.

"It's nine thirty," a little hoarseness in his voice. "I guess the sleeping meds really knocked you out."

"I keep missing breakfast."

"There's always cereal in the kitchen downstairs."

She swung her legs out of bed, slid forward, bringing the hem of her night-shirt riding up her thighs. "Is it hot out today?" She glanced around, needing to check on his eyes without seeming to check on his eyes. But she saw they were attached to her now, helping her, as she knew they would. This was the service of men's eyes: to help you find yourself when you were lost. She slid forward a little farther and leaned down to look under the bed for her slippers, knowing how this brought the hem of her nightshirt all the way up her hip. She pretend-ed to search the floor.

"There's news about Julia," the voice from the doorway informed her.

She straightened, froze, a slipper clenched in her right hand. "What?"

"She's coming back."

"When?" Her roommate was coming back, the pig to the pen.

"Around noon."

Parthia looked over at the mess of Julia's life, the battered journal she had almost finished reading, the scatter of papers spilled over it, the books, the drawers in Julia's bureau half open, the closet door ajar with its measly contents on display, the bib jeans, the ratty three-quarter length fake leather coat. Julia's smell was still in the room, the night cream and the unclean socks.

Scorn rose and then softened. She knew too much about the girl whose lifeless face she stared at as the stream floated her hair. "Don't be dead, Julia," she had prayed, dropping to her knees in the stream bed, her dress wet, her shoes ruined, peering down. "Don't be dead, please."

The eyes had opened then, glazed, looking up at her. Could they see anything? "Don't move, Julia. I'll get help," and she had gone screaming up through the orchard, screaming across the ball field, "Someone, help! Help!" The sound of her cry was stuck in her head. The sound of the cry from her dream.

She lifted a foot and put the slipper on. "How is she?"

"Pretty good, I guess." he said.

She lifted her other foot to receive the other slipper, gave him a wink of pink, then closed her thighs and stood unsteadily. But it had been enough.

"Thanks, Ed," she said, and met his eyes for moment. She was back in her own skin. She had trained him well.

"You're welcome," he said, not knowing why. Knowing why. Docile.

"I need my privacy now," and she walked to the door, beginning to pull up the hem of her nightshirt, sealing his eyes, soldering them to her. So he would come back again. When she needed him. She closed the door to an inch of the frame as the hem of her shirt cleared her hips.

•◆•

Win Lawrence noticed a striking looking blond woman walking the path around the upper lawn's perimeter and knocking on the door of the Tower. A real head-turner, and she knew it. He was waiting for Julia, a welcoming committee of one.

Then he saw her coming up the stone steps from the lower garden. She saw him. Her quick smile tugged at his heart. She was wearing the overalls he had seen her in when he picked her up from the stream. The same tee shirt. Both had been cleaned. Her red high-topped sneakers had new laces. She had a red kerchief around her neck. Her hair, he noticed, was pulled back into a bushy ponytail and gathered by a red band. In one hand she held a plastic bag, a bit of white fluff showing from the top---Athena, he thought. In the other a book. She came over to him, "Hello, Mr. Lawrence," she said in a hoarse whisper. "You're not here for me, are you?"

"Well, let's just say it wasn't out of my way to swing by."

"I'm checking back in."

"I see that," he said. "Any lasting damage?"

"My neck is sore; my throat, too. My voice—well, you can hear it---sounds a little leathery. I'm not looking forward to stares. But otherwise I'm OK, I guess." She smiled again at him, "Thanks for the visit on Monday, and thanks for Athena." Julia raised the plastic bag.

"I wonder what she will make of North Forks."

"Oh, she's glad to be here. I've told her so much about the place."

"Have you?'" he said and smiled. "Well, I'm glad to see you back."

"Thanks. Want to talk for a minute?" she asked.

"Sure," he said. "Where?"

"The Glass House?"

He knew it well. Its propane stove could keep it heated in the winter, and you could sit there, as he had once during a snowstorm years ago, with only a transparent membrane of glass separating him from the elements.

Julia sat and placed her bag on the floor, her book on her lap. He sat across from her in a patio chair. "What have you got there?" he asked.

"This? *The Dead and the Living.* It's a book of poems by Sharon Olds."

She handed it over to him. "Interesting title, he said. "Did they have that in the hospital bookstore?"

"No, but there was someone on my floor who had it." Win gave her an inquiring look. "A young man," she said in her rough whisper; "he was in for seizures. We met in the day room. He gave it to me." Julia saw the hint of a smile on his lips. "No, Mr. Lawrence. We just read some poetry to one another.'"

"This Sharon Olds any good?"

"I like her very much. Do you like poetry, Mr. Lawrence?"

"Can't say it's my strong suit."

"Want to hear one?"

"Sure." He passed the book back to her.

"It's called 'The Winter after your Death.'" Julia began to read in a breathy voice, but Win was already gone, for the title pitched him back to a winter night in this very place, snow swirling against the glass, and his heart like a chunk of ice. So he only heard a fragment: *"Deep in my body my green heart turns and thinks of you."*

When she finished, Julia looked up. She saw his lined face was pale, his gaze far away. "What do you think?" she asked.

Her words, a rope to a man overboard, pulled him back to the Glass House. It was summer, not winter; it was now, not then. "I like it," he said, hoping she believed him. "Perhaps some day you'll tell me what you find in it." Would his own heart ever be green again?

She closed the book on her lap. "I'm a little scared to be back, I'm not sure who I am right now."

"Maybe that's not a bad thing. I like the get-up, by the way."

"The bruise on my neck is pretty ugly," and she pulled aside her kerchief so he could see the purple discoloration of her skin, "I've got to cover it up some way."

"Ouch," he said.

"Yeah, but I'm alive."

"You certainly are."

"I keep expecting to fall back into being depressed, but I haven't. Yet."

"Maybe you won't."

"Can it be that easy?" she asked. "I've been thinking about that."

"I wouldn't call what you went through 'easy.'"

"Can I tell you something funny, Mr. Lawrence? The last thing I remember was the sound of a squirrel. It was at the end of the tree limb that I was...Have you ever heard the sound squirrels make?" He nodded. He had heard it often and smiled at the recollection; it was an odd, remarkable chortle.

"It's the funniest sound," she went on, "it's like a laughing duck with fuzz in its throat. I was standing on the stone over the stream. I had the rope tied. My weight was shifting. I'd passed the point of no return. Then there was this sound. I looked up and saw this squirrel at the end of the limb that was already dipping with my weight. It brought me back from...from where I was. And I remember thinking, 'Oh, there are so many things in the world to see and do, and I'm going to miss them.' But it was too late to stop. *So many things I will miss*: that was the last thought I had in my mind. Then I came to, and I was in water, cold water, and my throat was burning and my head pounded, and I was look-ing up into Parthia's face. It was like seeing the face of an angel. Seriously, Mr. Lawrence, I looked up into her face, and there were tears in her eyes. I thought for a moment I'd died and gone to heaven and that an angel was weeping for me; she was so beautiful." He said nothing.

"You came close."

"Then I was in the ambulance, and you were there. That meant so much. Not to be alone. You were a kind of angel, too, a guardian angel."

"Julia, I just did my..."

"I know," she interrupted him, "you just did your job. Still, I think you went a little out of your way."

"Not much. Really," he said.

"Don't worry, Mr. Lawrence, I'm not going to get all clingy. I suppose I'm always looking for a father figure, but I know the figure can never fill the space of the father I lost. Lost, but sort of never had in the first place."

"Shouldn't you be telling all this to Ms. Messenger?"

"I will. Actually, I can hardly wait to see her. I'm going to try to tell her ev-erything. I don't want to hide anything any more. Well, I better get on with it," she said. "Thanks for everything," and she got up and held out her hand.

"You're welcome," he said, holding her hand in his. Then she opened the door of the Glass House and closed it behind her.

He stayed. Was remembering the snowy night when he had sat in this very space, feverish and choked with rage, imagining his fist driving through the glass, imagining a blade of glass at his wrist, imagining his blood on the snow, craving oblivion, and suddenly Dean Venables was at the door, stamping the snow off his shoes and bringing a thermos of coffee and two cups. That was in the old days when North Forks was a forty-bed hospital, Gables a collection of drunks and psycho's of all ages, and Dean Venables a hard-working doctor who knew how to ease open the fist of a madman.

CHAPTER SEVENTEEN

Vale watched Claire Alexander pace her office. The aroma of her perfume filled the room, and she bloomed inside the scent like an exotic flower.

The visit was not entirely a surprise since Claire had left three messages on Vale's machine earlier that morning and in the last had said she was coming to the hospital with or without an appointment and hoped Dr. Messenger could find the time to see her. At this moment Vale was explaining to her why Parthia could not come home. "Not only can I not force her to do something she does not wish to do," Vale was saying, "but at this moment we would feel irresponsible to let her go. She is…just not ready to leave."

"And when might she be?" Didn't this woman understand? Time was running out.

"Mrs. Alexander, I cannot tell you." Vale resisted calling her Claire. She needed all the distance she could get. "It is not only my decision; I am part of a team of clinicians; and we all feel that Parthia is best served by remaining here for a while longer. We haven't even finished evaluating her. We are trying some medications, but we do not want to mask whatever it is that is troubling her. It is always delicate."

"But her father is dying."

"He is still at home?"

"He insists on remaining at home. He will…die at home. I'm still having trouble even saying these words. We have a physician, a friend, Claus Adenauer. Did I mention him to you? Of course, I did. I think you spoke with him. He and my husband have known each other for years. Actually before they came to this country. Claus is retired, but he is my husband's advising physician. There's a Doctor Phitzer from Sloan Kettering, who's in charge of the case. We have round the clock nursing care. There is nothing anyone else could do for him. He is dying. I know it. Wilhelm knows it. Parthia knows it. He is putting his affairs in order. He is waiting for his daughter to come home."

"I understand." Vale waited a moment, then began to probe. "Can you tell me something about Parthia's working life? What she was doing before she came home last time?"

Claire sat down and lit a cigarette. Vale could see weariness in her face. Like many beautiful women of her age, Claire Alexander looked better from a distance. "My daughter is a model. I call her my daughter, and she is in every way except by law. I thought often of adopting her; Wilhelm and I spoke of it, but in the end what would be the point? I never had a child, but I could not have given more love or attention to my own flesh and blood. Perhaps I gave too much." Claire sighed. "Parthia was a theater major at Sarah Lawrence, but nothing came of it. Lots of auditions, but no parts. She came home the summer after she graduated and moped around. I suggested she try to get some modeling work. As has often happened in the past, she just put herself in my hands. We hired a coach for her; then she took some classes at the Barbizon. Modeling is very different from acting; you don't have a script or a story. You learn to supply one and you learn to move in frames."

"This was how long ago?"

"Four years ago. I introduced her to a friend of mine in the industry, a man by the name of Biron Lord." Vale remembered the name. "It's his *nom de plume*, so to speak. Anyway, Biron took Parthia under his wing. I will tell you a secret, Mrs. Messenger. We paid him to 'discover' her. Not that he wasn't enthusiastic about her, don't get me wrong. And gradually she began to get work." Claire drew on her cigarette, then flicked the ash into the saucer.

"In time she was doing work for all the best companies. She has an Italian look, to her face, despite being blond, and that made her unusual. So she was an American face for *Biagotti, Calla, Versace, Mario Valentino*. She almost made the *Hidden Attractions* spread for Vogue. Things were building nicely, and she got a call from *Victoria's Secret* last fall. Brand new company, but a Wexner company." Vale had never heard of *Victoria's Secret* or Wexner and said so.

"*Limited? Lane Bryant?* No? Where do you shop? Mark my words *Victoria's Secret* is going to be big. There will be one in every shopping mall in America one day. Anyway, they were looking at Parthia. She would have been perfect, but irony of ironies, the agency that handled the account felt her face was *too beautiful*. Can you believe it?" And Claire blew smoke into the air to punctuate her incredulity.

"Anyway, things plateau'd after that from what I gather. There is a momentum to these things. The turnover is vicious. Besides, I think Parthia was getting bored. We saw her very little; she was living in SoHo in a dear little condo we bought for her. She had a trust fund from her father that allowed her to live well, not extravagantly, but she lacked for none of the necessities. Actually if she managed her money well, she wouldn't have to work, but of course, she wanted to work. We all need something to do, don't we?"

Vale nodded. "Please, continue."

"Well, that's it. I know she was close to Biron, and I got a sense that she was working on something with him. Well, you saw how she looked when she came here. You should have seen her when she came home. She gave me quite a scare. So perhaps she's doing something more in the art line. I don't know. She doesn't tell me much of anything. Unless she wants something. And now she won't talk to me at all. Why is that, Mrs. Messenger? Aren't you supposed to work with the family? Isn't that part of the treatment here?"

"Parthia is not a minor; she pretty much gets to run her treatment."

"Well, what's to stop her from running *away* from her treatment?"

"Actually, nothing," Vale said.

"She runs the show?"

"To a great extent it's her call."

Claire stubbed out her cigarette and seeing the red smudge on its filter, pulled out a small gold compact, flipped it open, scanned her face, then refreshed her lipstick with a practiced touch. She got up. As far as she was concerned, the interview was at an end. Who was this woman's superior?

"Mrs. Alexander, since you are here, may I ask *you* a question or two?"

Claire Alexander looked at her watch, a flash of gold and diamonds on her wrist, and then sat down. Vale contained her own irritation.

"Your husband, Dr. Alexander. Tell me about him. Professionally."

"My husband is a reconstructive surgeon. You do know what that is?"

"I believe I do," said Vale.

"Mrs. Messenger let me tell you a story about Wilhelm," and here Claire Alexander crossed her excellent legs and folded her hands over the leading knee, which brought her shoulders square. She gave Vale the benefit of her face in its frame of well-coiffed hair.

"Before I was Claire Alexander, I was Claire Summers. Does that name mean anything to you?" Vale shook her head. "Well, perhaps you are not much of a moviegoer."

Vale did not indicate whether she was or was not much of a moviegoer.

"Claire Summers was at the height of her powers in 1965. Think of Kathleen Turner, and you have a sense of me in my prime. I had the looks; I had the energy; I had the timing; I had the voice." Vale heard the mixture of pride and nostalgia in the woman's tone. "And then...well, then... I am amazed you don't remember this; it made the front pages of every film section of every paper." In 1965 Vale was in graduate school and marching against the war in Vietnam. Buddhist monks were immolating themselves in protest. If her life depended on it, she couldn't have told you the name of any movie that came out that year.

"I was in an automobile accident. I went through the windshield of a car. I was not driving." The memory made Claire shudder. "I lost my face." Vale came to full alert, the phrase ringing in her memory like an alarm bell. "I doubt you can understand what it means to have your entire life destroyed in a single moment."

Claire stopped, and once again Vale was struck by the weird mixture of self-theatrics and genuine feeling. "Please, Mrs. Alexander, go on."

In the spirit of suspense, Claire lit a second cigarette. "It is a very long story," she said with a sigh of smoke, "a story beautifully told in a made-for television film some fourteen years ago. I can get you a copy if you are interested. But the short of it is that after exhausting the resources of Hollywood quacks, after being told that my face was beyond repair, this face," and here she leaned forward as if to give Vale a closer look, "I heard about a reconstructive surgeon in New York by the name of Wilhelm Alexander. Photographs were sent; I flew east and the rest, well, you can see for yourself." Claire Alexander turned her face a little to one side and a little to the other so that Vale could admire Wilhelm Alexander's handiwork. "Could you tell?" she asked. "For one moment could you tell that my nose had been broken, this cheek crushed, these lips torn, my teeth broken, and that glass had been embedded in the skin? Go on, look." In spite of herself Vale leaned forward to look closely. The face hid its history perfectly.

Both women leaned back in their chairs. "Well?" Claire asked.

"A very good job I guess."

"A very good job! A very good job! Mrs. Messenger, you have no idea. It is as if you were to smash a priceless porcelain vase and then ask the restorer not only to glue it back together, but to do so in such a way that only a practiced eye could see that the vase had ever been shattered. He worked on me for two years. I gave myself over to him like a suppliant to a priest. I lived in the house, in the guest room. I endured untold hours of pain; I lived in bandages like a mummy; I studied the photographs with him, the drawings he made. Together we forged an astonishing reconstruction. At every stage we photographed the work, and it exceeded even his expectations. Only the voice," she touched her throat with her left hand; it rested there for a moment and the diamond caught the sun, "only my voice was beyond him. Torn chords can never be fully repaired. Scar tissue allows too little elasticity. My voice, well, you can hear it; it is not what it once was, and I could never work again in films. But those days were done for me anyway. I had found a new life. I had a mission to serve others. Wilhelm brought me back from the dead. There were so many people to help.

"Wilhelm presented our work at the annual convention of Cosmetic and Reconstructive Surgeons in Las Vegas in 1968. No one had ever seen anything like it. It brought him the chair at Mt. Sinai. It made him in a single stroke the most sought after reconstructive surgeon in America."

Claire sensed the story she was telling was somehow lost on this Messenger woman. She turned her cigarette in the saucer, putting it out. Well, she thought, it's not hard to understand; she knows nothing about beauty. "Anyway, we were married in 1969. I was 45 years old. I had been living for the past two years with Wilhelm and his daughter. He was a widower. I did not want to marry him until the work was done, but when it was, we stepped to the altar hand in hand. The surgeon and the movie star. Both with their losses. Both with their new lives. It was *made* for television. My husband is not a man who seeks publicity, but on this occasion, and for my sake, he allowed me to gather my lost world about me. I can't believe you saw no notice of this. But no, I can see your interests were elsewhere.

"So that, Mrs. Messenger, is Wilhelm Alexander, who until six months ago taught at the College of Physicians and Surgeons, maintained a surgical practice at New York Medical Center, and had a small very exclusive private practice in Babylon. The little Guest House in which Parthia tried to kill herself? It was converted from a three-car garage. It was my idea. I decorated it. It became the

refuge for our private clients who wished the best in care and complete ano-
nymity. You have no idea the faces he has worked on through the years. You
will hear that I said 'our private clients.' In 1970 Wilhelm began his private practice, and I was his office manager. We are as close as this," here Claire Alexander
held up the second and third fingers of her right hand as if she were making a
scout pledge. "Perhaps this gives you some idea of what it is that I am losing,"
and she lowered her hand to lap, and her shoulders sagged. She leaned back
against the chair, age and weariness showing. "Everything," she said simply, "I
am losing everything. Again."

"Mrs. Alexander I want to…"

"Won't you call me Claire, for God's sake?"

"Claire, then" Vale said, glancing at the clock. Parthia was due in her office
in twenty minutes, and Vale wanted to avoid the two of them crossing paths.
"Thank you for telling me all this. It is a remarkable story and it helps me understand Parthia. I have…"

"Does it? Does it? By all means let's understand Parthia. Be careful, Mrs.
Messenger, that *poor* Parthia does not manipulate you the way she has manipulated everyone in her life. She is selfish and she is spoiled. I suppose my husband
and I will have to bear some blame for that; I suppose too much love can be a
bad thing," though her tone said she did not believe this for a moment. "You
should have seen her when I met her."

"Well, actually," Mrs. Al…Claire, your story makes me wonder whether Dr.
Alexander ever did any work on his daughter? On Parthia." Vale held her breath.

"He most certainly did."

"Can you tell me more?"

"When Parthia saw what her father had done for me, she begged him to
do some work on her. Perhaps she was a little jealous, for I certainly had her
father's attentions. But she had mine. Almost from the moment we met, I em-
braced her. She had lost her mother you know, when she was very young." Vale
shook her head.

"You didn't know?" Claire leaned back and looked hard at Vale. "Mrs. Messenger, what have you been doing with Parthia this past…however long it's
been?" All Vale could do was shake her head; they had not made much headway
in developing a history. "My God at this rate Parthia could be here forever.

"So, in answer to your question, yes, Dr. Alexander acceded to Parthia's
wishes, though not till she was thirteen. To give you some idea of how badly

Parthia wanted this, she actually memorized whole parts of Vasari's essays from *Lives of the Painters*. She knew how to impress her father when she wanted to. And then, yes, he agreed to use his gifts to help her become who she wanted to be. What father, with such gifts, would not? And you can see, I trust, the fruit of their labor."

"I am beginning to," Vale said, to which she received a somewhat puzzled look. Questions begot more questions. But she needed to get Claire out of her office.

Moments later, with one final plea for Parthia to come home, Claire Alexander swept down the stairs. All that remained behind her was the scent of a rich perfume on the summer air and two cigarette stubs in the ash tray with the smudge of red lipstick on their filters like a harlot's kiss.

CHAPTER EIGHTEEN

After lunch Julia returned to the room she shared with Parthia. Would she ridicule her stuffed owl? Jean Newcombe was sitting on a chair in the hall. Not a good sign. "How you doing, Julia?" Jean asked.

"I'm pretty OK actually."

"Welcome back. Good luck."

"Thanks," Julia said and stepped into her room.

Parthia was standing by Julia's desk, looking down at the open page of her notebook. Julia cleared her scratchy throat.

Parthia turned, "I heard you in the hall. At least I heard a croak I assumed was yours."

Julia walked to the desk. Parthia stepped away. "Find anything interesting here?" Julia asked.

"I'm not much of a judge of these things, but I think your poetry is pretty good."

The sense of her privacy being violated warred with the unexpected pleasure of the compliment. Julia reached down and closed the cover of her journal. "I didn't expect you to read my diary."

"Your voice sounds really terrible."

"My throat's sore."

"You're lucky that's all it is," Parthia said. "Unless of course you really wanted to kill yourself. In that case you were unlucky. Which is it?"

Julia sat down on the edge of her bed. "I kind of left things a mess. Sorry."

"Don't worry about it." Parthia was looking at herself in the full-length mirror on the back of the door. "I've got an appointment with Messenger. You can clean up while I'm gone." She gave her hair a pat. She placed several cigarettes in a slim silver case, and slid it into her back pocket. "Come on, Newcombe," Parthia said, "don't let me out of your sight." Soon after they left, another person took the chair by the door.

Alone in the room, Julia sat motionless. Parthia confused her. At first there had been only two of her, Day Parthia with her cruelty and Night Parthia with her demons. Then, or maybe it had been a dream, there was a girl weeping over her, her face transfigured with a kind of terrible pathos. She wondered if she would ever get a glimpse of that Parthia again.

Julia reached in to her plastic bag, pulled Athena out, and looked into the glassy eyes. "What do you say, you wise old owl? Will Parthia make fun of you? And do I care?" Then, uncharacteristically, she set about bringing some order to her scattered belongings.

•◆•

"Julia's back," Parthia said, standing by the window, refusing to sit down on the blue chair.

"Yes, I know. I will see her later. What was it like to see her again?"

"I liked having the room to myself; she's a slob."

"That's all?"

"I feel awkward."

"Because…?"

"Because I feel guilty." The defiant chin did not seem particularly con-science-stricken to Vale. "I can't figure out whether I provoked her to try to take her life or whether I somehow saved her."

"Maybe neither. Maybe both. If that degree of despair was in her, maybe it would have come out one way or another. Better here than somewhere else. She would have regained consciousness. She wasn't going to die."

"It wasn't her time?"

"If you want to put it that way. But you got way under her skin, and it sent her someplace she hadn't expected to go to."

"Julia's a good person," Parthia said. "She's the ugly duckling, and I don't think she'll ever be a swan. It would take…" Parthia interrupted herself, her eyes darting to the ashtray on the edge of the desk. A quick crease furrowed her brow, then she tilted her head a little to one side and her nostrils flared.

"Claire's been here. I know the color of that lipstick and the smell of her perfume."

"She was. This is the second time. She was here shortly after you were admitted."

"Why didn't you tell me?"

Vale evaded the answer, "You recall I asked you if I could talk with Claire, and you gave me permission."

"You didn't call her in?"

"No I didn't. I had a message on my machine when I came to my office that she was just going to show up here at about noon."

"Yeah, that's her." Parthia leaned forward and reached into her pocket for her silver case. "Were you going to tell me that she was here this time?"

"It might have come up in the normal course of things."

"Let me guess why she came. She wants you to get me to come home." Vale nodded. "And what did you say?"

"That I didn't think you were ready."

"Too unbalanced?"

"I said you were a dangerous psychopath who was seducing all the men on the staff and planning your roommate's murder."

"You did not!" Here Parthia reached into the drawer of Vale's desk and withdrew the matches. She lit her cigarette and cranked open the mullioned widow a little wider.

"I told her it wasn't my decision alone; the clinical staff would decide. She says she's been leaving messages for you."

"I don't want to deal with Claire." Parthia turned to glare at Vale, "It is my prerogative isn't it? I can choose who I want to talk to and who not."

"Yes, you can."

"What else did she talk about? You ask her any questions? Or are you obliged to maintain some kind of confidentiality with her?"

"No, she's not my patient."

"Good. What'd you talk to her about?"

"She told me about this Biron Lord and how you had worked for him." Parthia snorted out a gust of smoke; the gesture did not cover a startled look. "No, about your regular work for him. I kept your secret." Parthia seemed relieved. "Claire also told me that your mother died when you were seven." Vale waited to see what Parthia might say. Parthia said nothing. "I didn't know that; I had assumed your parents were divorced. Pretty important thing to know about you."

"What else?"

"That your father was a reconstructive surgeon who had restored Claire's face."

"Oh yeah. She loves to tell that story."

"What do you mean?"

"What else did she tell you?"

"That your father did some cosmetic surgery on you." Off-hand as possible with these words, Vale watched the face before her for its reactions. But the face, seen only in profile as Parthia smoked, betrayed nothing. Was being a model like being a poker player, no tells?

"Did she tell you why?"

"She said that you asked him to."

"I see," said Parthia. Here she stubbed out her cigarette and sat in the blue chair.

"Do you want to tell me..."

"I don't go there," Parthia said.

"Go where?"

"I don't talk about my father."

"And why not?"

"Because I don't." Silence fell between them. "I need to get off status," Parthia said, "and I don't want you to twist my arm. I don't want you to make it conditional on my telling you things I am not ready to tell you. I don't want to be manipulated. I can't stand the confinement. I didn't do anything to deserve it. I am not a danger to myself."

Vale was dismayed that they were now engaged again in a struggle about Parthia's status. The seven hundred pound gorilla of her family history hunched in the room, and Parthia refused to acknowledge it. Vale came up against the limits of her role. She could not compel anything. "No," she said, "I don't think you are a danger to yourself, though I am not sure I can get others to agree with me."

"What's changed?"

"You were on limited ground and overstepped the boundaries."

"I admit that. I won't do that again. Listen, I've got a thing about being confined. It's...hard."

Vale had the strongest sense of the iron will that kept Parthia locked inside, the face that could freeze into a mask. "Parthia, will you tell me something about your dreams? In almost every nursing report I've read since you've been on SA, night staff says you seem to have very troubled sleep. Julia mentioned it to me also last week. Can you let me in just a little bit?" Vale coaxed. And then, on a hunch, she asked, "Do you have things you dream about again and again?"

"Maybe."

"Can you tell me?"

"Will you argue to get me off status?"

"I won't bargain with you. Tell me if you want. It's your choice." Vale waited for the slap of refusal.

Parthia withdrew another cigarette, lit it, snapped her wrist and deposited the match in the saucer Vale thought her hand trembled as she put her cigarette to her lips.

"In these dreams---I mean they're different but somehow all the same---I am walking up a long flight of marble steps. The steps are very wide. The place is familiar, like a palace or a great house of state. There are statues in niches, and there are many rooms." Parthia's tongue ran over dried lips. She drew in a lungful of smoke.

"In this dream I have white gloves on. Someone is holding my hand, but I can't see who it is. When I look up to see the person's face, I can't because it is hidden behind a mask of some kind. For a moment in the dream I think we are going to a masquerade ball, for the person, the man, holding my hand is not dressed in ordinary clothes. He's..." Parthia drew in and exhaled, "He's all in white. Kind of like a ghost or someone in the Ku Klux Clan." Parthia stopped.

"Go on," Vale said softly.

"We reach the top of the stairs, and we go into an enormous room. The room is deserted; there is no one in it, but there are pictures on the walls. I realize that I am in a kind of museum. I do not like it here. I don't want to go into these rooms, but the person holding my hand pulls me along, and I can't resist. I don't want to look at the pictures, but I do; I have to. I see they are portraits, you know like the old masters. Individual portraits of people dressed in fine clothes, but the faces are smudged, unclear." Vale saw that small beads of perspiration had appeared on her forehead.

"At first I think that the painter just did a bad job, but soon I realize that someone has come with turpentine or linseed oil and smeared the portraits until the features are blurred. They've been vandalized. For some reason I become very afraid at this point. I start to pull hard against the hand that is holding me, but I can't get away. More than that, I feel like I am losing strength."

Parthia got up and crossed to the window. She spoke with her back to Vale, her tone flat, her voice mechanical and punctuated by drags on her cigarette. "We go into a second room, and in this room there are not paintings but photographs. Life-sized photographs. But the wrong faces go with the wrong bodies. An old woman---you can tell by her hands and her ratty housedress---has the face of a young girl; a boy with a toy six shooter has the face of hobo; a bride stands beside her groom, but their faces are reversed."

A long silence followed. Vale said nothing, sensing that any word from her would break a spell, at the same time aware of Parthia's courage. Then she continued in a voice Vale had to lean forward to hear. "We go into one more room. I feel in the dream as if I am losing all my will. I cannot resist: I am losing the feeling in my hands; I don't feel my feet on the floor; I weigh nothing, and it is getting colder. The room is getting darker as if someone were turning down the lights very slowly. There is only one picture in this third room, and it is on the far wall. And the man with the white mask is pulling me towards this picture, and when I look at it, I see it's a picture of a little girl, an ugly little girl with yellow pigtails and braces on her teeth and bad skin, an ugly girl and the man lets go of my hand, and he takes a razor from his pocket, you know the kind of razor they have in barber shops, and he starts cutting out the face of the girl in the picture..." Parthia's free hand in the air holds the razor and pares at something only she can see---"and I start screaming only nothing will come out of my mouth and I am screaming and screaming as the man cuts away the face."

Parthia dropped her cigarette to the floor, and her hands flew to her face and covered it, the fingers, gathered under the eyes, curled to claws. Vale started from her chair, crushed the cigarette under her foot, and caught the hands before the nails could score the skin. "Breathe, Parthia," she commanded.

Parthia yanked her hands away and then covered her face, her teeth locked tight, ridges of muscle standing out along her jaw line.

"Come back," Vale said. "I'm here, Parthia. You're safe." Gently Vale drew Parthia's hands down from her cheeks. Parthia licked her dry lips. Vale saw her breathing was slowing, but Parthia could not or would not look up at her. Vale let go the trembling hands and sat down again. She was astonished at the transformation in the girl and the power of her dream.

"You are very brave, Parthia," was all she could think to say.

Turning, Parthia slumped into the chair. "Ms. Messenger, why do I feel so ashamed? I feel embarrassed, like I feel I can't look at you, or I don't want you to look at me." Having said this, Parthia slowly raised her head. There were tears on her cheeks. "You know what scares me the most about this dream, Ms. Messenger?" Vale shook her head. "What scares me the most is that there is another room." Here Parthia visibly shuddered. "In the dream when I am screaming and frantic, I look around for some place to escape to, and I see that there is another room, except that it is totally dark, and I know that whatever is happening here with the man in white, there---in that fourth room---it is worse." She looked down, saw the crushed cigarette on the floor. In a gesture Vale found oddly touching, Parthia reached down, picked it up, and put it down on the saucer. Then she looked directly at Vale. "Ms. Messenger, what could be worse...in the fourth room?"

• ◆ •

Crossing the grounds, Dean Venables spotted Win Lawrence on his way down from the dining room. He waited for him in the center of the quadrangle.

"I was looking for you," Dean said; the men shook hands.

"You got time for a cup of coffee?" Win asked.

"Only if it's fresh."

"You know me."

"I do," said Dean; "I do." They fell into step and crossed the driveway.

They climbed the B&G cement steps and walked down the hall to Win's office. While Win boiled some water on the hot plate and put two heaping spoonfuls of coffee in the French press, Dean took a chair and put his feet up on a make-shift coffee table. He surveyed his friend's domain: unfinished wood shelves with books and manuals stacked on them, bins where blue prints stood like umbrellas in their stands, the smell of sawdust in the air from the shop, and, coming through the door, the sound of men finishing a day's work, lockers banging shut, equipment being stowed. Dean smiled to himself; the arrangement they had devised years ago had worked out well.

Dean. "What have you been up to?" he asked.

"Finishing Lucore's perimeter. We're going to build watchtowers and install big klieg lights. Serge wants Dobermans."

Dean laughed. "Speaking of dogs, what happened with your decision to get a dog?"

"Postponed." Win poured steaming water into the press. "Dogs and sailboats don't usually go together." Win got out cups and a few minutes later filled them before sitting down on the battered sofa under the window. He put his boots up on the table opposite Dean's wingtips. "You want a tot of whisky in that? I've got some in my locker."

"No, this is fine."

They savored their coffee for a moment. "So how was your time sailing?" Win asked.

"Wonderful," Dean said. It was a passion both men shared. Though Dean no longer owned his own boat, he and his wife Rachel were often sailing on the Sound with friends and family. "You been out recently on the *Requiem?*" Dean asked referring to the old 30 foot Erikson Win would sail alone on weekends out past the end of Long Island.

"Not recently, but I hope to Saturday. I need to get away."

"Not surprised," said Dean. "I haven't had a moment to catch up since this whole thing with the Kessler girl happened. Wanted to check in with you. You were pretty close to it. Anything you want to talk about?"

Win looked at Dean over the rim of his coffee cup. "You being my therapist here?"

"An informed friend, maybe. I..."

"Spit it out, Dean. Delicacy doesn't become you."

"OK. You drinking?"

"Ahh, I see." Win put down his cup. "Maybe a little more than usual, but nothing out of control. This time I was at least able to be of some use."

"To Julia you mean."

"Yeah. Carrying her up from the stream, knowing she was alive. There was some relief in that. I've gotten a little attached to Julia. I'm not sure how appropriate that is."

Dean waved a dismissive hand. "I'm not surprised you're attached to her. Your history aside, it's a fairly intimate thing to save a life."

"I'm not sure I did any life-saving, but she certainly clung to me, and it felt good."

"How's she doing?"

"She came back today. I saw her. Actually, I went out of my way to spend some time with her. She seems...I didn't know her before, of course, but she looked, well, bright I guess is the word for it. I went to see her at North Shore. I went with Vale Messenger. Can it be that easy, Dean?" Win realized he was repeating Julia's question.

"What do you mean?"

"I mean can an experience like Julia's change a person, really change them?"

"Who the hell knows?" Dean laughed.

"But you're the doctor."

"Maybe, but I still don't know a thing."

"You knew enough to bring me coffee in a snowstorm."

"Well, I knew you loved your coffee. And this is up to your usual standards," Dean said, emptying his cup. "By the way, you have any impression of Vale Messenger?"

"I can see she cares. She sort of took me into her professional confidences about Julia."

"Good."

"Why good?'"

"I was thinking she could probably use someone to talk to. Pamela can be intimidating. Vale's still finding her way."

"I'm not sure I can be of much..."

"Nonsense," said Dean, "I've talked cases with you. You have an unusual perspective. You've been there and back. You remember that ballplayer we had here ...?" Dean was searching his memory.

"Gallagher, Tim Gallagher. He played triple A for the Mets and kept fucking up every time he got called up to the Majors. Then hit the booze hard."

"Right, Tim Gallagher. You used to play catch with him out on the ball field. You were the one he told about his father and the incest. He told you more about himself than he ever told me. You *were* his therapist as far as I was concerned. You have good instincts."

"For bullshit."

"Well, that's more than half the game. People trust you."

"Well, the other half of the therapy game is patience, and in that department I am sorely lacking."

"It's true," Dean said; "you do not suffer fools gladly."

"Except for you, Dean."

"Shhh," Dean said, "the walls have ears," and on that note, he put his empty cup on the table and let himself out.

CHAPTER NINETEEN

"Good morning," Ben Farmer said, opening their Friday meeting. "Julia's back and settled, and hopefully we've had our drama for the summer." Vale felt relieved that Julia's harrowing act might be construed as a scene in some familiar summer "drama." She wondered if she ever might have such a long view of things.

Edna White, reading the SA report from the night before, came to Parthia last. "She was complaining constantly of the intrusiveness of SA. Only person she seems able to work with is Ed Paley. I've got a funny feeling about this preference of hers."

Willa Maynard nodded. "I actually have some concerns about that, too," she said. "Parthia can be extremely seductive. The girls hate her, and all the boys follow her like dogs after a...well, you know what I mean. Of course, she gives no one the time of day, but she can cast a spell of sorts, and I think Ed may be a little overmatched. He's off today, but I mean to talk to him. I've been getting Jean to sit status when she's on duty, and another female mental health worker when she's not, but I wonder if Julia and Parthia need SA at all."

Farmer turned to Vale. "What do you think? And please spare us the preface about how inexperienced you are." Everyone laughed; Vale blushed. The room grew silent, waiting.

"This is a big weekend for Julia," Vale began. "Her grandmother is supposed to come visit. Julia is prepared for her not to show up, but I am still not sure how fragile she really is. I'm going to recommend the visit be on grounds, but that the restriction be lifted. As far as Parthia is concerned, she's opened up a bit, seems genuinely contrite about her actions. I'd like to respond to that."

"I will say this," said Willa, "that with people taking their summer vacations, we're spread thin. When Julia and Parthia are both in their room, it's no problem, but as soon as they leave, we need two people on them. Makes the other patients resentful."

Ben Farmer looked around the room. "OK," he said, "I would suggest regular check-in's, limited grounds, but no more SA. And they should not be allowed to go off together alone."

"Yes,' said Edna, "that's right."

The meeting adjourned shortly afterwards.

Back in her office she found two messages on her answering machine. "Vale, it's Win Lawrence. Give me a call when you get a chance today." She had brought her camera and suspected he was calling about seeing the site.

She listened as the second message began, *"For a crowd is not a company; and faces are but a gallery of pictures; and talk but a tinkling cymbal where there is no love."* She hit rewind and listened again to a woman's accented voice ---middle European? Slavic?---recite something that sounded faintly biblical.

Vale knew it was another message in a sequence she had taken at first to be crank calls. *I'm looking for Doctor A. I've lost my face* And *A pretty face is not an open book.* Now this. The random was starting to feel like a pattern. Who were these people leaving messages for her? She replayed the message a third time, this time transcribing it into her journal. Then she called Win Lawrence's number, and not reaching him requested that he call her later.

•◆•

Her morning sessions were full of testy, glimmering insights on the part of both Raymond and Liza-Jane. With a little steering from Vale, Raymond was able to connect his anger at Julia for her "hanging act" with his mother's suicide. Liza-Jane, an inveterate loner whose M.O was contempt, spoke of feeling some respect for Julia's courage at coming back and facing the music, which gave Vale the opening to remark that "facing things is not easy. Is it?" To which, damned if Liza-Jane did not actually tear up.

But the real surprise of the morning was Julia herself. Unprompted, she spoke about being sexually abused in her second foster placement. She described how it had begun, how it was conducted, and how long it lasted. This engulfing flashback was what had overcome her in her walk with Parthia. Much remained to understand, of course, not only why the abuse had gone on so long, but also what it had really been like for Julia, who had been twelve when it started. The text books said that girls who suffered abuse sometimes found guilty pleasure in the act, the acknowledgment of which was usually the last and most difficult piece to be admitted. There was the pleasure of power, of some momentary control, and then the pleasure of pleasure, the body's collusion.

What impressed Vale most, however, was Julia's last remark in the session. "I know we are both wondering whether this positive energy I have will last. In some ways it seems like a kind of high, a reprieve. It won't surprise me if I crash at some point." This self-awareness was more re-assuring than all the confessions.

Vale had a quick lunch, then went to a meeting about placement possibilities for Raymond. Back at her desk she finished up her notes on the morning sessions, made calls to the insurance company to argue for extending Julia's length of stay, and was about to write a quick note to Meli when Parthia's knock sounded on her door, and her phone rang at the same moment.

She motioned the girl into her office. "Vale Messenger here." Vale watched Parthia walk to the window, looking out. "Yes, what can I do for you?" Parthia was wearing a pale yellow dress today with blue cornflowers on it. "This is not a good time for me to talk." Summery colors, light, lovely. "Mrs. Alexander, I can call you back at four, but I cannot talk now." She noticed too the pale coral toenail polish, fingernails to match. Incarnadine was out, coral was back in. "No. Well, Good..." Cut off, she replaced the receiver.

"She's something, isn't she?" Parthia said.

"She is worried about your father."

"You notice he hasn't picked up the telephone,"

"And would that make a difference?"

"Frankly, I can't imagine him asking."

"That's not really an answer to my question. What if he did call?"

"He won't."

"Why is that?"

"Because he is Vill-helm Alexander."

"I don't understand."

"You wouldn't. You couldn't. Subject closed." Ice garbed in a yellow dress with cornflowers on it. No need for an air-conditioner with Parthia as your patient.

"I've been thinking about the dream you told me about," Vale began.

"What about it?"

"I was wondering if you have any thoughts about it. Sometimes we can't begin to think what a dream is telling us until we have shared it. Spoken it."

"I haven't thought about it."

"Would you be willing to think with me now, a little?"

"So what do you want me to think about?"

"Talk to me about museums."

"Talk to you about museums? Like, great museums I have known."

"Sure, why not?"

"Smoke first."

"The fuming defense?"

"Maybe, but I want a cigarette."

They enacted their little ritual, and when she went to stand by the partially opened window, leaning against the wall and looking out for a moment, Vale caught something in the angle of Parthia's head, a distant look in the girl's eyes, a sadness at the corners of her mouth, that struck her afresh with the sense of having seen the face before. The phrase "Great museums I have known" echoed in her mind, and she knew Parthia's was not a face she'd seen in any glamour magazine. Somewhere else. The hunch was insistent.

"I want to tell you something about Claire. It's sort of museumy. Claire's private museum."

"All right." Parthia might be avoiding something, but she was also volunteering something. They had time.

"One day, I was alone in the house in Babylon. I went snooping around."

"How old were you?"

"I don't know, fifteen maybe. I always felt that there were secrets in that house, but I could never find them. When I was alone, I'd snoop." Vale made a mental note: *What was she looking for really?* "This time I went into their bedroom, and I opened the drawer under Claire's side of the bed. I had never done this before. I found a box; the sort you might keep jewelry in. It was made of ebony and inlaid with mother-of-pearl. A treasure box. It was locked. I looked for a key and found it in the top drawer of the night table by the bed. I opened the lid of the box." Parthia tapped her cigarette ash carefully on the saucer on Vale's desk.

Under a covering of burgundy velvet Parthia had found tubes of creams and unguents of different scents. She knew instantly that they were sexual things, lubricants, stimulants of some kind, but the box was deep and she knew it had more layers to it, but she could not lift out the top shelf until she saw that there was a button on the front of the box. When she pressed this, the top shelf released, lifted up to reveal a second level. On this second shelf was a vibrator on a bed of burgundy velvet ---she knew it for what it was; Babylon girls talk. Beside it lay a variety of differently sized and shaped heads, each in its own fitted pocket. Parthia laid them out like exotic toys. She pressed the button a second time, and the lowest level was revealed where she found a stack of slender books, each with a soft cover and thick hand cut paper pages. And photographs. "I closed everything back up, but I took one book and some photographs back to my room, and I closed my door, and I looked at what I had found."

"The end of innocence," Vale said.

Parthia looked up. "Exactly," she said. "But I wasn't turned off. It wasn't like 'Oo, my step mother is a pervert.' No, it was more like having my first look into an adult world. Or like discovering that people hide parts of themselves."

"That people have other faces?" Vale offered.

"Don't interrupt me." Vale felt the force of a hard appraising eye. "You want to hear this story or not?"

Vale held up her hands; Parthia continued. "It took me a while to see that Claire was in each, sometimes the central figure, sometimes a player. I knew she had been an actress, but these pictures were not like, you know, from her Hollywood days. These were pictures of Claire after the surgery. Believe me, I'd seen enough before and after photographs---there's a whole album of them on the coffee table in the living room. This was stuff Claire had done since Daddy. I wondered if he knew. I wondered if he..." Parthia broke off. Vale completed the thought in her own mind. Parthia took a last drag on her cigarette, leaned over Vale's desk and twisted it on the saucer, a single thread of smoke rising. She came and sat down in the blue chair.

"Anyway, I was fascinated. The lighting was gorgeous, the color vibrant, and the figures---I didn't know what to call them, models or actors---were caught in carnal acts, poses really, in which there was an odd mixture of intensity and aesthetics. I wasn't really turned on, but I wondered where they were taken. In one there was a view out the window of the Eiffel Tower, but that could have been a set. Some of the pieces were very period---costumes and jewelry. Some were of banquet scenes, but all the guests were naked or masked in costumes, or caught in various, you know, acts. I wanted to steal them to show my girlfriends; at the same time I wanted to put them back and pretend I never saw them. But I never looked at Claire the same way again. When she sat at dinner with my father; when she entertained and people came to the house; when she went out to the city to shop, I imagined this other world that Claire belonged to, and I began to fantasize about it. A kind of theater world, a demi-monde, which she went to when she was done being a step-mother or a wife.

"When she introduced me to Biron Lord after I graduated from college and floundered out of the theater scene, I was sure that she was showing me the way into that world. Biron was the most fascinating man I had ever met. He still is. Crude and suave, funny and deadly serious, brilliant eye, brilliant sense of staging, and he knew how to sell you. He had some connection to Robert Mapplethorpe. You know who that is?" Parthia saw Vale's nod.

"Anyway I don't think Claire suspected that I had discovered this side of her. When I began to do some special work with Biron, I never told her. But perhaps she suspected."

The phone rang. Vale excused herself and picked it up. "What's up?" she asked, "I'm in session." Pause. Vale looked at her watch. "What time?" Pause. "Sounds good." Pause. "Yes, I brought it."

She put the phone down and saw that Parthia had her head cocked to one side and was looking at her with a curious expression. "Who was that?"

"Win Lawrence, the man who saved Julia. He wants to show me the place where it happened."

"Hmmm. Strange first date."

"Hardly. He needs photographs for documentation. I have a camera."

"How convenient. You'll ruin your shoes."

Fearful that they had lost the thread, Vale asked, "Was there more you wanted to tell me about the treasure box? About secrets in the house. About this Biron Lord?"

"You're just a bundle of questions aren't you? Shrinks are like detectives."

"Snoops?"

"Touché. No, nothing else. Box closed. Case closed."

"Parthia, when Claire told me that your father had done some reconstructive work with you, I wondered what Claire's role was. Towards you, I mean. In your life with your Dad."

"She made me want the things she wanted. I had no one. My mother was gone, and then there was Claire, all bandages and ballyhoo, and I felt my father and Claire were starting another life, as if they shared some great bond, and I was not part of it. They were like two people on a boat that was pulling away from the dock, and I was being left behind. And Claire, she kind of...I don't know, it's like she was saying, 'You want to be part of this new family, I'll show you how. I mean, of course, I wanted to be 'part of this new family.'"

"And also there must have been a part of you that resented the hell out of Claire."

"Yeah, sure. But I didn't really know that then. I just envied her, and when she made suggestions about what I should wear or do, I followed. And then, well, she thought I should have my nose done for my thirteenth birthday. And... Are you going to let me off status?"

"Won't you finish what you were saying?"

"I want to kill her."

"Because..."

"Because she used me."

"How?"

"I don't want to talk about it. You've gotten more out of me in a half hour than Mark Warren did in a year. So back off. Am I getting off this fucking status or not?"

"Yes, the staff had a discussion. But I have a question."

"Our time's up, Messenger. Besides, you've got an assignation. " And Parthia, summery in garb, wintry in mien, pulled the door sharply closed behind her.

Vale took fifteen minutes to record her impressions. She felt the same exhilaration she had felt before. It was as if she had picked up the scent of something. "Shrinks are like detectives." Clues and hunches. And legwork. Suddenly she had a plan.

• ◆ •

They met in the mailroom at four. Win saw she had her camera and thanked her for bringing it. They sorted through their mail. In her box Vale's found a notice for a hospital-wide schedule change: the summer Olympics were to be held next Wednesday. Sessions were cancelled, but it was a working day. Therapists were expected to come out and support their patients. Vale passed the note to Win with a questioning look.

"They do it every summer. Dean went to a boarding school where the head-master would declare a holiday for no good reason once or twice a semester. He loved it; all the kids did; he said it broke the routine. So he does it here, but calls it the "Summer Olympics". Patients enjoy it; it's the one time all the units mix."

They left the Administration Building and walked across the parking lot. "How was your day?" he asked her, and they made small talk as they passed beyond the Quad. The afternoon sun was snared in the tops of the big maples. A warm breeze, unhampered by humidity, carried the scents of dry earth, of cut grass, and the mixed fragrances of mid-summer flowers planted everywhere.

They stopped at the edge of the ball field. A game was in progress, Gables divided into two teams. Cries and voices, squeals and taunts reached them. They walked up the sideline. Frank Jessup was pitching. Vale watched him windmill a fast underhand pitch. Liza-Jane, playing third base, gave Vale a double-take as she and Win walked by. Catherine, Earl Andrews, and Raymond were in the outfield. Julia and Parthia were seated on the bleachers behind first base.

"Sometimes this place can look so normal," she said. "Kids playing ball. You'd never know that each of them was walking around with demons."

They followed the curve of the outfield behind the players past center into right. Catherine, idly throwing her glove into the air, turned to wave at them just as the crack of a bat sounded. Vale saw a well hit ball sail out towards them. Catherine was trying to get her glove on her hand, but was unable to locate the ball in the flickering light coming through the tops of the trees. Win Lawrence cut to his right, waited, and caught the ball waist high in the pocket of his hands. He hurled it all the way to Frank Jessup on the mound. Catherine gave him an appreciative look. Someone screamed, "No fair!"

Catherine looked at Vale. "Where you going, Ms. Messenger?" she asked.

"I'm going to see where Julia's accident happened," she replied.

"Accident?"

"OK," Vale said, "her suicide attempt."

"You better keep your mind on the game," Win said; "the same guy is at the plate. My catch didn't count."

They walked towards the weedy ground where the mowed field ended. "You look like you played some baseball in your time," Vale said. The catch had been instinctive and graceful.

"A million years ago," he said.

"Professional?"

"No, nothing like that, college then a summer of semi-pro, but I was mediocre."

"That's a little hard to believe," Vale said. They were following a rutted track through thickening undergrowth. Ahead of them old unpruned apple trees twisted in unkempt rows.

"When you play ball in school, you think you're quite a hotshot, but you discover pretty quick there's a big gap between Joe College and even a fair semi-pro ballplayer."

"I see," she said, but she believed she was only getting part of the story.

In silence they followed an overgrown dirt road into the orchard. She could see it had once been a lovely place. The evenly spaced apple trees had born fruit years ago. Now many broken boughs were strewn upon the ground. "What a shame to have let this go."

"You could bring this orchard back," Win said, "but it would take a lot of work."

"You like this place don't you?"

"This place? This orchard you mean?" Vale shook her head. "Oh North Forks? Yeah, it's a nice piece of land." Vale gave Win a look as if to say, *You know what I mean.* He did not rise to it.

Presently the fence came into view. "Ugly, isn't it?" Win said.

"Arresting," she said. The fence, bright wire and poles, ran to their right and left in front of a stone wall. "What do you want me to take pictures of?" she asked.

"Anything you want, I suppose. Lucore wasn't specific. I have no idea what he wants them for. He's just obsessive."

Vale freed her Pentax from its leather case and uncapped the lens.

She brought the camera to her eye. "How did you get down here?" she asked. The sunlight was rippling along the wire mesh.

"The four-wheel got me down the road easily enough and through the undergrowth. I stopped it over there by the wall, climbed over, and carried Julia up from the stream. Do you want to see the spot?"

"Sure."

She followed Win to the fence and peered through its web. Below in a shallow ravine, she could see the stream. She focused on shafts of sunlight coming through the trees and shimmering on the water. He came and stood beside her. "See there," he said, "putting a finger through the fence, "that boulder and big willow that seems to grow out of it?"

"Yes," she said. The viewfinder framed the massive stone gripped by ancient roots, a druidical willow, heavy-tressed, mysterious.

"Well there's a limb---there *was* a limb---that grew out over the stream. The rope hung from it." Vale imagined the limb and the rope.

Peepers and cicadas were sounding in the little dell; the occasional gnat or mosquito whined near her ear. The air was still; the breeze, such as it was, did not pass this way, but a marshy coolness came up from the stream bed with a smell of mud and stone.

Win turned his back to the fence and let it take his weight. He crossed one foot over the other and folded his arms. He looked down on Vale; she came up to his shoulder, no higher. She was standing with the camera to her eye, moving it over the scene. A finger of sunlight, finding its way through the branches of the trees, touched her hair, and he saw red highlights in the dark brown curls.

She had turned away from the stream to look back the way they had come. He saw there were strands of hair stuck to the nape of her neck, some moisture on her upper lip, a kind of glow to her skin. He saw something in her for which, at that moment, he did not have the right word, but later, returning to this moment as if he himself had captured it on film, the right word would strike him

The click of the camera's shutter distracted him. He looked where the lens pointed and saw how the dead apple limbs twisted against the sky. The camera moved. He followed its direction and saw how the rutted road curved into the tall grasses. Again it moved, and he saw where the alien fence seemed to attack the undergrowth.

'You like this place, don't you?' she had asked him. He did, the way the castaway loves his island or the fugitive his haven. He had often wondered if he had merely institutionalized himself at North Forks, here because he was not fit for any other place. Dean said it wasn't so, and perhaps it was the good man's weakness that he took Win in when it might have been the better part of wisdom to push him out. But to find a place where he could work and contribute, even distantly, to the restoration of people who suffered in a way he understood: that was reason to stay on. He had become a part of this place long after it had become a part of him. But here, in the shadows above the stream, ghosts were stirring. He spoke, "You asked me if I liked this place." Vale nodded. "I do. A fearful lot. A long time ago---at least it seems a long time ago to me---I came to North Forks as a patient." He came off the fence, turned and laced his fingers through the mesh, leaning his head against the wire. "What brought me here

was that I'd lost my wife and my daughter in a...you know I still don't know what to call it, an accident, an incident, an attack."

She turned to give him her full attention. "We were in Lebanon in 1978. My wife, Nayla, was a Beiruti. We wanted her parents to meet, Al..."---he had to clear his throat---"our daughter, she was seven. We were in a bazaar downtown. I had stopped at a booth to buy some fruit; they had gone ahead to look at children's clothes. There was an explosion; they were killed."

Her eyes never left his face it. Gripping the fence wire, he looked like a man in a cage. She saw his Adam's apple working in his throat, trying to swallow something down, or bring it up, and she saw the moisture in the corners of his eyes. "It was a nightmare. My focus was on getting their bodies home, getting them properly buried, and then for a while dealing with her parents, with my mother. Then...well, then I started drinking. It ran in the family, and it ran in me. Six months later, my business was in the shits, and my best friend, Dave, on the pretext of taking me to my boat because I was too bagged to drive, just kept on going and deposited me at North Forks. He drove off with my car, my keys, and my shoes. He'd let them know he was bringing me in. Venables was there in Admissions when I arrived. He put me to bed, and four days later I signed myself in. I was here for six months, all through the fall and winter. In the Spring of '76 I left, put my business back together---I had a company that repaired office equipment---sold it and took a job Lucore and Venables offered running B&G." His narration had passed its dangerous shoals. "I've been here ever since." Win pulled back from the fence, flexing his fingers. "Sometimes I think I should have left; but most days I feel I've found a place I can belong."

"I have a daughter," she said. "I don't know what I'd do..." She broke off unable to finish her sentence.

"It wasn't clear for a time there that I would survive."

The afternoon light was settling into a duskier blue. The silence around them deepened, as if for a moment the peepers and the cicadas had paused to listen. In the interval she heard the sound of water passing over stones. "I want to go down to the stream," she said.

"It will be hell on your shoes," he said.

"I don't care."

"O.K. The ground is fairly clear along the fence line; we can hug it for a ways, then make our way down to the stream."

She followed him. In a minute they rounded the last fence post. Win held out his hand to steady her, and they climbed over the wall. Then they made their way, through thicker undergrowth and over fallen stones hidden by brush, back until he cut to his right and down a narrow trail. The warble of the stream grew louder.

The ground was soggy here, and her feet squelched in the oozy soil. He was right; it was hell on her shoes. They reached the flat-topped boulder in the willow's clutch. Win climbed and reached a hand for her, hefting her up beside him.

She got her first clear view of the stream. It was twelve or fifteen feet wide and moved with a rustling speed over rocks and through the partial dams of fallen branches. She imagined that in the spring it might course with some power, for the slope would give the water speed. Just here the stream bayed out to make a pool. Downstream the water resumed its winding course. She saw a tire caught in the weeds, a frayed rope end tied to it. She looked back up and saw the fresh cut wound where a limb had been and its stacked lengths of sawed wood by the water's edge.

"She was just there," Win said and pointed to the pool. "I figure she waded in and got the rope end, carried it back up the bank then climbed up here." Vale was taking pictures fast. Seeing. "She tied the rope around her neck and just... swung out over the water."

"It would have been slow."

"Yes," he said. "It would not have broken her neck. She would have slowly strangled to death."

Vale imagined the body swaying over the water like a pendulum. "Dear Lord," she said.

"But the rope broke, and Parthia was here. It's possible Julia could have drowned if the water were an inch or two deeper."

"I don't know why I wanted to see the place."

"Makes it more real."

"For sure it does." She stared at the scene putting all the pieces together, the game of questions, the wall, the limb, the stream, Parthia's alarm, the fright, the dash for help, and Win. She turned to him, "What was it like for you?"

He gazed down at the pool. "At first," he said, "there was just the immediate crisis: make sure her neck wasn't broken---which I could tell it was not, and the nurse confirmed. Then getting her out of the water. I carried her up the slope and put her into the four-wheel. We brought her up to the main driveway. There was an ambulance there. I rode with her to North Shore." He stopped. She saw his jaw working. "That was hard. The last time I was in an ambulance..." He looked at her as if to ask if she needed him to finish his sentence. She shook her head then on reflex reached up and laid a finger against his lips as if to say, "No more."

•◆•

That evening, driving home, a recording of Mozart's concerto for cello and bassoon came over the radio. Win had to pull his pickup to the side of the road, his vision blurred by tears. And it wasn't just the memory that did it---of Nayla rehearsing that piece in their living room, the bow carving the air in her nimble hand, the cello between her legs where he had been so many times, the sound of long notes filling the room like a smoky fire, or of their daughter lying on the floor under a lamp turning the pages of a book---not just that, but the touch of a woman's fingers on his lips and the tears he saw rimming her eyes.

It was then that the right word came. It was not "pretty, for though she was petite, she was not so fine-featured or cute as to merit that word. Nor was she "beautiful" with all the glamour beauty conveyed. No, Vale Messenger could be---was in that moment by the fence---something else, something soft and intriguing and easy on the eye, sweet and good. "Lovely" was the word for it.

When he reached home, he found a message on his answering machine. "Win, it's Vale. I got your number from the switchboard. I'm going to the Metropolitan Museum of Art tomorrow. I've got a hunch about Parthia. It's too complicated to explain now. I'm going to be in the city around two thirty. Any chance you'd like to join me? Here's my number." He grabbed a pencil and caught the sequence. "If not, I'll see you sometime next week. And thanks for..." The machine cut off the end of her message.

CHAPTER TWENTY

Vale called Naomi that night to explain why she would not be out that weekend. "Field trip," she said, and then recounted Parthia's elaborate museum dream.

Naomi was of the opinion that it was likely a collage of delusion and memory packaged as a nightmare. "We know that moments of real life are the stuff of dreams," she said. "Here, if your hunch is right, those elements have been heightened to quite a terrifying degree. She is telling you a great deal, I think."

"But through a glass darkly," Vale said. She told Naomi of the damage done to the Guest House when Parthia had returned home.

"Good God, the rage inside her must be immense."

"I still feel I'm in over my head, No-No, but somehow not sinking. Not swimming but not sinking either."

"Dog paddling." Vale laughed. "Good for you, love. I've waited a long time to hear that sound again."

"That sound? Of me splashing?"

"Of you on the *qui vive*. You sound more alive than you've sounded---God, I don't know since summers on Fire Island. Go, girl."

They spoke of Meli and camp news. "Next weekend is the play. It's a Big Deal. I'll be going up for that. Elaine will be there..." They chatted for a while longer, then said goodbye. Only when she hung up the phone did Vale realize she had not mentioned Win.

She would have liked to sleep late on Saturday morning, but she had a maternal errand to run and a train to catch. She wondered what to wear. The city would be hot on this summer day, though all interiors, especially the Met's, would be cool. Short sleeves and then a wrap? Or perhaps the long sleeved cotton shirt she had found on sale at Marshalls? And shoes? Sneakers so much the best thing for the interminable marble floors, but then she'd have to wear white socks or half socks and that meant slacks or jeans. Finally Vale spied her navy cotton blazer, her Jordache jeans, and found a look she could live with.

In time to be at the stores when the doors opened, Vale drove to the Mall and had accomplished her mission by eleven. Off to Meli had gone "the surprise box": an assortment of stickers and a new album to stick them in--- and extras to trade; Judy Blume's *Superfudge*, just out in paperback; two six packs of raisins, no candy or gum allowed in camp; and a hairbrush, comb, and barrettes set in a turquoise color she knew Meli would love. Home by a quarter to twelve to shower and change. She grabbed an apple and two slices of bread with peanut butter to eat on the train.

She arrived at Penn Station in time to walk east in the bright sunshine and then rode a Madison Avenue bus uptown. Her father was on her mind, for this was the route she and Poppa Joe took once when she was girl and he her idol. She got off the bus at 81st, and she followed in their ghostly footsteps west to Fifth. She was remembering her excitement as she saw the great façade of The Metropolitan Museum for the first time, the four sets of double columns, the matching pools to the left and right, the gently rising staircase at the summit of which giant doors opened to unimaginable interiors. On that particular Saturday afternoon, lifetimes ago, she had seen falling from the roof an enormous silken banner, bellied by a wind, on which was written: **The World of Hieronymus Bosch**. She could still hear the guttural slur of the name in Poppa Joe's mouth as he read it to her.

Together she and Poppa had wandered into galleries in which small, jeweled objects glittered in glass cases, fragments teased, utensils spoke. There were statues without heads, stained glass windows that blazed, haloed saints knelt among crucifixes and thrones. Mile-high stallions bore aloft their battle-ready knights in bright chain-mail. On racks infinitely out of reach ranged an armory of axes and swords, bows and lances, pikes and halberds. "Halberd." In her little notebook she wrote this strange word down. Hall bird.

On that day her father had been animated at first, talked of many of the works on display without reading the legends printed on the walls. He was her own tour guide. She drank in the things he loved and loved them, too. But in time he tired, his stamina leaching from him. She knew the signs. "Poppa, can we get something to eat?" taking care of him, worrying.

"Yes, *schotzele*, come." Down one corridor they came to a great happy atrium, a restaurant. At the far end of a long rectangular pool, as its center boys in bronze rode spouting dolphins.

They went through the serving line. He got a cup and a little silver teapot; she got hot chocolate and a giant pretzel. He took out his paper. She sipped her cocoa, gnawed on her prize, and watched him, wanting to be off again. She saw the paper loosen in his hands. "Daddy, can I go look around by myself. Just for a little while?"

"*Gehe, schotzele*," he said. " *Ich habe mein nickershen.*" He often spoke to her in German, which she understood, but could not speak very well. He would have his nap; she could go. His little treasure.

So she went, as into a maze, chamber leading on to chamber, gallery to gallery, then up a flight of stairs and into an exhibition hall devoted to Hie-ur-on-ee-mouse Bosch.

There was enough of the cartoon and comic in these paintings to make them seem like the work of a child, a helter-skelter of forms and figures and doodles that danced. But the closer she drew to them, the more she saw the bird heads on human bodies, beaked pods, things gobbled, impaled, burning, twisted, maimed. She recoiled as if bitten; she returned to see more. Her eyes wandered dizzily over sparse landscapes and naked hills, through voids of darkness. She traveled to the tiny cities in the distance. The air swarmed with human insects. The pictures seemed to ring with shrill cries of pain. "Excuse me, miss," a uniformed man said, making her jump with surprise. "Are you here with someone?"

"Oh, my Daddy. But he's not here, he's down in the restaurant by the naked boys," and she darted away before the guard could capture her. She tried to retrace her steps, but she had taken too many turns---musical instruments gave way to giant stone faces, a stairwell brought her down to a corridor of mummies on their coffins, and beyond them the stone alleyways of tombs. She was a hall bird lost in a labyrinth.

But in time she found her father waking from his nap. "Did you have fun, my little treasure?" he had asked her in his mother tongue.

"Yes, Daddy," she had said, though it wasn't entirely true.

Now standing on the Museum's top step, the memory of that little girl disappeared as, searching for Win, she felt an adolescent flutter in her pulse.

When had she last felt…? And then she saw him at the curb across the Avenue. Waiting for the light to change, a head taller than most of the crowd, he wore pressed jeans, a sun-faded watermelon colored tee shirt, and boating shoes. He had a beige cotton jacket slung over his shoulder. The light changed, and as he crossed the street, he scanned the steps, saw her, and waved.

Vale had to check her shoulder bag, and then they passed freely down one of the corridors that led off the great atrium. They found a corner in which to talk.

In response to Win's innocent question: "So what brings us to the Metropolitan?" Vale sorted through the hints and hunches she had gathered in the past two weeks like so many pieces of a puzzle. In addition to Parthia's family history, as she currently understood it, she included the odd phone calls she'd received, a quick sketch of Parthia's museum dream, and her own dream of Oxford and Walter Pater, a thumbnail of Claire, and a few of Julia's insights, especially about the painting "The Scream." After fifteen minutes in which Win did not speak or ask a single question, she came to the end. "What do you think?"

"Let me see if I've got this right," he said. Above them a headless goddess leaned on a broken shield. "You think that this girl's father, Wilhelm Alexander, used his skills as a reconstructive surgeon to make over his daughter's face to look like some work of art. Is that's what you're telling me?"

"Well, I know it sounds far-fetched. But I keep feeling I've seen Parthia's face somewhere. I mean it seems familiar to me."

"But you said she was a model. She's been in magazines. Maybe you saw it there."

"You could be right. You probably are right, but I just wanted to walk around the museum to see if anything clicked. Her dream--- or maybe it's her dream mixed up with memory--- well, it's nagging at me."

"If you're right, it's not Parthia that needs to be at North Forks, but her father. Maybe Claire, too." He shrugged his big shoulders. "Wild stuff," he said. "I don't envy you. I'll stick to bricks and plants." He could see the concern on her face, an anxious look, fearing scorn. "So where do you want to start?"

"Maybe Greek. Maybe a painting---early or late Italian Renaissance. Could be something French even, Ingres, Manet. I don't know."

"OK," he said. "Anything in particular you want from me?"

"Not really. I mean you're here. Thanks for coming."

"Gave up a day of sailing," he said, but the smile on his face told her he wasn't complaining.

They passed through the rooms of Greek and Roman statuary, the decorative objects, the sacred relics, the kraters, the funerary urns, the incomplete mosaics. Increasingly pre-occupied, Vale began to move more quickly, her eye scanning, searching. Here and there she caught a hint, an echo of something. She hurried on as if pursuing some will o' the wisp, some figment out of focus, hidden in her imagination.

Gradually Win fell behind. He slowed to admire craftsmanship, to read a note on the wall, and he felt his spirits sinking, for he was remembering being here with Nayla. Her quartet had played for a fund raiser. Tuxedos and liveried waiters. Dim sum and champagne. No one listened to the music, everyone hob-nobbing, displaying their finery. It was as if the sound of her cello still hung in the air.

He had lost sight of Vale. She had sped on ahead. She might as well have come here alone. He stood in front of a funerary urn next to a tailored woman and her pinafore daughter. They moved away, and he stood staring at the urn with its central figure incised in red, a seated woman with a lyre against her breast.

"'Heard melodies are sweet, but those unheard are sweeter still.'" Vale was at his shoulder.

"Hunh?"

"Keats," she said. "Ode on a Grecian Urn."

"If you say so," his voice toneless, his eyes unwilling to meet hers. "I'm thirsty," he said, "Is there somewhere here we can get a drink?"

"Sure."

"Do you mind?"

She looked at her watch. "No, no it's a good idea. There's plenty of time. Let's take a break. Back this way," she said.

They threaded through galleries to the central corridor and turned right towards the restaurant, the pool, the dolphin boys. She half expected to see in the corner a tired man asleep with his paper on his lap.

She bought Win a beer. She got herself a cup of coffee. She bought two pretzels, and they found a table, sat, sipped and nibbled in silence. Where had he gone?

"I came here for the first time with my father," she said.

He looked up, then took a pull on his beer. His own father had never set foot in a museum. "Must have been nice."

"I..." she could not complete the sentence. There was something sullen in Win Lawrence.

"What?" he said.

"Nothing," but his attention was returning from wherever it had gone. "No really, what is it about your father?"

"I don't want to talk about him."

"Then why did you bring him up?"

"I don't know. I.. You seem far away somewhere."

"*I* seem far away. You're like a goddamn ferret."

She reviewed the past half hour and understood. "Sorry," she said. "You're right."

"Why did you want me to come here with you?" he asked.

"I don't know. Yesterday, down by the stream, I felt...scared I think."

"Because of Julia?"

"Suicide."

"You're in the wrong business."

"It's weird isn't it?"

"You want to talk about your father?"

"Maybe later." She wiped her mouth, and took a last sip of coffee. "When I come here he's on my mind. Sorry."

"Stop apologizing. You want to get back to the hunt?"

"I'm not going to be able to concentrate on anything until I've finished looking. You want to wait here?"

"No, I'll try to keep up. Let's go."

They left the restaurant and returned to the central atrium, took the stairs to the second floor and launched into the collection of European painting. Keeping Win at her side, Vale took a half an hour to look at the six rooms that housed the art of the 15th and 16th century Italy: Florence, Tuscany, Venice, Rome. She looked at representations of the Madonna, of Eve, of various handmaidens and mythological figures, and the more she looked the more she felt that Parthia's face belonged to this world, the slightly ovaled eyes, the long shapeliness of the nose, the clearly molded chin, the lips that were curving and full. It was as if Parthia was distilled from this tradition with its idealized beauty in which Greek proportions were filtered through Catholic spirituality, muscular classicism embodied in pale saints with their eyes cast heavenward.

"*A thing of beauty is a joy forever, / Its loveliness increases, it will never / Pass into nothingness...*" Keats again. "*Truth is beauty, beauty truth / That's all you know on earth and all you need to know.*"

What was this beauty the poet wrote about? Was it mortal beauty, or was it the beauty of art, a *thing* of beauty? Keats's aesthetic had something cold in it, and she had felt that same chill in the paintings she had just looked at. The flesh tones, perhaps sallowed by age, were a little deathly, the figures in their allegorical or religious settings representative, illustrative rather than individual and vital. These Platonists were infatuated with a beauty that stood beyond time, a deathless, "forever" beauty. Yet paradoxically such beauty was bound to death as to its shadow. Vale had taught a course on the Romantic poets. Robert was an art historian. In the good old days, they had talked about such things.

"Parthia," the very name meant virgin. Vale would bet that was not the name on her birth certificate. It was a later name, like the name attached to a work of art. *Parthia* was a figment made flesh. Granted it was a stretch to take the gaunt-eyed, suicidal girl, with the fading red streaks in her lusterless blond hair, and place her in this company of idealized beauties, yet Vale's imagination kept superimposing one on the other, and she couldn't shake the sense of something fitting. But in the end nothing clicked. They had come back to the top of the main staircase. She was tired.

"Nothing?" Win said.

She shook her head. "I feel the itch, I just can't scratch it."

"I don't know much about art history," he said as stood together looking down on the bustle below, "but aren't all those beautiful women of antiquity basically, you know, the same? I mean there was a certain ideal of masculine and feminine beauty, and, as far as I understand it, the painters sort of imposed those images on their models. Or copied one another."

"I think that's pretty true."

"So this face of Parthia's could be simply a face that resembles a classically beautiful face. I mean if her father was going to make her into something, then why not choose what had been regarded as classically beautiful?"

"I've been thinking the same thing. But I still feel it's more particular than that. And I think the classical painters, despite a kind of common ancestry in their ideal of beauty, stamped their figures with something distinctive of their own. A Raphael Madonna is not the same as a Titian."

"You take art history courses in college?" To him the previous hour was a blur of color, gilt frames, slow moving traffic, and watchful security guards.

"I did." She deliberated only half a moment. "And I married an art historian. Robert. He's about to become Associate Curator at the Frick."

"Really. I'm impressed."

"Well, don't be. He's a hell of an art historian, but he wasn't much of a husband."

"And as a father?"

"I really don't want to go there," Vale said.

"OK. So what's next?"

"I quit." They started down the stairs. "Unless..."

"Unless what?"

"Do you think we could take just a few minutes in the bookstore? Then we can find someplace to eat; I'm starved."

"Whatever you say."

Win browsed among the books on modern architecture, poring over Le Corbusier's *Chapelle de Notre Dame du Haut* at Ronchamps. He wished he could endow the new conference center with something of this whimsy and grace.

Meanwhile Vale passed slowly down the aisles. She turned over many pages, Raphael---so close, but too...what? Too fair and clean. Bellini: too hard-edged; Botticelli too soft; Bronzino: too masculine; Fra Angelico: too primitive; Andrea del Sarto: too decadent; Michelangelo, too muscular. Where to look? Where else? She took down a volume of Leonardo from the shelf. There were so few works in his hand; the Mona Lisa with her slightly bovine blandness stared out from the frontispiece. She realized this was all she really knew of Leonardo's paintings, and the Mona Lisa was hardly a model for Parthia Alexander. She paged through the early virgins whose faces were flat and shapeless; clearly the painter had been much more interested in composition, in drapery, landscape, perspective. There were sketches, cartoons, studies of cloaks, swirls of water, graceful hands. Then she came to two paintings, side by side on facing pages, that riveted her attention.

Each was called "The Madonna of the Rocks." Each showed virtually the same subject. One painting, owned by the Louvre, was dated in the late 15th century. The other, in the National Gallery of London, was dated ten years later and was attributed to Leonardo and his pupils.

In each the Madonna is set in a deep, grotto-like space that recedes through rock and winding waters to a pale blue horizon. In each her right arm reaches to clasp the shoulder of a kneeling Christ-child. Her left hand extends forward and hovers over the head of a second infant, presumably John the Baptist, whose little right hand is held up towards his cousin in a pose of benediction. But what caught Vale's attention was the figure in each painting which is seated to the Madonna's left and behind the baby John. Vale thought at first that it was a depiction of Mary's cousin Elizabeth, baby John's mother, but then she saw the arc of a wing, all but camouflaged by the shapes of rock and flora. It was an angel.

In the earlier painting the angel points a long finger of a raised right hand towards the kneeling baby Jesus across the picture plane, while the face turns towards the viewer. Vale noted the alert carriage of the angel's head, the high forehead and the strong nose. The lips were modeled with the hint of a smile, and the chin was well defined. Flaxen curls framed the brow. The eyes were almond-shaped with large, dark pupils.

The second paining was altogether darker, the massing of rocks more gloomy, the shadows falling more heavily over the figures arranged in the foreground. The detail in all the faces looked more worked. There was a smokiness in the shadings around the eyes and mouth. The Madonna appeared older, less innocent; there was more portent in her face. And so, too, the seated angel who, like the first, was posed in a three quarter turn towards the viewer. No smile played about these lips. The eyes no longer engaged the viewer's eyes. The look she gave the Christ child seemed almost forlorn.

The existence of the two paintings suggested a convention. In that era painters and their students knocked off copies of their own successes. The master's hand would show up here or there, the rest left to the artisans, the wanna-be's. Somewhere between these two examples, Vale suspected, there must have been others in which the standard elements were combined in different ways. Vale tried to set the angel faces against the mullioned window in her office where Parthia had stood so often, half turned away, or facing her in the blue chair.

She looked again and again as if to delay her growing certainty, its macabre implication. If there were a third painting that could combine these two… If there were such a face between the angel as a sunny girl and the darker later face…And then it seemed to her she saw it: not so much Parthia's face as the face upon which her face was modeled. She saw what Wilhelm Alexander might have seen in his imagination, saw for a moment into his mind, saw what he had tried to do. Figment into flesh. Not just to imitate the master, not just to step inside the oeuvre of Leonardo, but to imitate God. What had been a speculation, her hunch, now shuddered into fact.

Book in hand, she found Win and drew him into an unpopulated alcove.

"You've got something."

"I think so. You've seen Parthia, right? Of course you have; you gave her a tour of the grounds. Tell me what you think of these," and Vale opened the book to the pages that contained the Madonna of the Rocks.

Win bent over, looking carefully. "No she doesn't look like her," pointing to the Madonna's, "not at...Oh, you mean her!" Win's attention shifted from the Madonna to the figure in the foreground. Vale kept silent as Win looked.

"And what about this," she said, pointing to the image on the facing page.

He took the volume from her hands, tilted it to the light, looked back and forth between the two versions of the painting. "It's like Parthia is a kind of a cross between the two, but she's closer to this dark one, except for the hair. You'd have to put some straight spiky hair on this one, punk her up, but I can see it, yes, I can see it."

"Is this what you've been looking for?"

"I think it is. It's close. At least I feel I've found what's been nagging me for the past two weeks. I'm going to buy this."

"Good. Then let's get out of here. Let's head for a meal, and I want more than a beer."

They found a Good Humor man at the entrance to the Park and walked west along dappled paths, talking for a while about other things, about his boat and when he had first learned to sail, about her love of the water and Fire Island summers. He steered clear of loss, she of divorce.

Presently they came back to Parthia. "I'm curious," he said. "How do you understand what motivates an act of that kind. I mean it's not a single act, but a repeated act, almost a kind of ritual."

"You mean Parthia's father? Conventional wisdom would say love."

"What kind of love for God's sake?"

"The same kind of love that motivates almost everything a parent does. There's a psychologist by the name of Alice Miller. She wrote a book a few years ago, *The Drama of the Gifted Child*. She talks about the ways parents do things to their children, ostensibly done for their benefit, but actually out of the parents' own needs, to make them feel better about themselves. Little Suzie singing by the piano for mother's friends. Billy sweating off the pounds to make his weight for the wrestling team because Dad had been a wrestler in college. Miller sees selfishness at work. The parents' own unmet needs for recognition, for specialness, get transferred to the child. The child becomes a kind of object, an exhibit, a badge of sorts that the parent wears and from which the parent derives a kind of borrowed, even a stolen sense of self worth."

"'An exhibit.' Interesting choice of words. And you think that's what's going on here?"

"Well, Miller says that almost everything a parent does is done in the name of love. And the child interprets everything a parent does as an act of love. The child cannot imagine any other motive in the parent. So if the act hurts, the child assumes he or she has done something wrong, or that love is supposed to hurt."

"So Dr. Alexander does this---this body sculpting---because he loves his daughter?"

"In his twisted universe, yes. Perhaps he thinks he is giving her a gift, the gift of physical beauty."

"And do you buy this theory?"

"I don't have anything else to take its place."

"Vale, I'm hungry," he said. "Let's get out of the park and find a place to eat."

"But you've got to let me buy. You did miss your sailing day."

"You sure?" She assured him she was. "Then let me buy the wine."

"A deal."

•◆•

They found an Italian restaurant on Columbus Avenue with a booth at the back. Win ordered a bottle of Montepulciano. The waiter uncorked it and filled their glasses.

There was fresh bread on the table with a saucer of olive oil and garlic. The waiter came and took their orders. "How about telling me a little bit about your father now?" Win proposed.

She drew a breath and let it out slowly, measuring his interest and her stamina. She peered into the place where this story lay hidden. She looked up at him and saw him turning his wine glass between his hands.

"I don't know very much about his early life," she began. "He was born in Hamburg in 1911. The family was Jewish---you can probably see where this is going," she interrupted herself, suddenly apprehensive.

"I can't. Go on, please."

"He was the youngest son in his family. The baby. He had two older sisters and an older brother. I have seen a photograph of the family. It was taken on the occasion of my father's bar mitzvah. He is wearing knickers and a coat that looks too big for him. I always thought it must have been a hand-me-down. It's winter; there's snow on the ground. On the back of the picture is written the date, November 18, 1924." Vale took a sip of her wine; Win emptied his glass and refilled it. She put her hand over her glass when he tilted the bottle towards it.

"My father's father was a tailor, and my father was his apprentice. That is the way things were done then, but he did not want to be a tailor. He had dreams of being a writer. He told me once that his first paid job was as a reporter for a Yiddish newspaper in Hamburg. Later he wrote movie reviews for a monthly journal. He had studied English, which for someone of his social class was unusual, but he did it so he could understand American films. He particularly loved gangster films. I wish he had said the name of the journal he wrote for."

Win dipped a piece of bread into the saucer of garlic and oil.

"My mother filled in some of the blanks for me. My father had always wanted to come to America, and so in 1936, with money he had saved, he came to New York. It was going to be for the summer only. But in the course of the summer, things got suddenly worse for the Jews in Hamburg. His father was a swimmer; maybe it's where I get my love of the water. In July of 1936 all Jews were forbidden to visit the city's public swimming pools. It was a small thing. Much larger and more ominous things were going on. There was a song that became popular that summer. Roughly translated it goes: 'When the German marches into battle, he's in fine fettle, But when his knife spills Jewish blood, he really feels his mettle.' My father's father saw the handwriting on the wall. Do you know that in 1934 a Hamburg court stated that if a woman shopped in a Jewish store, she gave her husband grounds for divorce?"

At that moment, their dinners arrived.

She wondered if he knew about the Nuremberg Laws? Did he know that "Judah perish" was the slogan of Hitler's 1933 campaign? Did he know that professors, artists, and actors were all forced out of work after 1934?

They made small talk through the meal. He told her about the planned conference center, Dean Venables' dreams for a place where thinkers in allied disciplines, artists, academics might come together to talk about mental health and illness, about treatment, medicine, conversations across disciplines. She remembered Dean's question in her interview for the social work position when he had asked her about novelists she would like to confer on a case. Turned out they both loved George Eliot. Probably got her the job.

The waiter came to clear their plates. The last of the wine was in their glasses. In the silence, the specter of her father returned to the table. Win seemed to be waiting for her to continue, and, remembering his confession the day before, she gathered courage and picked up the thread exactly where she had dropped it.

"While he was in New York in that summer of 1936, he received a cable from his father, telling him not to come home, and he obeyed. Poppa stayed in New York. All he had with him were a few books, some clothes and that single photograph of his family and his bar mitzvah. He never saw any of them again. Like many who survived by mere chance, he never spoke of the past. Not to me anyway, and I think very little to my mother either. I have done some reading. I have done a certain amount of research. I visited Hamburg just after I got pregnant. I went by myself for a week. I found the place where my father's family had lived. I heard German spoken around me. He used to read to me in German when I was a little girl; it was my father's mother tongue." She put down her empty glass. "Can we get some coffee?"

Win summoned the waiter and he placed their orders, ordering for himself a Calvados. "You really want to hear all this?"

"I want to hear all this. How did your parents meet?"

"My mother was the daughter of a milliner from St. Louis. She had come east in the fall of 1939 to attend a conference of the International Ladies' Garment Workers Union; she was her local's representative. She had been staying with her cousin in Brooklyn and had caught her dress going through the heavy wooden turnstile of the subway station on Cortelyou Road. My father was on the subway platform that morning; he was going to the dentist. He'd Americanized his name by then. He was Joe Messenger, the New Yorker. Never without a needle and thread, he sewed her dress on the spot. She stayed on an extra few days to be with him. He showed her the sites. They had their first kiss on an April night on the ferry back from the Staten Island. My mother's 'few days' turned into twenty three years."

"Are you an only child?" he asked.

"No," she said, "I have an older sister, Naomi. Ten years older. They married and settled down in Brooklyn. They opened their own tailor shop together. Did quite well actually, though mother said father never lost his desire to be a writer; only he thought his English wasn't good enough. He did love to go to the movies though.

"Poppa was Jewish enough to think of Saturday as the Sabbath and secular enough to steer clear of the synagogue. When I was little, he'd leave mother and me and Naomi on Saturday and not re-appear until dinner time. He'd walk, go to a museum, take himself to a movie. I never knew what exactly. He wasn't a talkative man, but I longed to go with him.

"Then, finally, when I was ten, he started to let me come along. Sometimes. He was a fast walker, and I almost had to run to keep up with him. I was curious and questioning, and he began to tell me things, about the city, about the places we visited. He knew the city so well. Did you ever read Alfred Kazin's book *A Walker of the City?*" Win shook his head.

"Well, never mind, but that's what my father was, or really a bus-rider and subway-taker. In summer we went to Coney Island or east to the Rockaway's. We went to Park Slope, walked through the Brooklyn Botanical Gardens, listened to the gypsies in Prospect Park. On autumn afternoons we walked over the Brooklyn Bridge. We got lost in Chinatown and Little Italy, we explored the shops and bookstores of Greenwich Village, and neighborhood by neighborhood, Saturday by Saturday, we made our way uptown. All the way to the Metropolitan Museum of Art. Which is why he was on my mind today."

Win could see that she had gone as far as she wished to go. "Listen, Vale, I know what it's like not to want to talk about something."

"On a day like today, I miss him very much."

"Want to walk a bit?" he asked.

"Sure," she said, "I can get to Penn Station from Fifty Ninth Street."

He called for their check and would not give it to her when it reached the table. "No fair," she said.

"I know," he said. "Maybe someday you'll make me a home cooked meal."

They walked south; the city lighting up in the summer evening. As they came to the entrance to the downtown subway at Columbus Circle, Vale expected Win would be going with her to Penn Station, that he, too, lived on Long Island. But he stopped at the top of the stairs. "You know, I don't know where you live," she said, looking up at him.

"Around the corner from the Chelsea Hotel. West 24th St, to be exact. Used to be a manufacturing district, big lofts and huge service elevators. Just starting to get fixed up. I ran my business from one end of the loft, family lived in the other end."

"Oh," she said. "Well, then, goodnight."

"Goodnight," he said, and, for a big man, the quick stoop, the quick touch of his lips on her cheek, and the quick turn away, quite took her by surprise.

CHAPTER TWENTY-ONE

Vale brought Leonardo to North Forks on Monday morning. Though unde-
cided about what to do with it, she wanted its evidentiary weight on hand. She
put it on the top of her bookshelf, thinking Parthia might see it.

A phone call caught her on the way to morning rounds.

"Vale?"

"Yes?"

"This is Claire, I have asked my husband's physician, Claus Adenauer, to
call you. I don't seem able to impress on you the importance of Parthia's coming
home. Perhaps he can. I have given him your number, and he will call you at
half past eleven today. Please make yourself available."

Before she could even respond, she heard Claire hang up. She re-arranged a
session with Liza-Jane, and sat at her desk while 11:30 came and went. She was
leafing through the pages of of Leonardo and reading an elegant text when her
phone finally rang. She picked up and answered with her name.

"Yes," a voice said, "this is Doctor Claus Adenauer, Doctor Messenger.
Claire Alexander has prevailed upon me to call you. To speak candidly about
her husband's condition. We have spoken before."

"Yes, Dr. Adenauer, I recall. Please call me Vale."

"I would prefer to use your last name. What kind of a name is Messenger,
if I may ask?"

"The family on my father's side was German. Originally from the South;
later they settled in Hamburg."

"Ah, yes, a Jewish name, I believe." he said. There was a pause. "Wilhelm is not officially my patient, but I am a physician. I have known Wilhelm for many years. I agreed to consult."

Vale drew a pad to her and picked up a pen.

"Let me spare you the clinical details," Dr. Adenauer continued. "He has advanced pancreatic cancer. It is a fast moving killer. We are doing what we can in a palliative way."

"And do you have a sense of how long he may...? I am not sure how to put this. I'm sorry if this sounds calculating on my part. How long does your patient have before he will be unable or perhaps unwilling to see his daughter if she is able and willing to go home."

"Ach. That is impossible to say. Depending on his strength and, of course, his will, he might survive another two weeks, but almost daily his strength lessens. Also, his mind is affected. Pancreatic cancer is aggressive and its consequences far-reaching. The two weeks I just mentioned might be intolerable. As it is, he is under sedation much of the time." Doctor Adenauer paused, perhaps weighing how much to tell. "I expect..." he began, "I expect at some point in the very near future that my colleague will want to address the issue of his end. You will understand if I can say no more than that."

"Yes, Doctor, I can," she said, appreciating the delicacy of his position. "What was it in particular Claire wished you to tell me?"

"Just that Mrs. Alexander believes her husband's end will be made a great deal easier if he has a chance to speak to his daughter. He asks for her daily." Vale assessed the time frame the doctor offered. It would be Parthia's decision, she told him. "I know this quite well," he said. "I am, as I said, doing what Mrs. Alexander has asked of me. And so I have done."

Vale had nothing to lose by asking the question in her mind: "I don't suppose Dr. Alexander would feel comfortable having you talk about family history."

"Assuredly not. He is an immensely proud and private man. Now if you will forgive me, I must say good-bye."

A door closing firmly. "Thank you, doctor," she said.

•◆•

After lunch that Monday Parthia entered Vale's office wearing a short-sleeved sky blue summer dress adorned with tiny red polka dots. She wore thin gold sandals, her nails appeared trimmed and freshly painted in a bright scarlet. Her hair, purified of its tints and spikes, lay in curls on her head, and all marks of her ravaged face could now be hidden by artful make-up.

She was in this moment without fault or blemish, and Vale felt a certain discomfort in the presence of such perfection and poise. Parthia sat easily on the chair opposite her, crossed one leg over the other, straightened her back, and linked her hands over her knee in a pose reminiscent of Claire. Cool blue eyes looked at her appraisingly, "Mrs. Messenger. I am healthy. I've called my lawyer. I have work in the city. I wish to be discharged." The slightly imperious tone also reminded Vale of Claire.

Vale was taken aback. "What did your lawyer say?"

"He says that he can get a court order to review of my case by independent physicians. Within 24 hours."

"I see."

"He says that the fact that I am off status is tantamount to the hospital saying I am not a threat to myself. He says..."

"And what would he say to this?" And before she knew what she was doing, Vale had reached for Leonardo and threw it down on her desk.

Parthia, still languid, stood up and looked. " Ah, *The Paintings and Drawings of Leonardo Da Vinci*".

Vale waited, breath held.

"'Leonardo,'" Parthia said, "'is the greatest master of them all. The heavens often rain down the richest gifts on human beings naturally, but sometimes with lavish abundance bestow upon a single individual beauty, grace, and ability.'" Vale was aware of the stilted language, a change of tone. A recitation? A performance?

Parthia turned the pages. "'This is Verrocchio's *Baptism*,'" her voice took on a slightly sing-song quality. "'The angel on the left is attributed to Leonardo. And notice how the angel beside her gazes at the one to her right. Just so did Verrocchio the master gaze in wonder at the genius of his pupil. He was twenty three.'"

Vale stood and came round behind Parthia to look over her shoulder at the book, whose pages were turned by a languid hand. The tone of Parthia's voice troubled her. It was as if she were giving a museum lecture, but without animation or interest.

The voice continued, "'His first love was the observation of nature and the study of geometry. If you look at the *Annunciation of 1475*, you can see this attention to detail in his treatment of the angel's wing, the vegetation beneath the angel's feet. You can see, too, the characteristic landscape Leonardo favors, the receding horizon, his mastery of atmospheric perspective. Note, also, the profile of the angel Gabriel, and the shadow that falls on the grass.'" Vale looked at the profile and felt a chill.

"'Here is the *Mona Lisa*. Notice the mastery of '*sfumato* around the eyes and mouth. No one before or since has understood the subtlety of shadow as Leonardo did.'"

It was as if the small office in the Tower began to crowd with other presences. The subjects of these paintings took on a strange half-life through Parthia's words.

"'Here is the *Madonna Benois*. A mere girl really.'" Vale looked; and there it was again, the family resemblance, as if all the faces in Leonardo were aspects of single face, emanations of a single beauty. Parthia was turning another page in a dreamy slow motion. "Here is '*The Adoration of the Kings*.'" Vale knew that on the overleaf was the first of the *Madonna of the Rocks*; she felt the urge to take the book from Parthia's hands, to spare her. But Parthia was going on, "'He lost interest in it as he often did when his mind had already solved the interesting questions. But look at the face of the Madonna, the fond, indulgent, sad smile that hovers about the lips.'" Vale knew for a fact in this moment that Parthia was quoting the text, knew in a moment that this was the very book that the father and daughter had between them, the text of Parthia's transformation.

And now the page was turning, the drifting, dreamy voice going on, and it seemed to Vale that something strange was happening, as if Parthia was somehow disembodying or as if the images, the words, had triggered something in her. *Dissociation*: the word flashed in Vale's mind. "'And here we come to one of the unquestioned masterpieces, the *Madonna of the Rocks* in the Louvre. Genius is too pale a word for what he has done here with gesture, with the solid, yet precarious architecture of the cavern, the ledges of rock opening like jaws, the rough hewn shapes in contrast with the soft contours of flesh. Note the face of the angel on the right. Where have we seen it before?'" And here, as if the recording---for that was what it was like---had come to an end, Parthia stopped and for a long moment she did not move, her eyes seeing something now a long way off.

Still standing behind her, Vale's attention was caught by something behind Parthia's left ear, right at the edge of the hairline. She looked more closely. It seemed to her they were tiny incised lines, like scars.

Vale drew back then and sat down in her chair across from Parthia, her own heart pounding, for Parthia was turning her body a quarter turn, her head swiveling on her neck, her eyes looking through Vale, her gaze slightly down and over the left shoulder. She lifted her right hand from the book and reached it forward and extended the first finger of the hand as if pointing across at something, and it was as if worlds and centuries were collapsing, as if Parthia were being gathered into art, as if art were being embodied in Parthia, as if the genius of an invisible Leonardo were addressing the genius of an invisible Doctor Alexander, as if this confection of a woman had been asked to bear an unspeakable burden and was on the verge of some terrible dissolution.

Then, without a further word, Parthia walked to the door of Vale's office, passed through it, and pulled it closed behind her.

In the room, now emptied of her presence, there lingered the scent of her perfume. Sound returned. Vale heard the call of a hidden bird and the laughter of patients from the lawn. The book lay open on her desk, sunlight full on the page from which, it seemed to Vale, Parthia had arisen and vanished.

CHAPTER TWENTY-TWO

Win had spent much of that same afternoon in Serge Lucore's office on the third floor of the Administration Building, along with the architect and the general contractor, reviewing plans for the Conference Center. He had dressed for the occasion in his lightweight summer jacket over a clean denim work shirt, chinos instead of jeans, good shoes rather than his mud-caked leather work boots. Their palaver was thick with materials, time-lines, manpower.

The meeting ended, and with his head so busy transforming lines into solids, working out timetables, plotting temporary paths, detours, fencing, safety, fall rains, winter frosts, the unforeseen and the unforeseeable, that he fairly bounded down the stairs and almost ran over Vale coming out of the mail room.

"Whoa!" she said putting up a hand and laying it against his chest. "The speed limit is five miles an hour around here. Look at you," she said. "You have something special on for today?"

He liked the feel of her hand that lifted off his chest as he stepped back. Charged by his own excitement, eager to share it with someone, he said, "How would you like to have dinner with me tonight?" He surprised himself.

"You have something to celebrate?"

"Sort of," he said; "you could say that. There's a pretty decent restaurant on the bluff overlooking the harbor in Port Jefferson. I think you'll like it. Monday's petty quiet."

"What time?"

"I can leave any time, and I've got plenty to do. Your call."

She thought about her desk. "I can leave by five."

"Shall I give you directions, or do you want to follow me there?"

"Why don't you give me directions." They stepped into the mailroom, Win found a notice on the bulletin board---the announcement for the Summer Olympics--- and quickly jotted down directions on its back. She took it from him and ran her eye over his scrawl. "*The Walrus and the Carpenter?*" she said

"That's what it's called. Two gay guys run it. One of them has huge handle-bar mustache, and the other used to be a cabinet maker."

"Cute," she said. She'd love to go home and take a shower, but this wasn't a date, really. Just two colleagues having a bite of dinner after work. On their way home. To separate domiciles. "See you at five," she said.

Not long after five and having left word with the hostess to look out for his dining companion, Win was seated at a table on the patio, overlooking the harbor. He had a glass of Jack Daniels in front of him. His gaze scanned the traffic in the harbor: a passenger ferry labored slowly out of its berth and headed north through the mouth of the bay and into the Sound. Far out in the crook of the western arm of the breakwater, he could pick out the *Requiem*, riding on her anchor. Beyond her and over the top of the breakwater, he could see a few sails bent in the southerly breeze.

He did not hear Vale approach. "What are you peering at?" she asked.

He pushed back from his chair and stood up. "Nothing special. Boats."

"Is your boat here?" she asked and dropped her knapsack beside her chair.

"Yeah, as a matter of fact. She's out there," he said, pointing.

She looked. "Way out there?" All she saw was a line of boats anchored in the shelter of the breakwater. "Which one?" she said.

He drew her to the edge of the patio. "Look towards the far end of the moored boats," he said. "Look for a white hull, a single mast, and burgundy furling on the mainsail and the foresail."

She squinted into the lowering western sun. "I can't tell one from another."

"Well, it doesn't matter," he said. "Would you like something to drink?"

"How do you get out there?" she asked.

"I have an inflatable dinghy with a three horsepower motor. I keep it down in the harbor. There's a slip where you can tie them up, for a fee, of course."

"I'd love to see it."

"Whenever you say."

"Does this place do take out?"

"You thinking of going out now?"

"Why not? I'm mean your dinghy is down there isn't it?"

"It is"

"And your boat's out there, isn't it?"

"It is."

"So...?"

So thirty minutes later he was handing her aboard the *Requiem.*

They had both ordered hamburgers and fries to go, and Win, now bare-footed, was down in the galley putting them in the microwave. "You want to eat now or have a drink?"

"I can wait to eat, but I'll have what you're having."

Shortly he handed her up a plastic glass filled with ice, 7 Up, and a shot of Jack Daniels. The drink was strong and cold. He was cutting some cheese and laying out crackers on a plate. "No caviar?" she said in mock surprise.

"Hey, this is a short-notice charter. You want caviar, you got to call ahead."

"I'll remember that."

He climbed up the four-step ladder into the cockpit, setting down the plate of cheese on the bench beside her. "How about setting sail, mate?"

Vale had kicked off her shoes and had her feet up on the cushions with her back to the cabin bulkhead. "Really?"

"Sure. Unless you'd rather not."

No, no, she was happy to go for a sail. She watched as he turned on the ignition. She heard the throb of a hidden engine. "Tell me the names of things," she asked.

"Stern, taffrail, lines, halyard, boom, mast, cleat, tenders:" He named these things as he moved about, preparing to cast off. She sipped and watched, feeling like a girl being taken for a ride. "Compass, depth finder, winch, and wheel, of course." Which he now stood behind. "If you go forward and cast off the line, we can leave our mooring." Vale set down her drink in its cup holder, unwound the line from a forward cleat, and dropped its looped end into the water beside the moored dinghy.

As they passed the line of boats within the breakwater, Vale saw one couple having dinner, a hammock slung under a boom, the sound of music, and an older man with a pipe and a glass of wine. He waved. The *Requiem* bore into the opening, and in few minutes they were out into the Sound.

The warm, early evening wind played over the water. Win scampered forward and drew the tenders up on deck, then back at the wheel he brought the boat up into the wind and unfurled the mainsail in a series of fluid, unhurried motions. The sail bellied, and the boat got some way on her. When he cut the engine, Vale's ears tingled with the silence and then caught the sweet gurgle of water along the hull.

In another moment he had unfurled the big burgundy sail in front. "The foresail is called the jib. The biggest jib is the Genoa or Genny." The boat heeled a few degrees; they were headed away from the lowering sun, the water beneath them green and scalloped with small waves.

"There," he said, standing beside her, feet apart, his hands resting on the wheel.

She brought her drink to her lips and looked at him over the top of her glass. She wished she had brought her camera. He raised his glass. "Welcome aboard," he said in a funny formal kind of way. If she only knew how long it had been since he had shared the *Requiem* with anyone.

"This is lovely," she said.

They sailed. Vale made her way under the curving foresail to the bowsprit and leaned against the railing with her back to the stay. The wind ran its fingers through her hair. She returned, slipped past him and peered over the taffrail, watching the water flow out past the keel. The drink, the wind, the lazing lilt of the boat made her head light. It was all she could do not to come up behind him and wrap her arms around him.

"Time to eat," he said.

"How do you stop the boat?" she asked.

"Like this," and he turned the wheel with one hand, letting out the foresail with the other. The *Requiem* came up into the wind, steadied there. He took the line and wrapped it twice around the wheel, and the boat rocked gently on her keel. "As long as the wind doesn't change direction, we'll just drift with the current." He smiled, then went below to plate their dinners.

The faces of Nayla and Allegra looked out at him from their framed picture in the galley. What had loss been like in the age before photography? he wondered. Memory, left to her own devices, was merciful in her powers of forgetting. A photograph contradicted natural amnesia. What do you do with the photographs of the dead? Keep them on the shelf to stare at? Put them away in a drawer?

"So what were we supposed to be celebrating at *The Walrus and the Carpenter*?" she called down to him. "You seemed quite exhilarated when I saw you in that place that's so far away I can't even remember its name."

On deck again with their dinners, the sun dissolving into the darkening sea and the boat bobbing quietly, he told her about the Conference Center, and he was still talking---about getting bulbs in on the south side of the site before the first frost--- when he realized she had been quiet for a long time. "I hope I'm not boring you," he said.

"No, not at all. I was just thinking that all therapy ought to be done on a sailboat. It's so easy to listen out here."

"It's time we should start back," he said. The sun had set, and the sky was darkening in the west. He freed the wheel, turning it slowly. "I'm going to jibe, so watch the swinging boom." She ducked as the boom gently passed overhead. Their course now took them back towards Port Jefferson.

"It sounds like landscaping is one of the things you most enjoy about your work at North Forks."

"When I was a patient at North Forks, they had just put up a greenhouse. It's the Glass House now. One of the nurses spent time there with certain patients. She was raising some orchids. She got me hooked, and somehow that got me turned on to plants. Before that I pretty much worked on machines. I kind of ran the greenhouse in my last month as a patient. When I got offered the job as Director of Building and Grounds, I asked if I could build a new greenhouse and work on the landscaping."

They came in sight of the cut into the harbor. "How often do you come here to sail?"

"Almost every weekend. Sometimes after work if I've got the time. Like today. A few hours, and I'm restored. I've been known to sleep aboard and drive to work in the morning. There's a fair-sized bunk in the bow."

They fell silent again. He had turned on the engine. "Could you put the tenders down for me?" he asked.

Ahead of them in the bowl between the hills, the town of Port Jefferson was lit up for the night. Other boats were motoring in through the breakwater, furling sails, making for moorings and slips. They eased along the line of anchored boats and nosed gently towards the dinghy. At the last moment with the *Requiem* having almost no way on her, Win leapt onto the foredeck, grabbed the boathook, and caught their mooring line. He wrapped it twice around a cleat and looped a knot. The boat steadied, turned, and stopped, nudging the dinghy out of the way. It had been neatly done. Vale looked at her watch. It was just past eight. She didn't want to go home yet.

"Do we have to leave?"

"Heck no." He went down below and brought up a cotton blanket and draped it over her shoulders. "How about a cup of coffee?"

"Sure," she said and watched him light a kerosene lamp that glowed in the galley and put a fire on under a cast-iron teapot.

"What's Win short for?" she asked.

"Edwin. Never liked it."

"Why? It's a good literary name. There's Edwin Muir and Edwin Arlington Robinson, both pretty good poets. Muir was a bit of a mystic, as well. You're in good company."

"Well, I'm no mystic and no poet either. Kids called me Winnebago in high school. I was, well, kind of large." The kettle began to sing, and he poured hot water into a French press. Soon they had warm mugs in their hands. He held out a flask of Irish whisky, and on her nod poured a splash into her glass and his.

From somewhere down the line of boats, there was the sound of guitar and a voice singing softly. More stars clustered above their heads now. "God, this is unbelievable," she said.

"Can I ask you a North Forks question?"

"What's North Forks?" They laughed. "Sure."

"Did you show Parthia the pictures of Leonardo?"

She told him of their session and Parthia's strangely disembodied recitation, and her own most recent thoughts about the doctor and his daughter.

"You make it sound as if in some literal way he made her his creation. Body and mind. And you still think this is something done in the name of love?"

"I'm sure of that. And I imagine many kinds of love. I believe Dr. Alexander loved art, beauty, Leonardo, and his daughter. In some way it was all a kind of deeply perverted gift he was trying to give her. This doesn't mean it wasn't destructive, but not evil."

"And the difference?"

"Probably only in the intention. I don't think he did this only for his own pleasure. Nor do I believe he was a sadist. I don't believe he wished to harm her or to make her suffer."

"He did it for her own good."

"I've been thinking about this a lot. What's the best thing he could do for his daughter? It's not to give her an education, though he will do that. In order for education to be effective, you have to have an intelligence to go with it, and maybe he is not sure his daughter is so bright. And it's not money. He knows she will have money. Money is cheap and vulgar. No, the reconstructive surgeon believes that the most powerful thing a woman can have is beauty. That is the shrine at which our culture worships. Beauty is a great American industry. It confers status on a woman whatever her intelligence or class. Beauty opens doors. What father would not want his daughter to be beautiful? What father, if he had it in his power, would not tinker with nature to improve his daughter's native gifts?"

"Most fathers wouldn't. Jesus, Vale, most fathers aren't that selfish. Or that ambitious." Win was snugging the cover over the mainsail along the boom.

"But Dr. Alexander was," she said. "Apparently he was a father who wanted to take nature into his own hands and could. And did." And suddenly Vale felt the day's fatigue overtake her. "I think I better be getting home, Win," she said. "I'm bushed."

"I can have you to your car in twenty minutes," and in a moment he was handing her down into the dinghy. He locked the gangway hatch. The harbor waters were full of tremulous reflections. Above them the hills were black. A few last boats, their mast lights twinkling, slipped into moorings closer to shore.

He walked with her to her car. She rolled down the window. She looked up at him, his face lit by the streetlights. Small insects swarmed in the air. She turned on her driving lights. "Thanks," she said, "I'll remember this evening for a long time."

He squatted down so his head was level with hers; he only laid a hand on her shoulder." You take care," he said. "I'll see you tomorrow."

"I'll look for you," she said. He nodded, stepping back as she turned the key in the ignition.

As she put the car in gear and the wheels began to crunch on the gravel, he called out, "Talk to Venables about this Parthia stuff. I've got an appointment with him tomorrow at noon for lunch in his office to go over some Conference Center stuff. Why don't you knock on the door?"

"Thanks," Vale, said. "Maybe I will." Win watched her take the turn at the top of the drive. Then the car surged onto the county road and she was gone.

There was a message on her machine when she got home. Meli's voice, plaintive and excited. "Mommy, where are you? I just got out of rehearsal. It's sooooo cool. When are you coming? I miss you. Are you there? Boo hoo. Bye." Too late to call. First thing in the morning she'd hear that delicious voice and make her plans for the coming weekend.

Overtired, but unable to sleep, Vale found a movie on television, but she could not concentrate on it, her mind returning to Parthia, wondering how her afternoon and evening had gone. She'd make a quick call to the unit. She was just reaching for the phone when it rang. She heard the familiar voice of Edna White, and her perplexed heart knew in one piercing premonition that something had gone terribly wrong.

"Vale," Edna said, "Parthia is gone."

PART III

Without clear directions, Vale wanders through unfamiliar streets in a gathering dark. She is Messenger with a message she cannot understand, can't keep in mind, keeps forgetting. Now night is falling, and no streetlights illuminate her way. Suddenly out of nowhere a vehicle bears down on her, its lights shearing the darkness. At the last moment she manages to lurch aside, and the vehicle goes careening into an impenetrable gloom, taillights like two lethal red eyes peer back at her. *I should have seen it coming. I should have seen it coming.* The voice carps in the dreamer's ear until a clock, ringing, wakes her.

Morning. Vale groped her way into a shower, hoping its needles would revive her. A tribunal would be gathering at North Forks, and she had to hurry.

She hated her hair. It took forever to blow-dry, and she knew the day's humidity would kink her curls until she looked like a bush lady. She walked around the apartment, glaring at inanimate objects, banging the kettle down on the stovetop, cursing Parthia for breaking trust and bringing down a great deal of trouble on both their heads. *I should have seen this coming* was the refrain that harassed the drip of coffee into the Pyrex glass. And behind this self-accusation, a more damning judgment lurked: *It was my fault. I precipitated this elopement.* She had been a fool, a naïve, amateurish fool.

Now Parthia had cast herself out of North Forks and out of Vale's care and control. Likely she would never hear of her again, for it was against North Forks' policy ever to re-admit a patient who had gone AWOL. Vale now believed, however, that Parthia was more in need of hospitalization than she had been before. She imagined her out there, unraveling, perhaps delusional, in the grips of the demons Vale's impatience had let loose. She could still hear the singsong recitation of the regressed child.

She had just hefted her shoulder bag and had a hand on the door when the phone rang. "Hi, Mom," greeted her churlish hello.

"Melanie! Is everything all right?"

"Yeah, everything's great. I called last night but there was no answer. Where were you?"

"I was out, honey. I just missed your call. Listen, sweetie, you've caught me just as I was going out the door."

"How come? You never leave this early."

"Oh, there's stuff at the hospital I have to do. But I can take a few minutes." Vale sat down at the kitchen counter, her bag at her feet. "So talk to me."

"The play is going really great, Mom. We finished our costumes yesterday, and today we paint the set. It's so cool, Mom, and I'm part of everything. When are you coming? Are you coming up on Friday? Dad and Elaine are."

"No, sweetie, I can't get all the way there on Friday, but I'll drive half way, so I can be there by noon for lunch with you on Saturday."

"I can get a pass. We can go out for lunch. Can I bring Pia? She plays Tomasina. Mom, Guess what I..."

"Honey, I'm sorry. I just can't stay on the phone right now. Save all your stories. I'll be seeing you so soon."

"OK, Mom," Vale heard the disappointment in her daughter's voice.

"No, sugar..."

"It's OK. I gotta go, too. Bye." And she was gone.

Vale stared off into space for a moment. She'd make it up to her. Bring her a goody box on Saturday in addition to the one just mailed. Then she gathered up her things and headed for work.

•◆•

Staff meeting: Parthia was already a footnote in the life of the unit. Gone, out of their hands. Damage control the theme of the day. Picking up the pieces. Guilt in some quarters, relief in others. No one on staff was going to miss the entitled Miss Alexander.

Back in her office she faced an answering machine blinking with messages: several from various sectors of the hospital bureaucracy, Medical Records telling her the case notes were needed; from Legal, reminding her an incident report must filled out ASAP. Then Rivers, in a voice coldly official, wanting to talk to Vale sometime between twelve and one. Security informed her she could expect a call from the county Sheriff's Office. The Sheriff's Office? Good Christ!

And the next message was indeed from the Sheriff's office, requesting any information as to the whereabouts of Parthia Alexander. They had the responsibility to track down any involuntary admission who had eloped. Parthia had never signed herself in. Addresses, phone numbers, leads to people who might know where she had gone. What was Vale's responsibility to patient confidentiality and to the law? She had no idea.

Claire's voice, shrill with anxiety and peremptory in tone, demanded Vale call her immediately. "Your incompetence is terrifying," Claire said.

There was a call from Admissions, informing her that she was next in line for a new patient now that her caseload was lighter.

Then, fighting her own panic, Vale met with Liza-Jane and Raymond who were both prickly, sullen, and in some way angry at Vale. Had her perceived failures with Julia and Parthia made her patients feel she might be bad luck for them? Vale's hand trembled when she wrote her notes.

At noon she went to meet with Rivers.

Arlene, Rivers' secretary, stopped her. "Mrs. Rivers is held up," she said, "but Win Lawrence left word you are welcome to join his meeting with Dr. Venables. Please go in."

She had forgotten completely Win's invitation of the night before. "Really?" she said.

"Pamela probably won't be out for a half an hour. She's with Dr. Lucore. Go on in."

Vale gave a tentative knock on the door, and heard Dean Venables' voice tell her to come in.

When she entered, she saw the two men seated at the glass-topped coffee table at one end of the spacious office. Win, on the couch, was hunched over a paper plate. Dr. Venables, in the chair beside him, was getting to his feet. "There you are," he said, coming towards her now with an extended hand. "We thought you'd stood us up."

"Well, I never...I wasn't sure..."

"Nonsense," he said, extending a hand. "Please, Vale, make yourself a plate of food," gesturing to a tray of cold cuts on the sideboard.

She nodded to Win, and he, with a mouthful of sandwich, nodded back. Though she had no appetite, she put some things on a plate and poured herself a soda. Win made room for her on the couch beside him.

"Win and I have been going over the plans for the new Conference Center. It's a dream of mine to have a place where people can come together to learn, share stories, and form colleagueship."

"Sounds like a school," Vale said.

"In the course of this work we learn so much, and very few of us really are going to publish anything. I've often thought that they are different temperaments, doing therapeutic work and being able to write well about it. There are exceptions, of course. Freud was a brilliant writer. This will interest you, Vale. Do you know he was awarded the Goethe Prize for *The Interpretation of Dreams?* That's a prize given for literary excellence, not for scientific writing." Vale shook her head. She wanted to disappear. "So there are examples of fine clinicians who are fine writers, but more and more our field is clogged by research, by the need to prove and to document. Me, I've always been interested in cases and stories, but, of course, now the word 'anecdotal' is almost always accompanied by the word 'merely.' Pisses me off. 'Merely anecdotal.' Imagine. It's *only* a story. I mean what else could it be?"

"Eat your lunch, Dean," Win said. Vale could feel his eyes on her. He can tell something is wrong, she thought.

Dr. Venables laughed. "Win is the only person around here that will put pins in my balloons."

"An endless occupation."

"So, Vale," Dean said, "What's new?"

She took a swallow of her ginger ale and dabbed quickly at the corners of her mouth. "Did you know that Parthia Alexander has gone AWOL?"

Both men said, "When?" at the same moment.

"I found out last night when I got home."

"You're having some bad luck, aren't you?" Dean said.

"It's a little hard for me not to think I'm doing something wrong."

"Nonsense," Dean said waving his right hand as if he were chasing off a fly. "What's going on on the unit?"

"Patients are agitated; staff is concerned. There's a feeling of disruption. Maybe some relief, too. She was... well, she pushed a lot of buttons."

Dean nodded and seemed about to speak when two resounding knocks on the door stopped him. Dean went to the door and opened it.

Serge Lucore stepped in "I need to talk to you immediately, Dean," his tone demanding, his voice loud. He glanced briefly at Win and Vale.

"Come in, Serge," said Dean, sitting down behind his desk and drawing Lucore away from his guests.

"This is not a social call." Lucore paced in front of Dean's desk. "We've got a big headache. Another one. I trust you know about the Alexander girl."

"I just..."

"I had the Sheriff's Office on the phone fifteen minutes ago. They haven't been able to put any one on it. They were patronizing."

"Serge, I'm sure...."

"It's on the blotter, " Lucore continued, his face flushed. "No doubt some eager cub reporter will dig it up, spice it up, and write an article about a Loony on the Loose. There were police at the Alexander home in Babylon, and we're liable. Damnit, that's twice..." and here, as if remembering that the culprit was in the room, Lucore wheeled and glared at Vale.

"Messenger, I'm glad you're here. Seems to me I'm spending far too much time cleaning up after you. I'd like to understand why two of *your* patients have jeopardized the reputation of this hospital. This is just brilliant clinical work, Messenger, brilliant. Perhaps you should have stayed with literature."

"Serge, come on, that's unfair."

"Is it?" said Lucore," never taking his eyes off Vale. "Do you know what the law of averages would say about this? Messenger, I want all your case notes on my desk before the end of the day. They will need my reviewing. Once again we will have to go through the process of an incident report. Once again the Office of Mental Health will be looking over our shoulders. Once again, we are going to have to call in the lawyers. This costs more than we we pay you in a year. You are a very expensive employee. And you might be interested to know that we come up for accreditation review in the fall, and this is precisely the kind of thing that they look at. "

Vale gulped and nodded.

"Serge, if anyone should be reviewing Vale's case, it's me. I will take personal responsibility for this case."

Lucore faced his partner again. "Usually I stay out of your territory, Dean, and you stay out of mine. That's how it's been, and it's worked well. But I tell you this woman---" with a jerk of his head---"is jinxed. I took the trouble to look at her record; she's only halfway through her probationary period. If there is one more piece of crap of any kind, she's done. Finished."

Dean now rose from his desk chair, and Lucore took a step back. Vale and Win looked at one another. "Enough, Serge," Dean said.

"All right, I'm prepared to have you handle this situation, supervise it, call it whatever you want. But I'll tell you one thing. I want this Parthia girl found and brought back here."

"We don't re-admit patients who elope."

"Well, we're going to make a goddamn exception in this case. It's called controlling the story, Dean. My department. She's not just any patient, you know that."

"Let's let the police..."

"The police will do shit. You know damn well where this rates with them."

"Well, probably not very high."

"You've got that right. Not one in ten patients who run away from a psych hospital is found by the police. They go into hiding, and the police have better things to do."

"I can't pull a rabbit out of a hat, Serge."

"I want this Messenger woman to find the girl."

Before Dean could respond, Lucore turned again to Vale. "I want you to go after her, today, tomorrow, the next day. She's your responsibility. She came here having tried to kill herself. If she succeeds in killing herself, we could have a law-suit on our hands of astronomical proportions." Vale thought for a moment of Claire and shuddered. "I expect you to do whatever it takes to get her back here."

"But Serge," Dean protested, "Ms. Messenger is not a detective."

"She has more information than anyone about this girl, and what is more she has the time to pursue it. She has our time and her own." Lucore looked back at Vale. "Don't you think you might take some of your personal time find this patient of yours, Ms. Messenger?"

"Yes...I suppose..."

"Suppose! This is the time to show if you have any loyalty to us. Either get the girl back or get a new job," and with that Serge Lucore opened the door and slammed it behind him.

In his wake, there was a long moment of awkward silence. Dean sat back down in his desk chair and stared out the window.

Vale got up and began to clear their paper plates, the plastic cutlery, the empty plastic drinking glasses. She took a napkin and swept the table crumbs into it, folding it and putting it into the side pocket of her summer jacket.

Dean brought his attention back to the room, reaching for his humidor. He filled a pipe and lit it. "Vale, sit. Please. I'm sorry. That should have taken place between just the two of us. It must have been difficult for you both. Serge said some unconscionable things. You mustn't take him seriously. All I can say in his defense is that he worries over this hospital like a mother hen. He hates it when things are not under his control." Dean drew on his pipe. "As for that stuff about being personally and professionally responsible for Parthia's disappearance, it's just plain bull. It is not true, nor should you feel in any way obliged to pursue her. You are not a detective, you are a clinician---and I believe a very fine one. Serge cannot and will not hold you to that demand. You could bring a lawsuit against the hospital for that matter; it is harassment. He's just venting." Vale shook her head. "No," Venables went on, "I'm just saying that you need to focus your attention on the patients you have. This Alexander girl's running away from North Forks is my responsibility. I'm the Chief Clinical Officer."

Vale stood up; she needed to be on her feet. "With all respect, Dr. Venables..."

"Please, please, Vale, call me Dean." He met her eyes, and she saw that he meant it.

"With all respect...Dean,"---the name was not easy for her to say in this moment--- "I think I must do as Dr. Lucore has asked. I am concerned for Parthia; I do know the names of people she has mentioned in her sessions with me; and to keep my obligation to confidentiality I could not share these with the authorities. I have access to her step-mother and to her former therapist."

"But your work is here," Dean said. "It sets a terrible precedent. Frankly, I don't want Serge Lucore telling my clinicians what to do. I need to draw a line."

Vale thought for a moment. "Well, I understand that, but I would prefer... how to say this?'

"You'd rather the line were drawn around someone else?" offered Win.

"Yes," she said. "I want to help."

"Vale, I ask you to think about it this way," Dean said, putting his pipe down. "You have patients here; they are fragile, and they will have been impacted by this. More than that, if they see their therapist has disappeared and imagine you have gone off in search of Parthia, it will send the worst message. Make some calls. Use some evening time if you must. I cannot compel you, but I ask that you keep your post here." He put a hand on her shoulder, his voice gentle. "I meant what I said about your not taking Serge too seriously. We can't be that responsible for the lives of our patients. They come *through here*. We give what we can; they take what they take. At best we plant seeds. The most lasting seeds, Vale, are seeds of kindness. It's why I hired you. I could see... No don't, my dear. Please."

Vale reached blindly into her pocket for something to staunch the tears that, in the presence of just such kindness, could no longer be restrained. She drew out the napkin. As she unfolded it to wipe her eyes, the crumbs of lunch fell to the floor.

•♦•

Vale went downstairs to the Ladies Room and locked the door. She hardly recognized the face she saw in the mirror, eyes puffy, hair a mess, the mouth a tight line against more tears, the expression distraught. The last time she had seen that face was in the aftermath of Robert's announcement that he had a lover.

She washed her face, then climbed back to the second floor. At Arlene's nod, she knocked on her supervisor's door.

Admitted, Vale was directed to a chair at the round table in the center of the office. Rivers sat across from her. "Well this has certainly stirred up a hornet's nest, hasn't it? Serge Lucore was in my office---that's why I was late for this meeting with you. I can't honestly say I'm surprised this girl bolted. We never really had her."

Vale was caught off guard. She expected a dressing down, and Rivers seemed matter-of-fact. "I thought for a while I did," Vale said.

"Well, I am sure you tried. I will be going over the records, but I don't expect to find fault with her treatment, though perhaps..." The sentence was left unfinished. "We have a certain legal exposure; there *is* liability, but we have a good lawyer, we have insurance, and Parthia Alexander is not a person whom the gossip columnists follow. Nor is she by any means the first person to have jumped ship. You have no idea, Vale. This is a voluntary hospital. Our control is limited."

"Mrs. Rivers, there is one thing I haven't written in my notes yet."

"What is that?"

Vale then told her of the Leonardo episode, her hunches and their confirmations, her sudden confrontation of Parthia in their last session, and Parthia's surreal response.

Rivers listened without interruption. When Vale was done, there was a long, uncomfortable silence. Finally Rivers spoke. "Well, I am not going to second guess you. First of all, I am sure I never would have made the connection. I doubt there is one clinician in a thousand who would have. Whether you did the right thing in 'dropping the bomb,' as you put it, I am not going to try to judge."

Rivers' compliment---"one in a thousand"---surprised Vale and brought a blush. "What do you think I should do?"

"Frankly, I think you should do what you can to help the authorities find the girl while at the same time giving your work here the priority it deserves Dean is quite fanatical about his Olympics, and I don't want patients wondering where you are. They miss nothing and make up the wildest stories. I'd prefer not to do battle with Serge, so let's just see where we are as the week progresses. I will certainly give you Friday off if we have not had a satisfactory conclusion by then." Vale sat mute and immobile "Is there any way I can be helpful?" Rivers asked.

"I don't think so. To be perfectly honest, I was expecting...well, after Julia I thought..."

"Nonsense, Vale. You are new to this work, but you are not without dedication or talent. Dean Venables has made his errors in judgment from time to time, but by and large his radar is spot on. The excellence of this staff is largely to his credit. I have every reason to think that you will survive these rites of passage. However, you are making Dr. Lucore into an adversary, and I hope for your sake this can turn out well, or at least disappear without incident."

Vale swallowed. "Thanks, Mrs. Rivers."

"Vale, don't you think it's about time you called me Pamela." And Vale tried on the name, as she said her good-bye.

•◆•

In the swelter of her office, she pushed through some of the paperwork Parthia's elopement had generated; the rest would have to wait for Thursday. Then she went to the unit meeting about the next day's Olympics, where Dr. Farmer made it clear that though it might be a clinical holiday, that made it all the more important for increased vigilance. Everyone was needed to shepherd the unit. And he reminded them to be sure to see all their patients on Thursday. "You never know what the day might trigger." Then the hospital athletics director reviewed, in mind-numbing detail, the schedule of events, the teams, the places, and the times. It seemed to Vale the day threatened to be a three-ring circus filled with a thousand clowns.

Climbing somewhat wearily the Tower steps, she paused at her closed door, the space, once so quaint to her, was becoming an arena of trial. A cell. She saw the dreaded red light blinking on her answering machine. To her relief it was Win: "Vale, I was stunned by what happened in Dean's office. I'm taking the day off tomorrow, but I'll be around Thursday. Here's my home phone number in case you want to call." A number followed. She wrote it down. Sweet man.

A second message began: "Vale, it's Willa. There's something here at the desk you might want to take a look at. A package came in the mail for Parthia on Saturday. She left it behind. It's been opened and resealed, but maybe it has something to do with why she left."

Then a third: "This is Claire Alexander. What do I have to do to get you to return a call?" The usual phone number followed.

Aware that she had been avoiding this all day, Vale dialed Claire's number, and at the same moment Claire's voice came on the line, there was a knock on her door, and Julia Kessler's head appeared, looking in. Vale put a hand over the receiver.

"Are we having our appointment, Ms. Messenger?"

"Oh God, Julia, I forgot." Vale looked at the clock; it was half past three.

"Hello, who is this?" Claire's voice sounded in her ear.

"It's all right; we can skip it if you're too busy."

"Hello!"

"No, Julia, let me..."

"Is anyone there? Parthia, is that you?"

"Just a minute," Vale said into the receiver.

"Who is it? Is that you Messenger?"

"You want me to wait outside?"

"Yes, Julia..."

"Messenger, are you on the line? Goddamnit, will you answer..."

Just as the door closed, Vale heard the line go dead.

Vale redialed the number.

"Hello."

"It's Vale Messenger, I..."

"Did you just call?"

"Yes I..."

"What the hell's the matter with you? You gave me a terrible scare. As if I didn't have enough to deal with. Where's Parthia? Where is she? I can't believe your incompetence. I've had the police to deal with today. The last thing in the world I need. Where is she? Do you have any idea?"

And it went on from there, Vale defensive, Claire assaultive, the call ending with Claire's demand to be kept informed, and Vale's assurance that she would be.

Then she recalled Julia.

"You've had a hard day," Julia offered, when seated in the blue chair, facing Vale.

"I have, Julia."

"I'm sorry," Julia said.

"What's this been like for you?" Vale asked, trying to bring herself to her role.

"Well, to be truthful I felt I could breathe. Parthia took so much, and she gave so little. But... " Julia paused, seemed to make up her mind about something, then spoke again. "I wanted to like her; I tried to care; but in the end I felt rejected, and that hurt. And used, I suppose. When I discovered she was gone, all I could feel was a certain kind of relief, like good riddance. Is that terrible?"

"No, it's not terrible. Our feelings don't always flatter us."

"It's funny," Julia said; "now that I have said I feel happy that Parthia is gone, I feel even kind of sad. And scared for her. Worried."

"I'm worried, too," Vale said.

"She got a call over the weekend."

"Did she?"

"Is it all right to tell you?"

"Please, Julia, I need to do whatever I can to help her be found."

"It was from someone named Biron."

"How do you know this?"

"She told me. After dinner in our room. She said she couldn't spend the rest of her life here. She had work; there was a shoot she had to prepare for. Biron needed her."

"Anything else?"

"She got some kind of package Saturday. A fat envelope. It had pictures in it."

"Did she show you?"

"No, but I saw her looking through them after I turned out my light. She had very bad dreams that night. Worse than usual. She was remote on Sunday. I kind of thought she was---I don't know---like doped or something. Sunday night was bad again." Julia's account confirmed Vale's intuition that the work with Biron Lord had played a significant role in Parthia's behavior. "The last I saw her was yesterday afternoon. She was very different, kind of play-acting being really nice. Even gave Amanda a pack of cigarettes. Then she never showed up for dinner last night."

"Any idea how she might have gotten away?"

"Not really, except all she'd have to do is get to the road. Anyone driving, especially a man, would pick her up in a heartbeat. No questions asked, I bet."

"Thanks, Julia." The rest of the session was centered on Julia's weekend, and Myrna's surprising willingness to consider letting Julia stay with her when she was released from the hospital.

It was only after Julia had left and Vale was trying to think through the coming days that Julia's phrase "play-acting" hit her. Could Parthia's disappearance put at risk her weekend plans with Melanie?

CHAPTER TWENTY-FOUR

Friday morning, dressed and stressed, Vale sat nursing a second cup of coffee at the kitchen counter. She couldn't take her eyes off the sweep Tigger's tail on the big kitchen clock; she was waiting for Claire to call.

The hospital Olympics on Wednesday could have been a welcome interlude had she not been so distracted by the urgency of her mission and so unable to act on it. She had spent every spare moment dashing back to her office to make calls or hoping to find a message that would help her locate Parthia. She had called the Suffolk County Sheriff's office only to learn they could not divulge anything to her about the case. Which meant she had had to call Dr. Lucore's office and learn from his secretary that there had been no report from law enforcement. What she took to be Lucore's ultimatum---"either get the girl back or get a new job"--- haunted her thoughts.

She spoke to Rivers on the sidelines of a softball game, bringing her up to date. "Well, you need to be here tomorrow for the aftermath; patients need to be herded back into the routine. Take Friday if you feel you need to, but don't be surprised if you can't locate her. If she doesn't want to be found, well...you can only do so much."

After kickball, Vale had placed a call to Mark Warren, left a message, and at the end of the day, just as she was leaving for home, he returned her call. Yes, he was willing to talk to her if she came to his office. Did he have time on Friday? Yes, he could make some time Friday, say two p.m. She was desperate to ask if had any idea where his former patient might have gone. Had this ever happened before? Were there names Dr. Warren might be willing to release to Vale? Did he know how to find the mysterious Biron Lord? But he cut her short: "Friday afternoon, and be prompt, I have a patient at 2:30."

She had tried to locate Biron Lord. There were a dozen B. Lord's in the Manhattan Directory. She called them all, leaving a cryptic message where there was a machine to record it. No one returned a call. She remembered the names of two of the companies for whom Parthia had done work---Revlon and Cartier--- but she never found the right person in their publicity department to ask about Biron Lord. She had spent eons on hold.

It was only at lunch that she remembered the envelope that had come for Parthia. She retrieved it from the nurse's station, and its heft confirmed her suspicion that it contained the series of photographs Parthia had done with Lord, but, as Willa had told her, the envelope had been re-sealed, and in good conscience Vale felt she should not open it. Besides, it would not tell her Parthia's whereabouts. There was, however, a return address on the cover: *Graphic Images*, 115 Prince Street in New York. She got a number from information, reached a machine and a pre-recorded message which told her that the gallery was open by appointment only: If the caller was interested in making an appointment, please leave a number. She left her name and said she needed to speak to Biron Lord on a personal and professional matter. "It's urgent." Then, before hanging up she said impulsively, "I will come to the gallery around 3:00 on Friday afternoon."

When she could break away from "the comedy of errors," as she came to call the Olympiad, she had endured a maddening game of hide-and-seek with Claire. She suspected Claire would have leads for her, certainly a number for the mysterious Biron Lord, but when she called, only a machine answered, and when Claire did return her calls, Vale was not at her desk to receive them. The last words on her machine Wednesday evening, which she picked up Thursday morning, were Claire's promise to "make some time for you."

Thursday it rained. Wind beat against the little window of her cell. The big maple shook. All morning she worked to smooth her overtired and overwired patients back into their sessions and groups. She dashed to the dining room to put together a take-out lunch and sat at her desk to meet the demands of paper work, and pursue Claire. No luck at all.

Vale had left a message at the end of her working day that she was taking Friday off and would it be at all possible to see Claire at home? "You can call me at home this evening, but if not then, please call me Friday morning before ten."

She left her home number. Now past ten, Vale cleaned her coffee cup while overhead Tigger's tail moved its monotonous round.

The ringing phone startled her. "Claire?" she said, gripping the receiver.

"It's Robert."

"I'm waiting for an important call. What do you want?"

"Meli wants to know if you're coming up with us. We'll..."

"I told her I'd be coming up Saturday."

"OK. OK. I'm just..."

"Robert, I am communicating directly with Melanie. Butt out."

"She says she can never reach you."

"I haven't heard any messages from her."

"I just called to tell you we're staying at the Wainright Inn. Have you made res..."

"Robert, I need to get off the phone."

He broke the connection without a further word. No sooner had she replaced the phone in its cradle than it rang again.

"Hello," she said.

"Mrs. Messenger, is that you? It's Claire Alexander here."

"Yes."

"You are an extremely difficult person to reach." Vale stifled the retort that came to her lips. "Have you found her?"

"No. You haven't heard from her, I suppose."

"No. Not a word. I spoke to the headman at your place yesterday, actually both of them. One, Doctor Lucore, was very accommodating, assured me that you were fully committed to finding her. Then I spoke to the other person in charge there, a Dr. Venials---what a cold fish he is---and he told me that I should speak directly with you."

"Venables. His name is Doctor Venables."

"Who cares what his name is! I speak to so many doctors it's a wonder I can keep them straight. What can you tell me?"

"I was hoping that you could give me some ideas about where to look for her."

"I haven't a clue. Her apartment? I've called, of course. If she's there, she's screening her calls or not answering the phone. Where else could she be? I'm at my wit's end. I called Biron, but he made it very clear he wants nothing to do with this affair. I know the names of some of her friends, a Russian girl Tasha or

Sasha, something like that. And I have the names of some others of her friends in my address book, but I've been hesitant. I just don't know what to do. I don't want to be intrusive. I mean Parthia is a woman, a young woman, and I know she thinks I can be, sometimes, a bit...hovering. She has certainly made me aware she doesn't want me to mind her business. But then again, let's be honest here, where would she be without me? I don't know what I'd do if anything else happened to her. She's already given me the scare of my life." Finally a pause.

Vale looked at the clock. She would like to see that address book. And there was Biron Lord. Perhaps she could reach him. "Listen, Claire," she said, "I have to be in the city by two this afternoon, but I'd like to meet with you before. I can come to you."

"I am already late for a consult with the specialist about my husband. But I should be free by half past eleven."

"I can be there by half past eleven." It wouldn't leave them much time.

"Very good, I will expect you. You have the address?" Vale did, and they broke the connection.

Relieved at least to have some possibilities in the day ahead---Claire, Mark Warren, perhaps even the elusive Biron Lord--- she was on her way into the bedroom to put some things in a bag for the weekend when the phone rang for a third time. Her impatience faded as soon as she recognized Win's voice. She hadn't had a moment yesterday, nor had he, and besides, she told him, she had nothing to report. She told him her day's plans.

"So you're going to be in the city this afternoon? What's the plan after you meet up with Mark Warren?"

"I don't have one. But I'm going to try to find this Biron Lord, her photographer, at his studio on Prince Street."

"And what will you do if you can't find this Alexander girl before the end of the day?"

"I refuse to think about it. I'm packing for the weekend. I'll drive to Babylon to see Claire and then into the city. I'll head north after I catch a bite for dinner, and stay overnight at a motel to break up the trip. I have a date for lunch with Meli on Saturday."

"You're worried."

"I keep hearing Lucore's either-or in my head."

"Well, let me make you dinner before you head out. You could put your feet up at my place at the end of the day." He heard her silence. "I'll be home by five."

She thought for a second. "All right. Give me the particulars."

Win gave her the address and gave her his phone number. "Leave me message if you get delayed or plans change, and don't be put off by the look of the building. It's a loft in a refurbished factory. The neighborhood's safe, just unrefined. There's a parking lot on the corner."

"Thanks," she said, and they rang off.

• ◆ •

By half past eleven she was in Babylon, driving down a street deeply shaded by ancient sycamores. Hedges and gates hid the houses. Numbers were hard to find. Then she saw what she was looking for. She leaned from her car window at a closed gate and pressed a bell. In a moment the gates swung open.

She parked at the top of the drive, rang the front doorbell, and presently a woman in a maid's uniform opened the door and admitted her to an entry hall, furnished with two chairs and an antique drop-leaf table with a large vase of fresh cut flowers on it. A grandfather clock stood in a niche. "Mrs. Alexander, she be here soon," and the maid left Vale alone.

Caught between curiosity and good manners, Vale paced the foyer in slowly widening orbits until she passed into a central rotunda from which a staircase ascended to the second floor. She scanned the upper landing. A corridor. Closed doors. Behind one of them the dying father?

The clock was ringing the third quarter of the hour when Claire emerged from a book-lined room and offered Vale a perfectly manicured, diamond-heavy hand. "Thank you for coming, my dear. Please, come into the living room." Vale followed Claire into a spacious room, furnished with all white furniture. Sliding glass windows looked out on the garden, where a man on his knees was tending a bed of roses.

Just inside the door, Claire pressed a button, and in a moment her maid appeared. "My usual. Anything for you?" Claire asked, turning to Vale.

"A glass of water, that's all. Thank you."

The maid disappeared, and Claire settled herself on the couch, Vale across from her in a wingback chair. Between them lay the coffee table upon which was displayed a large photo album with a leather tooled cover.

Claire was shaking her head; she had a slip of paper in her hand. "Do you know what the word en-ce-phelo-pathic means?" she asked, sounding out the word.

"I'm not sure," Vale said.

"Apparently, it means the brain is sick. My husband has not been himself. He is very agitated, and sometimes he makes no sense when he is talking. Or he starts talking in German, and I can't get him to talk to me in English. Dr. Phitzer told me that liver functions are often compromised by pancreatic cancer and that this encepheloparthia is the result." Vale heard the slip of the tongue. "My husband appears to be losing his mind. For example, he cannot endure the smell of smoke on my breath. Fire, fire, that's all I hear about from him. *Feuer*. He reverts to German. I hate that. I feel excluded." Claire put the piece of paper down. "There is no hope at all. Which I already knew. The disease is in its final phase. My husband's life can be made less painful; it can be prolonged in some ways; it can be, Phitzer intimated, it can be *hastened*, but not by him; he made that very clear." Claire reached over to a gold box on the table and withdrew a cigarette. With the snap of a gold lighter, smoke rose in the air. "But the end is very near, and now there is this brain sickness, this...I hate to use the word, this kind of madness." She drew on her cigarette again. "Dr. Phitzer says he has done all he can. He knows of Claus and suggested Willi might talk to him, as our friend and physician, about helping my husband to end his life." Claire tipped the ash off her cigarette into a crystal bowl. "I dread this. It's macabre," she said, looking across at Vale. "I have such terrible decisions to make. Wilhelm is in a great deal of pain, and Claus has him doped up most of the time."

"I'm sorry," Vale said, her sympathy warring with her impatience. "Mrs. Alexander I have so little..."

"Must I keep insisting you call me Claire? Here you are in my home. You are my guest. I am *Claire!*"

"Claire, yes, I have an appointment in the city. I have to..."

"What time is your appointment?"

"Two o'clock."

"And where?"

"The Upper West Side."

"But it's only noon. You are driving? Yes. Well, if you take the Triborough, it's only a little over..." Claire glanced at a gold clock on the mantelpiece. "We have at least half an hour."

At that moment the maid returned with a tray and offered Claire a drink that looked like a Bloody Mary and Vale her glass of ice water. Claire put out her cigarette, drank several swallows, then spoke, "This afternoon the plumber will be coming to re-do the bathroom in the Guest House."

"Claire, you mentioned something about an address book?"

"Would you like to see it?" Claire asked, brightening. "Come let me show you." Here she downed the last of her drink.

"The address book?"

"No, silly, the Guest House."

Vale began to protest, but Claire was already on her feet, sliding open the French doors, and leading the way across a patio onto a flagstone garden path at the back of the house, talking over her shoulder as she went. "We provided surgery and aftercare for those who wanted privacy, a retreat, and a doctor available at any time." Along one side of a great hedge, Vale saw a swimming pool and behind it a bathhouse. On the other side, and hidden from view until she turned a corner, stood a stucco, single-story building with its own fore-garden, patio, and barbecue grill. "I loved hosting the celebrities who came here. I spoke their language after all. And, of course, I had a daughter under my wing, our ugly duckling who was becoming our swan." Claire opened the gate for Vale and then the front door.

"Claire, you mentioned an address book."

"In a moment, dear. In a moment."

Once inside Vale could see that the Guest House had been freshly painted and decorated. Just short of gaudy, brightly colored furniture in a very feminine design showed ruffles and frills. Hollywood meets Art Deco. A kitchen fronted by a counter occupied one end of the spacious living room. There was a second smaller room with bookshelves from floor to ceiling---paperbacks and popular fiction on the shelves---and a daybed along one wall, a television and stereo system along the other. Through curtained windows you could see hedge, trees, and garden. There was privacy, comfort, and quiet.

"Lovely," Vale said. "Everything looks brand new."

"It is. Parthia destroyed the place that night before she...did what she did. She had broken lamps, a chair. The mirror above the vanity had been smashed. The sheets had been slashed with a kitchen knife. She'd taken a knife to the pillows and the chairs. There was wine spilled all over the rug. It was carnage, absolute carnage. Then I found her, saw the pills, and I realized she had had a fit."

As she was hearing these words, Vale was looking past Claire into the bathroom. She saw stains on the floor---blood? Spilled wine? Lipstick smears?---

and in a sudden flash her memory produced a frozen image: a sink, a pair of tailor's shears, and her father's slumped, motionless form. "Oh my God," Vale breathed.

"...I was just so damn angry. It wasn't as if I didn't have enough on my hands without this. Vale, are you all right? You look quite pale."

"No, no I'm fine. It's just that I've gotten to know Parthia and being here..."

"Did you ever learn why she did this?"

"Mrs. Alexander, I can't really..." Vale interrupted herself, seeing what was coming, "Claire, I can't really talk about what Parthia told me."

"I understand. Of course. Privileged information. That's it, isn't it? Yet I am supposed to tell you all sorts of things. Well, let's go back to the library and get that address book you are so damned interested in."

Moments later Claire was seated behind a Queen Anne's desk, Vale on a loveseat in front of it. She had rung again for her maid, and a fresh drink was in her hand. "So what do you want?"

"You mentioned having some names. Can we start there?"

Claire opened her leather secretary and read out names, addresses and phone numbers. Vale wrote them down on a page in her notebook. When Claire came to Biron Lord, she cleared her throat. "Biron is your best bet. He and I have been close in the past. We still are. Biron has done so much for Parthia, and she put a great trust in him, I believe. I have his home number in the city. I told you I spoke to him. He knows nothing and wants no involvement. He has a house on Fire Island, but I don't have that number." Claire dictated the city number. "And this is the number of his agency." Vale took it down. "He also has a gallery, *Graphic Images* on Prince Street in the Village." Claire provided that number, though Vale already had it. "You may be able to reach him through Parthia's agent, Blaire Whittemore. This is his number." Also, she had the names of restaurants and bars where Parthia often went.

Capping her pen, Vale thanked Claire. "Do you think I might use your phone to make a call or two?"

"By all means," Claire said. "I'll wait for you in the living room."

Vale called Biron Lord's home number and left a message on his machine with Win's number and the fact that she could be reached at that number after five. Biron's voice seemed distantly familiar, a smooth baritone with a campy edge to it. She also called Blaire Whittemore, whose secretary took Vale's name and informed her that Mr. Whittemore was in Toronto for his summer vacation. He might call in, though it was unlikely. As far as reaching Parthia's friends, Vale suspected none would be at home in the middle of a summer Friday. She would try them tonight.

On the desk before her Vale saw two pictures side by side in a single frame. One was a black and white photograph of a plain young girl in a school dress uniform who clearly did not wish to have her picture taken. The other was Parthia, dressed as if she were going to a party, wearing an evening dress. She held a corsage in her hands. A phrase from Claire's lips came to mind, "I had a daughter under my wing, our ugly duckling who was becoming our swan."

A daughter under my wing... Melanie.

She went to the living room, where she found Claire seated on the couch, the album on the coffee table open before her. "Did you have any success?"

"I left messages."

"Yes, well, it's Friday."

"May I ask you a question?"

"Certainly, darling. Sit down. Would you like anything else to drink?" Claire had a fresh one in her hand.

"No, thank you." Vale sat down in the white wing chair. "Can you tell me about your husband, Mrs. Alexander? Can you tell me about the work he did on Parthia?"

"But what has that got to do with finding her?"

"Mrs. Alexander, I found out something about Parthia. I think it may have caused her to leave the hospital. It had to do with how she looks. With what her father had made her look like?"

"I don't understand," Claire said. She lit another cigarette.

"Let me show you something." Vale took out the Leonardo from her shoulder bag. She carried it over to Claire. Her bookmark made it easy to find the page. "I assume you have seen this picture."

"Of course," Claire said, "many times. And in the original." Claire gave Vale an appraising glance. "Parthia told you; I'm impressed."

"No. I felt I had seen Parthia's face somewhere. Not in a magazine. Somewhere else."

Claire nodded. "Isn't the resemblance amazing?" She leaned forward, squinting slightly. "The man is a genius."

"Leonardo?"

"No, Wilhelm. My husband."

"He created Parthia to look like this?"

"Of course. You think it was an accident?"

Claire handed the book back to Vale. "You really don't understand anything about this kind of work, do you?" Vale sat down again with the book closed on her lap.

"There is reconstructive surgery, and there is cosmetic surgery," Claire began, as if offering a child an elementary explanation. "In the past the former was used to repair damage of the sort that I suffered. It is structural work with bone." She took a long drink and dabbed at her lips with a white handkerchief she drew from her pocket. "And there is cosmetic surgery which, with the exception of changing the shape of a nose, involves working with skin. What Wilhelm has been doing over the last twenty years is bringing these two fields together, or rather turning the art of cosmetic surgery into a means by which an ordinary face can be deeply transformed. Almost single-handedly he has pushed out the frontier of this science. His work has proved that it is possible for any woman, no matter how plain, to become her own perfection. And the work may begin early. Wilhelm showed that with Parthia. A person need not go through adolescence as a wallflower. She may be a rose. Or an orchid. Imagine, Dale, to be able to choose your own face."

Claire took up her drink. Finding mostly water and ice in her glass, she rang again. Her maid appeared, whisked away the glass, and in a moment returned with a full one. Vale imagined a pitcher in the refrigerator, always full.

"My husband has a supreme aesthetic sense," Claire went on, her face now flushed. "He had the artistry to realize what he could envision. You think I exaggerate, Mrs. Messenger? Someday perhaps you will see the pictures he took of the work he did on me. He is meticulous in recording what he does." Claire rested her hand on the album before her. "No one who has not seen it can appreciate his art. Da Vinci? What did he do? Worked in paint. Turned clay or wax into bronze. Very impressive. But Wilhelm worked in flesh. Think of that." Claire sipped her drink. "One day I will publish the work he did on Parthia. It will astound the world."

"So what happened to Parthia?"

"I told you I don't know." Claire lifted her glass and drank.

"No, I am not asking you where she is. I am asking you what her father did to her."

"*To* her? *To* her? It was all *for* her. Don't you get it? First of all, Parthia is not her real name. Or rather, that is not the name on her birth certificate. The eight-year-old girl I met was 'Paula.' Willi called her 'Paulina.' She named after her maternal grandmother I believe. Paula had been born with a lazy left eye. It has some fancy name. The eyelid drooped. Early on she had a simple surgical procedure that lifted the lid. But she was a homely girl. Like her mother. Bavarian with a small undistinguished nose and a..."

"Wait, Claire. Stop! How did you get her to co-operate? How did Parthia---Paula---Did she consent to this?"

"Of course, she did. I told you in your office that she wanted it desperately."

"Tell me the story."

"We made it into a kind of game. We showed her pictures. We talked to her. She wanted us to make her beautiful. At first Wilhelm refused. But she persisted. No, he said, not yet. She wasn't ready. She was too young. She pleaded with him. Really, you can't believe how much she wanted to become beautiful. And he said, No, he wasn't sure she really wanted it. If she got perfect grades in school, he would know she really wanted it. If she stopped picking at her nails, if she ate as he told her to eat---he set many conditions to make her prove she really wanted him to do this difficult thing for her. So all through sixth grade and seventh grade she worked like a child possessed. Then finally he said he might be able to do something on her thirteenth birthday. Her birthday is the 23rd of May. That's when we began, the day she turned thirteen. It was her birthday present, and each year for four years it would be her birthday present. She would have her father all to herself, and he would work on her. Together they looked at pictures and made decisions. What did she want to be? They would go to the Metropolitan, to the Frick. Each Christmas we took her to Europe, and we looked at all the great art in all the museums. Of course, like her father she loved Leonardo Da Vinci best of all. So one shouldn't be surprised that they actually chose a face from Da Vinci. But Wilhelm was that kind of genius, you understand. If Leonardo Da Vinci lived in the 20th century, he would have *been* Wilhelm Alexander."

"And your role in all this, Claire?" steeling her voice against a rising inner rage.

"Yes, I had a role. Thank you for seeing that. Wilhelm always said he could not have done it without me. Paulina was a little frightened at first. I soothed her, repeated my story to her again and again. Showed her the pictures. It was our fairy tale. And then, of course, he could only be with her for so long. He had patients; he had his work; he was a very busy man. And perhaps, well, you know, he was a little distant with her, a European father. He was not demonstrative. So I kept her company while the bandages were on. The first weeks of June were always a quiet time. She rested. We watched the soaps. I had done the soaps a hundred years ago. We'd go through catalogues and shop for clothes. She was learning to love clothes. She was learning to love all the things I loved. She was my daughter in all but blood. I doted on her, absolutely doted on her. I suppose I did it in part because I wanted to thank Wilhelm for restoring my life, but I loved her, I really did, and here was a chance to help shape her into a beautiful, talented child. It was as if the three of us had been brought together by fate to participate in a great experiment."

The grandfather clock was ringing, the third quarter hour. Vale stood, putting the Leonardo and her notebook into her bag. "I understand," she said. "I understand."

"I'm so worried about Parthia," Claire said then, looking up at Vale and tears showing in her eyes, a hand reaching out to detain her. "If anything happened to her, it would kill her father. What a terrible thing to say. I mean he is dying. What I meant to say was that it would give him added pain. He did it all for her. You have no idea. I would do anything to spare him that. She is everything to him. You must find her, Dale, you must help her." A slight slurring had begun to take the edge off Claire's syllables. "She's such a bright future. She's his legacy, his greatest gift to the world. Just going through a bad bit right now. You can help. I know you can. I can see how much you care. Oh, do, Dale, I mean Vale. Vale and Dale, they are the same thing aren't they? Hill and Vale, Hill and Dale."

"I must leave. Mrs. Alexander."

"Yes, I suppose you must. Forgive me, if I don't see you out. I am quite done in for some reason."

"I can find my way," Vale said, and with the weight of Leonardo back on her shoulder, she closed the front door behind her.

CHAPTER TWENTY-FIVE

Mark Warren, Ph.D. Gold lettering on the door.

The man who let Vale in was so like her image of him that she did a double-take and wondered whether she had met him somewhere before. Tall, round-shouldered with a pale complexion and a close-cropped beard of gray and brown, he greeted her with a knuckled hand and the unnecessary mention of his name. Unnecessarily she supplied hers.

"You are late," he said, as he brought her into his office which was appointed with tan leather furniture, an analyst's chaise longue, and floor to ceiling bookcases on the wall behind his desk. The effect was imposing. "You might have called."

"Yes. I am sorry. I drove into the city and got a late start." Half their time was already gone.

He motioned her to a seat across the desk from him. He sat down in his swivel chair and tilted back in it, his thumbs tucked into the pockets of his vest. On the mahogany surface between them sat a pad of paper, a quiver of sharpened pencils in a carved wooden jar, and a polished brass magnifying glass. This last seemed to suggest the penetration of the analytic eye. Or perhaps its need for assistance.

"Do you have any news of her?" he asked.

"No, not yet."

"And you think I may be of some use to you?"

"Can you tell me, Dr. Warren, how it happened that Parthia came to see you in the first place?"

"Yes. Well, I have a certain reputation in her industry," he said. "I see a number of models and artists. They are often hysterical types, as you know, narcissistic, demanding, empty. My approach---a steadiness, nothing flashy, but dependable and, if I may say so, smart---gives them a certain stability. They like to talk; I am a good listener. I have seen some of them for years. They lead such irregular lives; they need someone with whom to make sense of it all."

"I see. And may I ask how long you had been seeing Parthia?"

"She came to me for the first time three years ago. It began well, and then she missed appointments. I haven't heard from her in more than a year with the exception of a call to me a year ago, in May, requesting an appointment. For which she failed to appear. Then there was a message from her that June, to which I responded and reminded her she was responsible for payment. There has been no communication since."

"Was there anything in particular she seemed to be working on in her sessions with you?"

"Yes. Mostly it was her relationship with her step-mother. With Claire Alexander. You understand, Ms. Messenger, I am speaking to you in professional confidence now and will do so only up to a point. I take the doctor-patient privilege with great seriousness. There is an inordinate amount of gossip and an almost incestuous intimacy among the circle of women and men I see."

"I am here in an emergency, Dr. Warren. I need information; I need to find Parthia. I have my own therapeutic relationship with her."

"I understand, and I will do what I can." He turned a few degrees in his swivel chair so that he was no longer facing her. "What brought her in to see me in the first place was her desire to individuate from her step-mother. So, in a general way I can tell you this is what she worked on. Though "work" is perhaps too strong a word for her complaints, her recriminations, and her envy. Parthia felt herself to be dependent on Claire Alexander. She had never been able to break free of her; she needed her and resented the need. She played out this ambivalence in all kinds of ways, at times going on endlessly about what gift to give her step-mother for her birthday, at other times coming in with detailed reports of furious spats. I was never successful in getting Parthia to talk about her biological mother, but I gather that she had been a very lonely child before Claire came into her life. I always believed a great deal of negative transference attached itself to Claire that was likely displaced form another source, her anger at her biological mother's abandonment."

"And did you have..." Dr. Warren raised a finger.

"Additionally she was succeeding in her career in modeling, and success breeds its own anxieties. Yes, you were going to ask?"

"And did you have an understanding of her history? Of her relationship with the father, for example?"

"No, I did not. I know her father was a reconstructive surgeon, but he never came up in his daughter's sessions or at least not beyond a mention in passing."

"You didn't find that odd?" Vale wasn't sure she believed him.

"Odd?" Dr. Warren considered this a moment. "Perhaps you have not been exposed to the psychoanalytic process, Ms. Messenger. In our work a relationship evolves slowly. The analyst is not a fact-finder. That her father did not come up in our sessions may be due to the intermittent nature of Parthia's appointments. I sensed that her father was and had been the one stable element in her otherwise changing world. The transference between us had not yet developed to the point where I was able to infer much." Vale speculated on Parthia's choice for therapist of this distant, dry man.

Dr. Warren continued, "Her father had provided very well for his daughter---she had her own co-op in So-Ho that she could not have purchased out of her income alone---but he was just not much a part of her life, and she seemed quite content with that."

"You told me over the phone that Parthia was not willing to see you when you visited her at Good Samaritan. How come you were there at all?"

"Claire called, prevailed on me to go. As far as I was concerned, Parthia had terminated with me. She was not my patient any longer, nor did she seek to be. I had heard---I won't say how---that she had become involved with a man named Biron Lord. Perhaps you have heard of him?" Dr. Warren looked up and registered Vale's nod. His nose wrinkled for a moment as if a foul odor had reached it; then he continued. "I had heard stories of Lord, and I was concerned for Parthia; it did not seem like a good career move, shall we say."

"What can you tell me about Biron Lord?"

"What I know is hearsay. I believe he preys upon young men and women who begin as his subjects in legitimate commercial enterprises. My impression is that he has collected a number of unstable people about him. He sounds like a charismatic narcissist who adopts birds with broken wings and persuades them to let him exploit them in the name of art. He is utterly irresponsible, like a doctor practicing without a license. He thinks he is some kind of shaman. I believe he is only a sham."

"I am trying to find him. Are there any names you can give me of people who might know Parthia or know where she is?"

"I'm sorry, Ms. Messenger. I realize you are only trying to do what is right and necessary by your standards, but I cannot divulge the names of other patients of mine, of other people I know through the disclosures of my clients who might know Parthia. You will have to find her whereabouts from some other source."

"Fine," said Vale, rising from her chair. "I understand your priorities."

"They are not priorities, Ms. Messenger," said Dr. Warren, rising also, "they are professional standards."

They had reached the door of his office when a last question occurred to her. She had nothing to lose by asking. "Did Parthia Alexander ever say anything to you about Leonardo Da Vinci?"

"About Leonardo Da Vinci?" He paused with his hand on the doorknob. "What a curious question. Why do you ask?"

"Oh, he came up in one of our sessions. She seemed to have some interest in him."

"Well, oddly enough, yes, though in a very indirect way. Parthia went to London...it was late June of last year if I am not mistaken. Wait a moment if you will. I can be more exact." He walked back to his desk, pulled out a file drawer, reached in for a folder, and laid it open. Vale could see neatly penned session notes, a small sheaf of them. There was also a brightly colored card. He picked this up and looked carefully at it. "Yes, here it is. It was a card she had bought at the National Gallery in London. It shows one of Leonardo's paintings." He brought the card closer to his eyes to read the legend on it.

"*The Madonna of the Rocks?*" Vale offered.

"Why, yes," he said. "How did you know?"

"Just a guess. And did she write anything on the card?" she asked.

"It says---I can divulge this I am sure ---'Wish you could see what I see.' That was all. I never gave it a second thought. It was the last I heard of her until Claire Alexander called me."

Dr. Warren closed the folder and replaced it in the file drawer. He looked up at Vale. "Is there some significance to this?" he asked. "I simply assumed it was a version of 'Having a wonderful time, wish you were here.' I was actually a little flattered that she wrote."

"You would have to have been a genius to have seen the significance in her remark." He looked momentarily crestfallen. "I wouldn't give it another thought." With that she thanked him for his time, and let herself out, leaving Dr. Mark Warren to make of her remark what he chose.

•◆•

She found a pay phone at the corner, popped in a dime, and rang her work and home answering machines, pinching the phone to her ear with a raised shoulder and ready to jot down information on a page in her notebook. Among the messages on her machine at home was one that jolted her. A male voice, providing no name, startled her with the words, "At first we see through a darkened glass, but soon we will see face to face." Nothing further. *Biron Lord*, the name flashed into her mind. It was the same voice she had heard on his answering machine, and now she was sure it was the same voice that had been "looking for Dr. A".

Vale began calling the numbers of Parthia's friends that Claire had given her. She drew blanks---numbers out of service, no answer, messages on machines---until she dialed Sasha Tartikoff, who was not at home, but whose machine gave a number to which day-time calls could be routed. Vale dialed it.

She was surprised to hear the receiver lifted after three rings. "Sappho East," a husky woman's voice informed her.

"Is this Sasha Tartikoff?" she asked.

"No. You want to speak to her?"

"Yes, please."

"I'll see if she can come to the phone." Vale waited. The husky voice came back on the line, "Give her a minute."

Three dimes later, a voice with a strong Slavic accent picked up the receiver.

"This is Sasha. Who is this, please?"

"My name is Vale Messenger. I am a...a friend of Parthia Alexander."

"And you are calling me why?"

"I am trying to find Parthia."

"You have tried her apartment?"

"Yes, I have."

"Well, I do not think I can help you. Part'ia has been out of town. There vas rumor…" the voice reconsidered, "I do not know vhere she is."

"Do you have any suggestions about how I might find her?"

"I am sorry, but I do not know you. Perhaps you are creditor or jealous wife," Sasha laughed.

"I assure you I am neither. Can I meet you?" Vale heard the note of desperation in her voice.

Perhaps Sasha heard it too. "I am in rehearsal. Sometimes we take breaks. You understand me?"

"Yes, I understand. I'll take my chances. It is important to me, Miss Tartikoff. May I come to the theater?"

There was a pause. Someone else's voice calling "Places" was audible in the background. "Da, yes. As long as you are patient person. Maybe around 4?" Vale assured her of her patience, and in response to her question about where to come, Sasha concluded the conversation with an address on St. Mark's Place.

By the time she rang off, Vale's blouse was clinging to her back, and she felt no nearer to her quarry than she had been twenty-four earlier. She had to get out of the sun. She was thirsty, and she needed to eat.

She bought a bagel and cream cheese and a bottle of ice tea, retrieved her car from the garage and threaded traffic south towards Prince Street. She was oppressed by thoughts of her daughter and of Robert and Elaine already in Vermont.

She forced herself to consider the matter at hand. The words on Parthia's postcard came back to her: "Wish you could see what I see. See me." Vale shook her head at the concision of those words. Casually scrawled on a post card, they certainly suggested the airy cliché Dr. Warren had heard. Parthia had flattered his ego with her hint that she was having a wonderful time and wished Warren was there with her. But in the light of all Vale now knew, the words carried a different intent. "Wish you could see what I see" seemed to Vale a kind of appeal. "Take out that magnifying glass of yours and look at this image. See what I see." But the plea had fallen on deaf ears.

•◆•

According to the register beside the street door, *Graphic Images* was to be found on the fourth floor. She pressed the appropriate button, and after a very long moment, a buzzer admitted her. On the fourth floor she read the names of galleries: *Apertures, Hard Edges, Nouveau Clique,* and, at the end of the hall, *Graphic Images,* behind a closed white door with "By Appointment Only" incised on a rectangular brass plate.

Vale knocked, then leaned wearily against the wall. She heard the approach of feet, and then a dark-skinned young man opened the door: he was slim as a cigarillo, and wore a white apron over a black tee shirt and black jeans.

"Can I help you?" he said, the trace of an accent in his voice.

"I am looking for Mr. Biron Lord."

"*Mister* Biron Lord," he repeated, raising an eyebrow. "He is not here."

"Could you tell me where he is?"

"And you are?" The slim man put an arm up on the doorframe, blocking entry. Vale looked past him and saw photographs mounted on white walls.

"My name is Vale Messenger. I..." without thinking she reached into her satchel and pulled out the manila folder and held it out to him. "I am trying to return this to the person to whom it was sent."

"And why would you wish to return it?" The guardian of *Graphic Images* continued to regard her with a faint smile, but took the envelope from her and turned it around to read the name of the intended recipient. "Ah," he said, "Parthia."

"You don't know where I could find her, do you?"

"I thought you were looking for *Mister* Biron Lord," the young man said.

"May I know your name?' she asked.

"I am Adin," he said; "I develop pictures for Biron. I developed these. You have seen them?"

"No, I have not."

"That is too bad," he said. "They are very good."

She set down her bag on the floor. "Look Adin," she said, "I want you to take something on faith. Do you know what that means?'

"Yes," he said, "I know what that means. To believe without having proof."

"Exactly. I want you take something on faith: it is a matter of very great importance to me that I find Parthia Alexander. I can't tell you why."

She could see he understood, for the look of irony fell away, and he handed the envelope back to her. "I do not know anything about where she is," he said.

"Can you help me to find Lord? He may know."

"Biron is not here," he said.

"I know he has an unlisted number. Can you get it for me?"

"In the city? Out on the island?"

"Both. Either."

Adin paused, considering. "This I will do." He left her standing at the door and went into a back room. Vale took a step forward and glanced at the pictures on the wall. Now she knew that the headshot she had seen on the morning she waited to meet Parthia for the first time was Lord's work, and she thought again of Mapplethorpe. The images on the walls were all striking, even shocking, done in a highly finished style, vivid contrasts of black and white, primary colors where colors were used. Naked figures, singly, in pairs, groups, poses. Like Mappletho-rpe, it seemed the subject matter was meant to strike the eye hard, to alarm, to arouse, even to disgust the viewer. It would have been too glib to label the work sado-masochistic, though the term sprang to mind. Was Parthia among them?

Adin returned with a small scrap of paper. "I believe," he said, handing it to her, "that I heard your voice already on the answering machine. You called. I did not make the connection.'

"Will you be talking personally to Mr. Lord today?"

The smile returned to Adin's face. "I do not think so," he said; "he is already away for the weekend. It is summer. A slow season for us."

"Can you tell me something about these?" she asked, gesturing to the walls.

"These are the first in each series."

"Series?"

"Yes. Biron composes photo essays. Each of these belongs to a series."

"How do I see the rest?" she asked.

"This is by appointment with Biron only. But," he said, pointing to the envelope she had in her hands, "you have those."

"Thank you," she said.

"You are welcome. I like that you asked me to take something on faith. It is a nice way to speak to a person. I wish you well in your search," and with that he closed the door.

She stood in the hallway considering her options. It was a few minutes before four. She dreaded returning to the heat outside. It was a trek in the hot afternoon to St. Mark's Place, but before setting out, she found a phone booth and placed a call to the number Adin had given her, but was rewarded only by a blithe and by now familiar baritone letting her know that, "You have reached the Mad Hatter, darling. If this is the March Hare, leave a message." Wearily she spoke into the receiver. "Adin at *Graphic Images* gave me this number. My name is Vale Messenger, and I need to speak with you, Biron." Then on an impulse she added, "Unless you are too scared to talk *face to face*." What did she have to lose? "I am in the city and will be until about 8. You can reach me..." and she gave the number at Win's. Then she tried to reach Blaire Wittemore, but was told by message the office was closed for the weekend.

Like a weary pilgrim, she shouldered her bag and hailed a cab.

•◆•

A billboard in front of Sappho East announced the coming production of *"Antigone Revised*, an all–woman rendition of Sophocles." Vale was admitted by a sunburned girl in the lobby, who directed her through a black curtain to the theater, and then resumed stocking a small concession stand. Sasha's name had been the password.

Black walls, black seats, and a black stage gave the place its aura of eternal night. A rehearsal was in progress. A lighting crew was tinkering with gels and spots on a catwalk overhead. Vale found a seat in the last row. She knew Sophocles' play and soon enough figured out how it had been "revised."

Judging from the costumes or lack thereof, Corinth was more like a nudist colony than a Greek city. It was ruled not by King Creon, but by an Amazon Queen played by a black woman, magnificent in stature, bare-footed, with one breast revealed by her open purple toga. They were doing a scene where Antigone was requesting the body of her slain lover--- brother in the original--- and the Queen was refusing her the last rites.

A female chorus of four women---naked to the waist---moved in stylized turns and counter-turns, commenting on the argument. Then, in a flashback scene, the lights came down to a moonlit blue as the two lovers mounted a raised circular platform at the center of the stage from which four spokes extended. As the two undressed one another from their iron and bronze battle gear, four members of the chorus leaned on the four spokes, and slowly turned the platform. Not only did this afford a view from all angles, but suggested the wheel of fate on which the lovers were entangled. Fade to black.

Vale waited as the director gave her notes to the cast. She thought of another rehearsal, a universe away, where Melanie prepared for her summer debut and her mother's open arms.

A voice startled her, "I am Sasha. You are, Wale?"

Sasha was more striking from a distance; up close Vale could see pitted marks on her cheeks that marred her complexion. "Yes, thank you for seeing me."

"I got twenty minutes," Sasha said, "then we start Second Act. Can I ask that you to do a favor for me?" And in response to her nod, Sasha said she needed a cup of coffee and a sandwich. Tuna fish, or chicken salad. "Can you do this Okay? A deli is next door." Vale asserted that she could and would. "Heavy with the cream and the sugar, please. I will use the bathroom while you are going."

Ten minutes later they were seated side by side in the same back row. Sasha took a swallow of her coffee and bit into the sandwich. Vale sipped a cup of iced coffee. "I am sorry," Sasha said between bites, "there is not wery much time, but you can see we are hard working. How much do I repay?"

"Please, let me." Shasha nodded her thanks. "When do you open?"

"Next Friday. But tomorrow and Sunday we are not rehearsing. There is cabaret here this weekend. It is, well, wery low budget." Her Slavic accent colored the vowels and consonants. "Thank you, this sandwich hits the target. Is that the way you say it, 'hits the target'?"

"Hits the spot," Vale corrected.

"Hits the spot. Yes." Sasha drained her coffee. "So you are looking for Part'ia. You are not family I do not think." Vale shook her head. "A friend then?" A certain wariness had entered the girl's face.

Vale weighed her varying obligations. "How well do you know Parthia?" she asked.

"Oh, I know her," Sasha said, "and I do not know her well. We are part of same crowd, but we do not get wery personal unless we are lovers. Even then it can be not personal."

"Parthia is my patient. I am a therapist." Vale saw brown eyes take her in. "I am concerned about her. I have not heard from her when I expected to."

"This is not so unusual I think, for Part'ia?"

"I am afraid she may be in danger, a danger to herself. Do you understand?"

"You are concerned about her, that I can see from your face. I can feel that you are not trying to make trouble for her. She has maybe made trouble for you?" Vale gave a slight shrug.

"Can you help me find her?"

"I do not know where she is, but have you heard the name Biron Lord?" Vale nodded. Sasha reached into the side pocket of the light cotton jacket she

wore over her nakedness and drew out a pack of cigarettes. She fingered a dis-
posable lighter; the flame for a moment lit up her face. She turned aside to spare
Vale the smoke.

"Five minutes, people," came a call from the stage.

"He is photographer, does many kinds of things, many kinds of shoots.
Some of us make extra money on side. He…how do I say this… he works with
us in special way. It is difficult to describe. When you have done this work with
Biron, you are connected to him. It is not that he has power over you. Or maybe
he does. Is that you have shared with him something wery private, wery deep.
He can touch the soul. Once you work with him, it is like you are family. I think
Part'ia would go to him if she has run away from you. You will have to get her
back from him I think."

"But first I will have to find him." Vale looked down to the stage where
performers were assembling, the chorus finding its places.

"Sasha," the director called up to her.

"With Biron it does not work that way. He finds you."

"Sasha, we are all waiting for you." The director's voice brought their interview to an end.

"I wish you good luck," the big girl said, standing. She turned, put the cigarette to her lips, held it there, and smoothly removed the cotton jacket from
her naked shoulders. Then with long strides she descended the slope of stairs,
tossed her jacket to one side, her cigarette into a red bucket, and leapt lightly
onto the stage.

•◆•

As Win had forewarned, it was an unprepossessing neighborhood; five story
buildings giving no outward hint of residential possibility. She found a space
around the corner and left nothing in the car. Now standing before his building,
Vale felt some hesitancy about this arrangement. She was not fit company, wilted from the city's heat and from the failure of her searches. Only Melanie was
on her mind now. But she rang the bell and while waiting plotted her course;
she might get as far north as the Massachusetts' border.

"Come on in, Vale," Win's voice called from the box by the door. There was
the snap of a metal lock retracting. Once inside she summoned the elevator and

rode it to the fifth floor where she found Win waiting for her. "You made it," he said as she stepped off onto his floor. "Welcome."

"Hi," she said. "By chance any calls for me?"

"No," he said. "None."

He relieved her of her overnight bag and led her into what was, she saw, a single great room, his loft. The old tin ceiling was painted white, and every fifteen feet or so a large barroom fan turned; skylights opened to the late afternoon air.

Win had quartered the cavernous space into something like rooms, an office with drafting table and shelves near the entrance, then a wide corridor with two rooms on one side, a bathroom between them. At the farther end there was an open area that contained a living room, dining room area, and a kitchen. The back wall was green with plants that rose from floor to ceiling around tall windows. Orchids, wide-mouthed-exotic, bloomed on winding tendrils.

"This place is amazing," she said, as she followed him towards the living room. "How long have you lived here?"

"About twenty years. It was a real dump when I bought it. I used it as an office for my business; then when I married, we took over the south end and walled it into two separate spaces. Then, after I... afterwards when I started to work at North Forks, I took the wall down and made it into what you see now. There is some privacy, but it's still open."

"*Very* nice," she said.

"Can I get you something?"

"I'd like to use your bathroom. Would it be possible to take a shower?"

"I put fresh towels out on the hamper. You can use the spare bedroom. There's a robe on the back of the door."

She came out twenty minutes later, a fresh blouse on and make-up reapplied. He was in the kitchen chopping vegetables. "So much better," she said. "Thanks."

"I'm just finishing up the preparations here, nothing fancy. Do you want something to drink?"

"What are you having?"

"Gin and tonic. But there's a half-finished bottle of Chablis in the refrigerator."

"A small glass of wine would be wonderful. Can I use your phone? I need to check my messages."

"Sure. Use the one in my office down the other end."

There was a single message on her machine at work: From Lucore demanding an accounting of her time by day's end. She called her home phone and listened to Naomi wishing her well on her trip and asking her to be sure to send love to Meli. Then, surprisingly, Lord's voice, "'A man's face is his autobiography. A woman's face is her work of fiction.' Thank you Oscar Wilde." The click of disconnection followed. No other messages.

Vale set down the phone, wondering when Lord had made his call. Had he gotten her latest message? She dearly wished for the opportunity to slap his taunting face.

Vale heard kitchen noises from the far end of the apartment, but she sat in a stupor of her own weariness. The drive to Vermont seemed beyond her. Maybe she could make it to Brewster---three hours, go later, after the big traffic surge.

She called North Forks and left a message for Lucore. She knew he'd be gone for the weekend. Though his imperative would not take motherhood into account, she wondered whether it would matter if she hung around the city tomorrow? Her options were exhausted. And to wait for nothing when she could be with Melanie? It was a little before six now; she could wait until eight---at the latest--- and still get a good start on her journey.

She came back to the kitchen, offering no response to Win's glance. She picked up the wineglass he had set out for her and wandered into the living room where in one corner a stringless cello stood, its foot driven into a pedestal of charred rock. She looked at it a long time, aware of his eyes on her.

"I can have dinner on the table any time you want," he said. "It's pretty informal."

"I need to eat," she said.

He served up a salad of mesculun greens and sweet baby tomatoes. He'd made guacamole with the tang of lime and garlic, and a pico de gallo with corn chips for dipping. Then from the oven came a basket of warm tortillas and from the refrigerator bowls of various fillings. Eating tacos became a slightly comical affair. More napkins were needed.

He asked about her day, and she told him of her meeting with Claire, of Mark Warren, the trip to *Graphic Images*, Sasha and the scene at Sappho East. He laughed at some of her descriptions.

"And what about tomorrow?"

"I'm giving it till eight tonight. If I don't hear from Lord, or better yet Parthia herself, I'll get started on my trip. I don't know. I'm at a dead end." She finished the last of a taco, and felt somewhat restored. It would be nice to lie down for a bit, but that was more comfort than she was prepared to invite. "I dread talking to Lucore."

Win was silent, looking away.

"What?" she said. He looked up. "You look like you aren't saying something."

"It's none of my business."

"What do you want to say, Win? Tell me."

"Go to Vermont," he said.

"But Lucore..."

"Fuck Lucore. Sorry," he said. "Listen, Vale, you are doing the best you can, and one day isn't going to make a difference. If Parthia is going to...well, you know...she will do it whatever you do. Keep your priorities straight. Melanie is your daughter."

She hardly needed reminding. Vale thought of his daughter's death and how in retrospect any lost moment with her must haunt him now "I told Lucore I would keep after this." And Meli that she'd be there.

"And you will. If Dean knew you were thinking of giving up your day with your daughter, he'd...I don't know what he'd do. But he wouldn't permit it."

"You really think...?"

"I do."

"OK," she said. "I'll just rest a bit. Thanks. Let me help you clear..."

"Don't be silly. Go put you feet up for a while." She felt giddy with the relief of a decision made. She'd face Lucore's music on Monday, if it came to that.

On the nearby bookshelf, she saw an old Norton Anthology of American Literature among books on horticulture and sailing. It brought to mind something she had been thinking about. "Have you read any Nathaniel Hawthorne?" she asked from the living room.

"*The Scarlet Letter* in high school. Why?"

"I've been thinking about a story of his called *The Birthmark*. It's a very simple story, really." With a dishtowel in his hand, Win stood at the end of the couch.

"Tell me," he said.

"A man marries a beautiful woman. I think her name is Gloriana or Georgiana, something like that. She is more than beautiful. To her husband she is sublime, an angel. Only she has a small birthmark on her cheek that mars her otherwise perfect beauty. Hawthorne tells us the mark is in the shape of a tiny hand. The husband becomes obsessed with this single blemish. He decides he wants to have the birthmark removed. He looks everywhere for a medical procedure that will accomplish this. Finally he finds a doctor who promises to remove the mark. The husband is overjoyed; the procedure seems to work, but as the mark fades, his wife grows sick, and just when the mark completely vanishes, her beauty perfected, she dies."

"So this doctor was not a surgeon?"

"No. This was before cosmetic surgery. There's some potion or ointment."

"I can see why you might remember that story," he said, turning back to the kitchen. "You want some coffee?"

"O yes, milk and sugar."

Later, sitting across from one another in the living room, Vale was telling Win about the prank phone calls she'd been receiving. "They all come from Lord. From the beginning. In some ways his calls have been clues. In other ways simple harassment." She looked at her watch. It was 7:30.

"But you said there were different voices."

"Well, a lot of his associates are actor types. Maybe he got them..." But Vale didn't really have an explanation. "I don't know."

"Biron Lord's the mystery man," he said.

"I am sure Claire is or was seeing him the way Warren clammed up when I asked him about Claire. Which reminds me," and here Vale walked into the spare room and came back with a big manila envelope. She put it in his hands.

He hefted the envelope. "What's in it?"

"Photographs I assume."

"You haven't looked?"

"No," she said, "I haven't. They belong to Parthia."

"Well?" he said. "What gives?" At that moment the phone rang. He looked at her.

"Get it, please," she said. "I left your number for him."

He went to the kitchen and lifted the receiver from its cradle on the wall. "Hello," she heard him say. There was a brief pause, and then "Yes, hold on a second." She caught his glance and walked quickly down to the far end of the apartment and lifted the receiver.

Win did not listen to the conversation. He heard brief words from Vale, stretches of silence, and then he heard her voice and a tone of urgency, an insistence, even a kind of pleading. He put the envelope aside on the top of the bookcase and went to pour himself another cup of coffee.

In a few minutes Vale returned. "That was Biron, the prankster, the manipulator. He says that the best chance I have of seeing Parthia is to come out to Fire Island tomorrow."

"She'll be there?"

"He didn't promise. He was so...so cagey. So fucking pleased with himself."

"And what did you say?"

"I begged him to tell me where she was. He wouldn't." Vale's face was pale and her eyes restless. "I said I'd come."

Win was quiet. There was no reason to argue. "When?"

"He said come in the later afternoon. Ferries run almost hourly from Patchogue to the Pines. It's one of the gay communities on Fire Island. I've never been. He said to come alone. He gave me an address."

"I'm going with you."

"But Biron said..."

"Vale, this is ridiculous. It's too cloak and dagger, too manipulative, to use your word. Let me go with you."

"I need to think about it. I need to get home and call Robert. And Melanie... I have to…" The room swam, and Vale reached out to steady herself. She was going under. Win reached out also, and there was a staggered moment between them, a missed hug of comfort, a muted wish. Then she was turning away. His big hands hung in air where she had been, then dropped to his side.

She fetched her bag.

He opened the door.

The elevator swallowed her last words to him. "I'll call you."

Late that night Win woke, and unable to fall back asleep wandered into the kitchen for a glass of water. Moonlight shone through the skylight. The apartment was silver and silent.

There on the bookcase where she had forgotten it lay the manila envelope. He picked it up and felt its weight. He sipped from his glass. Then he carried the envelope to his drafting table, turned on the high intensity light, pried open the clasp, drew out the stack of photographs, and looked at each in growing amazement and concern.

CHAPTER TWENTY-SIX

"**I don't want to talk about it**," Vale said to Win as they sat side by side on the upper deck of the ferry, waiting for it to cross the Great South Bay. Mare's tails streaked the hot afternoon sky. "It" was her phone call with Melanie.

"Fine," he said and took out the newspaper.

Her irritation with him had begun when she realized she had come home the night before without the envelope from *Graphic Images*. It had not been where she had set it down. A quick call to Win that morning reassured her that he had it, and when she asked if he had looked at them, his casual "yes" opened a distance between them: she the conscientious therapist playing by the rules, he the man who could play by his own.

The ferry edged from the pier, made slow passage in the channel, then opened throttle, passing the breakwater. Out of the corner of her eye, she saw he had taken out the Times and in the face of her "I don't want to talk about it" had folded it down against the wind, his eyes hidden behind his sunglasses. He wore a white tee shirt, black hiking shorts, boating shoes without socks, and a faded blue Brooklyn Dodgers baseball cap. A sailing bag was tucked on the deck between his knees. She refused to notice that he had great legs.

She carried an overnight bag. Might as well be prepared, they had agreed that morning. For what? Who knew? Now she regretted letting him come, resented his detachment, worried the question of his interference, rebuked herself for her irritation, replayed in her mind Melanie's cry of dismay, her own ineffectual words, the empty morning, this blind mission to the Pines, and this inscrutable companion. She had hardly slept, and one cup of coffee too many made everything jangle.

"It was awful," she wanted to tell him. "Melanie just cried and cried." Which, of course, gave Robert the chance to be the totally understanding Dad.

Up through their feet came the low thrum of the diesels. The boat turned into the channel past the green buoy and headed towards the low silhouette of Fire Island. Biron had said come alone. Was Win going to queer the possibility of her meeting Parthia? *Queer.* She smiled sardonically to herself. She and Win might not be the only straight people on the boat, but they were certainly in the minority. Toy-poodle-bearing boys, naked to the waist, with buffed muscles and gold chains posed and played on the metal benches that lined the upper deck. Oddly paired women—large and small, the ample with the thin, the old with the young--- chatted and laughed with one another. Vale remembered the yellow-slickered little girl on an empty deck in the rain. It seemed so long ago. She had the stills in her mind, that dash of yellow against the blue and gray. Her heart wrung for Melanie.

Beside her Win lifted his cap and ran his hair back with his hand. She saw he was reading an article about the yacht races at the Summer Olympics. She could feel the tension between them. "The big lug," she thought, "I'll be damned if I am going to be his damsel in distress."

The voyage to the Pines passed in silence, and at one point Vale found herself staring at two women who stood at the rail. One was black and muscular, the other slender and redheaded. Every now and then the black woman leaned her head down to speak in an upturned ear. Vale was sure she had seen them in one of the photographs at *Graphic Images*; she had a queasy sense they were heading in the same direction.

Later, armed with sandwiches bought in a market where the ferry tied up, they carried their lunch to the beach. They sat on Vale's towel, their backs supported by dune fencing. Vale, impatient with her own hesitation, finally spoke. "So you looked at the contents of that envelope I left behind."

"I thought you left it *for* me to look at," he said, trying to make light of the accusation. She glared at him. "Is that what's been bothering you?" he asked, surprised.

"Will you take off those sunglasses for a minute? I can't see your eyes."

Win lifted his sunglasses and set them on his brow. "I looked," he said.

"You had no right," she said.

"You're right, I didn't. I had a whole bunch of reasons for wanting to look---mostly they had to do with this Lord guy, not with Parthia. I wanted to know what he was into. But I knew it wasn't really any of my business. At the same time it felt like it was."

"And?" she asked.

"And what? There were pictures."

"I know that."

"A lot of them. I looked at each one; then I put them back."

"And?"

"Vale, what do you want to know?"

"Nothing. I mean I want to know what you saw, but I shouldn't know anything. They belong to Parthia. If anything comes of them, I need to hear it from her. Damn!" she said and looked away from him. "What's done is done," she said as much to herself as to him. "There was one picture I saw of Parthia at the gallery yesterday," she said. "In it she was bound in rope from neck to ankle and wore a white death mask."

"Yes," Win said, "it was the first picture in the series."

"Does she wear that mask in every one of them?"

"No," Win said, "sometimes her face is bare."

"OK," Vale said, "that's enough. I'll just have to go on, knowing what I do and not knowing what I don't. I envy you being able to look. She isn't your patient. You can do what you like, but it feels intrusive and unfair." Vale leaned back against the slats of fence.

On his side, Win felt justly rebuked. He half wished he could undo the searing impression Lord's pictures had made on his mind. The young woman, met only once, and whom he had driven around when she first arrived at North Forks ---and whose face he had found in a forlorn angel in the Leonardo book--- had become in the space of a midnight voyeuristic hour a savage, writhing figure of torment, naked in every possible sense of the word, even when masked. Her *danse macabre* shocked him, and he was a man not easily shocked. But the photographs also evoked a terrible, helpless pity, and he felt, in a way he had not before, that Vale's mission, whatever its outcome, was immensely brave. Like a descent into the underworld.

A Frisbee sailed in their direction, tilted up and hung, rotating on its axis in a dreamy slow motion. A young man, lithe and fleet, snagged it, spraying up sand on them, and sprinted off with an apology thrown back over his shoulder.

Vale came to her feet, brushing herself clean. Win got up also, shaking out Vale's towel and folding it. "Sure would be nice to go for a swim," she said, but she had already turned her back on the water and was climbing the wooden steps to the boardwalk that traversed the dunes.

•◆•

She had to ask directions twice before she found South Bay Walk, a street over-arched by bamboo, holly, willow, and pine.

"The pines don't look healthy," Win said to Vale's back. She had been watching the numbers change and began to figure that the house they were looking for might be the last or the second from the last on their right, perhaps at the edge of the bay.

"This community is called 'The Pines,'" he said, "but the pines look like they're dying."

"It's a blight," she said, hurrying on ahead, thinking of the slow moving plague called AIDS. "There's a bug---they call it the turpentine bug---that's de-stroying the black pine on the island. People say it will wipe out the entire population."

He heard the impatience in her voice. "I can see they're replanting," he said, "western cedar, willows, Russian olive."

But she was not paying attention. "Here we are," she said, stopping them in front of a high, gray, vertically slatted fence. The house announced itself only by stenciled numerals on a call box and the words "The Mad Hatter" scripted above a mail slot.

"What's our game plan?" he asked.

"I don't have one." She put a hand to her hair in a fruitless attempt to tidy it, then leaned on the call button. No response. Napping guests? Stoned around a hookah? A party gone to the beach? No one was home. She pushed on the bell again. Vale felt the beginning of a great weariness. Then the little box at her fingertip squawked, "Who's there?" It was a young girl's voice. Not Parthia's.

"Vale Messenger," she replied.

"A messenger?" The voice said. "What's your message?" Vale looked again at the address on the front of the gate and at the piece of paper she held in her hand.

"No, my name is *Vale* Messenger. I'm here to see Biron Lord. Is this...?"

"Wait a sec." Vale imagined her name was now being conveyed to someone else. Then a buzzer sounded; there was the click of a retracting lock, and the gate released inward. Pushing lightly against it, she stepped through it. Win followed.

No one greeted them. They were in a kind of vine-dense fore garden: a jungle of wisteria, cat briar, and clematis clung to the armature of dead pines and concealed much of the house from view.

They reached the front steps by a meandering path, and before either of them could knock, the door was opened by a girl of no more than nine or ten with a blond ponytail and shining blue eyes. She wore a wet and brightly spangled bathing suit and was so different from what Vale had expected here that she wondered again whether she had gotten the address wrong. Was this Alice in the Mad Hatter's den?

Water dripped from the ends of the girl's blond hair. "Hi," the little girl said, "Uncle said to let you in, show you where things are and tell you to come out back. My name's Aurelia, but everyone calls me Aurey." She swung the big door open and they came in, introducing themselves on the way. "You can just put your things there, if you want---" Aurey motioned to the wide pew-like bench in the vestibule. "The bathroom's right there," she was dancing on ahead of them and pointing to her left. "The kitchen's over there," gesturing to her right. "Uncle's out in the pool." And with that she ran to the back of the house and disappeared through open sliding glass doors into the glare of the afternoon sun.

Leaving their bags, they followed Aurey's wet footprints into a spacious clerestory living room that ran the entire length of the back of the house. It had a stunning view of the Great South Bay. A spiral staircase climbed to an overhanging balcony. Vale, accustomed to the spectacle of Fire Island real estate, headed for the bathroom. Win, on the other hand, studied the layout of this playhouse with its theatrical balcony above and bedrooms, he assumed, behind it; the open lower floor with a kitchen and dining room on one side; a media center and some kind of office or studio next to it. An enormous three-sided sectional occupied the center of the room and faced the water. Easy chairs were scattered about, companioned by low bookshelves with lamps on them.

Through the glass doors Win saw a swimming pool that extended towards the bay. On either side of the pool, shrubs and flowers grew in large wooden tubs and rectangular planters. Chairs and lounges were arranged in casual clusters. At the far end of the deck a sailboat was tied to house's own dock.

Vale was back at his side. "Fitzgerald once wrote, 'The rich are not like us,'" she said.

"You ready?" he asked.

"No." she said. "Sorry I've been so crabby. I'm glad you're here."

He saw that she had touched up her lipstick and had taken off the faded sunhat so that her hair blossomed its dark curls around her head. He wished the occasion were different. "I'm sorry about prying," he said.

"I would have done the same."

They stepped through the curtains and onto the deck.

Two girls---one of them Aurey---and a laughing man were playing water-basketball with whoops and shouts at the far end of the pool. A couple lounged on the deck; the man was reading a copy of Barons; the woman had her nose in a paperback. They glanced up briefly when Win and Vale stepped out of the house, made desultory nameless greetings, and returned to their reading.

Not quite sure what to do with themselves, Vale and Win walked towards the far end of the pool and looked at the water game with more interest than they felt. The two girls clung like limpets to the man in the water---*Uncle* Biron Lord?---who, with a red and white perforated ball in his hands, was toiling towards the basket. Draped on his shoulders, lunging desperately towards his outstretched arm, the girls tried to drag him down. Suddenly he took a gulp of air and went under; they held to his diving form for a moment; Aurey went down with him briefly, but he held his breath too long for her, and she surfaced, rubbing her eyes with her fists. "Where is he? Where is he?" she screamed, and the other girl pointed to the figure now crouched at the bottom of the pool, the ball in one hand, the ladder gripped with the other. They circled above him and then clung to the ladder, catching their breaths.

The underwater figure had not yet stirred. "Come on, Uncle!" Aurey screamed and beat at the water with the flats of her hands, but the man on the bottom remained motionless. With every passing second the girls became more frustrated.

Win selected a chaise and extended himself on it. Vale sat down next to him. Beside her was a glass-topped table, on it a small camera. Tiny as a toy. She was tempted to pick it up, when suddenly the figure on the bottom of the pool pushed off from the bottom and rose rapidly to the surface, angling towards the basket. The girls screamed and set themselves in motion from the ladder, but he shot past them and with an extended right hand dunked the little basketball through the hoop.

"No fair!" the girls screamed. Aurey retrieved the ball, but the man was hauling himself out of the pool, laughing down at them.

"Enough, for now," he said. They swam to the pool's edge and looked up at him with adoring eyes. "I have some guests. Maybe we will play later." Aurey made a grab for his ankle, but he was too quick and skipped back. "No, no, no," he said. Aurey stuck out her tongue. Lord laughed, then the girls looked at each other, at Vale and Win, and turned away.

"Race ya," Aurey said and churned off with her companion instantly giving chase. Vale watched the girls swim to the far end of the pool where Aurey, with her head start and perhaps a year on her companion, was first to touch. In this moment she was seeing the sleek form of her water-daughter at play in the waves. She bit her lip.

When she lifted her eyes, she saw the man she knew was Biron Lord reaching down for a towel and running it quickly over his face, arms, and torso. He was a ropily muscled man, whose tanned face came to a point in a salt and pepper goatee. He had gray hair, worn long enough to be gathered in a ponytail. Creases showed around his eyes. Fifty, Vale thought. Maybe older.

"You met Aurey," he said. "The other one's her sister, Calydon, Cally for short. He gestured to the adults who were being implored by the girls to join them in the pool, "Those are their parents, or mother and step-father to be precise. She's my half sister, Felicity, and her husband is Gerard." Lord's voiced dropped to a stage whisper. "He's in business of some kind on Wall Street. Nothing I can understand, leverage and bonds and underwriting. Completely arcane, probably shady, but, of course, he's richer than God. Which is a requirement for Illicitly, as I like to call her. He won't be around much longer; she's already tired of him---hubby number three. But he keeps her in satin and pearls. You can meet them later. Or not. They'll be sailing back before dinner; that's his boat." They all looked for a moment at the sailboat tethered to the dock. "She drives me nuts and he's a bore, but I love the girls and they love me. I feel like I may be the most stable man in their lives. Which, believe me, is not saying much." He stopped as abruptly as he began. "And you, no doubt, are Vale Messenger."

"I am," she said and extended a hand. Lord took it, shook in briefly, and then turned her hand palm side up. She started to pull away, felt him grip her hand, and then relaxed. "Are you going to hold my hand or read my fortune?" she asked.

"You never know," he said. "You can tell everything from the hand. Do you know the Chinese believe that the hand is the map of the entire body? He flattened her palm and ran his fingers over the pad below the thumb, "This is the heart, and here," he applied a light pressure along the outer edge of her palm, "is the spine. "Here," he lightly pinched the soft valley between her thumb and first finger, "are the lungs, and here," bringing his fingers to the center of her hand, "are the internal organs, kidneys," he moved his thumb along a line of invisible points on her palm, "pancreas,'" he moved his thumb again, "liver," again his thumb moved, "and spleen. And here, "pressing into the cleft of her palm just above her wrist, "the gen-i-tals." He released her hand, his eyes still on her face, watching her. "Moist hand, cool to the touch. You are a nervous messenger, Messenger."

"What I am is beside the point. I am here to find Parthia."

"All in due time," Lord, said, "all in due time." Lord picked up the little camera, small enough to fit into his hand, and directed it towards Vale without bringing it to his eye. She saw his thumb depress the shutter, heard the faint whirr of film advancing.

Vale glanced at Win. "This is Win Lawrence," she said.

"I asked you to come alone." Lord's gaze remained steadily on Vale.

"I found that request sufficient grounds to insist on coming," Win said, removing his sunglasses.

Lord turned to look at Win. "How gallant," he said. "And what relationship do you have with our Messenger?" The eyes came back to Vale, a faint smile on his lips, "It is Ms., isn't it? I don't see a ring."

"Vale will do fine."

Eyes back to Win. "What's up with you two?" he asked again.

"He's…"

A sharp glance at Vale: "Do you always answer for one another? How *in-time*," he said.

"I'm at North Forks," Win said.

"Are you? You don't look like no therapist," Lord drawled.

"I'm not."

"A patient then?"

"No," he said.

"Ever been one?" Lord asked, and suddenly the small camera in his hand was pointed at Win. Vale heard the click and whirr.

"None of your business," Win said, "and let's can this camera thing."

"No can do. Get used to it, Lawrence; you're on my turf now."

"Win's Director of Building and Grounds," Vale put in. Lord was relentless.

"But not always, right, Mr. Lawrence? We have been on the inside I think. Win Lawrence, what did you *lose*?"

"What makes you think I lost..."

"Loss is the ticket to the loony bin," Lord said. "If you dig deep enough, it's always loss." Vale saw Win's color change even under his tan. Lord saw it, too; perhaps he saw the working of the muscle in Win's jaw. Click, whirr. She saw Win's eyes turn a cold gray. "And will you look at those eyes?" Lord said, the tone neither baiting nor ironic. "You see that look only in two kinds of men, Messenger," speaking to her but never taking his eyes off Win's face. "You see it in men who have been to prison or men who have been to war. I was an army photographer in Vietnam; I should know. Which was it for you, Mr. Lawrence?"

Again the camera came up. "Hold that pose," Lord said and leaned in, this time he raised the camera to his eye. Vale saw the muscles stiffen in Win's arms as if he had been jabbed with a needle. He's going to hit him, Vale thought with a gasp, but instead Win lifted his sunglasses and put them on his face.

"Think I'll take a look at that boat," he said, and got up from the chaise and walked to the back of the deck.

"What's between the two of you?" Lord asked.

"We're colleagues," she said.

"That all? What's Mr. B and G doing here with you on your rescue mission?"

"He's a friend."

"Sons and lovers perhaps?" Her reaction: click, whirr. "No, I can see not. Not yet. But the thought has crossed our minds, hasn't it?"

"It is none of your business," Vale said.

"It is absolutely none of my business. I am a curious person. It's my nature. I push on doors. Sometimes they open; sometimes not."

Win had returned and stood to one side. "You have quite a way about you, Lord," he said.

"And how is that? And shall we call each other Biron and Win or keep to this formality?"

"Let's keep the formality," said Win.

"How very English." Lord said and patted the chaise for Win to sit. "What is this 'way' I have about me, Mr. Lawrence?"

Win sat down beside Vale again. "You assume the offensive from the start. Your eyes watch, your words provoke, and then with that little camera of yours you record reactions. I get the oddest feeling of being seen and toyed with, of being both a person and a specimen."

"Bravo, Mr. Lawrence, no one has said it better." Lord looked at his camera for a moment fondly. "I cannot do what I do or be who I am without a camera in my hand. It's like a novelist, I suppose, who in a far more secretive way stores up everything he sees for some future story. I am a *provocateur*, as you have astutely observed. This camera is like an appendage. Whenever I have the time, I develop the film and discover what it is that Biron Lord has caught in his net. Sometimes the pictures are out of focus, half out of the frame, sometimes sharp and clear. Always they are immediate."

"An amateur Andy Warhol," Win commented.

"After Andy everyone's an amateur," Lord said. "So what did you lose, Mr. Lawrence?"

"You first, Lord."

Biron Lord paused. He looked down to the far end of the pool where Aurey and Cally had hoisted themselves up onto red floats and lay adrift on the turquoise water. "I lost the only man I ever loved," he said after a pause. "This house was his. Tommy was a very successful set designer. We lived as a couple for fifteen years. Faithful as a pair of churchwardens. He was a drug user from time to time. It killed him. He died a year and a half ago. AIDS. He left me this. I am an amputee." The recitation, without a trace of self-pity, held a note of bitterness and sorrow.

Win shook his head, then looked down at his folded hands. "I can't talk so easily," he said.

"Easily?" Lord said. "Does it seem easy? Maybe I've just told my story more often than you have, that's all."

"Maybe," Win said, "but this isn't the time or place." Win got up and again walked away from them towards the bay. Vale saw him lift the sunglasses off his nose. A hand passed over his eyes.

"Do you always...are you always so direct?" she asked.

"I try to be."

"And are you so willing to be direct yourself?"

"It depends."

"On?"

"On where I feel the other person is coming from."

"And where do you come from?"

"Sometimes I come from curiosity, sometimes from compassion, sometimes from a desire just to shock or surprise, sometimes from a desire to mess with someone's head; sometimes with a desire to be helpful. I just can't stand conventionality. Do you have a family?"

"I have a little girl, Melanie. She's ten, away at camp. Off limits."

"Off limits because...?"

"Because I am not here to provide you with information about myself, and I'm not here to learn about you. I am here only because of Parthia, my concern for her, my wish to find her, and to get her back to North Forks."

"You made that clear."

"You said you might be willing to help. "

"But first I must learn about you, Messenger."

"To learn about me? Or to test me?" Win was back, circling, protective.

"Parthia has asked me to tell her what I think of you."

"And why is your opinion so much to be valued? Or put another way, why is she so hesitant to trust her own?"

"You would have to ask her those questions."

"But she's not here to ask."

"What can you do? It's a cruel world."

Vale was quiet for a moment, taking her own counsel; then she looked up. "Listen, Lord, here's the deal. I am first and foremost Parthia Alexander's therapist. I take that responsibility seriously, and I will not reveal anything that has happened between her and me in our treatment."

"Understood, Messenger. You have the instincts of a lawyer."

"Is Parthia here now?" she asked.

"In this house? No."

"Is she on the island?"

"She may be. I am not sure."

"So what do you want to know?"

"I want to know why you are so anxious to get her back to the hospital." Lord leaned back in the deck chair, the camera cradled in his palm.

"I believe she needs treatment."

"But she did not ask for *treatment.*" Irony glazed the word. "Claire and some physicians took that decision away from her. You don't think she would have put herself in a place like North Forks, do you?"

"Probably not. But it's where she ended up."

"But now she has run away."

"I think she needs psychiatric care."

Down at the other end of the pool, Cally and Aurey began to call him. "Uncle," they called, "come play!" Lord waved a hand.

"Frankly," he said, "I am not in a position to judge whether she does or does not need psychiatric care, but I have a fairly low opinion of the profession. I can see the value of brief spells in a hospital if you have a condition that medication can treat, but as a place for therapy, well, it seems poorly designed for that."

"I'm not going to get into an argument with you. In Parthia's case I think the hospital could be a good place for her for a while."

"And are you a good therapist for her?"

"I am concerned about her, concerned enough to be out chasing around after her on a perfectly beautiful summer weekend."

"So you care about her?" Lord leaned forward, fixing her with that intense gaze of his.

"I do, but I care about all the patients I see."

"So she is just another patient to you, whom you care about?"

"I'm not going to fence with you, Lord. If Parthia has made you her protector, then you will have to make up your own mind what to do with that charge. I think you are in way over your head. You are taking on a great deal of responsibility for someone who is as fragile as I think Parthia is. And," she added, "as alone."

"Parthia has friends."

"Perhaps she does, but I am not sure how well any of them really knows her. She is not someone who easily lets herself be known, and I don't think I am breaking any confidences by saying that I don't think she entirely knows herself."

"Who does?" Lord said. To Vale it was a question that didn't deserve an answer.

"May I put in something here?" Win asked.

"Fine by me," Lord said.

"You did that series with her, and my sense is that you get to know your subjects pretty well." Lord looked at Win, waiting. "What do you think she needs?"

"I think Parthia needs to get away from Claire Alexander."

"Anything else?"

But Lord was getting up. "I need to play uncle for a while. They'll be going soon." He dropped his towel to the chair, set the small camera down on the table, and slipped quietly down the rungs of the ladder into the pool. The girls were for the moment distracted by something their mother was saying to them. He drew in a deep breath, submerged, and pushing himself off the side of the pool, set himself off towards the floating girls, a shark without a fin.

He stopped under the unsuspecting girls. Then he surfaced between them, upending them into the water. Their screams filled the air, and after much splashing and futile retribution they lost themselves in a game of Marco Polo.

"Well," Vale said, "what do you think?"

"He's holding all the cards."

"What do you make of him?"

"I can't put it together yet," said Win. "At times he seems rude, vain, and very controlling. At other moments he seems direct and clear. Lord, the uncle, is warm and playful. As far as his relationship to these young women he photographs, the jury is definitely out."

After a while Lord got out of the pool and came down to their end. "Felicity and Gerard will be leaving soon. The girls are going to shower and change; I'm going to give them a snack. You two are on your own for a while. Place is yours. There are upstairs bedrooms with bathrooms. You might grab a room or two for yourselves just in case you decide to stay over. They'll probably fill up before the night is out, and it's first come first served here. I'd make a snack for you, but it's family time. Mi casa es su casa."

He ushered Felicity and the girls into the house. Gerard remained with his nose in his financial magazine.

"I'm going to swim," Vale said to Win, heading upstairs to change.

For the next half hour Vale swam, then dozed on a chaise longue. Win got into a conversation with Gerard about his sailboat, went aboard, and then when Gerard was called inside, Win sat on a lounge chair, reading *The Awards Quarterly* from the American Orchid Society.

Felicity and Co. left with hugs and waves. It was half past five. The girls had loaded water pistols on board and gave their uncle a final salvo. He ran to get the garden hose, but they were out of range by the time he got it turned on. The arching beam of water, caught by the breeze, misted out over the water in rainbows. Gerard's sloop shook out her canvass. A light wind filled her sails, and she went away on a reach, the girls at the stern blowing kisses to their uncle and he to them. Win watched, missing the *Requiem*; Vale her Melanie.

Then Biron watered the plants by the pool, the whole place suddenly quiet in the absence of his nieces. He shut off the hose and went into the house, leaving the lavender and shocking pink impatiens glistening with water, the deck darkened in pools. The stillness of the afternoon settled down on them, drowsy and spacious.

Presently Lord came back bearing a tray of cheeses and English biscuits; these he set down on the table near them and wordlessly returned to the house. Music reached them, light and Latin. He came out now with three wine glasses in one hand and a freshly opened bottle of wine in a silver bucket in the other. He sat down beside them.

"I love this time of day," he said; "the burn is out of the sun, but not its warmth." He tilted the bottle of wine and filled their glasses with a wine pale as summer wheat.

"Quite a life," Win said. It was hard to stay angry with Lord; he could be gracious. "What do you do?" Win asked, "When you're not here?"

"I'm a photographer. But you know that. I take fashion photos, my day job; and I do my art on my own time. I have a gallery, which you visited I believe," he said to Vale.

"How does your gallery operate? Adin wouldn't tell me much of anything," she asked, sitting up and wrapping the towel around her. The wine had an overtone of pears. How easy and tempting it was to slip into the mood of Fire Island on a summer Saturday evening.

"Certain people I work with approach me to do a different kind of work with them. Sometimes I approach them. We come to an agreement. I have a certain reputation."

"And what you do is…?" Win left the sentence unfinished.

"We undertake a kind of exploration together, a journey. There is a bond of trust. There is no time limit; there is no idea beforehand of what we will find. I record the journey. I help them to stage an aspect of their inner lives, if that doesn't sound too hokey."

"And who buys the pictures?" Win asked.

Lord sipped at his wine, its pale gold lit up by the sunlight. The shadows were lengthening around them. "You find the market; the market finds you. I don't mean to sound vague." Biron gestured to the world across the bay, "All kinds of tastes, all kinds of dishes. What I do has a clientele and a more refined one, a more selective one, than you might think. As edgy as my work is, it is not pornographic."

"And the distinction?" Win asked.

"I think, honestly, the only distinction in the end is intention, that of the artists involved. Is your aim to provide masturbatory fodder? Or is your aim to reveal something new? In that latter endeavor sex, the body may be a means, but it is not the end. This work we do is a way of revealing the hidden. It's what's hidden after all that can amaze you."

Vale broke in. "It seems to me that the real issue with pornography is shame. Do the participants in the act feel ashamed of what they are doing? And does the viewer?"

"Ahh, but that would depend, wouldn't it?"

"It would. But you as the---what shall I call you?---the director, the chronicler, you would know, you could know, whether what your players did made them feel ashamed." Biron started to speak but she went on, "I mean people may be put under a kind of spell---mesmerized, seduced beyond their usual boundaries---but when they look back at what they did, they can feel a sense of shame for having done it. In such a case I think the work is pornographic---even if the subject is not explicitly sexual. A person has become an object, exploited." She waited for his rejoinder; it did not come. "You were going to say something?"

"Not important. Have you seen the series I made with Parthia?"

"I have not."

"Really?" he said. "May I show it to you? I would be very interested to have your opinion." He started to get up.

"No," said Vale, "if Parthia wants me to see them, she will show them to me."

"You know, Messenger, you can sound quite prissy every so often."

"Mr. Lord," she said, "I have spent summers on Fire Island. I know how to let my hair down out here. Believe me I can enjoy myself, but not here and not tonight. I am working, on duty, and on my best behavior. I may sound prissy---frankly I sound a little that way to myself---but I have a relationship with Parthia and until she breaks that, I will act with her trust in mind."

"Quite a little speech," Lord said. Vale saw that the camera was back in his hand, the hand angled towards her.

"With all due respect, Mr. Lord, Fuck you." And with that Vale got up, leaving her glass behind her, and walked into the house to shower and change.

• ◆ •

Vale finished blow-drying her hair and heard the shower running in the shared bathroom. She also heard the bell chime a number of times, and at each ring she had gone to her window to see who came through the gate. Parthia was not among the arrivals.

She gave the face in the mirror a smirk, then took a few steps down the hall and rapped on Win's door. She heard his "Come in," entered, and found him standing before a dresser mirror, running a brush through his hair. He wore a black tropical short-sleeved shirt over faded cargo pants. His face glowed from the day's sun.

"You don't look any the worse for wear," she said.

And she felt him assessing her in the blue sleeveless summer dress she wore, earrings, sandals, hair loose, glossy with highlights. "You look lovely," Win said.

"Oh for another time and another place," she said. "You ready to take on this evening?"

"Normally about this time, I'm anchored all by my lonesome and cooking dinner in the galley. No parties. No bright lights."

"Sounds great." She thought of his boat, rocking at its mooring.

There was a wicker chair in front of the window, and she sat down in it. His room, like hers, had two twin beds, small bureaus, and a door that led to the shared bathroom with its small sink and stall shower. On the wall above the beds was a blow-up of the nieces. It showed them encircled by bright red inner tube, probably in Biron's pool, their bodies siamesed together, heads side by side, two grinning, gap-toothed peas in a pod. Melanie would love it here. "What do you think about staying the night?" she asked.

"Prefer not to, but willing to if it means we can do what you came here to do. When's the last ferry back to Patchogue?"

"Midnight on Saturday night." He shrugged. "You're being a hell of a sport," she said.

"Oh, it's not that bad. Actually, I'll be fine. I can disappear into the woodwork or walk back up to the beach and sit by the water."

"Don't you dare."

Win walked over to her with an extended hand. "OK," he said. He pulled her gently to her feet. "Let's go."

CHAPTER TWENTY-SEVEN

From the balcony they saw Lord coming in from the deck, dressed now in an unbleached cotton caftan, his hair pulled back in a ponytail, and smiling like the Cheshire cat. He saw them at the top of the stairs. "Ah, our honored guests. Please, you two, stay there for a moment. Let me introduce you. People," he declared. Silence fell, faces upturned.

"Oleander and Nadine," Biron pointed to two women at the entrance to the deck. Vale had seen them come in and recognized them from the ferry and the gallery. A black and a white hand rose to wave. "Chad and Evan, in the kitchen." One round, the other thin: they bowed in unison. "Sasha and Merlyn," Vale caught the actress' eye and smiled. "Adin and Shin Shin." Adin smiled up at her while Shin Shin had eyes only for Win. "And Paula and Francesca,"--- transvestites?--- standing in the glass entrance to the television room. "Some of these folks work with me," he continued, "others play. Everyone's a gossip, but usually no one remembers anything the next day. OK, everybody this is Vale Messenger and Win Lawrence. They're friends of mine, so treat them with respect. And you two, no rules." He gave Vale a particular nod. "No one is taking notes."

"Sing something," Francesca said. Vale blushed.

"None of that," said Lord

They came down the stairs, and people drifted back to their conversations.

In the course of the next hour, the chimes rang several more times. Never Parthia. For Vale there was a hint of Hallowe'en; people dressed up and strutted, posed, laughed, goosed one another. Everyone knew everyone. Win and Vale nodded hellos, were shooed out of the kitchen, sat for a while at the end of the deck, staring at the bay, then feeling anti-social, wandered back inside. "No need to smoke a joint," he said to her; "the second hand smoke will do you in."

The cheese tray was international; there were open bottles of wine; beer nestled in a large copper ice chest on the deck. Something Asian was playing over the speakers. Sticking close together, Win and Vale circulated until Shin Shin managed to get Win out on the deck, and Adin got Vale into a conversation about books. He was a great fan of Hermann Hesse. The sun bulged on the horizon, then slipped below it.

Later, dinner, and a meal that passed in slow stages as a surreal extravagance of color and taste, laughter and story, the whole affair a high-end cousin to the casual bacchanals she knew from other times and other places on the island. Biron was at times the master of ceremonies and sleight-of-hand man, quick with his wit and camera; at other times he all but disappeared.

But she tracked him, listened to his voice when he was holding forth at the other side of the room, charted the eddy of those around him, noted his use of touch, of kiss and caress. Even when she was engaged in conversation----with Chad about a new restaurant in the city; with Adin about Lebanon; with Sasha about Antigone; and with Win--- periodically comparing notes--- she kept an eye on Biron as the fly might keep the spider in view.

So perhaps it was not surprising that in an aimless but almost inevitable way she found herself browsing the room they all called his "studio". Nor should she have been surprised when she turned from her casual inspection to find Biron standing at the door, his amused eyes watching her. He leaned against the doorframe. "Welcome to my inner sanctum," he said.

"Biron, voices have been showing up on my answering machine. First a voice with a request to speak to Dr. A. Then voices leaving messages with quotes." She looked at him directly; he did not look away. "Have you been fucking with my head?"

"I have."

"Why?"

"I don't like shrinks, never liked shrinks. Don't like Parthia in the clutches of the drug pushers, the electrode-prodders, the people who never live life but analyze it, the old maids with their air of superiority, the flatulent psychiatrists, the whole industry of mental health and illness. I think hospitals are deadly."

"How did you get my home number?"

"I have to protect my sources."

"Claire," said Vale.

"Claire and I go way back."

Vale thought about the pictures Parthia had discovered in the treasure box under Claire's bed.

"It was hostile," she said.

"But they were also clues. You can't tell me that I didn't get you thinking. Ah hah, I can see that it did."

"Don't do it again."

"What would be the point?"

"You mind fucker," she said, surprised at her vehemence. But she did not leave the room. "What do you do in here," she asked, "over-expose people?" He chuckled at her pun and did not correct her.

At the center of the room two chairs faced one another, one straight-backed, the other swivel. From the ceiling a microphone hung on its thin wire; a tripod stood at an angle.

"Interviews," he said, crossing the threshold. "I'm working on something a little different. Sort of the next evolution from the series idea. I'm interested in voice now, in story *and* photograph. A soundtrack of someone telling a story, and images—slides--- taken of the teller's face as they tell. I want to see if I can capture moments when the words and the expression are mutually revealing."

He opened up a cabinet, drew out a camera and fixed the camera's base to the tripod. He had graceful, dexterous hands. "You see," he said, "most people's faces reveal nothing. They are masks. Over the years---from earliest childhood really---we learn to control the muscles of our faces. Boys learn not to wince or cry. Girls not to smile or laugh too much. Never to show anger. The cool face that betrays nothing, that's what we aspire to. We go to films or theater to see expressiveness on the human face. Painters by and large are hopeless when it comes to facial expression, except for very subtle, contemplative faces. Like the Mona Lisa." Vale became instantly more attentive. "Painters' models after all can't hold the look of surprise, or sorrow, or joy for very long. Facial expression---natural facial expression---is fleeting." Biron was attaching a lens to the camera body and then a cord with a little plunger on its end. He positioned the camera on its tripod so that it faced the swivel chair. He looked through the viewfinder, adjusted the angle, tightened it in place.

"But the problem with film and theater," he went on, "is that the face is not really the subject of the viewer's attention. The whole body is, the body in motion, I am interested in the face as it reveals feeling in the act of telling a story. Frames. Stills. Stilled Life. I want the viewer also to be a listener. In that act the photos become points of emphasis, accent moments." Biron was standing behind the camera now adjusting its focus. He went to the wall and turned the rheostats so that the lights came up. He took a light meter from off a shelf. "Vale would you put your hand there," pointing to the head rest of the swivel chair. "Now tilt it, no the other way so that the palm catches the light. That's it." Biron made an adjustment to the shutter speed or the aperture.

"Sometimes the images I get from the story stand free of the story. They are a series of facial expressions, often subtle, sometimes appearing to tell a story of their own. Walker Evans in the subway. That kind of thing. Other times I transfer the pictures and the sound to a videotape. Do you know the work of Ken Burns? He did a video piece on the Brooklyn Bridge two or three years ago. He uses stills and zooms into the them in a way that gives you a sense of the still as a kind of scene in which the camera pans and moves into for close-ups. With the right soundtrack or voice-over it's very powerful. Entrancing really. I want to do something similar with personal story. The everyday. Not the actor. Not the scripted drama."

"I see," Vale said, her mouth a little dry.

Biron now went to a switch on the wall and turned a dial. She saw a small red light blink at the base of the hanging microphone. He opened a cabinet and punched the buttons on a console. Vale saw the big wheel of a tape recorder begin its spool from left to right. From one side of the room he drew forward a table and placed it to the right of the straight-backed chair. He brought an ashtray over and set it on the table. Then he left the room.

Vale walked to the straight-backed chair and sat on it, the camera at eye-level. She peeked through the viewfinder. She looked up at the microphone. She walked to the cabinet and saw the tape slowly traveling. "Testing, testing," she whispered.

Biron returned with two wine glasses in one hand and a silver ice bucket with a bottle in the other. She heard the rattle of ice cubes as he set it down. He closed the door and adjusted the blinds, shutting out the living room from sight: the sound of the music and voices suddenly inaudible.

He had brought in champagne. "Son of a bitch," Vale thought, watching the bubbles effervesce in the fluted glasses as he poured.

"You called me a mind-fucker a moment ago." He took a sip of his wine and sat down in his chair.

"I did. I think you are."

"In your experience is fucking---I don't mean mind-fucking now---is fucking a reciprocal experience?"

"Of course."

"Then why is it that mind-fucking seems exclusively to have a negative connotation? You'd think mind-*fucking* would be an extremely pleasurable experience; instead it's second cousin to brain-washing." Biron took another sip of his champagne.

"Is one of those for me?" Vale asked.

"Don't be coy," Biron said. She crossed the room and picked up the glass, tilted it to her lips, felt the tingle of the bubbles on her tongue. It was a very dry champagne, very cold. "What keeps good mind-fucking from happening," Biron continued, "is that it ceases at some point to feel consensual. It becomes a kind of power trip."

"Yes," she said, "that's right." Interested in spite of herself.

"But it could be like a dance, two people mind-fucking. I wish there was a better word for it."

"In the eighteenth century," Vale said and slipped into the swivel chair---just for the comfort of sitting down---"the word..." She stopped as Biron reached for the cord with the plunger and carried it to the side pocket of his caftan. The motion was casual. *Is that a plunger in your pocket or are you just glad to see me?* she thought, smiling to herself.

"What was that little smile?" he asked.

"What smile?" she said.

"You're being coy again, Ms. Messenger." She made a face. "You were saying something about the eighteenth century?" The camera was silent.

Had it started? "I was saying that in the eighteenth century one word used for sexual intercourse was conversation."

"And there's the word intercourse itself. It's a word that means both talking and fucking."

"And congress," she said, "a deliberative body and the sexual act."

"A *deliberative* body, I like that. So what are we to surmise from this, Ms. Vale Messenger?" If the camera was taking her picture, it was soundless. She tried to see the flick of the shutter. There was something snake-like about the camera's cold eye.

"I don't know," she said. "And really I don't care." Her mind was pre-occupied with something, understanding it for the first time. Usually behind the camera, she was now in front of it, fascinated by its power to provoke both shyness and a desire to disclose. Here in this room, concealed, with a man focusing on her, focusing a mind, an ear, and a lens, she felt a dangerous recklessness. It was not impossible to imagine a person's desire to take off their clothes. Add some champagne, some grass, and one could go quite far. The fact was that for all his guile and magnetism, there was something safe about Biron. It puzzled her.

"So is therapy mind-fucking?" His question brought her back. "Is there erotic excitement in therapy?"

"I haven't got the faintest idea what you are talking about."

"Coy again. Come on, Messenger, what's the excitement in therapy? What's the charge? What are you in it for, really?" Vale flashed back to the moment in Claire's Guest House, the sudden revelation.

"What?" Biron said. "Just now, what went through your mind?"

God, she thought, he doesn't miss a thing. She was seeing the sink, the slumped body; she was hearing the water from a tap, left running so the blood would drain.

"Tell me a story," Biron said.

She shook her head, but heard herself say "Which story?"

"About your father." How the hell did he...? Lord was like an animal with a keen sense of smell. Even her resistance laid down a scent.

"Why him?"

"Little girls and daddies. There's always a story there. Beautiful. Sad. Wounds and wishes."

"Why should I tell my story to you?"

"Because you want to."

"What makes you think I want to?"

"Because you're being coy and defensive, because you sat. Because you ate the pomegranate seeds."

"Can I trust you?"

"Tell me a story about your father."

"I don't want that kind of intimacy with you."

"Why not? Because it will be one-sided? Because you are afraid that you will feel things more deeply, more purely even, remember things more clearly? Because something in the way you have always told the story to yourself will have to change because you will be telling it for the first time."

"Not for the first time. I've told the story many times."

"Which story?"

"The..."

"Yes?"

"No."

"A story," Biron said, "brings back the dead. Tell me the story about your father. I want to hear you speak, Vale."

And then she understood. She knew the desire he felt to hear, to know. It was what she felt with Julia, Liza-Jane, Parthia. To be told their secrets. Trusted. To enter a mysterious place, unlit passageways, the sense of hidden forces. The secret, the search for it, the discovery of it: that was the fascination. The mind-fucking. The yielding.

"When I was sixteen years old, my father committed suicide," she began, "I never saw it coming..."

•◆•

Midnight and the last ferry had come and gone.

Vale, a little tipsy, exhausted, and lonely. Her sense of failure in her mission and in her daughter's life weighed on her heart as she went in search of Win. She did not find him and pained herself with the thought he might have been seduced by any of the women who had rubbed his flank in the course of the night.

When she saw the closed studio door closed, she wondered if Biron had lured him into confiding, but she found the thought too far-fetched. Biron was good, but not that good. More likely he was getting some air. Went to the beach. Maybe in bed. Perhaps in hers. No. Silly thought. Good of him to brave this for her. She'd see him in the morning.

Vale labored up the stairs and cast one last backward glance from the balcony at the dim scene below with bodies entangled. Shin Shin and Adin were spooning on the rug like two cats. Chad and Evan were sitting together at the dining room table, long cleared, talking with another couple whose names Vale could not begin to recall. From the entertainment room came the sound of a movie on the television. Outside there were naked bodies in the pool. Others at the far end of the deck. And below her, the final image of their satyricon, Oleander, black as a Masai, lounging against the sofa and Nadine on her back with her head in her lover's lap. Nadine tugged at Oleander and pointed up to Vale. They whispered something to one another, and Oleander began stroking Nadine's breasts with one hand, the other found its way under Nadine's short skirt. The outline of that hand moving under the fabric like a small animal made Vale flush. She saw Nadine's knees part, bringing the short skirt up until Vale could now see the caressing black hand as it worked in the fur where Nadine's legs joined. Enough, she thought, her nerves frayed, her senses sated and starved. She waved goodnight to them. Nadine touched her fingertips to her lips and blew Vale a kiss.

In her room Vale turned the shower to a cooler setting, raising goose bumps on her skin. The lonely animal of her desire was prowling. Colder. She panted to catch her breath under the icy spray. Then she shut off the shower and dried herself. She slipped into the cotton nightgown and thought for a moment about leaving the bathroom door ajar, not knowing whether Win was in bed or not. Then, prim and proper, she locked the adjoining door. She got into bed, forcing her mind back over the previous two days. It was hard to be clear-minded with a pulse going in her body, an itch that wanted scratching, and in her mind the carping of self-rebuke and second-guesses. Her room was filled with moonlight. Bamboo leaves brushed back and forth across her window. She saw the full pouting lips of one of Win's orchids pouring its profusion of petals down a long green stem. She saw the chorus of dancers sway above the twinned lovers on a darkened stage. She saw knees part. If someone had passed by her room a few moments later, they might have heard a moan and wondered if a sleeper were distressed in the grip of a dream.

• ◆ •

But her sleep was shallow, and some time later when some noise from the house reached her, she woke to see her windows streaked with rain. The sound again: somewhere in the house the distant insistent twitter of a telephone. It stopped. Had it been answered? She did not hear a voice; she heard nothing. A wrong number? Or perhaps someone had answered and was whispering into a receiver. It must be very late. It didn't concern her. No one knew she was here.

She drifted, restless, woke again---had she slept at all?--- and now from somewhere in the house, a voice. She pulled on the terry cloth robe and slipped into the bathroom between her room and Win's. Before returning to her room, she tiptoed onto the balcony and looked down on the darkened living room. She was surprised to see Biron, sitting on the sofa. A coil of smoke from an untended cigarette rose into the air, silvered by the light of the pool. She turned to go back to her room, but her weight pressed a creak from a floorboard, and Biron looked up. "Just thinking about you," he said, his voice slurred slightly by fatigue or drink or both. "Give me a minute, will you."

"Biron it's late, and …"

"I want to talk to you about Parthia."

Vale felt her way down the stairs and came to the sofa, taking her seat at one end of the sectional where she could face him. He wore a red silk kimono, tied at the waist; his gray hair, loosed from its knot at the back of his neck, hung to his shoulders. A telephone lay on the table between them.

"Why are you here?" Biron asked, looking over at her. "Why really?"

She thought the answer was obvious, but Biron's gaze, no matter how late the hour, possessed that infernal directness she had found so compelling. Instead of answering she got up and walked to the kitchen. She ran the hot water, wet some paper towels, and pressed their heat to her face like a compress. She dried off and poured herself a glass of water.

She returned to the sofa and sat, took a drink and regarded him with a more wakeful eye. His face seemed older, the lines more evident. Closer to sixty. Outside a pale blue mist hung over the pool. Rain ran watery streaks down the sliding glass doors.

As if reciting a memorized lesson, she spoke: "Parthia was remanded to the hospital by two independent physicians. Under such an admission, a patient forfeits certain freedom. When such a patient leaves the hospital without the appropriate discharge, she is considered legally the hospital's responsibility. There are liability issues."

He did not speak, as if waiting for the more unofficial version. She sighed. "The owner of the hospital threatened that I might lose my job if I didn't get Parthia back." Vale took a drink from her glass. "Frankly, I am not sure how much that has to do with my being here, but it is a factor."

"But not even that makes up the whole reason?"

"No," she said, "not the whole reason." She looked away from him and out through the glass doors into the ghostly light of the pool. When she looked back at Biron, she found that despite his fatigue, his gaze rested patiently on her face. What did it matter?

"I told you I'm new to this work. It is a second career for me. I've only been at North Forks since March. Aside from the fact that I have a daughter and need to support her, I do this work because…well, I like it. A lot. I didn't at first, and there are parts of it I'm still getting used to, but the people I work with care. And I think being a therapist may suit me, my talents, my needs." She sipped from her glass again and pressed on. "Often, too, I feel unable to make anything better. In some way by the time a patient reaches a psychiatric hospital, things have progressed pretty far, so it's an uphill battle."

She paused. His question was in fact her question: Why this care for Parthia that trumped her daughter's weekend. "I am still trying to figure out where to stand in relation to my patients. With each one there is a proper distance, and that distance changes over time. I need to be close enough to touch and be touched, but not so close that I become entangled. With Parthia I was still reaching out for her, towards her, but I think I may have reached too far. I didn't know her boundaries." Biron cocked his head. "I found out something about her and put it before her in a way that I think frightened her away."

"Can I ask what that is?"

"It is not appropriate for me to tell you. But I feel in my eagerness to let her know I had discovered a kind of secret about her, I was tactless. Perhaps I was showing off. Or maybe I was impatient. Angry even, wanting her to take herself seriously."

"You think you drove her away?"

"She was only barely there, still trying to assess whether this was something she could want for herself rather than something that had been imposed on her. One thing I will tell you: her father is dying." Biron nodded. "Ahh, of course, you would know that. But I think that the series she had just done with you broke her open, and that break has something to do what happened to her as a child at her father's hands. Also, I don't think she can come to you for help. I don't think it's what you have to offer." Vale sipped again.

A gust of wind threw rain against the glass doors. "I see," he said.

She expected his defensiveness. Instead he was silent. His cigarette had gone out, and he lit another. The flare of the match lit his face, naked in its weariness. And sorrow. "I've been trying to reach her myself. Not just tonight. During the week. I think she called a little while ago. I didn't get to the phone in time." His head was a dark silhouette against the windows and the haze above the pool.

"I'm worried about her. I'll admit that. Maybe more worried than I want to let on." He shifted his body so that he was facing her now, one leg on the pillows, the other foot on the floor. "I haven't done so many of these series that I can always predict how they'll turn out. How they'll affect the performers. And with Parthia..." he hesitated.

Vales eyes, fully accustomed now to the bluish half-light, saw his awkward attempt at a smile. "What?" she asked.

"As you said, she is very alone. Oleander and Nadine, Chad, Evan, Bruce and Perez...most of the series I have done were with couples. Parthia, well, that was a solo." The cigarette burned between still fingers. "I have a sort of gift, you know. I can get people to trust me. To trust me a lot. But I don't always know what to do with their trust."

"Will you help me?" Vale asked.

"How can I help you more than I am?"

"You're judging me."

"No, I'm..." and then he stopped himself. "Yes, you're right." His eyes appraised her. "I don't like shrinks. You know, art is the product of an unquiet mind. Pills and talk and an endless babbling about mothers and dads seem to me a kind of anesthesia. But that's just me."

"Perhaps that is true for artists; maybe they need their angst. But I am not sure Parthia is an artist. I am not sure she can use her pain."

"She wants to be," he said, "but she is not. I mean she is gorgeous; she was made to be a model, but she's..." He broke off.

"Yes?"

"*Lost* is the word I was going to use. It seems so damning."

It was, Vale realized, the very right word. "'Lost' is not a terminal diagnosis. You can help me."

"How?"

"Well, mostly you have to throw your weight behind me. If she asks you what you think she should do, you should tell her to come back to North Forks, come back into therapy." Vale paused, wanting to be very careful. "I don't say her life is in your hands. I don't hold with that. But I do think you have a role to play in her life, that you have already done much, much that might be, in the end, positive."

"Parthia doesn't know you're here," Biron said. "I am not under orders to check you out."

"You made that up?" Vale felt a stab of frustrated rage. "Why?"

"Donno," he said. "Wanted to see who you were."

255

"Great!" Vale said. The whole trip was useless.

"It doesn't mean I don't have some influence with her."

"But you haven't spoken to her."

"Not yet. But I'm here by the phone, aren't I?"

And she saw that he was in his own way maintaining a kind of vigil. "But have you called her tonight?" she asked. "Have you told her that you believe she should seek help? Can you do that?" Biron slumped back onto the sofa. With his long hair on his shoulders and the kimono drawn about him, he seemed like a weary geisha without the painted face. Vale stood. "I'm doing all I can, Biron. I think that if she heard from you, really heard that you are worried about her and wanted her to come in out of the cold, so to speak, it just might make a difference with her. At least you will have tried."

CHAPTER TWENTY-EIGHT

Parthia wakes from a drugged sleep into the drape-drawn darkness, and she stares at the ceiling until she can assemble the fragments. To make some kind of pattern in her mind. She has been asleep forever, dreaming the same dream. It lies in wait for her just on the other side of sleep, her own private Hades. She cannot bear to be taken again.

She turns on a lamp, and her head throbs. She gets out of bed, puts on the white robe with the ornate L on the breast, and goes into the bathroom. She turns the tap on hot, soaks a washcloth, and puts her face into it. Then she takes out all the vials of pills she has brought with her and makes an inventory. Not enough. She does not want to wake again to her stomach being pumped under the glare of lights. She does not want Claire hovering by her bedside with her questions, her contagious, uncontrollable fright. She needs more pills.

She sits at the edge of the bed. A wave of dizziness floods her. The room spins, steadies.

Out in the street a siren sounds. She pictures an ambulance parting the traffic on Lexington Avenue. A figure under a white sheet, hoses attached, under a mask.

On the television she never turns off, gangsters in the back of a black sedan pull up to a house in a neighborhood of wealthy homes. Like Babylon.

She tears her eyes away from the screen and stares at the phone by the bed. She lifts its receiver, hears the hum of its dial tone. Puts the receiver back down. Picks it up again. Puts it down. Then she lifts it a third time and with something like dread dials into her answering machine.

Caesar Romero is entering a house and slowly climbing a curved staircase. He has a gun in his hand.

She presses the receiver to her ear, afraid of what she might hear. An unlit cigarette dangles between her fingers. She comes to her feet, ready to run, as the messages begin.

"Parthia, darling. Where are you?" Claire's cloying coo. "Your therapist left a message on my phone. The new one, not that wonderful Mark Warren. I didn't think you should have stopped seeing him. Anyway this one, Dale Messenger her name is, wants to meet with me. I'm not sure what to do. I'm worried. Please don't scare me like this. Call me. Please."

"Parthia, it's Claire. I'm going to be seeing your Miss Messenger later this morning. Everyone is looking for you. Your father took a turn for the worse last night, but I haven't told him anything. Perhaps in some way he knows. He keeps asking for you. I don't know what to say. Call, Damnit!"

"Hey girl. Where you at? It's Oleander. Nadine and I are going to the island this weekend. Biron says you're on the loose. Come join us. We'll be in the Pines Saturday, do the dinner thing, crash, probably be there most of Sunday too. Check in, baby, when you can."

"Parthia, it's Vale Messenger. I'm in the city trying to find you. Here are two numbers where you can reach me. Call any time. Any time." Two numbers followed.

"Parthia, it's Claire. I had a talk with Vale Messenger this morning. She impressed me as a very sensible, straightforward person. Perhaps a little officious. But she means well. I had bad news from Dr. Phitzer. You must come see your father. Before it is too late. You will be sorry if you don't. You owe him this much, Parthia. You owe me this much." Fuck you, Claire. "You little bitch, come home." Ahh, the truth at last.

"Hey kid, I just talked to your shrink. She's been trying to reach me. Looking for you. Hard working girl. Anyway, she's coming out to the island tomorrow some time. I told her she might have a chance to see you here. I don't know where you are. I'll let you know my take on her. On the other hand, you can always show up. Any way in particular you want me to play it? Give me a ring."

"Parthia, it's Vale again. I want you to know what's going on since I'm poking around in your life trying to find you. I spoke to Doctor Warren yesterday. I can see why you did not give him high marks. I went down to Sappho East and talked with Sasha. She didn't know where you were. I've called Biron Lord. I am going out to Fire Island this afternoon to see him. Maybe you're there. He led me to think you might be. I hope...." The message was broken. *Hope.*

"Parthia, it's Biron." His voice was slightly thickened with booze. "I think you should come on out to the Pines. It's Sunday already. Ollie and Dine are here..." There is a pause. "Also your friend from North Forks. Your therapist, Vale Messenger. She's here, too. Looking for you. She wants you to think about going back to the hospital. You know I don't like shrinks, Parthia, but if I did, I'd like this one. That didn't make any sense did it? Well, g'night."

"Parthia, S'me, Biron. I can't sleep. Seems like I'm callin' you all a time now. Lissen, kid, I'm worried 'bout you. Yeah, right. Me. Don' be scared, kid, but come in outa the rain. Got a warm bed here for you. Make you a good breakfast. Chad and Evan are here. Whole gang. Most left I think. We all missed you last night. We may be fucked up, but we're family." There is the sound of a belch. "'Scuse me, darlin'. I can't seem to sleep." There is a long pause. "You still there?" the voice asks. "I miss..."

"Fucking thing. Cut me off. You there? Oh right, I'm talking to your machine. Had a fabulous dinner tonight. Got these innerlopers from the loony bin." Biron laughed at his own slurred joke. "Innerlopers. Tha's pretty good, don't you think? " Another pause. "Parthia, I like this Vale person. You could do worse. She's got a lot more on the ball than that Warren jerk. Talks sense, this Vale does. Guy with her had a hard time." Another pause; Parthia heard a swallow, the clink of glass against a hard surface. "Shit. Spilled my drink." There is a jarring knock on the recording. "Sorry. I dropped..." The message is broken.

Biron again: "Where was I? Oh yeah. This guy from the nut house. Name Lawrence. Talked about his wife and kid. Lost them both in a bomb thing years ago. Hard for me to restrain ..I mean retain...my artistic oddjetivity. Good face this man. Win, tha's his name." The baritone was starting to mumble. "'zema as a kid maybe. ' lissened. You know me, good liss'ner. Big ears. Big heart." There is a catch in the voice, a sound something like a muted sob. "Thought about..."

"Parsha, did I call you arready or 'm I jus' talikn' to you in my head? You still there? You goddamn better be still there. You got me scared now, girl. Come on, answer me, damnit. Don't do this to me. You makin' me think about Tommy. But this is all 'bout you, 'bout stayin' alive. We're here for you. Gotta come in outta the rain, sweetie. Rainin' hard here. Rainin' on the fishies in the deep blue sea. Come home, come home to…" There is another jarring clunk and this time the line goes dead. No more messages. All gone. All gone.

She sits holding the silent receiver against her ear. She pictures the big living room in the Pines. She sees Biron seated on the sofa, the black windows in front of him streaked with rain, perhaps the pool glowing blue in the night.

She lowers the receiver to its cradle. On the screen Caesar Romero is standing over a young woman, lying asleep in a bed. As he leans over, the coin he wears around his neck swings free, glimmers in the moonlight in the room, hangs over the face of the sleeping girl like the silver disk of a stethoscope.

CHAPTER TWENTY-NINE

"So where were you last night?" Vale asked.

Though they had risen at different hours, they had met in the kitchen twenty minutes ago as if by design. They co-operated on a pot of coffee and found enough croissants in the freezer to feed the French Foreign Legion. Win had asked her about her night, and she had told him of her time in the studio, though she spared herself the details.

Now they were sitting, shoulder almost touching shoulder, at the far end of the dock, their bare feet dangling over the edge and the house fast asleep behind them. Before them the bay spread an expanse of calm water. The residue from last night's rain and the heavy morning dew sparkled in the beds of the flowers and, where the sun warmed the pavement, a faint evaporation rose into the air, like the steam that rose from the cups of coffee each had by their side.

She asked her question again. "I lost track of you at one point. Anything you want to tell me?"

"Sometime late, after the last ferry, I was with Biron. In his studio." Out in the bay a solitary fisherman in his dinghy cast his line. "I'd had a little too much to drink."

"Really. How did he...?" She thought better of the question.

"How did he lure me in?"

"Yes, I suppose that's what I was going to ask. What made you go?"

Why had he done it? How was it possible to trust Biron Lord with things he had only told Dean? Strangers on the train? Or some very real, complicated power that had ensnared him? "I have a hazy recollection."

"Well, peer through the haze for me, unless what you're saying is that it's none of my business."

"I'd say we're pretty deep into one another's business."

"But old habits die slowly?" Vale said looking at him over the rim of her mug.

"Meaning?"

"Habits of privacy. Of solitude."

He leaned to his right and nudged her with his shoulder. It was playful and she leaned against him. They remained so.

"At some point I poked my nose into Biron's studio. Actually I had seen you come out. I guess I was curious. Adin had developed some proofs of the pictures Biron had taken in the afternoon. There's a darkroom somewhere in the house."

"Any good?"

"Flattering, no, but his timing is frightening. I said something to him about it, and he shrugged it off." Win sipped at his coffee.

"Sounds uncomfortable." Vale eased her shoulder off Win's and pulled her feet up on the dock, then turned her body so that she faced him.

"He's quite the interrogator. We sat in his studio. He brought in a bottle of single malt Scotch. Place is soundproofed. You couldn't hear the music. Well, I guess you know. I just started rambling." Win stopped, remembering the entire conversation with uncomfortable clarity.

She saw a softness in his face, and it reminded her of the time they were together down by the stream. He had been leaning against the chain-link fence with his arms folded. Letting her in. Like now.

"He asked me what was between you and me." Vale stiffened. "He said he saw all kinds of tiny interest marks, little glances as if you and I were in some sub-audible conversation with one another."

"Not always sub-audible," she said. Still, she knew what Biron meant.

"I said...well, you know...I kind of dismissed it. Said we were just thrown together because of this thing with Parthia and he said 'Bullshit!'" Win flashed Vale a smile, but his eyes were searching her face. "So I asked him what he thought was going on."

"And?"

"He said he thought you were sniffing me out. He said that you were ---and I quote--- 'like a vixen around the tail of the old fox.'" Win glanced at her and then out over the water.

Vale tried to stifle a smile. "Not so old," she said.

Win brought one knee up and crossed his arms over it, chin on his forearms. "Later Biron said that he thought I was deciding whether to come out of hiding."

"Hiding?"

"Yeah. He said that I'd been in a bunker with my hands over my head. He asked me if I could still hear the explosion."

"Jesus," Vale said. "Did he know what he was saying?"

"It rocked me," Win said. "I think it was just a metaphor for him...but he's really tuned in. Biron puts the pieces together very fast and then sort of climbs inside your head and puts words to what he has seen." Out on the water an early sail flashed in the morning sun. "Well, somehow that got me started, and I just talked. About my wife's death. About my daughter's. About the way I tried to deal with it. About North Forks." Then after a pause, "About you, too."

"About me?"

Win swiveled his body towards Vale. He laid his toes over hers. Vale shivered up the whole inside of her body.

"I told Biron that I did not know how I felt about you," he said, "and Biron said---I mean at the time it seemed like a great kind of wisdom; maybe it still does---he said that there are all kinds of...of loves and all kinds of ways they are born. There's a kind of love that grows out of chemical heat and a kind that grows out of respect and interest. It starts in the head, in the mind, 'not in the balls,' Biron said. That kind of love thrives on difference and requires words. He said," and here Win looked down, unable to meet her eyes, "he said that this would be a good kind of love for me."

Win knew his eyes were watering, and his cheeks burned. He swallowed hard, forced himself to look up, and went on. "He said that I need words the way a plant needs water. He said I am in danger of drying up." Win looked away again, unable to continue. Vale drew her toes from under and laid them over his. He had brought tears to her eyes, but she bit down on her lip and held still. His voice was very low. "He said that I need to learn to talk, to share myself. He said I need to come out of hiding and discover that lightning has struck; it's come and it's gone. The trees have been blasted, but the sap is still running.

'You've survived,' he said to me, 'but surviving is the beginning, not the end. You have to live again.'"

This account had cost Win. Vale could not know how much, but she saw his breathing change, saw the clenching of the muscles in his jaw, and then---as if he could not bear the emotion any further---he rounded his shoulders and lowered his head between the taut weave of his arms. She saw how the sun had weathered and bleached his hair. It was long around the ears and needed cutting. She watched the knotted muscles in his shoulders tremble; then helplessly she reached across the space between them and rested a hand on the top of his head, stroking his hair.

"And I'll tell you one last thing, Vale," he said looking up, his face naked with its grief. "In that moment I had a vision of Nayla's face. And Biron said to me---God only knows how he knew it, and I know this sounds utterly crazy---he said, 'Listen to what she's telling you.' And I swear I heard them---my daughter too, Oh God her face was so clear--- and they were telling me to come out of hiding and to live."

•◆•

Later, they were seated at the dining room table with a second cup of coffee. One by one and two by two most of the overnight guests had appeared, poured coffee, made their greetings, wandered off to the deck, the pool. Now Chad and Evan were in the kitchen, putting away the dinner dishes, getting ready to make breakfast. A pitcher of freshly squeezed orange juice was standing on the sideboard beside a half dozen inverted glasses. Biron was doing laps in the pool, and Vale had been looking at the Sunday ferry schedule.

Now Oleander, dressed in something flowing and African, unwound down the spiral staircase. She saw Win first, "Biron get you in his toily toils last night?" she asked, winking at him. She did not wait for an answer, but crossed behind Vale and gave her a peck on the top of her head, then disappeared into the front hall. They heard the door open and moments later she was back with the New York Times wrapped in blue plastic.

"Is that what I think it is?" Win asked.

"It is," Oleander said, dropping it on the table in front of him. "Came over on the first boat. Gets delivered."

"I feel like one of the lost boys in Never Never Land," he said to her back as she entered the kitchen. He pawed into the Times. Vale plucked the Book Section.

Oleander re-appeared. "The boys are taking orders. What do you want for breakfast?"

"I can go with the flow," Win said.

"No, no, no. Must challenge the lads otherwise they grow fat and lazy. Something difficult." Then seeing him hesitate, Oleander came over and rested her hands on his shoulders leaning over so that her musky hair fell over his face for a moment. "Give them something *hard*."

"OK. I'll have eggs Florentine with a side of Belgian waffles." She patted his head. "Just kidding," he said, "scrambled eggs and toast will do just fine."

"I'll let them know," she said. "Vale?"

"Surely we can manage to squeeze in a few more calories. French toast perhaps?"

"Hey, honey, you're in the swing of things now," Oleander conveyed some message to the kitchen and then swept out to the deck. "Yo, Biron, my man." Apparently he could not hear her voice through the steady thrash of his crawl. She leaned over the pool and gave his head a light slap when he made his turn. Something was spoken between them. Oleander looked at her watch. Said something. Biron responded, then resumed his laps.

"Chow in a half hour," Oleander said as she breezed back into the kitchen, "but coffee now."

Nadine appeared on the stairs and made her entrance. Win looked up and saw that her red hair was tied up on the top of her head and that she wore a silk smoking jacket tied loosely at the waist. It looked like she had nothing else on beneath it. He realized for the hundredth time that they did things differently here in the Pines. But then, he reminded himself, these were models, show people who worked hard for the bodies they had and were used to being seen. Liked being seen. His gaze followed Nadine as she passed onto the deck outside, peeled off the jacket and plunged into the water with hardly a splash. Then, surfacing, she began her laps, her white legs flashing. When he turned his attention back to the table he saw that Vale was looking at him, smiling.

"Never Never Land and no Captain Hook," she said.

"It's always like this?" he asked.

"Always, and the flesh never wrinkles and no one grows weary and no one grows old."

"Yeah, I hear you." Win watched as she returned to something she was reading in the Book Review. He kept an eye on her above his Sports page, saw her play with a curl at her temple, and he could see her seated thus, so absorbed, as if they had been having breakfast together for years. Past years? Or future years? He tilted the Sports page, but continued to look at her above its edge. He saw her smile to herself as if she had read something that pleased or amused her. Then she looked up, catching his eye.

"Walk with me to the end of the dock?" he said.

"Sure," she said.

Biron and Nadine were ploughing past one another in the pool. Serious swimmers. Good ones, Win thought. He caught the flash of Nadine's buns, and as she turned at the pool's end the small, pink tipped breasts, jeweled with water. He felt a playful tug at his arm.

They sat again on the breakwater. More fishing boats now idled on their anchors. From somewhere came the sound of singing, a trained tenor doing its warm-ups.

"So," he said, seated beside her, feeling the warmth of her flank against him, "is there any news about Parthia?"

"I got up in the middle of the night and found Biron in the living room. He wanted to talk. He was a little drunk, lonely. I didn't know he'd been with you, but now I think some of what went on with you must have stirred up his own grief."

"But this was about Parthia?"

"He'd been trying to reach her, leaving messages for her. But he still wanted to know why I was after her. I told him the truth. Then I told him I needed him to try to influence her to come back to North Forks. I knew he was ambivalent about it to say the least. I wanted him to put his weight behind it; I wanted him to care." The tenor was no longer doing his warm-ups; he was singing an aria now. Looking to her left along the bay line, Vale saw him at the end of a boat dock. She could almost see the music pouring from him.

They both listened. Win shook his head as if Fire Island kept surprising him. "Biron probably has some influence with Parthia," he said. "What did he say to your request?"

"Only that he hadn't been able to locate her. That tells me something. Apparently they haven't spoken directly since she left North Forks."

"You think she's going to show up here?"

"I don't know. I looked at the ferry schedule. They come and go just about every hour. If she hasn't come by three o'clock, I'm going to give it up. We should get back. Any later and the traffic will be horrendous for you getting off Long Island. "

"So, we'll wait and see," he said.

"Yeah," she sighed, "wait and see."

"Easier said than done."

"Sometimes I think this therapy business is about dealing with feeling helpless."

"I have orchids in my collection that took three years to throw their first spike. That's the stalk that supports the flower. And until that spike shows, you don't know whether anything will ever come from the plant. I feed them. Give them the sun and humidity I think they need. Stress them, and wait."

They were silent, her mind traveling. "After Robert..." she began and stopped. It was so very complicated. But also, she saw, very simple. "I think I made a decision without knowing it. I decided to go it alone. On some level with Robert and with my father I felt betrayed."

"Blind-sided?" he offered.

"Yes, exactly. And I think I got scared, really scared, that I was always going to miss something important, something that would come back and bite me." She turned to look at him. "I need to go slow. I.. with you, I mean. Us. If we are an *us*." God, the man knew how to be still.

Win reached out his hand and rested it on the deck between them, palm up. She could see the way dirt had worked deep into the roughened skin. The stains of earth. His hand made a kind of nest and her hand, shyly, settled into it. She felt the big fingers close gently over hers. Say something, she pleaded, but he did not, only gently folded his hand around hers.

"Win, there's something I haven't told you."

She lifted her hand from its cradle in his and got to her feet. He was looking up at her. "My father killed himself. That's how he died. It's what I couldn't tell you when we were at the museum. Somehow Biron pulled it out of me." Win got to his feet. "I'm still carrying it in me," she said. "Maybe more than I know. I am not sure I ever understood..." She tilted forward and let her forehead rest on his chest. "I'm not sure I ever understood what a mystery he was to me. This work I am doing now..."

"Shhhh," he said. Gently his big arms encircled her, offering protection. Somewhere under her breastbone Vale felt something shift, open, flutter.

"Hey, you lovebirds," Nadine was calling. "Breakfast!"

• ◆ •

The remains of the meal lay uncleared around them

Much to Win's amused chagrin Chad and Evan had indeed produced eggs Florentine with thinly sliced fried potatoes tasting of garlic and rosemary. There were Belgian waffles, light as clouds, for which they had heated maple syrup and butter. There was French toast, crisp on the outside, moist within, and dusted with buttered cinnamon. Fresh pots of coffee appeared unceasingly. Adin and Shin Shin, Sasha and Merlyn, and others, whose names Vale could not remember, filled out a merry table. Vale kept an eye on the time. It was fifteen minutes to two.

They were in the midst of the Times crossword puzzle. "A nine letter word beginning with 's' and ending in 'd,'" Nadine said, who had the puzzle next to her. "And the definition is '"Unlike an omelet."'"

"Scrambled," said Chad immediately.

"Looks right," said Nadine, and there was a flutter of applause. She read out the next definition, "'Michelin's grade.' Five letters and it begins with...'"

"Tires," said Biron, jumping in.

"'S,'" said Nadine.

"Stars," said Win, but before the verdict, the phone rang. Biron went to the studio and closed the door behind him.

Silence reigned until Biron returned to the table; it was as if everyone knew. He spoke to Vale. "Can I have a word with you?" She got up and followed him out onto the deck. The early afternoon sun was beating down on the pool and the bay. They stood under a big umbrella at one of the glass-topped tables.

"That was Parthia," he said. "She's here. In the Pines."

Vale actually felt a little weak in the knees and sat down. Biron drew up a chair beside her.

"You OK?" he asked.

"Yeah. I'm fine. It's just..." she drew a deep breath letting it out slowly, "What did she say? What did you say?"

"She's been at the café in town. She came in on the one o'clock boat. She asked if you were here. I said you were. She said she'd like to talk with you. I told her I'd bring you to the phone, and she said, No, that she'd meet you on the beach at the end of this street at two." Vale looked at her watch.

"Anything else?"

"Yes, she said bring the money, no guns, and if the Feds are watching, the deal's off." Vale's mouth dropped open, and then she reached over to punch Biron on the arm. "Well, it does have the feeling of intrigue," he said. "She asked me not to tell anyone else she was here. "And by the way, I did call her back last night. I left a message. Several I think. I said she should trust you. That I did." He paused, looking briefly at Vale and then away. "I told her also that I was worried about her."

"Thanks, Biron." Vale started to get up. Biron placed a hand on her hand restraining her for a moment. "I know a lot about this girl. A lot. If you ever need..."

"No, Biron. I appreciate where you're coming from, but this will be between Parthia and me."

"Fair enough," he said.

"I'm going to my room for a minute," Vale said. She walked through the glass doors, leaving the glare behind her, her eyes unable to focus in the shadowy interior. She supposed that they were all looking at her. Some part of her registered an obligation to Win, but she did not stop.

Some moments after she had gone upstairs, Win excused himself and made his way quietly to the door of her room. It was open a crack and, knuckles poised to knock, he glanced through the opening and saw something that stopped his breath. There on the floor before the window, hands clasped against her breast, her eyes closed, Vale Messenger was on her knees, her mouth moving in an inaudible prayer.

•◆•

Standing at the top of the stairs that led down to the beach, Vale saw Parthia's huddled form below her on the lowest step. Her arms were clasped around her knees, the knees drawn up under her chin, the articulated bones of her spine sharp as knuckles. Under the brim of the sunhat, blond hair lay on the nape of the neck in golden wisps. Beside her a small drawstring bag. On her feet not golden sandals, but flip-flops. Vale was afraid to see what five days had done to that face.

Beyond the stairs the narrow beach was spangled with blankets on which scantily clad men and women lay reading or asleep. A few swimmers bobbed on modest waves. Some gulls floated on the water a stone's throw from shore. "Give me strength," Vale whispered; then, her hand on the wooden railing, she was descending the steps. Her shadow fell over the huddled form like a wing.

PART IV

Dr. Claus Adenauer closed the bedroom door; from his breast pocket he removed the handkerchief he always carried, and out of habit mopped a brow that was in this moment rather dry and cold.

Claire had summoned him while he was still at breakfast with Ruth. "Willi"---she never pronounced it the German way---had taken a turn for the worse during the night, she reported. Pain beyond reason. Uta, the nurse, woke her when he insisted she come to him. He was sure that there was a fire on the grounds. His yellowed eyes wide with terror. "*Feuer! Feuer!*" he was screaming. Nothing would convince him all was well until the fire marshal came at dawn. "I was embarrassed. What could I do? He's awake now. He wants you to come." Claus had given his wife a quick kiss and hastened away.

As expected, he had found nothing new, only the erratic erosion of Wilhelm's strength and sanity. He'd adjusted the analgesic, and in the spell of lucidity that followed his old friend had spoken with unprecedented candor about certain matters—memories--- that were rising to his mind in vivid assaults. At times Claus felt like a priest listening to a confession; at other moments he was the sinner of a shared crime.

Then with a sudden clinical objectivity, Willi had spoken of final things. "I know that I am losing my mind," the dying man said in the formal German of their academic days. "I know the day draws near when I may not be able to make a rational decision. These terrible dreams become worse. These memories. Demons. I do not wish to die any sicker of soul than I am." *Geistkrank* was the word he had used. "You understand that, Claus. That would be unacceptable to me."

Claus nodded. "*Ja, naturlich.*"

"I want to see my daughter. I do not think I can wait much longer. I do not know where she is or why she does not come. Do you?" The old physician shook his head. "Ahh," groaned the sick man. "So what to do?"

"Perhaps we must have a plan?" Claus offered.

"Yes," his patient had said at last. "We must set a date, a time. 'A deadline.'" A pale smile passed over his lips, for he had used the English word. "And we must prepare. I believe it is to be soon. Do you concur, Herr Doktor?"

He did. Yes. Soon. Claus wondered whether he would have the nerve to manage his own end with such determination.

They needed time to make the final arrangements, and Wilhelm wished to be left alone in the house with his physician and friend, for he had records he wished Claus to dispose of. To that end he would require some hours without the nurse or Claire to interrupt. He would need Herr Doktor Adenauer to go to the pharmacy for him; he would write a prescription in his own hand. Let there be no impropriety. He had thought of a harmless ruse that needed Ruth's cooperation: perhaps she and Claire might go tomorrow afternoon to the Cloisters to see the Bruges tapestries? Wilhelm would talk to his wife. Claus would talk to Ruth? *Ja.*

Claus sighed. He should never have agreed to act in this manner. But what could he do? Claire's pleading had prevailed over his better judgment. "A friend is what he needs now," she had said, "a physician who is a friend." What Willi needed was absolution. But who could give it? Such a thing was beyond him. He was not a psychiatrist, nor a priest. And always, making his task more delicate, was the prospect of preparing Claire for the harsh reality of a definite end. He replaced the handkerchief in his pocket, and after assuring Claire her husband was resting, he went home to confer with Ruth.

•◆•

When Vale reached her office that Monday morning, she was not surprised to find her answering machine already flashing with messages.

One from Claire---whom Vale had called the night before to notify her of Parthia's return---now distraught and pleading for a further conversation and hinting at ominous developments. A final shriek before breaking the connection: "I must have an answer. Is Parthia coming home?"

Pamela Rivers, calling to make sure Vale came in to see her at her earliest convenience. After morning rounds, perhaps. A steely summons gloved in Rivers' impeccable professional courtesy.

Some kind words from Win, to let her know he was thinking about her and hoped to run into her before the day was over. "By the way, I've got tickets to a Yankees game on Wednesday night. How about going with me?" Sweet, she thought, and *Take me out to the ballgame* began to play in her mind.

And one from Robert, wondering why he had not heard from her. He reminded her, unnecessarily, to call Melanie. "She really missed you. I know how important your work is, but this is ridiculous. She..." Vale deleted the conclusion. She would call Melanie that evening. She dashed off to the morning meeting on the unit.

Though she received a few perfunctory congratulations as the staff gathered, the underlying mood was one of unexpressed displeasure: A very difficult young woman, who had defied them from the first, was now back for another round of testing their patience. Parthia was once again on status, and the repercussions of her return and the special treatment she required were sending eddies among the inmates of Gables. For all her dedication, Vale's championing seemed somehow self-indulgent and excessive. She could not speak of Lucore's dictum. It did not bode well that Parthia had come back to the unit Sunday evening in a stupefied state---everyone assumed she was on something. Nor had it helped the night staff's mood that Vale had lingered at the nurse's station in order to respond if Parthia needed her. A poor message, Edna thought, altogether too accommodating. On top of it all, Ed Paley had called in sick that morning, so the staff was short one person on a day they could have used extra hands.

Vale was speaking of her need to assess her patient's condition when she was summoned from the meeting by a phone call.

"Good morning, Vale; it's Dean. I got the message that you found your quarry. Congratulations. I am very pleased and relieved. I am sure you are also."

"She's had a hard time, Dr. Venables. Actually, she seems to have broken down in a way I am not sure how to assess. We're waiting for her blood work. I haven't had a session with her yet."

"I see," Dean said. "When did you actually get her back here?"

"Around six. It was a bit of an ordeal."

"I'd love to hear about it sometime," he said by way of ending the call.

Without thinking she replied, "When might be a good time?"

"Ah," he paused. Had she been importunate? "Let me look at my calendar. I'll leave a message on your answering machine." With that he rang off.

By the time she returned to rounds, the meeting was breaking up. From across the room Ben Farmer gave her a nod. In it she read a support that steadied her.

Back in her office, she placed a call to Claire, and for once got her on the first ring, but immediately Vale heard a hand cover the receiver. Then Claire returned, "Listen, Dale, I can't talk right now. I am speaking with Claus about my husband. He had a terrible night. Call me later."

"Mrs. Alexander, I have a busy morning ahead…"

"What? I'm sorry what did you say? No I really can't talk now. Call me later. Please." And Claire broke the connection.

Vale called Pamela Rivers' office and was told to come over immediately.

In deference to both their schedules, after offering Vale a glass of sparkling water which she refused, Rivers came right to the point, requesting a full update on "the Sunday expedition," as she called it. Then she listened to Vale's account in silence, and after a moment spoke. "I took the Alexander girl's file home with me this weekend. I've read the transfer record, your in-take, your session notes. I've reviewed the treatment plan. It occurred to me that there might be something you've overlooked." Vale's stomach dipped; she thought of her missing Julia's birthday. "Have you ever heard of the Stockholm Syndrome?" Rivers asked.

Vale had a recollection of something in a textbook, but she would not like to be examined on the matter. "What are you thinking?" she asked

"Well, as you know, it takes its name from an event that occurred in Stockholm about ten years ago. There was a botched bank robbery, and a group of hostages was forced to spend six days with their captors in a bank vault. At the end of their captivity they actively resisted rescue. They refused to testify against their captors, even raised money for their legal defense. According to some reports, one of the hostages eventually became *engaged* to one of her jailed captors. There was a rash of public opprobrium, but some smart Swedish psychiatrist looked twice at the conduct. In the end he identified their behavior not as a form of passivity, but as an adaptational response to fear."

Rivers took a sip of water from her glass. "Since that time there have been other events which have showed similar features, and so it came to be called a syndrome. The defining feature is that the victim goes through a transformation of sorts. There's thought to be some kind of personality change. The captive has been broken down and in some way reconstructed. There is always fear involved, extreme fear, and to cope with this fear, the person adopts behaviors, patterns of thought, designed to lessen fear."

"What kind of rehabilitation has worked with such people?" Vale asked. "Are they restored to their previous personalities?"

"In most cases yes, though with a certain lingering features of post traumatic stress. In fact, I think you should review the relevant material in DSMIII; it's 309.81, I believe." Rivers offered Vale a pad and pencil, and Vale wrote a note to herself. You might want to look at some of Robert J. Lifton's work and Robert Spitzer's as well." Again Vale scribbled the information. "This Stockholm Syndrome always refers to brief and intense experiences of fear, of a kind of short term brainwashing."

"But longer term abuse...?"

"You learned that Dr. Alexander operated on his daughter, repeatedly. Such treatment over time, and at the hands of a parent no less, could constitute a far deeper personality disorder. A person undergoing such abuse might split off a part of herself, especially if this treatment lasted for several years. It struck me that Parthia was, in a sense, kidnapped by her own father and experienced what might seem a ritual of torture. I mean that is how it might feel. Frankly, I cannot imagine what marks it would leave, or of what duration."

"I was struck by a word you used a moment ago," Vale said. "You spoke about a person being broken down and 're-constructed.'"

"Yes."

"As you know, Wilhelm Alexander was chief of cosmetic and *reconstructive* surgery at St. Luke's Hospital." Vale tore the page of notes from the pad.

Pamela Rivers started to say something, thought better of it, then glanced at her watch and rose. Vale stood also. "I have nothing to offer you by way suggestions for treatment. You couldn't have a better ally than Ben Farmer." Rivers went to her desk, picking up a manila envelope, "Or Dean Venables, for that matter. Make use of all our resources." She crossed back to Vale and handed her the envelope. "I found some references for you, some articles that may be useful. There is no case of this sort that I have ever heard of, but these may be helpful."

They were standing at the door as Vale took the envelope, opened it and slid her notes into it. Her supervisor continued, "I reprimanded you not long ago for your somewhat novelistic way of writing up your patient notes. I'd like to withdraw that criticism. It is refreshing to read what you say about your patient. You have a gift. Who knows, you may want to write this up someday. It is 'one for the books,' as the saying goes." Rivers opened the door. "I wish you luck, but I will not be surprised if you find nothing works." Apparently she saw Vale's expression change, for she added, "I just don't want you to blame yourself. You will realize that we all come up against things in our patients we cannot change. Sometimes the damage is just too grave."

CHAPTER THIRTY-ONE

That same Monday, after Uta had fed her husband his lunch, Claire sat in the chair beside his bed. She was twisting his linen napkin in her hands, twisting and untwisting it as if she were wringing the scrawny white neck of a tiny bird. Then she smoothed it out in her lap, pressing her palms against it, flattening it, looking down at the wrinkled square of white cotton. She glanced at the crowded night table before her where a picture in a silver frame showed a handsome couple, he in black, she in red, seated at a table beside a low stonewall. Between them a bottle of wine, two glasses ready half-filled. Claire drew some strength from the picture.

The afternoon light now glowed in the curtains at the bedroom window. Her empty cup rested in its saucer on the table by the reading chair. On a table under the window sat a stack of photo albums, some magazines, a new Hollywood novel. The massive canopied oak bed on which they had slept the nights of their years together had been disassembled and put away in the garage, replaced by cold, stainless steel. An IV bottle leaked nourishment and oblivion into her husband's left arm. Wires running from her husband attached to a monitor on a high metal stand gave a read-out of vital signs. A catheter's tube snaked out from under the white sheet into a plastic bag that hung on the side of the bed, a bag half filled with chartreuse urine. A call button was taped to the rail; it would sound downstairs and up. Next to it a plunger under his thumb that could deliver an additional dose of morphine. A night table was crowded with bottles of pills. On an ample fold-out table across the room there were washbasins, bedpans, soft towels, unguents for his sores. Disease had displaced everything in this familiar room, yet she would have it no other way. He could be at home; he would be at home. Thank God at least for that. What more could she do?

In Wilhelm's book-lined study down the hall, the nurses on rotation had set up a cot for themselves, a few personal items, a change of uniform. They had access to their own half bath. Everything that could be done was being done to give the dying man comfort and attention. Claire slept in the smaller bedroom that adjoined the one in which her husband lay.

As he slept his ragged sleep, Claire went to the table and picked up the scrapbook that told the story of her tragic accident, her despair, her miraculous restoration. Her husband always kept scrupulous records and photographs of his work. She could see the time-lapse progress of his devotion to her, how bit by bit, over the span of two years, he had brought her face back from the dead. It had been the most terrible and wonderful time of her life.

When they came to do the television movie ten years ago, she had played herself in the final scenes. Some they had shot here in the house. The film had ended with her talking with the filmmakers about making a film about her recovery that the viewer had just seen. A neat script. Wilhelm, ever shy of publicity, had agreed this once to stand, though surely not to bask, in the light of his own success. After that, well, he became the surgeon to the stars. The familiar story soothed her.

Claire picked up a second volume of photographs, a cavalcade of faces---breasts, hips, fannies---from stage and screen, mostly women, of course. Diane Vreeland had written about Wilhelm in *Vogue*. Claire knew the quote by heart:

> In my opinion, in the next century so many physical problems will
> have been surmounted that a woman's beauty will be a dream that will
> be completely obtainable...The future holds a golden world.

This doyenne of fashion had seen in his work the opportunity for every woman to achieve through art a beauty only a very few possessed by nature.

She had just picked up a small Moroccan leather album when the feet of the figure on the bed began kicking, throwing off the light blanket which covered them. The feet were restless, twitching as if they were trying to take the immobile body somewhere. She stood and covered the feet again and laid her hands over them to quiet them; they jumped under her fingers as if jabbed by small bolts of electricity. She thought to summon the nurse, but the nurses were useless. The way the legs jumped of their own accord frightened her as if the sleeper were caught in a dream, attempting to flee from a pursuer. She squeezed his foot. He did not wake.

She studied the face, gaunt and yellow from jaundice. The skin had tightened over the forehead, sagged around his closed eyes, pouched flaccid along his jaw line. Whiskers bristled on his chin. His mustache needed trimming. He had been such a handsome man. Only a few months ago they had strode through the chapels of the Cathedral in Toledo looking at El Greco. For Wilhelm the Spanish masters---El Greco, Zurburan, Murillo---held an abiding fascination. On that occasion she had remarked to herself on his bearing, the difference in their ages inconsequential in Europe, where it was taken for granted that a man of such aristocratic presence would have a handsome younger woman on his arm.

They had eaten a meal on the veranda of Vente de Aires, he in his black suit with the white Egyptian cotton shirt buttoned to the neck; she in the red dress, arms bare to the warm Iberian night. Under flickering candles on the patio, a gypsy had played ballads on his guitar. She gave the waiter her camera, and he had taken their picture. Later a private car took them back to Madrid.

El Greco could paint him now, a yellowing death's head on a white pillow, the encroaching shadows.

A rasping of breath calling her name brought her back suddenly to the room. "Have they put out the fires? I can smell the smoke."

Dr. Phitzer had explained all this to her: the olfactory miscues, damage to the nerves. Technical words. Her husband was losing his mind. Don't contradict him. Play along. Reassure him. The yellowed eyes stared at her. Dried spittle was caked at the edges of his lips; his face was twisted in a grimace of panic.

She had never seen such a look on her husband's face, a face that had always seemed carved from a fine pale wood in which even the wrinkles of age had been incised with a craftsman's hand, a lean, long face with a strong nose and a cap of straight white hair. Wilhelm Alexander had cheated time until this assault had wrinkled him almost unrecognizably. In a single predatory leap, age was consuming him before her eyes "Yes, darling," she said now. "The fire marshal was here early this morning. All is well."

"Ah," he said, *"Danke Gott."* The eyes found her face, searched it, blinked once as if clearing the image of a dream. Then the chest heaved; the feet between her hands stiffened. She came around to his side and was reaching for the call bell---this was beyond her, too much, too much---when his hand seized hers. His fingers gripped her hard. "*Vo ist miene kinde?*"

"I don't understand you," she said, though she did.

"*Meine kinde,*" he said, his voice made hoarse by pain. "My daughter. Where..." His throat thickened with phlegm, and he started to gag. She wrested her hand free and pressed the call button, and almost instantly Uta appeared at the bedside. She lifted his head and slapped him sharply between the shoulder blades. A gobbet of phlegm flew from his throat and landed like a slug on the sheet. Uta removed it with a swipe of a tissue. She whispered something to him in German, and he shook his head. Then she laid his head back onto the pillow and wiped his forehead with a washcloth. "*Ich muss miene kind...*" but the last words were stopped again by a seizure of pain. Gently Uta pressed the plunger; in a moment the body relaxed, the eyes, rolling up into the skull, closed. Claire dismissed her with a glare, hating the fact that Uta could speak to her husband and understand him in his mother tongue.

Soon Wilhelm's eyes opened. "*Wasser,*" he said to his wife. Claire placed the elbowed straw between his lips. He drew on it. Water dribbled down his chin, but slid down his throat as well. His voice was weak, and Claire had to lean forward to hear it. "Have you spoken to her?"

Claire did not know what to say to her husband's question. "I don't know when she will come." In response Wilhelm closed his eyes. Claus had urged her to tell her Willi the truth. There were decisions to be made; he must be in possession of the facts. Easy for him to say. But he was right; she had waited long enough. "Darling, I have something to tell you." She had hoped to spare him this. His blue eyes were clear in the rheumy folds of their lids. "Parthia is in a hospital." She saw him start. "A mental hospital. I think the thought of your illness was unbearable to her. She had...well, a kind of breakdown."

"When?"

"A few weeks ago."

"You mean all this time when I thought she was somewhere working..." Suddenly the face froze and the pallor changed. Claire could almost see the wave of pain pass over his body. Sweat started out on his forehead. He shook his head and ground his teeth. Then the pain passed; his eyes closed. "Water," he whispered. She fed it to him. "Go on," he said.

"When she was last here she took some pills. They made her sick."

"But you said she was called away to the Southwest."

"I know. I didn't want you to be troubled." She watched him close his eyes. The head nodded once as if he understood.

She wanted to tell him about the smashed furniture, the torn sheets, the half naked body, the ambulance and the vigil at Good Samaritan. She wanted to tell him about Parthia's mutilated face. She wanted to tell him of her frantic phone calls, of the maddening Dale Messenger, of the escape that Parthia had made, her return. She wanted him to know how brave she had been, wife and step-mother, how alone. But she would not trouble him. "Parthia is apparently not herself yet," she went on. "She is in a place called North Forks on the North Shore. She is under psychiatric care. The very best. She is really fine, just a matter of regaining her strength."

"So you think she will come?"

"I...I cannot say."

The man on the bed lay quiet with his eyes closed for so long that Claire thought he might have fallen to sleep. When he spoke, she thought she had missed several transitions. "Listen, my love, there is a Raphael tapestry on loan at the Cloisters. I had very much wanted to see it. Will you go for me tomorrow, go with Ruth, and tell me about it?"

"But now?" she protested. "To be away from you?"

"It will do you good, a little breather. And you will bring me back something beautiful. You will tell me what you saw. Do this for me?"

"You're sure?" The gray head nodded. "If this is what you want."

"Yes. More water, please. " He drank. Then his eyes closed, his breathing slowed, and he fell asleep. Mercifully the feet were still.

Sitting by his side, Claire resumed twisting the white napkin in in her lap, twisting and smoothing, twisting and smoothing, and staring at the photograph of the handsome couple in the silver frame. She could almost hear the sound of the Andalusian guitar.

•◆•

Vale and Dean sat at the informal end of his office, she on the leather couch, he in the chair to her left. "Thank you for making this time for me," Vale said.

"Tell me about it."

"Do you want the whole story or the short version?"

"Give it all to me," he said, and as she began to speak, he reached over for a pipe, filled it from the humidor, lit it, and listened.

Her narrative, full but with the personal details edited out, ended with her account of finding Parthia on the beach. "I sat with her on the steps. I was shocked really with how she looked, shaky and unsure of herself, broken down." Vale returned in her mind's eye to the sight of the young woman seated beside her on the wooden steps, whose fingers could not stop picking at her cuticles, whose eyes skittered in their sockets, and whose voice was croaky. Vale had wondered if she was hallucinating.

"I asked her where she had been the past five days, and she told me she had been in at the Lexington Hotel in the city. I asked her what she had been doing and she said, 'going a little nuts.' She was trying to be casual about it, but I think she was telling me the truth. She was scared." Vale looked at Dean and found comfort in his listening presence.

"I told her I had been looking for her, that I was concerned about her. I said I wanted to take her back to North Forks. We could go together and that I would stay with her until she was settled. Then I told her I would help her get her life back. 'I don't want my life back,' she said, and I said I'd help her make a new one."

Vale was remembering the look on Parthia's face of hope and fear. She had reached over then and taken the hands that fluttered in Parthia's lap. Orphan hands with no one to hold them, the cuticles torn, the nails bitten down to the quick. She held the hands gently, firmly in hers, not letting them escape. They tugged weakly, then went slack. "I don't want to go back there," Parthia had said. Then the eyes had looked away, and the hands had pulled away. "But I have no place else to go."

"She is depending on you, Vale," Dean said, interrupting her memory.

"This is the first time I've felt it." Dean looked quizzical. "Felt like I've got someone's life in my hands. She's breaking down, and I don't know how to stop it."

"You can't. I mean we could give her drugs and arrest this, but I don't think we should."

"But isn't the whole point to help them get control over their lives."

"Yes, of course. But actually some of them need to break down."

"Why?"

"Because they already have."

"I don't understand."

'I'm not altogether sure I can explain it, but in my experience what used to be called a "nervous breakdown" in some cases actually seems to be a necessary kind of re-enactment of a breakdown that occurred once before. A replay of a moment of psychic death which the patient both fears and needs to revisit."

"Why to revisit?

"In order to repair the death that occurred. To realize that life has gone on. That there is hope. That one is not locked in that past."

"How...?"

But he was gong on. "Vale, there are some things one only understands in this business through experience itself. The books just can't give it to you. Parthia may need to go *through* something, not be pulled back from it. Stay with her. Something inside her is desperate to heal, and she believes she can do it with you."

"I'm frightened," Vale said. "Of failing her." And what else? the kind eyes asked. "Of failing you." The kind eyes smiled, the head shook slightly. "Of getting lost in her madness."

"Ahh," Dean said, "just so. Madness is a formidable adversary." He set down his pipe. He stood and ushered Vale to the door. "All I can tell you is keep the connection you have worked so hard to make. It is her life-line."

•♦•

Vale saw Julia later and learned that things had gone unusually well with Myrna. "It's like she and I have been locked in some kind of mechanical dance," Julia said, "and for some reason this time it was different. I didn't react in the places I always react, and because I didn't, she didn't do the things she usually does. We actually joked a little."

"And you stayed overnight in her apartment for the first time in how long?"

"Almost three months."

"A good sign."

"Grandma says I can live with her when I get out, until I get a direction."

"What do you think?'

"I need to. Gramma's halfway house." Vale smiled. "I'd like an overnight pass for Tuesday. I want to see if I can find some work. Would that be OK?"

"I think so. I need to talk to Myrna." Julia nodded. Then Vale asked, "How is it having Parthia back?"

"Scary. You know how, before, she was restless at night and Miss Calm and Collected during the day. Now it's just the opposite. During the day she is bizarre and jumpy. Changes her clothes all the time. Spends a lot of time in the bathroom. She's reciting things, lines from a play. I don't know what. Then at night." Julia paused… "at night she sleeps without moving at all. It's like she's… well, she's immobilized in some way. Frozen. She's in exactly the same position in the morning she was in when she went to bed. Flat on her back, her arms at her sides. She keeps her feet outside the sheet. They stick up. It gives me the creeps."

"Because?"

"It's a little like the room becomes a morgue at night. All you'd need is a ticket on her big toe."

•◆•

"So what's this about a ballgame?" she asked Win when she reached him on the phone at work.

"I've got two tickets for a Yankees game Wednesday night. Any chance you'd like to go?"

"I've never been."

"Never been to a baseball game? You're kidding." She head him chuckle. "So, want to go?"

"I'd love to," she said, "but it doesn't strike me as the best place to have a conversation. We've got some catching up to do."

"How about you pack a change of clothes. We can leave from here together, go to the city for a quick meal, take in the game, and I can drive you up here on Thursday. The extra room is always available."

Ah yes, she thought, the extra room. "Sure," she said. *Take me out to the ball game.*

"You hear anything from Melanie?" Win asked.

"I got in too late last night to call. There was a message on the machine. I can't call till suppertime tonight."

Vale heard his silence on the line. She let it hang there. "I miss my little girl. Still."

"I'm sorry, Win." Paltry words. Losing Melanie…unthinkable.

"Is Parthia settled in?"

"She is, I guess. I had a talk with Dean earlier today. I just have to get used to the fact that everyone in this business is basically winging it. I keep thinking there's supposed to be some kind of map for the territory. Dean says there isn't one. As for Parthia, she's supposed to be here for a session in two minutes."

"I'll let you go, then. If I don't see you before, let's meet up in the parking lot at four on Wednesday."

"I'll call you if anything unexpected happens."

"I hope nothing does."

"Me, too," she said.

•◆•

Parthia pulled on a dress. She hated how it looked. She took it off, threw it on the bed, found her black jeans and a black tee shirt on the floor of her closet. They needed washing, but she put them on anyway. Then she could not resist the gold sandals, and then the mirror demanded a quick smear of lipstick. Earrings. No, fuck it, and goddamn it. She slammed her closet door, but she could not leave her room without going back to the mirror once, twice, and a third time until her obedient hand fingered two small gold hoops onto each ear. "There," she snarled at the face in the mirror, "Are you satisfied?" *Meine kleine Prinzessin,* the voice in the back of her mind murmured approvingly.

Parthia stepped past Jean Newcombe. She passed under the red Exit sign at the top of the stairs. Exit. Exit. Exit. On her way out she lit a hungry cigarette and walked onto the brazen lawn. She wished immediately for her dark glasses. Humid, listless air smothered her and drove her immediately towards the big beach tree. Her head was full of voices, a staccato of urgings, warnings, invitations, mechanical, distant, irrelevant, tugging at her, pulling her, giving her information she had no interest in, for which she had no use. Among these voices, one persisted, her name, repeated once, then again, a voice calling her name through the high branches of the tree. She looked up, the sun spiked into her eyes. She found the source of the voice, Messenger leaning out her office window, looking down. "Parthia," the voice said, "it's time for our session."

Parthia took a final draw on her cigarette, dropped it onto the grass, then head down, she walked across the neon lawn to the entrance of the stone tower and plodded up the stairs to her inquisition.

Messenger met her at the door. Parthia felt the eyes on her, searching, examining. *Somewhere there is a world of the blind.* She longed to be among the sightless and unseen. She glared back at Messenger, then went to the window, turning her back. She felt the stickiness of eyes on her skin. Why had she agreed to come back here? Where was the potion that would shut down the brain? She shivered though it was humid and close in the stone, walled room. She was a swimmer weighted with lead.

Silence, except for the tick of the desk clock, the distant white-noise of crickets in the heated air. A scent of dusty earth and dried grass, and tea rose.

Tick, tick, tick. Too weary to stand, she stepped back into the room and found the seat in which she always sat. It was like accepting a sentence, the doom of the blue chair. She refused to look at the woman in the other blue chair. She fixed her eyes on the pattern in the rug. Her eye looped along its intricate border, dizzying itself.

" Parthia, I..." Vale began.

"Can we not talk?" Parthia asked.

"Is that what you want?"

"I can't take this," she said, a hand gesturing to nothing, to everything. "I'm here. Just let me be."

Vale took this in. Assayed it. All right, she thought. Anyway, she did not know where to begin, and it seemed important not to interrogate. Perhaps for the moment it was enough that Parthia was here, had roused herself from her room, a kind of complying. Best to be quiet. She imagined Dean with his irresistible warmth, his confidence. He would be able to reach this one. He would know how to unlock her secrets. But she did not.

And so time passed, and she saw Parthia's eyes droop. The figure slid down in the chair until her head rested on the curved back, the legs extended. Then gradually the head bowed. The flesh on the face slackened. Her breath sounded louder in the room. Parthia slept. Was this by any stretch of the imagination part of treatment or was it the sign of treatment's failure? Was Parthia over-medicated? Under-challenged? Over-resistant? Under-attached?

Vale watched Parthia and found, notwithstanding her questions, that she was satisfied to sit and guard that sleep. The summer cicadas ground out their music. The humid air pressed its weight upon her. Her mind took her to the seashore. There was Melanie skipping along the water's edge, but big waves were starting to roll in. A distant roaring in her ears. Melanie called to her mother, and Vale slipped all the way into the dream.

The ringing of her phone startled her awake.

Parthia was gone.

Vale flushed with embarrassment at the thought of Parthia waking and seeing her therapist asleep. Vale had abandoned her.

She picked up the receiver and said her name.

"Mrs. Messenger, it is Dr. Adenauer."

"Yes."

"Mrs. Alexander informs me that Parthia is back in the hospital."

"Yes, she is."

"And?"

"And it appears that she is somewhat the worse for wear."

"I'm sorry, I don't understand."

"She's had a hard time."

"Mrs. Messenger, you know why I am calling I am sure. I wonder if you can tell me whether your patient will be able to make a brief visit home to see her father."

"I haven't proposed that to her, Dr. Adenauer. She certainly hasn't volunteered it."

"I see. And will you propose it?"

"I am not sure."

"Mrs. Messenger, it is not my job to tell you your responsibility as a therapist. I do want you to be in possession of certain facts. I believe I can say with certainty that this is the last week of my patient's life. It is now a matter of days. I have had a confidential conversation with Dr. Alexander. We cannot wait much longer for the daughter to come home. If I had a crystal ball, which I do not have you understand, I would say Friday is the likely time."

"I see," she said.

"It would be irresponsible of me not to tell you of this fact. All I can say is that the time is short, and with every passing day his mental presence---no, his presence of mind---deteriorates. He is less and less able to be alert and awake."

"I understand, doctor, and I understand that my patient's father very much wishes to see her."

"He does."

"And do you know why that is, doctor?"

"If I did, would that make any difference?"

Vale considered this. "I don't know. If there was something I could tell my patient that might give her some idea of what he wants from her, perhaps..."

"Ah, yes. Well, let us say that merely the sight of her face, just that, would do a great deal to ease him." Vale bit her tongue. "Perhaps you can tell your patient that."

"Doctor Adenauer, thank you for your call. I will do what I can."

"I am sure you will. I am sure Mrs. Alexander will stay in touch with you."

"No doubt," Vale said.

•◆•

When Julia returned to the room, she was taken aback to discover that Parthia had taken a lipstick and written in bold red letters on the wall by her bed the word EXIT.

She went into the hall and asked Jean Newcombe, who was sitting status, to look at it. After doing so, Jean went to the hall phone and called down to the Nurse's station. Willa Maynard came up and confirmed the report.

Parthia was curled up in her bed, a tray of half eaten food on the chair beside her. Her back was to the room. Willa tried to engage her and was met with a "Leave me alone," which, under the circumstances, she found mildly reassuring. Then the two staff members withdrew to the hall. Julia could not overhear their conversation, but presently Jean opened the door wider and set her chair on the threshold.

Julia sat on the edge of her bed, staring at the unmoving form across the room. Then she got up and went downstairs, explained to Willa what she wanted to do, and was given a pair of scissors. Twenty minutes later, Julia placed beside Parthia's bed a jar filled with cut flowers. They leaned their colorful heads towards the sleeping girl.

CHAPTER THIRTY-TWO

After breakfast on Tuesday, Ruth came in her chauffeured car to fetch Claire who did not for one minute like leaving her husband, nor did she understand the reason for this errand. But as the car traveled towards the city, she allowed herself to settle into the soft leather seat and into the sympathy of a woman of the world. When Ruth offered her a glass of sherry from the bar, she took it gladly.

They sipped in silence. Ruth could see the lines of fatigue and worry around her friend's mouth. Shadows showed under her eyes that not even Claire's practiced cosmetic touch could hide. "So," Ruth began, "tell me how does it go with you."

Claire needed no prompting. "I am furious with Parthia, just furious."

"But Parthia is in the hospital. Perhaps she cannot help it."

"I don't believe it. It's her therapist who's obstructing this. Dale Messenger. Everything goes through her. It's maddening. Christ, with modern medication these psychiatrists can get anyone up and running."

"You make it sound like she is in the machine shop."

"Well, I'll tell you this," said Claire, turning in the seat to face her friend, "I don't think anything is broken. My God, we made that girl into a thoroughbred. You should…" Claire stopped herself. She sipped at the sherry, her face flushed. Some miles passed in silence. Then Claire spoke again, leaning forward and putting a ringed hand on her friend's sleeve. "Ruth," she said in a stage whisper despite the fact that the glass was closed between the driver and the backseat, "have you ever seen pictures of Parthia before…when she was a child?" She was aware, as she asked the question, that she was about to violate one of the few taboos of her marriage. But someone had to know her sacrifices, her achievement. Parthia was, after all, her triumph also.

"No, That I have not seen," said Ruth. She knew there was some secret about the girl, and she suspected her husband knew far more than he ever told her, but then Claus and Wilhelm were old friends.

Claire reached down into her handbag and withdrew the Moroccan leather album, the size of a wallet, and opened it. It held photographs in an accordion of plastic sheaths. Claire held them high, and they spilled down in a cascade; then she passed them to Ruth, who then flicked the switch on the inset reading light behind her head.

The color photographs were arranged in chronological order. The first picture showed a little girl seated in the lap of a large woman, a nursemaid perhaps, who had broad Swabian features, very pink cheeks and blondish hair worn in a bun. Her smile was wide, and on her lap a small round girl held a small red rag doll in her fist. The lid on the little girl's left eye drooped, so that the eye was almost hidden. "2" was written on the lower left hand corner of the picture.

In the second picture the little girl was standing beside the same woman; only now it was apparent that the pair was mother and child. Both wore matching folk dresses and blouses. The similarity between them was obvious; they had the same wide noses, the same broad foreheads, the same heaviness in cheek and chin. The little girl was looking up at her mother, smiling and holding her hand. Both eyes were equally open. "5."

Ruth flipped past a few other pictures of mother and child and came to one in which for the first time the young girl appeared alone. She was seated as if posed for a grammar school picture. She was rosy and decidedly plump, but the skin of her face seemed marked with blemishes. Her hands were folded awkwardly in her lap. "6"

Then there were two pictures of the girl with her father, each, to judge by what they wore, taken at the same time, all bearing "6" on the border. In the first of these, the two of them were playing chess. The child wore a blue smock that concealed her body. She was seated on a hassock, chin resting on her fist, as she stared not at the board, but at a handsome man in a white shirt and vest who, with one hand on a knee and the other poised over the board, seemed intent on the game. The look on her face was one of sheer adoration.

The next was taken on the same occasion, for the girl was dressed identically, but now was seated on her father's lap, a book open before her from which apparently she was reading, The title was legible: *Grimm's Fairy Tales.* The little girl has just turned as if to ask her father a question. This time she seemed a little worried.

In the next photograph the girl was seated in what looks like a dentist chair. She was holding a mirror and looking at her face in it. She wore pink pants and a blue short-sleeved shirt. She was missing a front tooth. The camera had been positioned so that the viewer saw the face of the girl and the face in the mirror. In both the child looked apprehensively at the camera. "7."

"8." The girl was alone. Her straight hair was now longer; it fell to her shoulders. She was standing somewhat rigidly, arms at her sides, with her hands balled into fists. She was frankly fat now, porcine, and did not appear healthy; her cheeks were mottled as if she had a rash. Her eyes looked down. She was standing against a plain, white background on the right edge and across the top of which ran a set of numbers. Using them it was possible to measure her height and width. She was four foot six inches tall. Ruth did not try to figure out her girth. She leaned forward to press an intercom.

"Mam?" a voice sounded from the front seat.

"Hans, it is a little chilly back here. *Bitte*, lower the AC."

"Yes, Mam."

Claire saw where Ruth had come in her perusal. "Her mother had died earlier that year," Claire offered. The child did look a sight. Claire felt almost apologetic on her behalf.

The next picture was a surprise to Ruth. It showed the fat little girl sitting on a hassock beside an armchair in which a woman was sitting whose face was almost completely covered in bandages. The camera had caught a frozen smile on the face of the little girl. "9."

The following eight pictures were, Ruth discovered, actually four groups of pairs, all taken against the white background. In each the girl was naked except for panties. Each pair showed a front view and a side view. The pictures struck Ruth as having a purely clinical intent, and it would be easy for anyone to estimate the changing size and shape of the subject. The legends followed the girl from "9" through "12". Ruth spread them on her lap and scanned them closely.

"You can see what we had to work with," Claire said. And a moment later she added, "And what we accomplished."

Indeed the pictures told a story. "9" showed the girl attempting to hold in her stomach and stand straight. She was biting down on her lower lip. By "10" the girl's hands hung at her sides. Though still fleshy, she no longer looked fat. Her hair was shorter. By "11," the process of slimming was complete. Ribs could now be seen beneath pre-pubescent breasts. The girl had grown to the height of five foot two.

In "12" the change was even more dramatic. Small breasts had arrived. The body had muscle definition in the legs and arms. There was hardly any body fat to be seen. The girl looked athletic. He hair was worn very short. She had grown another inch to five foot three. The face was still plain and marked, but wore now a look of determination. It stared into the camera with the chin pushed slightly forward and the shoulders back. In profile the back was ramrod straight. She wore braces on her teeth.

The next picture, "13" was a portrait. The face filled the frame. There had been no attempt to gild the image. One could see clearly the imperfections in the skin, the rash and blemishes that persisted despite the fact that the girl had a healthy color in her face. The nose was straighter, its breadth magically re-duced, but the face was still plain, the eyebrows heavy and slightly overhanging. The lips were thick.

There followed a series of pictures in which first the eyebrows, then the chin, then the lips were shown in before-and-after versions. What followed was a portrait of the face entire, and Ruth felt momentarily confused. Was this the same girl? It was as if the pieces of a puzzle had fallen into place, a face assembled from parts, a stunning sum. "17," and the girl was now a young woman. Dressed in a black leotard, hair longer and curled, she bore almost no resemblance to the child whose history Ruth had been following in time-lapse sequence.

Three other "17" photos followed, all taken apparently at the same time, for the girl wore the same black leotard. Clearly she had received dance lessons, for in one of the pictures the girl reached her arm forward in a port-au-bras, and in the other she rose on the toes of one foot with the other foot resting against the inside of the knee. The bare arms were slender; the legs long and lean. But it was the face that stunned Ruth, for now only the blue eyes resembled the face she had seen in the earlier photographs. Though the hair was still short, it was a paler blond, and worn with curls gathered softly around the forehead and ears. The eyes seemed set wider apart, or perhaps that was due to the narrowing of the bridge of the nose and the plucking of the eyebrows. The cheeks looked soft, but there was a sense of the bones under the skin. The chin had lost its squareness and was rounded, but it was the lips that drew Ruth's attention. The lower lip was small, almost tucked in under an upper lip that was wide and a little flat. The mouth in one picture looked almost severe, but in the next it showed a set of flashing white teeth in a wide, winning smile. The eyes blazed out at the viewer almost defiantly. The hands were long and shapely, the fingers slightly tipped with a pale coral polish. The neck was either longer or the girl had learned to carry her head high, for there was a great sense of pride in the body. She was a perfect beauty.

"Astonishing, isn't it?" said the voice beside her. "Look here, look at this last one. Do you remember this?"

It was a picture taken at Parthia's eighteenth birthday party at the Plaza Hotel. In this particular photo Claire was wearing a burgundy sleeveless dress that showed off her figure. Her head with its mass of strawberry blond hair was turned towards Parthia, on whom she was bestowing a benevolent smile. Parthia faced the camera, her face devoid of expression and apparently indifferent to the attention that was being heaped on her. The contrast between her cool demeanor and the evident exultation in Claire's face was striking. Both women wore matching sets of diamonds in their ears. Though Claire wore rubies at her throat and Parthia sapphires, the necklaces had been identically designed. There were other matching touches, orchids at their waists, gold charm bracelets on their wrists. They looked like sisters if not in feature or coloring, then in the sense of style, the glamour, the class.

Ruth remembered the night very well, for, uncharacteristically, her husband had had too much to drink and had actually made something of a scene with Wilhelm. The men were in the bar, and the party was winding down. She and Claire were somewhere else, and no one who reported on the incident was able to tell what had been said since the men spoke in German, but it took a year before the two men resumed a civil friendship. Ruth and Claire had conspired to mend their husbands' estrangement.

Ruth sighed, folded the photos into the album and handed it back to Claire, who kept them on her lap, her fingers worrying the plastic edges. Neither woman spoke, each in her own thoughts, each gazing out opposing window.

The car had passed under the silvery span of the George Washington Bridge, the Cloisters two exits away. Ruth was still digesting the story composed in the album, filling in the missing pieces, wondering and imagining. It had been done so well, so secretly, that she had always supposed the homely young duckling had turned gradually and naturally into a swan. But now she saw things differently.

On her side, Claire had much that she expected to say when Ruth had finished, regarding the evidence in the case against Parthia. She was still full of charges and accusations. But for some reason she found it took some work to get the photographs to tell her their old familiar story of sacrifice and triumph. She missed her husband very much.

They arranged for the car to pick them up in ninety minutes. Before they ascended the stone steps to the Cloisters, Claire found a public phone and called home. Uta informed her that Dr. Adenauer was with her husband. All was well.

The Raphael Claire had been sent to see turned out to be another sad symptom of her husband's dementia. The tapestries in question had yet to arrive at the Cloisters---they would be on display after Labor Day. So this was a precious day lost.

They drifted to the South Garden, where the herb garden scented the air with thyme, basil, rosemary, and lavender. The fountain plashed in its basin. Below them the river hardly moved at all, a foil of brilliant light.

Ruth had brought a book and read in the shade; Claire, restless, wandered the rooms. For a long time she gazed down on one particular bronze effigy of a knight, lying on his sarcophagus, hands crossed on his sword, his beard trim. Briefly she laid her hand over his and felt the chill of bronze.

She found Ruth in the Garden. "Take me home," she said.

• ◆ •

Parthia looked a little brighter to Vale that Tuesday afternoon. No new bizarre behavior had alarmed the staff, and with Jean Newcombe's assistance *Exit* had been cleaned off the wall. Parthia, whose moods swung across a broad spectrum, seemed at this moment composed, if frail, and Vale thought this might be the moment to broach the issue of her going to see her father. After a few preliminaries, she asked her if she wanted to know what was going on at home.

"I suppose I should know. Or that you want me to know. So go ahead."

"Here are the facts as I know them. I received a phone call yesterday from your father's physician-friend, Dr. Adenauer, who informed me that your father was not only failing fast physically, but that his mind was going."

"Bet he's planning to put the old boy out of his misery."

"Euthanasia is illegal, and Dr. Adenauer is in a delicate position, but he tells me with some assurance that your father will not live past this week. His best guess is this Friday."

"Three days from now?"

"Yes."

Vale watched Parthia rise and go to the window, her arms hugging herself. She stood there looking down at the upper lawn. Then she returned and sat back down. "I don't know what to do." She looked down at her hands where they rested in her lap. "I want my Mommy," Parthia said, making a joke of her words.

"Tell me about her."

"I can hardly remember her. There's a picture in one of the rooms of our house, in my father's house, of a woman in a silver frame. She's my mother. But I can't remember her voice, or her smell, or anything we did together. It was so long ago, and my father never spoke of her after she died. "

"What was her name?" Vale asked.

"Eva," Parthia said.

The name surprised Vale. Her father's pet name for her.

"What did you call her?"

"My mother?" Vale nodded. "I don't remember. Mummy, Mama. No, Mami; I called her Mami."

"'Mami," said Vale. "M-a-m-i?" Parthia nodded. "Did you and your mother speak English together?"

"English, yes, Daddy insisted that English be spoken in the house. Very strict about that. Mother's English was not good. She was often embarrassed. She was quiet."

"My father was German, also. But he wanted me to know German as well as 'American', as he called it, so I had a second language as a child, though I can't speak it now." Parthia seemed indifferent to this information; she was somewhere else. "Did you and your mother... sometimes between the two of you, at night, a song, a story?"

'*Guten abend, guten Nacht/ Mit roeslein bedacht...*" Parthia's dry voice carried a broken melody. "Where did that come from?" Something was coming with it, a sense of dark and cold, candles flickering in a room, a box, the flash of her father's hard stare. "I'd like to go back to my room now and rest."

"Before you do…"

"What?"

"About going home?" Vale asked.

"I feel I should, but I…" Her hands were busy in her lap with their terrible uncertainty. "Claire wants me to come so that Daddy can say his farewells to me. It was why she called me home weeks ago; she wanted me to be near him while he…" She broke off and then resumed, "I… I couldn't." Parthia stated this as a simple matter of fact. "I went crazy when I went home. Something came over me. I trashed the Guest House. I wanted to burn it to the ground. If I had had a can of gasoline, I would have set fire to everything. Instead I cut everything to shreds."

"You were angry."

"I was beside myself with it. Literally. I wanted to kill him, and I was furious that he was going to die without my having had a chance to kill him. Crazy, hunh?"

"Intense. Not crazy."

"Claire wants some sort of death-bed scene now. She always wants things arranged just so. I am to come home and play my part, the ingénue role to support the leading lady while she weeps and carries on." Vale suspected that Parthia was not far wrong. "I have not had a single call from my father, not one. She says he wants me to come home, but you'd think he would want to tell me so himself." Parthia looked up. "You notice everything goes through Claire."

"And would you go home if your father asked you himself?"

"It would depend on how he asked me and what he wanted. I haven't talked to my father for several years. He has never once called me since I came here. He is a remote man. 'Cold' doesn't get the half of it."

"Perhaps he doesn't know you are here," Vale said

"May I have a cigarette please?" Vale helped her light one. "What does 'father' mean?" Vale saw Parthia's anger returning. On balance, she would rather see fire than ice. She smoked in silence, and Vale remembered the uncanny pun Parthia had used in their first session: *the fuming defense.* Parthia was fuming now. Then she put out her cigarette in the saucer.

"I am his seed, and I am the work of his hands. You know that this face"---and here Parthia reached up and mashed her cheeks together so that for a moment the perfect features were crushed into a grotesque mask--- "is not my face." The words came almost garbled through the distorted mouth. "My father did not want *me*. Did not want her, Paula. If he was to have a child he wanted Parthia, and he made me want her, too."

Parthia dropped her hands from her face, and the red lines from the pressure faded back to peaches and cream, one mask substituted for another. "Father!" she said. "I wish I had been an orphan."

"You were," Vale said.

"You have no idea, Ms. Messenger, how much I hate my father. No idea at all. If I went to see him, it would be to see his suffering not to relieve it." The hands had loosed a corner of flesh by the right thumbnail and tore at it, a bright red line of blood appeared. She pulled off the skin and put it into her mouth.

Vale had nothing to say. She handed Parthia a Kleenex, and the girl looked down at her hands. "My father would take my hands and clip my nails and cuticles; I was no longer a child when he did this. I could not stop picking; it angered him; he did what he could to make me stop. He would collect the parings and put them on a saucer. He would say," and as Parthia continued, she captured the faint unmistakable trace of a German accent, "'If you vish to eat your flesh, zen perhaps you shall eat zis for dinner.'" Vale felt her stomach turn over. "He made me wear white gloves whenever we went out in public. I felt so ashamed. When he came home from work, he would..." but Parthia broke off here.

Vale saw Parthia's hands knit into fists. "Call her," Parthia said. "Call Claire. We will see what my father does." Then she rose and seemed to grope her way to the door and down the stairs. Watching her from the window, Vale saw Jean pick Parthia up and escort her back to the unit.

She dialed a number she now knew by heart. An unfamiliar voice answered, and to her question replied, "Yes, this is the Alexander's house."

"May I speak with Mrs. Alexander, please."

"Who may I say is calling?"

"I am Vale Messenger. She will know..."

"Ah yes. I am Ruth Adenauer, the doctor's wife."

"Has anything...?"

"No, no, Claire cannot come to the phone now. I shall tell her you called. Is there anything you want me...?"

"Please tell her I need to speak with her in person."

"I understand. Does she know how to reach you?"

"Yes, I am sure she does."

"Good bye then. I will tell her."

"Thank you, Good bye."

At least, Vale thought somewhat to her surprise, Claire was not entirely alone.

CHAPTER THIRTY-THREE

Claire reached the top of the stairs as Claus was leaving her husband's room. "How was your trip to the Cloisters?" he asked.

"A wild goose chase. Why are you here?" her voice rising.

He laid a finger over his lips. "He is resting now." In spite of his attempt to lead her away, Claire opened the door and looked in. The drapes were drawn, and the room was in deep shadow. Uta was adjusting something on the IV. Claire searched her husband's face from the doorway. On the flat and lowered bed, his hands folded on the coverlet, he seemed not to be breathing at all. An effigy. She gave a frightened glance at the doctor, who motioned her away. They stood together on the landing. "Is Ruth here or did she go home?" he asked her.

"She is here," Claire said.

"I need to talk with you. Perhaps you would like to have Ruth with us also?"

"Come down," she said; "we can sit in the living room."

Ruth came in from the kitchen and sat in on the sofa. Claus stood before the fireplace in which no fire ever burned. Claire went to the sideboard to pour herself a drink. Then she squared her shoulders and looked straight at the round little man opposite her. "So," she said, "what do you want to tell me?"

Claus looked at his wife. She gave him an almost imperceptible nod. "Claire," he began, "you know the pace of this cancer is very fast." Claire nodded. "We have been doing everything we can to keep your husband comfortable, but it has become very difficult. He is weakening and his mind is going."

"Yes. Yes, I know this. Tell me something I don't know."

Adenauer went on, a meticulous man, delivering a speech he had prepared in his mind. "For some time now he has persisted on the strength of his very considerable will power alone and his wish to see his daughter. I am afraid what I am doing now is…keeping your husband alive. He knows it, and I know it also."

"Keeping him alive? What does that mean? Of course, you are keeping him alive. I want you to go on 'keeping him alive.'" Claire took several swallows of her drink. She felt the touch of panic.

He went on in as calming a voice as he could muster. "He has been waiting for his daughter. He has asked me to do what I could to help him wait. We have managed to buy some time, but…" Here the good doctor let his shoulders finish his sentence in their slight lift and fall.

"But what? What are you telling me?"

"I am telling you that this morning your husband and I spoke, and he asked me to help him end this waiting." Did she understand?

"Asked you this morning? While I was gone! Is that why he wanted me away?" Dr. Adenauer did not indicate yes or no, but waited out the first salvo of Claire's anguish. "And you spoke? He spoke to you, but not to me about this. Why?"

"Perhaps because he needed to be in control of his own destiny." Claus said, for that was the simple truth of it. "Perhaps because he could not face doing this to you."

Claire knew the ring of truth when she heard it. *In control*. It was what she so admired in her husband, the deep power of his control. And no, he would not want to plead with her; he would not wish to ask her permission. Now he was marshaling this control one last time. "He's giving up, isn't he?"

"He is in a great deal of pain when he is awake. You cannot perhaps understand how much. The delusions persist. And when he is unconscious, well, he feels he might as well be dead."

"He's giving up *waiting*. That's what I mean." Claire was pacing the living room now. "He has given up on Parthia coming. His own daughter is not going to come! What do you think of that? Tell me! He gave everything to her. He made her what she is!" She looked hard at Dr. Adenauer. "When?" she barked at him. "When does he want you to kill him?"

"Claire please, we must not speak that way," Ruth rose and closed the open living room door.

"Oh! What shall we call it?" Claire exclaimed. "It's all words. Words! You have been ineffectual. All your science. For what?"

"Call it mercy," said Ruth. "Think of him, Claire. He has done everything he can to stay alive for you and for his daughter. He can't any longer. He shouldn't be asked to."

Claire stopped in her furious pacing, dazed like a beast into whose side someone has shot a dart. She found the nearest chair and slumped into it. Ruth came and sat on the footstool, taking Claire's hand. "When?" Claire asked again, this time wanting an answer.

"As soon as you..." Here the doctor took a breath; he had never dealt with anything so delicate. "A few last days."

"Damn that girl, damn and damn her to hell," said Claire, snatching her hand from Ruth. She went to the bar to make herself another drink.

Behind her back Ruth and Claus exchanged looks. "Perhaps she cannot come," Ruth said. "But it is time to let him go."

"That's not your husband up there," said Claire, wheeling on Ruth. "See what you say when it is." And with that she left the room, slamming the door behind her.

Ruth mopped up the spill on the sideboard. "Is there something we can do?" she asked her husband.

"*Nicht*," he answered her, shaking his head.

From upstairs they could hear Claire's voice shouting at Uta. They heard footsteps on the stairs, then the front door opening and closing. Ruth got up and left the living room. Moments later she came back. "Claire told Uta to get out; she said she didn't want any strangers around any more. The poor girl is standing on the front steps; she doesn't know what to do."

"Uta should not be dismissed. I shall go up in a little while. Wilhelm should not be left alone for too long. Go; call Uta back. Have her wait somewhere out of sight. Claire is being impulsive." Ruth left the room and returned shortly.

"Will it take long?" Ruth asked. "I mean when you decide to help him go?"

"No," said her husband with a sigh, "not long. I will add something to his drip. It is...easy. I doubt there will be a post-mortem inquiry."

Ruth was just sitting down again when the living room door was flung open. Claire had a telephone in her hand. "Call her!" she said advancing on Dr. Adenauer. "Call her and tell her."

"Call whom?" Claus asked.

"Call Parthia. Who else? Or call her fucking therapist! Call someone! You're a doctor; they will listen to you. Tell them!" The phone quivered in her outstretched hand

Claus took the receiver. Ruth spoke then, remembering the earlier call, "She called," she said.

"Who?" Claus and Claire spoke the same word at once.

"Vale Messenger. Just when we got home."

"What did she want?" Claire asked.

"To talk to you."

"I'm done talking to that bitch. Pleading with her for my own daughter. The ungrateful slut. Make me a drink."

Claire might not have been on screen for many years, but she could command a terrible presence. While she paced the room, Claus went to the bar and mixed her another drink, a weak one.

"Claire, please sit down, please." Ruth settled an arm around Claire's shoulder and guided her to a chair. "I know this is what you have feared. One is never ready..."

"I shouldn't have left him today. I wanted to stay with him." Then Claire turned a ravaged face towards the doctor, "He has decided hasn't he? He's set a date." Dr. Adenauer nodded. "When? When, damnit? Tell me."

"Friday," the doctor whispered. "A little time. But not too much."

"Will I at least be able to say good-bye? Will he even hear me?" It was grotesque, this scheduling of death.

"I think we can. Yes. He is a strong man. We have not exhausted all our resources." He handed Claire the glass.

"Thank you," she said. "I'm sorry. I'm..." She drank, shaking her head. "I'm not ready. I want to be...calm and beautiful for him. Tomorrow is Wednesday. Thursday. Friday. Two days. If she does not come tomorrow, then she will not come. She torments me. I must order flowers, lots of flowers; I want the room to be beautiful." She thought of what she would wear. The red dress: he would remember. It was the last image she wished him to have of her. God, it was unbearable.

She drank again. "Call the hospital, Claus. Ask for that Messenger woman. You've spoken to her before. She'll take your call, tell her. Tell her to get to Parthia." Claus hesitated. "Do it now!"

"I don't know the number."

Claire reeled it off.

Claus dialed, a cautious eye on Claire as if he expected her to pounce on him. There was a pause during which Ruth and Claire watched Claus intently as he made his request of the operator and listened to the reply. "Can you find her? This is an emergency." Again he waited. A much longer interval of silence. Then they heard him say, "Is this Mrs. Messenger?" He gave a glance at Claire, "Yes, this is Doctor Adenauer. Mrs. Alexander is here, and she urges in the strongest possible terms"---Claus saw Claire nod, her eyes never leaving his face---"that Parthia come home. Tomorrow, Thursday at the latest." There was silence in the room as Doctor Adenauer listened. "I see," he said. "Yes, I see. In that case…"

But before he could finish his sentence, Claire had leapt from her chair and seized the phone. "Messenger," she cried, "I don't know what you just said to the doctor, but I can guess that Parthia is too sick to come, or some such shit. Well, you tell her for me if she doesn't come, I'll make sure she doesn't inherit a cent from her father. You get that!" And not waiting for an answer Claire dashed the phone against the floor, where it bounced off the thick pile carpeting.

Ruth picked it up and replaced it on its cradle. Claire was half way out of the room when the phone rang. Claire returned and answered it.

"What do you want?" she asked. Then listened. Then spoke, "So my word is not enough? Her father's physician is not enough?" And to the answer, "I see."

She hung up the phone, her mouth in a hard bitter line. Ruth and Claus looked at her expectantly. "Messenger says Parthia wants her father to call her himself if he's so anxious to have her come home."

CHAPTER THIRTY-FOUR

When Julia returned to the unit on Wednesday after her overnight pass, she was stopped in the hall by Jean Newcombe. "Parthia keeps lying on top of your bed, Julia," she told her.

"What do you mean?" Julia asked, startled at the thought. She remembered catching Parthia looking through her journal, reading her books.

"She started lying on it almost as soon as you left for your pass. I reported it to Willa. We told her not to do it, but almost every time she gets up to go to the bathroom, or to meals, she comes back and lies on your bed. I was told she was sleeping in your bed last night. I'm sorry. She stuffed pillows under her sheets so it looked like she was asleep in her own bed. We don't know when she got up and got into yours. They put her back in her own bed immediately. We changed the sheets on yours this morning."

"What's going on?" Julia asked.

"Damned if we know. Her boundaries are getting pretty fuzzy, I guess."

"What should I do?"

"Don't know that either. We decided to see what would happen when you got back."

Julia, frightened, stepped into the room. Parthia was lying on her own bed with earphones over her ears, her back turned towards the door. The flowers by the bed were wilted, but Julia was amazed to see her own red kerchief under the glass, a square of color. She noticed, too, an indentation on her coverlet.

She made a little extra noise in putting her clothes away in the drawers. She went into the bathroom and closed the door a little hard.

When she came out, Parthia had rolled over. and though the headphones were still on, she was watching Julia move around the room. Julia lifted a hand as a wave. Parthia did not respond. There was no communication between them.

Later, Julia went out and cut some more flowers. She brought them to the room, threw the wilted flowers into the wastebasket, freshened the water in the jar, and arranged the flowers in the glass. Day lilies were in profusion now, purple phlox, small white daisies. Julia set the jar down on the bedside table, her movements followed by large blue eyes.

•◆•

Parthia had been the subject of a unit meeting Wednesday morning.

"I don't know whether any of you are cat people," Ben Farmer said, "but whenever I go away, I find the cat has been sleeping on my pillow or sitting on my reading chair. Never happens when I'm home."

"So what's that about?" Vale asked.

"Contact. Missing me."

"You think Parthia's missing Julia?" Willa asked. "Come on."

"Stranger things have happened."

"Maybe Parthia wants to *be* Julia," Al Ramsey suggested; he was the unit's veteran social worker.

"Who knows?" said Farmer. "I'll be interested to know what Julia makes of this, Vale."

"I will, too."

They did talk about it later in their session after Julia told Vale she thought she might have a job in a bookstore biking distance from her grandmother's house.

"I read the report about Parthia being on your bed. It is inappropriate, and at the same time we don't want to make too big a deal out of it."

"I don't mind," Julia said, "really."

"Still, Julia, it's a matter of boundaries."

"She used to go through my stuff when I wasn't there," Julia said. "Actually she knows pretty much everything. The 'question game' and all. So it's not a matter of feeling intruded upon."

"But keeping boundaries is an important issue for you."

"I guess. It just feels good to have her want to be in my space. It's kind of like wanting to be close to me."

"It may not be that simple. Feelings are not always the best guides; they can be warped by experience. Sometimes you need to look objectively at a situation. In this case, I think what is right for you is that you push back. It's not acceptable behavior. You need to confront it. I am sure this feels risky to you, but we can explore together the right way of getting this across."

Julia cringed inwardly at the thought of pushing Parthia away.

"And this cutting flowers for her?"

"Is that a problem, too?"

"Why are you doing it?"

"Well, I did it because...to make...I just thought it would be...I want to be.. to have..."

Gently Vale prodded, "Finish your sentence, Julia, 'you want to have' what?"

"A friend. I never had a friend, and I never thought I would have one." There were tears in Julia's eyes.

"Parthia cannot be your friend," Vale said, easing the hard fact across to her patient. "Not yet anyway. Hospital friendships can be very tricky."

"With all respect, Ms. Messenger, Parthia seems really alone and scared. She's been lying in my bed. It's kind of a pathetic way of trying to be close to someone. I know it's a weird and intrusive thing to do. Yet it also comes across to me as a reaching out. I am reaching back."

Vale felt a surge of pride and pleasure in the young woman before her. "So what do you want to do, Julia?"

"I want to be permitted to respond to Parthia, not as some sicko, but as a person in pain. I want to treat her the way I would want to be treated."

"She may turn on you in an instant, you know."

"I suppose she can."

Vale sat back in her chair, regarding the young woman before her, the mark of a rope burn like a pale pink necklace round her throat.

• ◆ •

The call for Parthia came in at a little after noon. Al Ramsey was at the nurse's station. "Gables," he said.

"Yes, hello," a voice said in his ear, a voice with very little strength in it and with an accent Ramsey could not place. "My name is Wilhelm Alexander. I am Parthia Alexander's father. I would like to speak with her."

Ramsy asked the man at the end of the line to hold. He launched himself upstairs, greeted Jean Newcombe, who was doing the status, and knocked on the half-closed door. "What?" a voice said.

"Parthia," Ramsey said, "your father is on the phone."

There was a long silence. Had she heard him?

"Parthia, it's your father, he's..."

"Tell him I will call him back."

"When?"

"I don't know."

"Can you...?

"Leave me alone!" the voice screamed out from the other side of the door.

Ramsey went back to the nurses' station where he passed on the message. To the caller's "When?" he could not give an answer. Then he called Vale's line to pas along the information.

Fifteen minutes later therapist and patient were seated in Vale's office, Parthia behind the desk for easier access to the phone. She had swiveled the chair so that she was partly turned away from Vale, but even from this angle, Vale could see the whites of Parthia's knuckles as she gripped the receiver.

"Let me speak to him," she said peremptorily into the receiver. There was a silence, then Parthia's head flinched back on her neck as if she had been slapped. "Yes," she said, "I can hear you." She was holding the phone away from her ear as if it were a feral thing with the power to do her harm. "I know," she said. And then a moment later, "I know," again. There was a longer pause while Parthia listened, and during it she half turned to find Vale with her eyes. Vale was astonished at the look on her patient's face, the look of a small frightened child. "I...don't know if I can," Parthia stammered. "I know what you want," she said. "I have always known what you wanted." And then as if that statement had taken all her strength, she placed the receiver on the desk. Vale reached over and picked it up. She heard a voice at the other end of the line saying "Parthia, are you there? Are you there?"

"Dr. Alexander," she said, "I am Vale Messenger, your daughter's therapist. I think she has said all she can say right now."

"But I need her to come home," the voice labored and wheezed.

"Sir, do you know where your daughter is? Has your wife told you?"

"Yes," the voice said.

"Sir, I am not sure what Parthia will decide to do about coming to see you."

"But I am her father," the voice said, as if he were invoking a law obligating daughters to the will of their fathers.

"I know, but the decision is hers." Vale heard the click of the line going dead.

Parthia sat in Vale's desk chair, her knees tucked up under her chin and held by encircling arms. Her whole body was shaking.

Vale went to her, squatting down so that she was at eye level, brushing the hair back from the forehead, pressing a Kleenex into her clenched hands. Parthia made no attempt to use it. Vale stroked her shoulders. They trembled under her hand. "That was very hard for you," she said; it was not a question.

"I don't know whether I can..." and broke off.

"Yes," said Vale, "I see that. You don't have to." Until that moment Vale had not known the depth of terror the girl carried in her bones. It now seemed an extraordinary act of courage to have made the call at all.

"I don't think I can face my father. When I picture going home, I picture sitting with him in a dark room, so dark I can't see him, and he can't see me." She looked over at Vale. "That's weird isn't it?"

Vale thought of how rape victims had been helped to encounter their perpetrators who, when blindfolded, gave the victim a psychological advantage. The eyes, Vale understood, the eyes held all the power.

"I think you can ask for whatever you want. He has called to see you. You can set the terms. If he doesn't like them, well, too bad. You have yourself to take care of. That's the most important thing."

"You really think...?" leaving the question unfinished.

"I think you can ask for what you want. Period."

Again they sat in silence. Vale could see by the tilt of her head that Parthia was trying things on for size. "I don't want Claire there. I don't want her listening. I don't want her anywhere near."

"It's your call."

"Claire was like a procuress for him." Parthia looked at Vale searching her face. "Do you know what I mean?"

Vale nodded. "I think I do," she said,

Parthia unclenched from her position, put her feet on the floor, stood. She walked unsteadily to the window. "I hurt all over."

"Take the time you need, "Vale said.

"There isn't much time, is there?"

"No. There isn't."

"I get just about ready to say I'll go, and then my stomach turns over, and I think I am going to be sick."

"I'll go with you if you want me to. We certainly won't let you go alone."

Parthia turned from the window. "You want me to go?"

"No, I'm just reminding you that you do not have to do this alone. I think that when you picture going you leave me out of the picture."

Parthia thought for a moment. "You're right, I do. When I am with him, I am always alone. No one is there, except Claire."

"Two against one."

"I was always less than one."

"What I want," Vale said, "is for you to make this decision. I will stand behind you, or beside you. Or in front of you for that matter. But the choice is yours."

"God, I'm scared Ms. Messenger. I'm really fucking terrified."

"I know."

"Give me a little more time," she said. "Could I maybe talk with you later this afternoon?"

"I could see you at three."

"I feel like such a baby."

"Well, baby yourself then. It's all right."

At three fifteen and no sign of Parthia Vale called the unit. Ten minutes later Jean Newcombe knocked on her door with Parthia in tow.

Vale was alarmed by what she saw.

For the first time Parthia appeared disheveled, hair awry, lipstick smeared, eye shadow on one eye only. Her tee shirt was untucked and the ends of her fingers were pink and red where the cuticles had been torn. There were welts on her cheeks as if she had walked through brambles. Her eyes jittered in her head. Her hands went to her face in patting and gripping motions. This, Vale thought, is madness. She nodded her thanks to Jean. Parthia sat on the edge of the blue chair, swaying.

"Parthia," Vale said, trying to call the girl's wandering attention. The blue eyes flitted to the source of sound, found Vale's face, seemed to awaken for a moment of recognition, and then slid away. Vale understood, as she had never understood before, how in the old days the spectacle of madness had bred a certainty of demons.

"Parthia," Vale said again and this time leaned forward and gently took the girl's hand.

"What?" Parthia said, her eyes slewing round to meet Vale's. A weak smile passed over dry lips then faded. "I can't," she said weakly. "I can't."

"Yes, I can see that. Can you find any words at all to tell me what is going on with you?"

"Can you help me get the bandages off?" Parthia said, running her tongue over her lips.

"Bandages?" Vale asked softly. "What bandages do you mean?"

"These," said the girl lifting her hands to her face. "On my face. I'm hot; my skin itches," and Parthia began to claw at her cheeks with her nails. Vale reached over to stop her. "Got to stop the itching."

With one free hand, Vale reached for her bag and withdrew a tube of skin lotion. "It just so happens I have the latest medication for itching skin, Parthia," she said unscrewing the cap with her teeth, then briefly freeing her hand to squeeze some of the lotion onto her palm.

"My name is Paula."

"Of course. Sorry."

"My skin itches so badly."

"Would you like me to put some cool cream on them for you?"

"Oh yes, please, please. When I ask Claire to, she says I must be patient that it will all be worth it in the end. But the itching is so bad. I can't sleep at night unless daddy gives me something to help me sleep. I look like a mummy."

"Here, dear Paula," said Vale. "It might sting just a little at first, but that will help the itching go away; then it will feel cool." Vale gently rubbed the girl's inflamed cheeks.

"That's good. It stings a little, but it's soothing."

"How long have you had the bandages on?" Vale asked.

"I don't know. I kind of lose track of time. I wish Daddy did the operation in the winter when it's cold, but then I would have to miss school. I need to get perfect grades. I can't miss school. I get my reward when it's over. We go to Europe. I wish it could be just me and Daddy and not Claire. Mustn't say that. Don't tell."

"No, I won't tell." Vale reached for a little more lotion. "I'll have a special doctor come and see if he can't give you something to help you sleep a little this afternoon. I'm sure the itching will be better too after a little while.'

"I don't want another injection. Daddy gives me so many injections. I don't want another inj..." The figure in the chair was stiff and upright the hands reaching to stop the massage on her cheeks.

"No, no injections. Just a pill to help you relax and sleep," Vale said.

"Who are you?" frightened hands now gripping Vale's, and pulling Vale around before her.

"My name is Vale Messenger," she said, sitting down.

"What are you...? I..." Then Parthia covered her face and eyes with her hands. A tremor passed over her body. Then, the head lifted and Vale could see Parthia was back. "Ms. Messenger, I can't get a grip on myself. I've been... somewhere else. I was back there in my father's operating room, the one in the basement. I had bandages on my face; they itched so much I wanted to tear my skin off. I...I feel so embarrassed," said Parthia. "I don't remember what's happened. Dr.---I mean Ms. Messenger. I want...I'm scared."

A half hour later, with Parthia back on the unit, Vale sat in her office feeling a little shaky herself. She placed a call to Dean, and Arlene put her through.

She brought him up to date. He said that it made perfect sense to him that Parthia would experience this sudden loss of ground, this resurgence of powerful memory, this regression. Her father's immanent death must raise to the surface of her conscious mind the wreck of old deeply buried agonies. "This is a good sign, especially the part about Paula. Don't let them over-medicate her. You can work for a long time before the symptoms flush out into the open. The beast is in view. Make sure she gets rest. She will need her strength, but don't let them give her anti-psychotics. You want the psychosis. It's the code. You want to know what she's going through." There was a pause. Then he said, " What you are doing, Vale, is what I call 'primary care.' In our work we very rarely get the chance to reach this level, the level where trauma occurred, and its consequences were actually formed. You are on holy ground."

•◆•

Wednesday half past three, Vale's phone rang.

"Is this you, Messenger?"

"Mrs. Alexander."

"I understand Parthia is not coming home. I get it."

"She can't, Mrs. Alexander. She just can't, and you'll have to take my word for it."

"I give up, but my husband will not. He says he wants you to come in her place."

"Me?"

"He wants to tell her something, and he knows she will not listen to him."

"He could tell you."

"No, he insists on speaking to you."

"I see."

"Listen, I don't like this situation. You don't belong. His daughter by rights should be at his side. But he is asking for you. It's Friday. Do you understand? Friday about the middle of the day. Curtains. Don't ask me why then and not Saturday or Sunday. It makes no sense."

"And he wants me there? When?"

"Soon. Tomorrow morning."

"Claire, I can't get away without notifying my supervisor and my patients. I can't come tomorrow."

"Then come Friday. Come early in the morning. At nine. After that it will be too late. Do you understand?"

"Claire, I don't know whether..."

"For Christ sake, Messenger, is this so much to ask? The man is dying. It's a simple request. Just show up. If not, well the hell with you. The hell with all of you!" And the line went dead.

• ◆ •

Finding she could leave work earlier than expected, Vale left a message for Win, altering their plans. She had time, she said, to go back to her place. Could he pick her up there? She gave him the address, directions, and her phone number.

Once home she caught a quick shower, and changed into jeans and a blue denim shirt with pearl buttons. She packed a few toiletries in a big shoulder bag, pondered what to wear if she slept over, decided on pajamas, felt like a fool, and was spared more indecision by Win's ring at the door.

They chatted, listened to the news---Mondale had chosen Geraldine Ferraro as his running mate---and were spared rush hour traffic jams. Once arrived at his apartment, neither said anything about the sleeping arrangements, but

Vale found the little room prepared for her, fresh towels on the bed, the top bureau drawer empty, a glass shelf in the bathroom cleared for her toiletries.

Win had prepared a cold pasta dinner; then they threw the dishes into the sink and headed for the subway. He was in a hurry, no more wanting to miss the opening pitch than a theater-goer wants to miss the rising of the curtain. He carried a green poncho over his shoulder for her. "Always good to be prepared. Forecast said there was a chance of rain."

On the way to Yankee Stadium, he talked about baseball, telling her more than she wanted to know about the Yankees and the Minnesota Twins. Half an hour later they were passing through the turnstiles and into the belly of the stadium with its maze of ramps and corridors, its concession stands and bathrooms along the walls, its barkers with their wares of scorecards and Yankee paraphernalia. She heard the distant roar of the crowd seated above them. They walked up a ramp and into a vast space that opened about her, filled with the clamor of a many-tongued multitude.

They found their seats up behind third base under the overhanging upper deck. Win was rattling off the names of players. Vale was taking in the color, detail, spectacle, and variety of this enormous theater. Then an invisible voice sang out over loud speakers, "Oh say can you see, by the dawn's early light...," and twenty thousand people stood under the banner of a tired old anthem. She slipped her hand in Win's and squeezed it. As the last chord faded, and the crowd began its rolling cheer, she stood on her toes and leaned towards his cheek with a light quick kiss. "Thank you," she said, "this is just what I needed."

"Yeah," he said, "it gets me every time. Even though I hate the Yankees with a passion."

With so much to understand and Win so interested to explain it to her, the early innings whizzed past in a series of long duels between pitcher and batter, short sprints after rabbit-fast ground balls, one stupendous fly that was caught in deep center field.

With the novelty fading, the middle innings dragged, and the slatted wooden seat grew harder under her. Other concerns, held at bay, returned, worrying her mind. She replayed in her mind the brief and broken conversation with Melanie of two nights before and felt queasy again with the sense of a new distance between them, of something important she had missed. Perhaps it was the first of many things that she would miss, the sum total of which would constitute her daughter's independent life. Melanie was for the first time out of reach.

Win's touch on her sleeve brought her back to the ballpark. "Look," he said to her.

It had begun to rain, a slight thickening of the air into moisture, a haze that captured the light of the field and softened it. The game was going on, but with all its edges slightly blurred, as if something like a pale translucent veil had fallen over the entire scene.

Despite the rain, no one moved from their seats. Newspapers spread like triangular caps over glistening heads. The better equipped huddled under the tents of raingear and umbrellas. On the field uniforms clung to shoulders, a batter wiped his hands continuously. Motion slowed.

Then, as players slogged and balls went sailing, there was a crack of thunder almost directly over their heads. It made Vale's heart lurch. Before its echo died, the rain became a downpour. Below her in the box seats and across the field in the bleachers and the exposed upper decks, she saw fans scamper for protection, and many to the exits. She watched as a grounds' crew in double time drew a tarpaulin over the field as neatly as making a bed. The outfield grasses sparkled now; small puddles formed in indentations. Time seemed to stop. Music came over the loudspeakers, but was muffled in the hiss of falling water. Finally, a voice announced that the game was being called. The Twins were ahead by a run; in the record books the game was theirs. There were a few boos, laughter, distant cheers. The masses, dispersing from under the eaves, streamed to the exits.

"Shouldn't we be going?" Vale asked Win, who had not moved.

"There's no hurry," he said. "The subways will be packed with wet bodies. Are you warm enough?" She was. Despite the torrent the night was still humid. Win put his feet up on the empty seat in front of him. There were only a few fans here and there, mostly couples like themselves who sat under the awning of the upper deck and stared, transfixed as the tarp over the infield filled up with water and light. The green expanse beyond it shimmered like a veldt in a monsoon. The rain poured down now, arcing off the bottom lip of the upper deck in spouts and waterfalls. The bright lights caught the lines of rainfall in endless patterns. The stadium whispered with a sound as peaceful as the sea.

Vale leaned against Win; the barrier of the metal arm of her seat between them dug into her ribs. She trembled, though she was not chilled. In this all but deserted amphitheater under the canopy of rain, she felt small and young and unequal to the demands of her days. Win tugged at her arm, bringing her to her feet, and he drew her down onto his lap. He wrapped an arm around her shoulders, and she leaned back against him, letting her body relax against his, feeling his chest, the warmth of him, smelling a trace of garlic on his breath, a whiff of beer. He drew the slicker over her shoulders as together they watched the rain falling endlessly from the dark. Then a grid of lights blinked off. Then a second rack of lights snuffed out. The field before them receded into a watery haze. The tarp had become a shallow, silver pond.

Slowly she lifted herself away from him and stood up. He stood also. They were holding hands. It was like standing in a great cathedral, she thought. His hand squeezed hers and, leaving behind the surreal gloom of the field as yet another grid of lights blacked out, they followed the concrete ramp to the inner corridors and wound their way down towards the street. There, as if waking from a spell, they sprinted towards the subway and took the journey home.

Vale woke in his big bed, the space beside her empty. She lay in the drowse of morning, aware of her skin, warm and soft to her own senses, a purr of ease in her stretch.

Where was he?

She got up and put on her pajamas, and without a glance in the mirror, without a visit to the bathroom, she padded out in bare feet to find him. She saw him from the bedroom door, down the hall, at the far end of the big space; he was standing among his orchids in the light that came down through the skylights above him. He did not sense her, and she watched him, from this distance, where he stood standing in some reverie, some stillness. And as she watched, she felt this girlish desire rise in her to run down the hall and to leap into his arms.

"Win," she called.

He turned and saw her. She saw a smile break out on his face, and before he could say a word, she was running towards him. He opened his arms, and she leapt.

CHAPTER THIRTY-FIVE

Now she is frozen in a grip of fire. She is a bandaged face in a hall of mirrors: *l'enfant dans l'enfer.*

Now she is a little girl, wandering through the gloomy, unlit rooms of a great house: "Mami! Mami!" she cries. She gets a glimpse of faded flowers in one of the rooms, of candles flickering... "Mami, come out now!" But Mami will not come out. The little girl has to find her, but the house is too big; it seems to go on forever. "Mammmmiiiii!"

Now she thrashes from side to side, terrified, knowing she is dreaming, but unable to wake. Locked awake in the dream. Buried alive. She does not want to go any farther into the corridors... Mami is not going to come out. Ever again.

Eyes open. She stares up at the slope of a roof over her head. Heat. There is a small window beside her covered in iron mesh Light is filling the window from a pale blue sky. Thirst. The window is closed. Coop. Chicken coop. Cooped up... The coop is hot. Her face is stinging as if she had a sunburn... *Dance in the flames / Burn up your names.*

Thirst, a dry tongue touches dry lips. There is a small chest of drawers at her feet. Without moving her head she shifts her eyes to the right and sees that woman seated on a chair by the doorway. Her face in shadow. Claire? It is Claire waiting for the bandages to come off. She sees a white porcelain washstand in one corner of the room. Thirst. Bedside table. A glass of water. Slowly she begins to lift a hand towards the glass of water. She cannot move her hand. She tries to move the other. It too is bound. Then she begins to scream, her voice in her own ears hoarse and desperate as if she is being suffocated.

• ◆ •

Vale was in the middle of her session with Julia that Thursday morning when a call came from the unit.

"I'm sorry, Julia, I have to look in on Parthia." The girl nodded and rose. She understood; she soothed the flame of protest with reason, and it submitted.

The night before Parthia had awakened from her sleep with a shriek and thrashed her way out of bed, stumbling like a blind person, knocking into the desk chair, overturning it, cursing with the pain of a bruised shin, then raking at her face with her hands. Terrified Julia had run towards her trying to keep the hands away from their furious work, but Parthia had hurled her away. Already red welts showed drops of blood. The mental health worker sitting status came bursting into the room; together she and Julia tried to restrain the claws. Back-up arrived, pushing Julia aside; they subdued Parthia and put her in a camisole; then the needle sedated her. They carried her away. It took an hour for Julia's heart to steady.

"We'll finish our session before I leave for the day, I promise."

Now, seated beside Parthia in the converted attic room under the eaves where a single patient could be kept in seclusion, Vale lifted the plastic bottle and offered refreshment to the young woman who lay back on propped pillows as weak and wan as someone in and out of high fever. Scratch lines ran down Parthia's cheeks like the tracks of bloody tears. The marks were exactly like those Vale had seen on her admission.

Gratefully, eagerly the lips sucked, a tongue licked over blotchy lips; a trickle of water ran down the chin. Vale reached over and dabbed at it with a Kleenex. "Thank you," said the small voice. "Why am I tied like this?" she asked raising her hands to the length of their tether and letting them fall back by her side.

Vale removed her compact from her handbag and flipped open the mirror. She held it so that Parthia could look at her own face. "You have been tearing at your face," Vale said. Parthia kept her eyes fastened on the small cameo of her face in the quivering glass. All she could think of was that her father would be very angry with her. Vale was still talking, "I'm sorry," she was saying. "This must be very hard for you to be so helpless."

The word brought Parthia's full attention back to her therapist. "How long will I...?" and again she lifted her hands to the length of their tether and let them fall.

"Until we can be sure you won't tear at yourself again. Or, if you prefer, we can put the gloves on you."

"The gloves?"

"Yes, they're specially made gloves that will prevent you from using your fingernails. They are locked at the wrist so you can't pull them off." The treatment of the mad had not much changed in three hundred years.

"No. Not gloves."

In the past twenty-four hours Parthia had unraveled beyond what Vale had ever seen in a patient, beyond what she had thought possible. Madness, a fury deaf to all interruption.

"What is this place?" Parthia asked. "Why am I here?"

"It's called the Quiet Room. A patient is put here only when they need to be restrained. You will have someone here to help you with what you need." Parthia looked down, appeared ashamed. Vale reached a hand out and lifted her chin. "Parthia, what do you remember?"

"I was in a house. It was dark. I was looking for Mami. She was dead. There was a room in which she had been laid. I could not go in." She lifted her head from the pillow, "May I have more water, please."

Vale filled the plastic bottler from the bedside pitcher and held it for Parthia to drink. She was remembering Melanie, home from school with a flu, the trusting eyes looking up over the rim of the Cinderella cup, the cheeks blushed from fever, the small hot hand over hers. "What else?" Vale asked.

"Is my father...? Parthia could not finish the sentence.

"There is no news. The time is very short now."

"I know I should go, but I can't. I don't know what's happening to me."

"Right now you need to rest."

"Will I be able to get up?"

"Of course. We will let your hands be free as long as you are awake and aware. You can go to meals if you want. Attend a group. At night we will need to bring you here until we are sure you have your self-control back." Parthia nodded. "I'll undo you now," Vale said.

"Thank you," said Parthia.

Vale bent over and uncinched the canvass strap that held Parthia's right hand to the metal frame of the bed. Then she stood and leaned over the girl to do the same with the other hand.

Vale felt the grip of Parthia's hand on her wrist. She did not pull away. Parthia tugged on the arm. "I'm so scared."

Vale cupped the girl's cheek for the briefest caress. "I know," said Vale. "You must be."

"I am losing my mind," Parthia whispered as if it were a secret to be kept from the girl seated by the door. "I feel like I can't hold it still. My mind has a mind of its own." And she smiled weakly at her own sad joke. Vale smiled also. "I wish you could stay with me," Parthia said.

"I know," Vale said. "I'll stay for a while. Close your eyes. You are safe. You need to rest."

Parthia's stared at Vale, and then slowly her eyes closed.

Down at the nurse's station Vale left explicit orders that she was to be called if there was any change for the worse.

•◆•

The rest of her day passed without incident.

She spoke to Rivers about Claire's request and was told that the matter was entirely up to her. It was certainly an unusual request, and Vale should keep uppermost her patients' well-being. Did Parthia know of the summons, and had she expressed herself in the matter? Vale told Rivers that Parthia was psychotic. "Ahh, then, you will have to decide on your own."

Vale was aware of a kind of inward reflex to turn toward her sister. Naomi would advise, Naomi would know what to do. And Vale was aware that she was denying that turn. It alarmed her to think she was cutting herself off from solace and wisdom, yet she felt that this was her ordeal to see through. It was not that she felt any glimmer of confidence in what she had done or the outcome ahead, but she felt in some way that Win anchored her; Dean and Rivers guided her; and her own instincts, though often contradictory, had not, so far, proven disastrous. And further, dimly sensed and cautiously nursed, she felt something happening in her own heart. Perhaps it was– – –well, surely it was in part due to this warmth, this heat, that came to her from Win and which, God knows, she returned–––but it was also something that included her patients, all of them, not just Julia and Parthia, who had occupied the foreground for several weeks. What that feeling was did not give its name to her, but it was a mix of tenderness, care and carefulness, respect, amazement. Murky, yes, impenetrable this valley of shadows, but there was something singing inside her, a keenness, alert and profoundly interested. She no longer wondered about this therapy business. She wondered deeply about her ability to do it; she was humbled; but she no longer doubted the value, the power, of the work itself. "Primary care," the phrase came back to her, and Dean's words, "You are on holy ground."

When she saw Julia again that afternoon, she signed her out for a weekend pass to start Friday evening. She had her last session with Liza-Jane, who was handling her termination from the hospital by talking tough, saying how glad she was to be getting out of this "fucking nut house." Raymond had finally decided to re-apply to college and had brought his application to her office. Together they had filled it out. It was a big step for a learning-disabled young man. His father was willing to let Raymond live with him for six months while he got started. Raymond had been clean for two months and was regularly attending the hospital twelve-step group. He had a sponsor.

Before looking in on Parthia, she was able to reach Melanie, and they had a good talk. The cloud had lifted. Meli was only three days from coming home. Robert was picking her up on Saturday. They were going to the Mystic Seaport Museum and the Aquarium. They would stay overnight and take the ferry across the Sound on Sunday morning.

They chatted about what they would do together during the rest of the summer, about Y-camp during the August days, weekends with her father and Elaine.

"They're moving." Meli said.

"When," Vale asked. For the first time she was getting information from her daughter and not from Robert.

"This month. Daddy starts his new job after Labor Day."

"Excited?" Vale forced herself to say.

"I guess so," Meli replied. Then quickly changed the subject, "Will we be going to visit Aunt Yes-Yes?"

"Definitely."

"Positively?"

"Absolutely."

"Doubtlessly?"

"Actually, sugar, the word is 'indubitably,'" and Meli, ever avid for words, sounded this one out.

"Bye, Mommy."

"Bye, my darling."

On her way to Gables at the end of her day, Vale took a detour up to the worksite for the conference center. The project was gathering momentum now. A yellow tape marked the area off; a big maple had been cut down and its roots dug up. She caught sight of Win, walking down from the Administration Building. He saw her and waved. "What are you doing in my neck of the woods?" he asked, when they met; he restrained the impulse to throw his arms around her.

"Just wanted to see you."

"Me, too."

"I'd love to say come into my office, but I don't want to deal with the gossip. You have any plans for the evening?"

"No, not really."

"You getting ready to leave here?"

"Just need to look in on Parthia," she said, as they skirted the worksite, reached the service road, and turned up hill towards the rear of Gables. "You want to have a drink or something?"

"'Or something?'" she smiled.

They passed the parking lot. Vale was conscious of people emptying from the units and offices, heading home. She felt conspicuous.

"How about dinner at my place?" The words were hardly out of her mouth before she realized she had nothing to offer.

"Sure," he said before she could recant.

"Give me a head start." She looked at her watch. "Come at six."

"I can shower here. I always keep a change of clothes in my locker."

"How do you feel about Chinese take-out?"

"After caviar and lobster thermidor it's my preferred diet."

"I'll do Chinese take-out. You bring something to drink."

"You like Sake, don't you?"

"You know I do."

"Then we're set. See you soon," and as he passed her to go back down the hill, he brushed briefly against her flank.

She learned from the duty nurse that Parthia had taken a lipstick and drawn marks a foot apart from floor to ceiling on one bathroom wall. Vale went up and found the girl in bed with the sheet pulled up under her shin. She was not restrained, which Vale took as a good sign, but she was shivering. Vale fetched a cotton blanket from the linen closet in the hall and laid it over her. Then she sat down beside Parthia, taking her hand, feeling the tremble slowly subside. "Do you have to leave me?" Parthia asked.

"I do," Vale said.

"What is happening at home? With my father?"

"The end is near." How helpful the old euphemism, how true. "Claire reports your father wants me to come."

"Really? Why?"

"I don't know exactly. Next best thing to you, I guess."

"Are you going?"

"What do you think I should do?"

"I don't know. What will you do?"

"Sleep on it, I think."

"Can I see Julia, Ms. Messenger?"

"Jean is here, Parthia. She'll..."

"But..."

"Yes?"

"Just for a while. I want her to...to read to me."

•◆•

Vale called ahead to the Chinese restaurant. She had never asked Win what he wanted. They had a sea bass special and chicken with cashew nuts. By the time she got home it was ten to six. She turned the oven on low and transferred their dinner into casserole dishes. Then she dashed through the apartment, stashing unread newspapers, closing the hamper on her dirty laundry, seeing the disarray of her desk. Yesterday's clothes went under the bed. She changed her earrings, applied a touch of lipstick, and set the little round table.

Ten minutes later, Win was at her door, bearing in one hand a bouquet of flowers, in the other, a bottle of sake. As Vale ushered him in, she was aware that he was the first man to cross her threshold since she and Robert had parted. Suddenly the apartment felt small, revealing, unprepared. Traces of Melanie were everywhere, the refrigerator a collage of her pictures, the little bedroom a menagerie of stuffed animals. What would that be like for him?

While she put the flowers in a vase, he poured some sake into a pitcher and set the microwave to heat it. He read the signs of her domestic life, bookshelves everywhere, a desk in a corner with a typewriter on it, warrens full of letters, bills, envelopes. And photographs on the walls, some merely tacked up, others in frames. "These yours?" he asked.

"Yes," she said, pretending not to notice or care. She brought their food to the table. "Chopsticks or fork?" she asked

"Fork," he said.

"These all taken on Fire Island?"

"They are. Come on and eat."

But he lingered, looking. She had several black and white blow-ups of dune fencing, throwing long shadows on the sand. There was a surf-fisherman at dusk, his line bent hard with the weight of a catch, and beyond him a full moon was rising over the sea. Either a lucky shot or the result of hours spent waiting and seeing, he surmised. There were several pictures of monarch butterflies in the dune grasses. "I like these," he said. "All of them." She could tell he meant it.

"Thanks. I used to take a lot of pictures. Let's eat," she said.

As they ate, some part of him, estranged for years from a domestic life, a woman's touch, a child's presence, stirred. The small kitchen was clean and bright. Through the open door to Melanie's room, he saw a panda on the bed. The door to Vale's bedroom was open. Evening light filtered through gauzy curtains. The room was the color of a soft June sky.

Vale, too, was sensing him in her space. The sake demi-tasse in his fingers was a kind of metaphor, as if a giant had stumbled into a children's tea party. He needed the acreage of his New York loft or the space of the sea around him. He dwarfed her table, and she feared the dining room chair might crack under his weight.

Then she was remembering the heft and bulk of him naked beneath her and then above her, a mere night ago. His body so near now raised her pulse. She liked the light in his hair, the working hands with a broken nail and a mending scab, the shy, uncertain blue eyes. Her heart seemed to swim like a loose fish under her breastbone. Had she not the single burdening question of what to do about Claire's request, she would have skipped dinner and taken him right to bed.

Later, with the dishes quickly disposed of, they were seated in the living room, he on the wicker chair, she on the couch. They had the last of the sake between them, a small carafe set in a tea kettle, keeping it warm. They sipped their thimble cups, and she broached her dilemma, "Claire Alexander conveyed to me that the old man wants me to show up at his bedside tomorrow morning since Parthia can't come."

"That seems a bit outrageous, doesn't it?"

"It does." She looked over at him, the tanned sun-creased face---not all those creases were from the sun, she knew---looked back at her with attentiveness.

"What's going on with Parthia?"

"Psychotic," she said. "Or in and out. She clings to me as if she was three years old, and I'm responding to her. I mean how could one not?"

"You sound like you're afraid of something."

"I suppose I am. I'm afraid that I will make a mistake in judgment, get too close so that I can't see what to do, or will in some way act out of some kind of self-interest and lose sight of what's best for Parthia. I know I've been missing Melanie terribly."

"You think Parthia is kind of filling an empty place in your life?" Then he smiled a little at her, seeing in her face a sudden vulnerability and confusion. "Maybe," he said, "you have a different empty place. Not one left by a child."

She wanted to say, "Look who's talking." She wanted to say, "Less empty than it was a week ago---a day ago." But she said nothing.

Win saw fatigue in the lines around her eyes and mouth. He realized he was drawn to this face, serious sometimes, playful at others, a face that had shown him its passion. He remembered watching her read the book section of The Times at Biron's, intent, amused, intelligent. "In everything you do, you lead with your heart," he said to her. "I'm not sure you really know how rare that is. And it's an intelligent heart. It is a heart that is connected to some intuitive, instinctive sense of people."

"But how do you know? I mean you haven't seen me with patients?"

"I've seen you with me," he said.

She patted the couch beside her, and he came over and sat. She took his hand in hers. She wanted to move that hand over her body. He turned his hand palm up. "So what do you think you'll do?" he asked.

"I'll go," she said. "I'll go tomorrow morning to the Alexander's house and stand in for Parthia. I'll be her witness or proxy. I would have liked to ask her what she wanted from me, but she was in no shape to think about this."

"Do you want me along tomorrow by any chance?"

She shook her head. "No, it's strange enough, but thanks. And thanks for listening. I've got to call the unit and tell them I'm not going to be in till noon."

"Anything I can do?"

"Yeah, put on some music," pointing to her CD's and the stereo.

"Anything in particular?"

"Surprise me." Then she went into the bedroom with the phone and closed the door, crossing her fingers that all was well, or at least stable, at North Forks. It was, and in two minutes she had fresh sheets on the bed.

CHAPTER THIRTY-SIX

The ring of her phone awakened Vale from a deep, dreamless slumber.

As she moved away from the body beside her, she felt the night air on her skin. Win stirred, but did not wake. She closed the bedroom door behind her, carrying the phone with its long cord to the kitchen.

Tersely Celia, the Gables' night nurse, gave Vale the news that Parthia was raving and vomiting. "Sorry, but there's a note here saying you wanted to know if there were any changes. Shall we sedate her?"

"No. Tell her I am coming. Thirty minutes."

Vale started the coffee while she ran some water over her face, threw on a pair of jeans and a tee shirt, and caught her hair in a ribbon. She left a note for Win: "Gone to NF. Parthia. Half past four. May be back by the time you get up. If not, call." Cup in hand she got in her car and raced to North Forks on deserted roads, her mind gripped by visions of the wretched girl. It seemed as if her father's dying was releasing some toxin into Parthia's psychic bloodstream.

Now Vale stood at the door of the Quiet Room with the night girl on SA. "She's been having a pretty hard time of it. She threw up after dinner---induced, we thought---and then we heard her retching in the bathroom every few hours since then. We kept her hydrated. Fed her some ice-cream, some dry toast. She was hungry, but she wasn't able to get to sleep. She'd sort of slip into a kind of delirium, kept crying, "Mami, Mami.' It was a heart-breaking sound. Then an hour ago she had the heaves and was screaming, 'I want to see her. I want to see her.' We thought she meant you. We had to restrain her hands again. She did finally fall asleep on her own just a little while ago."

Vale entered her patient's room and pulled up a chair beside the bed. She did not loose Parthia's bonds. She just sat and watched.

At first Parthia had seemed somewhat calm; then a twitching began in the feet and legs, small fluttering, warding off gestures with the tethered hands. The head began turning from side to side in widening arcs. The feet kicked at the sheets. Then Parthia began panting; sweat soaked the thin nightdress, and her eyes were squeezed shut. Reddish discolorations showed up on her cheeks, on her throat, her chin, her eyelids, around her mouth, along her hairline. Everywhere the knife has been? Vale wondered. What might the body, hidden under the sheet, reveal?

Then the features of her face began to twitch and contort; and suddenly the lips were pulled back into a horrible grimacing grin as if invisible fingers stretched them. The eyes shot wide open, staring and unseeing, and the hands at the end of their bonds quivered in the air. Then her whole body arched as if it were trying to get away from the mattress, as if the mattress were charged with an electric current. Parthia's mouth opened to a long raving scream. Then her body fell back to the bed, breathing slowed to something like normal, the eyelids fluttering briefly, then she woke. "You're here," she said in a hoarse voice.

"Yes," said Vale, and she reached over and untied the girl's hands.

Parthia rubbed her wrists, then reached for the plastic bottle and drank.

"What about my father? Has it happened yet?

"I will be going to the house this morning, soon."

Parthia was quiet, then whispered, "You're brave." Parthia handed the empty bottle to Vale and lay back.

"Can you tell me anything of what you have been going through?"

"Dreams," said Parthia in a low voice, "dreams that seem to go on forever. I'm watching them, and then I am in them. They're all about Daddy and me. In one of the dreams I am in a museum, again, but not the part of the museum where they display the art. Not like in those dreams I told you about. I'm in the workshop part of the museum where they, you know, work on the art."

"Where they do restorations?"

"Yes, that's it, where damaged works of art are restored. And in one of these rooms is my father. He's wearing a white smock and a stethoscope; he looks like a doctor but then he looks like an artisan, like a restorer. There's a statue in front of him. It's a bigger-than-life-sized statue of a fat little girl. She is very

ugly. 'Little piggy,' the man is saying, 'what shall we do with you, *schweinchen?*'
It's a very realistic statue; you'd almost swear that the stature was a real girl
standing very still and holding her breath. Then Daddy in the dream picks up
a tool; it's a knife, like a scalpel, but he uses a mallet, and he starts to cut away
at the skin of the ugly fat girl, and she can't move, because she's a statue, but..."
here Parthia squeezed her eyes shut as if to block out the picture "...she is feeling
it. All of it!" These were the last words Parthia seemed able to speak. She was
overcome with a tremor that passed over her body making the skin mottle.
Then the head titled back, and from deep in the throat a single piercing "NO!"

Vale reached out and pulled at her hand. The muscles were locked and the
skin ice cold. "Parthia," she said, "Parthia, open your eyes. Look at me." The eyes
remained shut, the girl quivering, head straight again, lips sealed. She seemed
caught in a vise. "Parthia," and then in a flash another name came to her, "Paula,
she said leaning forward, "Paula, wake up. It's only a bad dream."

The girl on the bed writhed once more; the hands came up and thrashed
the air, inadvertently striking Vale. Vale was about to try to grab the flailing
hands when they stopped and dropped to the bed. Then the limbs went slack.
Parthia's eyes fluttered open. "What did you say?" she asked in a weak voice.
"What did you call me?"

"I called you Paula." Vale reached over with the washcloth and dabbed at
Parthia's face. The scabbed welts were bright red.

"I want my mother," Parthia said, tears welling out of her eyes. "I am so
scared. She left me alone with him. Why did she leave me alone with him?" But
the words were hardly out of her mouth before she said," I'm going to be sick."

Parthia pushed past Vale to the bathroom. She just made it through the
open door before she doubled over and began retching, the sound hoarse and
harsh in her throat, the meager contents of her stomach spewing out. Vale
stood at the bathroom door, watching Parthia on her hands and knees in the
shower stall, a creamy puddle of bile gathering over the drain.

Then Parthia's hands gripped the aluminum edge of the stall. She straightened her arms and legs at the same time until her body was a drawn upwards
in a triangle, and using a terrible kind of force, barked and barked from deep
in her throat, like a wild wounded dog trying to expel something. From her
mouth flew small gobbets of vomit and spittle. Her face was crimson with the
strain, the welts on her cheeks strident. Vale reached over and held the girl's
burning forehead in her hand. Again and again some spasm twisted the girl's

innards, but now nothing came out of her mouth; spittle dangled from her chin in long threads while the sound, a choking caw, echoed and was amplified in the enclosed shower stall, the sound of a wounded animal, growing hoarse with its efforts, the whole body trembling in the strange inverted posture. Vale was astonished at the girl's strength. "Exorcism" was the word that came into her mind.

Finally the body slumped to the floor, coming to rest against the wall. Her hair was pasted against her forehead and the nape of her neck. Vale reached into the shower stall and turned on the faucet, washing the swill of puke down the drain. Then she shut the shower off, closed the lid of the toilet and sat down. For a while the two women remained as they were---Parthia with her back against the wall, legs straight out in front of her, chin against her chest, panting. Vale seated, watching, seeking to understand this stormy catharsis.

Parthia sighed and looked up, eyes watery, her face waxy. "I stink," she said.

Vale reached into the stall and turned on the water again; she adjusted the temperature, then closed the stall door. "Can you stand up?" she asked.

Parthia gathered herself and with Vale's help wobbled to her feet. She leaned against the wall, her breath shallow, her color ashen. "Dizzy," she whispered.

After a few moments she was able to stand unsupported. "Let's get you cleaned up," Vale said.

Parthia nodded. "Can you help me?"

Vale reached down and pulled up the hem of Parthia's nightgown and lifted it over the girl's upraised arms, aware of the young woman's body, seeing red marks around the breasts and buttocks. Vale opened the stall door and with a steadying hand passed Parthia into the stream of the shower and closed the door. Through the stippled glass she could see the girl standing in the spray, one hand gripping the railing along the back of the stall.

Vale sat back down on the closed lid of the toilet while Parthia washed; the steam rose around her, misting the mirror. She had a picture then---it had come to her when she saw Parthia's body distorted through the mottled glass of shower door---of the girl's flesh subtly stitched with scars, tucks, folds, places where fat had been suctioned out and the skin sutured closed. Once she had seen tiny scars behind the ears, but now others, around the ankles or knees, showed like minute signatures of the hand that made them, the restorer's hand.

The intimacy of the acts to which Parthia had been subjected were violations of a father's will onto the child's flesh. A kind of terrible incest. Parthia was like some totem figure, a libidinal object that had been charged with her father's obsession. Were the girl not there before her, her torment all too real, Vale would have had trouble believing that such monstrosities were possible. What were human beings capable of?

Then she heard the water stop. The shower door swung open, and Parthia stood naked, gleaming and apparently unashamed in front of her. "Well, you look better than you did five minutes ago," Vale said, amazed that the body showed no sign of its secrets.

She handed Parthia a towel, and the girl dried herself. "Let me see if I can find something for you to put on," Vale said, and searching through the drawers in a bureau in the Quiet Room, she found a pair of hospital drawstring pants and an oversized white cotton tee shirt.

Parthia was brushing her teeth. Vale left the clothes on the toilet seat and then set about remaking a bed with clean sheets and pillowcases. When Parthia came in from the bathroom, brushing out her hair, Vale had the pillows plumped and the sheet drawn back. Parthia crawled back into bed. "I'm so tired," she said, "but I am afraid to go to sleep. My dreams are so bad."

"I'm sorry," was all Vale could think to say.

"So you will go to see him?" Parthia lay looking up at Vale.

Vale had feared the question would set off another sequence, for Parthia's present calm seemed as shallow as a half held breath. "I will," she said.

"You're my understudy," she said with a weak smile.

"I think the word is stand-in," Vale said.

"You could tell Claire to go fuck herself," Parthia said. "Who does she think she is?" Vale did not answer. Parthia was quiet, thinking. "But why are you going?"

"I'm not entirely sure," Vale admitted. "Maybe I'm curious about him."

Parthia nodded. She closed her eyes, then squeezed them as if trying to blot something out of her mind. Vale saw sweat break out on her forehead. "You will tell me what happens?" the girl said.

"Yes, of course."

"Everything?"

"Yes, I shall tell you everything." Again Parthia closed her eyes. "I wish they had anti-dream medication. Could you...?" then Parthia blushed.

"What?" Vale asked, thinking she was going to ask her to stay with her.

"Could you...tell me a story?" Vale thought of Melanie, the words a refrain from their bedtime ritual that went back years.

"What would you like to hear a story about?"

"I don't know. You choose."

Vale thought for a moment; then she had it, a version of a story Poppa Joe had told to her a long time ago. "OK," she said. "It's a kind of fairy tale."

"Not Grimms'," Parthia said, eyes wide.

"No, no. Very different." Parthia slid down on her pillows so she lay flatter now, her eyes fastened on Vale with a hint of apprehension.

"Once upon a time..." Vale reached out and took Parthia's hand. "Once upon a time, in a distant country there was a Queen who had a daughter. She was the Princess. She was in all respects a fine and lovely Princess and of an age to be courted. In fact a ball was being planned for her birthday some months from now, and at that time the Queen would entertain suitors for her hand."

"Where's the King?" Parthia asked.

"There is no King in this story. Maybe the King died." This seemed to satisfy Parthia. "One day, out of a clear blue sky, the Princess got up from the royal dinner table at which there were the usual courtiers and ladies-in-waiting, and crawled under it. No one knew what to make of the act, but it being the Princess, no one said anything. Everyone went on with their meal as if nothing had happened.

"The Queen, of course, was astonished. She looked under the table and asked her daughter what she thought she was doing. The Princess replied that she was now a chicken and that she would eat the scraps that fell from the table. The Queen could not imagine what had put that idea into her daughter's head, but thought it best to humor her for the moment. At the next meal, however, the very same thing happened, and the next after that. Now the Queen was not only a little embarrassed by the Princess' behavior, but she was concerned that her daughter had...well, lost her mind." Vale whispered the words as if they were a secret to be shared only with the listener.

Parthia nodded. "Like me," she said.

"So the Queen summoned the court physician. He had the Princess put to bed, let some blood as was the custom in those days, and gave her various remedies. Two days later and back at dinner, the Princess once again slipped under the table, claiming that she was a chicken and that the scraps dropped by the guests would be quite enough for her.

"The physician was summoned again; other remedies were attempted, but nothing worked. At every meal the Princess could be found underneath the table and no one could do anything about it."

"Perhaps," said Parthia, "she was afraid of getting married."

"It's a thought," said Vale.

"I'm hungry," said Parthia.

"I bet you are," said Vale, "but I'm not sure it's a good idea for you to eat anything yet. Your stomach's been pretty upset."

Parthia reached for her water bottle, sipped, and lay still. "Go on with the story, please." She folded her hands on the sheet and closed her eyes.

"So time passed, and the Princess continued her bizarre behavior. Despite her best efforts to keep things hushed up, for this would surely dash the Princess' chances for a husband, word got out. Over time any number of quacks presented themselves to the palace in the hopes that they could cure the Princess. All failed, and the Queen, weary of being practiced upon, let it be known that the penalty for attempting and failing to cure the Princess' condition was death. That quieted things down considerably. The Queen gradually resigned herself to the fact that her daughter was mad." Vale saw now that Parthia was still. She went on in a voice lowered and slow.

"Then one day there was a knock on the palace door, and a woman presented herself to the gatekeeper. She said that she had come to cure the Princess. The gatekeeper thought the woman was a hoax, for she seemed quite ordinary in a gray smock and gray jacket, but he knew it was not his decision to keep her out. He left her in the reception room and went to inform the Queen. The Queen summoned the stranger and told her the penalty for failure. 'I understand this quite well,' said the crone (for this is what she was). 'Then you may try your best,' said the Queen, 'I pray that you may succeed.'"

"This is a good story," Parthia mumbled; "I've never heard it before." Her pale face was soft.

"That night at dinner, the Princess appeared as usual, and as usual she slipped quietly under the table and disappeared. Only this time, and to her considerable surprise, she found a stranger under the table with her. 'Who are you?' asked the Princess, alarmed. 'Why,' said the woman, 'can't you see? I am a chicken. And you?' 'Well,' said the Princess, 'I am a chicken, also.'

"The two eyed one another for a moment. Then the Princess said, 'How nice it is that you join me. I was a little lonely.' 'I too am glad to have company,' said the woman, 'and I can see there are some very good things to eat here.' For indeed the Queen made sure that fine delicacies were left under the table so that her daughter might not starve." Vale saw Parthia's eyes closing again.

"And so it went for a number of days, meal after meal, the two grown women behaving like chickens under the royal table. The Queen grew increasingly perturbed. In private she berated the crone for exacerbating her daughter's condition and threatened her with death. But the crone urged patience. 'These things take time,' the old woman said, 'these things take time." Vale saw that Parthia's breathing was regular, slow and deep. "These things take time," she whispered to the sleeping girl, perhaps to herself as well. "Time."

Vale sat in the stillness of the room, and her own exhaustion overtook her in a wave. She leaned back against the chair. She heard a slow drip of the shower and the sound of morning birds. The window above the bed showed dawn's hue. The house around her seemed as if it were suspended in time and space like an ark, its cargo of secrets and suffering known only to a few. For a moment this vessel seemed to ride on a quiet sea.

Vale looked at her watch and sighed. It was almost six. She was expected at a house in Babylon at nine. There a man she had never met, but with whom she felt she had been engaged in some surreal struggle for the soul of a girl, was presumably preparing to die. Finally she would have a face to go with the story she had been attempting to decipher for weeks. Parthia was the book he had written in his private code and for obscure and terrible purposes. "And it shall be a sign upon your flesh…" The line—biblical wasn't it?---floated into her tired mind. She was half adoze herself, holding vigil over her charge who seemed, for once, asleep without her terrible dreams. "Rest," Vale whispered, "rest." And Vale let her eyes close. Did she sleep? Perhaps, but the sun was only beginning to catch in the treetops, when her eyes opened.

Vale got up and went to the door. She looked back once on the sleeping maiden---like a figure in a fairy tale she thought not for the first time---then passed into the hall, smiling at the wide-eyed sentry. "She's resting now," she said.

At the top of the stairs she met Julia, who was carrying a small jar of flowers in one hand and a book in the other.

"Where are you going?"

"To the Quiet Room."

"Julia, this is irregular. Parthia is..."

"Ms. Messenger this is a nut house. Everything is irregular, and I know Parthia is going through a bad time. She wont hurt me, and I won't hurt her."

"No, I'm sure you won't. What are you going to do?"

"Sit with her."

"She's asleep."

"That's all right. I can read. Will you tell Celia it's all right for me to be with her?"

"If she becomes violent..."

"Don't worry Ms. Messenger. I know I'm not a staff member. I just don't want her to be alone."

Vale nodded, then went down to the nurse's station and told Celia how she had left her patient. "Don't restrain her hands if you can possibly avoid it." She left orders for how Parthia was to be handled under certain eventualities, and then made her way to her car, feeling she had already worked a full day.

The thought of Julia seated beside Parthia offered Vale some strange resolve; it seemed to her a very brave, a very beautiful thing.

CHAPTER THIRTY-SEVEN

Claire decided she did not want sleep that night; she wanted to remain awake in order not to miss a single moment of her husband's life---*I am like one of those wives of ships-captains who pace their widow walks, looking for a lantern from the sea.* But by midnight---with the Adenauer's long gone and Uta restored, thank God, to her place---the book she was reading by his bedside kept slipping out of her hands, and whatever it was that Claus had given her husband seemed to sink him below any agitation.

She realized that she could not tolerate for the whole night long the sight of his expressionless face, the sound of his ragged breath, the odor of decay. A beard of several days' growth stubbled his cheeks and chin; they had not been able to shave him. The hair, thinned and white, fell over his forehead. Sharp angles of bone showed through the bed sheet. Somewhere inside him the cancer was growing, multiplying, shredding his nerves, consuming body and mind. She could sense it in the room with her, faceless—lethal.

Notifying Uta that she was taking a break, she went to her own bathroom and looked through the medicine cabinet for something to get her through the night. Faced with the vials of her pills, she considered for a moment taking an overdose of some narcotic and meeting her husband in the afterworld. She had played Cleopatra once in summer stock: "'I have immortal longings in me,'" she said to the mirror, wishing for a robe, an asp, and an audience. But the face that looked back at her was not that of an Egyptian queen. Weariness and worry had smudged her eyes, pulled at the corners of her mouth.

She lifted the skin; wrinkles flattened and disappeared. She pulled at the skin under her chin. And her hands, she looked at her hands: That was where age told most, the knobbing of the knuckles, the liver spots. But that, too, could be fixed. She knew whom Wilhelm would recommend.

She filled a glass of water and swallowed one of the amphetamines.

She went to her clothes closet, found the red dress, and laid it out on the bed. Then she took out her black chiffon dress with the black beading over the bodice, held it up in front of her, and studied the woman in mourning who stood before her The funeral itself would be a demanding event. Though Wilhelm did not have close friends---with the exception of Claus---there were many people, both colleagues and patients, who would come to mourn him. Ruth had assured Claire the funeral arrangements were all in hand, awaiting only…

How odd, how unnatural to stage a death, she thought. It was a kind of murder and suicide at once. Though they had not set a precise time, the phrase "around noon" had been floated and agreed upon. But why not "around two" or "around four thirty five?" Why not sunset, moonrise, midnight? It seemed so arbitrary to her. She threw the black dress down on the bed. Too much. It was all too much to bear. And to bear alone.

Heedless of the time she dialed Biron's number. She'd get his machine, she knew. "Biron, it's Claire. I need you, darling. Willi is dying…will be dying. To-morrow. High noon. A complete melodrama, and I have no one here for me. That Messenger woman may be here around nine. I can hardly bear to look at her. Come, darling. Spend a few hours. Just be here if I need a shoulder to lean on. Be a good boy. Come."

She began to feel the drug's jangle of vitality. Biron would not come, she was sure. Such an egotist. Ruth and Claus would be here. Perhaps that horrible Messenger woman. She would need something to serve them.

She went to the kitchen, looked through the refrigerator, then inspiration struck her: the Bavarian coffee cake. She found her old recipe--- not hers actually, it had been Eva's. Did she have the ingredients? Why, yes, she did. She even found an unopened bag of walnuts. How odd: Eva. She did not think about her from one year to the next, yet in this instant she felt an odd kind of kinship with the woman whose place she had taken. A vanished sister. Yes. A single photograph of Eva in a silver frame sat on the mantle of the guestroom in which no guest ever stayed. A ghost room, that's what it was.

Claire made herself a cup of coffee, put on an apron, and set about mixing flour, kneading it and setting it aside. She would make it just the way Willi loved. While the dough rose, she vacuumed the living room, plumped the pillows and changed the towels in the downstairs bathroom. She returned to the kitchen, kneaded the dough again, set the timer, and went back to the living room.

She turned on the television. Every now and then she would catch one of her old films on re-run. Her first part had been as a chorus girl in *The Great Ziegfield*. She was just nineteen, and Ray Bolger had danced with her after a shoot one night at the Mocambo. But there was no Claire Summers to be seen on late night television, and impatient with other faces and other scripts, she turned off the set.

When the timer rang, she went back to the kitchen, broke up walnuts, sprinkled on sugared cinnamon, raisins, and twisted the dough into a braided circle. A little after four, she put it aside. She would bake in the morning. The smell would fill the house. She took another pill. Would Parthia come at the last minute? Hateful girl. If she did, she would see how a woman could behave.

What to do now?

Claire switched from coffee to tea and on impulse dashed her tea with a splash of vodka. A tea-toddy. She giggled to herself. She walked into the library where her scrapbooks were arranged in leather bound sequence. Clippings, photographs, the script from *An Unforgettable Face* with all those autographs. Reviews. When she died to whom would these go? Who would care for the story they told? Not Parthia. Claire felt angry, but there was something else, too, the edge of a new and nameless anxiety. She picked up the big scrapbook that told her story and placed it on the coffee table in the living room. "The family Bible," Parthia had called it once. So it was.

The silence in the house was oppressive, the steady tock of the grandfather clock in the hall measured time in deafening intervals. Shut the damn thing off--- she went to the hall, opened the glass front of the case, and stopped the pendulum. There in the foyer she saw her handbag. She withdrew the Moroccan wallet with the pictures she had shared with Ruth and carried it like a trophy to the coffee table and set it beside the big scrapbook.

Through the living room window she saw that the night was lifting; the trees and shrubs in the garden took form. She could tell by the pallor of the light---the dewy weight on the lawn---that it was going to be a humid day. Then she went upstairs to bathe and dress.

• ◆ •

Win woke and found the bed and the apartment empty. He padded around like a bear in an unfamiliar cage. He had brought his toothbrush, but that was all. He saw Vale's note, was amazed that he had not awakened when she left, then he remembered their lovemaking and its wake of exhaustion. He had always thought his marriage had been satisfying in the bedroom department, but he had to admit that Nayla was perhaps on the quiet side as a lover, responsive, tender, but also in some way delicate. And, of course, for years there were the ears of a small child only a partition away. Vale was, well, not delicate.

When he reached the hospital, he went to the cafeteria and made a take-out of French toast and bacon and filled his mug with coffee. Chad and Evan would have been appalled at the fare. Back in his office, the shop not yet stirring, he called Vale's number. She answered on the first ring. "When did you get home?" he asked.

"About half an hour ago."

"We must have passed each other. I should have waited."

"No, it's just as well. I feel like hell. Pretty soon I've got to change and get ready."

"What happened with Parthia?"

She gave him a review. "Maybe I'm being quixotic, but I hope that her father's death effects some change in her."

"Quixotic? Did Sancho Panza ever get his adjective?"

"Panzaic?" Vale offered.

"Sanchesque?"

"Oh, yes," she said, "I like that. Sanchesque. That's you. To a tee."

They talked then of literary characters whose names became adjectives, of her nostalgia for teaching. "I used to get my madness in the pages of a book," she said.

And who had written well of madness? And who of orchids? And then she really had to go.

"What's the weekend look like for you?" he asked.

"I'll be good for nothing tonight. Sunday Melanie comes home."

"Does she? So soon?"

"We've got plenty of time," Vale said, reading his mind.

"I hope so."

"Win, I was wondering if I could come out on the boat tomorrow. Do you think that would be possible?"

"Really? Sure. You can count on it."

"I'll call you tonight. I'm running on fumes, and the day is just beginning."

"I'll keep you in my thoughts," he said. She had no idea how much she was already a part of them. "'Good-bye, Lady Quixote. Watch out for the windmills."

"Thanks, Sancho." There was a brief silence on the line, within it a kind of mute flutter of affection that never rose into words, and then at the same moment they broke the connection. Win recalled Vale on her knees that Sunday morning at Biron's. *Pray for us sinners, now and at the hour of our death.*

• ◆ •

Claus Adenauer was sitting at the kitchen table, nibbling a coffee cake and sipping coffee. He had come down from checking on his patient. "I have done what I can for him," he reported to Claire. "He is resting now, and I would like him to stay quiet and undisturbed for as long as possible. When is this Vale Messenger from the hospital coming?"

"If she comes. I told her to be here at nine."

The doctor shook his head, "This is very difficult to arrange. She must not stay long. There can be no..."

"I must see him last," Claire interrupted. "But I do not want to be there when you...you know." She could not finish her sentence.

"This is not an exact science, you understand."

"What does that mean?" Claire asked. She paced the room now, twisting a white linen handkerchief in her fingers. She wore the red dress, with red alligator skinned shoes, ruby studs in her ears, and an onyx broach on her bosom, her one nod to black. People might be shocked that the widow wore red, but she was not a widow yet, goddamnit it. "I want his eyes open when I see him. You understand?"

"I do not know how well I shall be able to keep Wilhelm going. He is very weak, and each time I give him the medicine he needs in order to be alert, he is left weaker still and in more pain after it. He will not have time or energy for very much. He is suffering, and his mind is more than ever not under his control."

"Listen, Claus," said Claire, standing over him, "I have been up all night. Do you understand? I have not had one wink of sleep. That is *my* husband up there. He is my life; he has been my life. I deserve a few moments with him, and I need them. I need to see him and have him see me. I need to say goodbye, and I do not want to say good-bye to a man who is unconscious or out of his mind. I don't care what you have to do, but I want you to give me that. At least that."

It was useless to explain it to her. "I have brought you something," he said, opening his black medical bag and reaching in for a small plastic bottle that he handed to her. She took it and unscrewed the top. Four small green pills spilled into her hand.

"What is this?" she demanded.

"You asked me to bring something. This will help. Take one now, and another in three hours. They will make the morning more tolerable for you."

"I don't want to be a zombie," she said, but was already moving to the sink and drawing a glass of water.

"You will not be a zombie. I know you wish to be with him and to have all your wits about you." He watched her swallow a pill.

"Ruth will be here in a few minutes," he said, glancing at his watch. It would not be soon enough for him.

"When can I say good morning to my husband?" Claire asked.

"Let me have a second cup of coffee and perhaps another slice of this delicious cake. Let us wait for Ruth." They did this, making small talk while Claire, unable to sit still any longer, made fresh coffee, took fruit from the refrigerator, washed the grapes, filled a bowl.

Ruth arrived at the kitchen door at half past eight, and Claus went one more time to check the status of his patient. Ruth indulged in Claire's coffee cake, commented on how well she looked, and took down names Claire dictated of people she wished to notify of Wilhelm's death.

The door chimes rang. Claire glanced at her watch." She's early," she said and went to the hallway. But it was Biron, dressed in linen slacks, a Hawaiian shirt, and sandals. He looked bleary-eyed himself. He put his lips to a powdered cheek, then slouched into the living room where he kicked off his sandals and sprawled on the sofa. Claire left him there and went to the kitchen where she prepared a tray of cake and coffee and carried it to the sideboard in the living room. "I can't thank you enough for coming. I look awful don't I? It's been an ordeal."

"I'll be here if you need me," he said, and he closed his eyes.

Claire left him and went up to her husband's room, but to her disappointment found him asleep with Uta in the reading chair by the bed. Claire bustled uselessly, plucking flowers into a better arrangement, emptying the wastebasket near the bed, putting a new CD on the changer. She found his eyes on her at one moment, and she saw recognition register in them. She came to him and brushed her lips against his ---only with the self-control of an actress did she master her recoil at the smell that came off him. His eyes went to the water beside the bed, and she tipped a straw into his mouth. She must get him shaved, she thought, the hair brushed, clear the rheumy gum from the corners of his eyes. This would never do, but as she brought the hairbrush and a warm washcloth to the bedside, he lifted a hand and waved her away. The effort cost him; she saw his hand reach for the plunger clipped to his bed sheet, then saw it stop. She saw his lips move in an effort to speak, but no words came from him. Again his eyes asked for water and this time as she drew the cup back from him after he had drunk, she heard his voice. "Is she here?" he asked.

"Not your daughter, no. But her therapist, Vale Messenger, she may come. I ordered her to come."

The eyes wandered around the room, then came back to Claire's face. "Yes. Good. Bring her to me please, when she comes. Then leave us alone."

"Save something for me," she said. Did he understand her? The hand rose weakly from his side, its fingers pushed the air.

"He's at death's door," she thought, and in her state the cliché took on a vivid reality for her. It could have had the power to frighten her were she not subtly, mercifully removed from the sensation of fright. She floated over her exhaustion and anxiety in a kind of cloudy self-command. She saw everything, but felt little as if this staged finale were only another scene in life's tragic play through which she moved, Garbo-like, her great inner grief concealed behind a mask of remarkable bravery.

• ◆ •

Vale took stock before the full-length mirror in her bedroom. "You look like you're going to a funeral." The face that looked back at her wore a rueful smile. "Well, you are."

The hair had been momentarily tamed, and the navy blue linen suit fit her well. It would wrinkle, but it was the best thing she had. She'd debated the stockings, then decided to wear them. Her best black shoes pinched a little. She ran some lipstick over her lips, worked the gold stud earrings into each ear, gave herself a last appraising look, and realized in a bitter moment that she was dressing for Claire. It galled her. Her father came to mind. Not as she had last seen him, but younger, dressed for one of his Sabbath adventures, jaunty, with a twinkle in his eye. *I'm dressing for you, Poppa.* The thought squared her shoulders.

It was just after eight thirty when she broke a sweat on her way to her car. She was tired, gritty-eyed, punchy. She would be grateful to pull over and close her eyes.

When she arrived in Babylon twenty minutes later, she found the gates of the Alexander house open. She drove the long driveway between tonsured hedges and spreading rhododendrons, and parked in the shade of the big maple that flanked the turnaround at the columned entrance. She steeled herself for the unpleasantness of Claire's reception.

Claire did not receive her. Her maid wordlessly ushered her into the house and left her to find her way. There was a smell in the air, faint but unmistakable, the smell of reefer. She'd heard of prescribing cannabis to deal with pain. Was Claus Adenauer so enlightened a physician? She stepped into the living room and there, lounging on the sofa, shoes off, bare feet crossed, was Biron Lord, an unlit, half-smoked joint in the ashtray.

"Hi, Messenger," he said to her. A big photo album lay propped open on his stomach.

"What in God's name are you doing here?" Vale stepped into the room and saw that there was a sideboard with a coffee urn on it and wedges of coffee cake.

"Help yourself," he said.

She poured herself a cup of coffee and sat down in the chair across from him. "You're the last person in the world I expected to see here." And she had to admit to herself, it was a relief. He may not be a friend, but in some way he defied the ghoulish spell of the place.

"Yeah, Claire called. It's D-day. Wanted a shoulder to lean on."

"So the two of you are..."

"I did some work with her years ago," he said, "after she got her life together. She missed being in front of a camera. Now she's...well, a patroness of sorts."

"What kind of work?" Vale asked, remembering the photographs Parthia had found. She was amused to play cat to his mouse for a change.

But Biron ignored the question. "Have you seen these?" He lifted up the album from his lap.

"No. Are those the pictures of Claire's reconstruction?"

"Claire's miracle. Claire's fairy tale. Yeah," he said tossing the book back on the table top, "every step of the way. They tell quite a story. A helluva series."

"Is everything a series with you, Biron?"

Again he evaded her question. She rather envied his ability to do this. "How's Parthia?"

"It is none of your business, though perhaps I owe you some thanks."

"Think nothing of it. Could you give me a slice of cake?" Vale went to the sideboard and brought him a slice, carrying it to him on a napkin. "Parthia's not coming apparently," he said.

"No, she's not."

"Claire said she had asked you to come in her place."

"'Asked?' Well, Claire is ..." She did not finish the sentence.

"Why are you here?"

"For Parthia."

"I think there's more to it than that."

"Biron, this is not the time or the place for another third degree. OK, yes, I am curious about him, about Doctor Alexander. But that's not why I am here. God, you're insistent."

"OK," he said. "You want a toke."

"Jesus Christ, no. You're something else."

"I scared Ruth and Claus. They vacated back to the kitchen. Scandalized. Meanwhile the old fart is administering illegal doses of God knows what to off the old man upstairs, but turns his nose up at cannabis. Go figure."

There was the muffled sound of feet on the stairs, and Claire entered the living room. She was dressed in red, heavily made up and seemed to wear as much jewelry as her frame could bear. A sorry masquerade. "I see you are here," she said to Vale with a smile on her face that came nowhere near her eyes. "Olivia did not inform me." Vale doubted that. "Come, I will take you up to him," she said. The voice was imperious. Vale rose. "Biron, would you open a window please," Claire said; "this place smells like an opium den. And watch the crumbs. I just had the furniture cleaned."

At the door Vale turned back to glance at Biron, who had not moved. He was watching her, and suddenly there was a camera in his hand.

•◆•

Vale followed Claire up the stairs, feeling sullen and ill-used. "You have ten minutes. Do not tire him and do not exert him," Claire said. "There is a call button by his side. Press it if you find you are out of your depth. Be careful what you say to him. He is not… Never mind." Then, opening the door, Claire turned to Vale, "I detest you," she hissed, as Vale passed through.

The door clicked in its lock behind her. Standing beside it, Vale paused to let her eyes adjust to pale light that filtered in through drawn curtains. Music played from hidden speakers, and a mélange of floral scents poured from half a dozen vases arranged around the room. A single standing lamp between the night table and a reading chair illuminated the man on the bed.

Even from this distance, she could see that the face was jaundiced, mottled, and stained. The hair lay unkempt on a yellowed brow, and a yellowed arm extended on the sheet to receive an IV's drip. A plastic bag clipped to the bed frame gathered green urine. A monitor on a wheeled metal stand registered the blip of a pulse. Vale had not prepared herself for the starkness of his condition.

She cleared her throat. The eyes of the cadaverous man opened. A hand raised a few inches off the sheet in a beckoning gesture. "*Wer ist hier?*"

Who is here? The German of her childhood clicked in. Her father here with this other father. Odd. Comforting.

She crossed the room, aware of the deep silencing pile of the carpet beneath her feet. The closer she came, the stronger the fermenting smell of his decay. She breathed shallowly through her mouth. The eyes in the skull watched her draw closer. No expression could be read on lips concealed under a mustache. She stood now at his feet.

"*Wie heissen sie?*" A pause in which she did not answer. "Don't you speak any German?"

"I understand a little," she said. "I don't speak it."

"What is your name? I am sorry I cannot remember."

"Vale Messenger."

"Messenger? *Der Engel?*"

The angel? "No, only your daughter's therapist."

"My daughter. Parthia." The eyes closed. *"Oder ist Paulina?"* Or is it Paulina? The eyes opened, but now they seemed focused on something far away. "Do you know the little fairy tale of Paulina, *Die geshicte mit dem Feuerzeug?* We all learned it as children."

The little match girl? "No," she said, "I do not know the German version of the story."

"'Paulinchen war allein zu Haus / Die Eltern beide aus.'" Little Paulina was alone in her house. Her parents had gone out. "It has a...what is the word? When something is repeated? A refrain. *'Du lichterloh, Du lichterloh.'* You will burn. You will burn. Only his lips moved, no sound coming from him. Then, "Is her face healing?"

"Whose?"

"My daughter's? I was concerned that scars might show."

Vale was confused. She did not think Dr. Alexander had seen the marred face of his daughter a month ago. "Her face is healed," she said. "Perfectly."

"Come, sit down, please." She came around the side of the bed and sat on the edge of the chair. *"Der Engel der Tod,"* the voice murmured to itself. *The angel of death.* "Ohne Barmherzigkeit." *Without mercy.* "Thank you for coming. *Danke.*"

"Your wife wished it."

"You know my daughter?"

"Yes, I do."

"Where did you meet my daughter?"

"She is a patient in my hospital."

"Your hospital? I did not know... Oh, yes. Claire told me. *Ein Sanitorium?*"

"Yes," she said, "a sanitarium."

"Is she a good patient?" he asked. "She was always a good patient with me."

Vale shuddered. "Yes, she is a good patient." She watched the old man register her reply; his eyes closed briefly as if he were taking it in like a swallow of something sweet.

"Does she talk about me?"

"No, she does not."

The blue eyes closed again, as if the lids were too heavy to hold open. "Is she angry with me?"

In spite of herself, Vale bristled. "Doctor, I am not here to speak for her. Your wife wished me to come."

"Do you know her history?"

"I know that you worked on her. Remade her. I know that you took as your model a face from Leonardo Da Vinci."

"No, not a model. *Nicht eine Kopie. Die vorstellung.*" Not a copy, the idea. "*Verstehen sie?*"

"Yes," she said, "I understand."

He nodded, opened his mouth to speak, perhaps he had volumes to tell her---reasons, methods, intimacies---but the only sound she heard was a sigh, as if it were too much now to recount or explain.

But it was not enough for her, this sigh of resignation or exhaustion. So she asked the question that had festered in her from the beginning, asked not on Parthia's behalf, but on her own, out of her need to understand what it was that prompted this human soul to its evil. "Why?" she asked, "why did you do it?" *Warum:* that was the word for why. "*Warum?*" she asked, leaning forward. But he seemed beyond questions and answers now. She was too late. How awful if Parthia had come.

Then his voice startled her. "When I was a young man, the great Weimar experiment was underway. I wanted to be a painter. I met Kandinsky once." A note of pride rose into the voice; a sigh followed. "But my father had other plans for me. When the Republic dissolved, there were difficult choices to be made. National Socialism had no place for artists of the sort I had dreamed of being. *Sieg Heil!* " A phlegmy cough shook him. "And then ---" but this sentence was also interrupted as a contorting wave passed over the withered features; the teeth gritted; the body stiffened; sweat stood out on the skin. Then the body shivered into its bones. "*Deutchland, Deutchland uber alles.* Everything changed." The red tongue emerged again and attempted to moisten withered lips. "*Wasser, bitte.*" The old man closed his eyes, wincing. "So hot," he said, "I am burning up. Burning up. *Ich brenne. Ach, das feuer...*"

Claire had said something about his hallucinations about fire. Vale brought the plastic cup and straw to his lips, struck by the fact that only hours earlier she had done the same thing for his daughter. He drank, nodded, and she returned the cup to its place on the night table. A dribble of water ran down his whiskered chin and disappeared in the gullies of his throat. She sat back down.

"There are two cats, Minz and Mantz. They warn her. '*Die Holtzen brennt gar lustig, hell und licht / Das lackert lustig, knistert laut.'*" *The match burns cheerfully, bright and light. It crackles and pops.*

"Warn her? Who?" Vale asked.

"*Paulinchen. Miau! Mio!* They cry to her."

He was getting away from her. Was this what she had come for. Delirium? Fragments. Yet another madness. "Sir, you wanted me to come?"

"*'Die Flamme fasst das Kleid. / Es brennt die Hand, es brennt das Haar...'*" *The flame touches the dress, burns the hand and hair.*

Vale saw a spasm cross his face; the eyes squeezed shut so hard the whole face pinched around them. The breath caught in his throat. "*Ach du lieber,*" he whispered through clenched teeth. Should she summon Dr. Adenauer? She was lifting off her chair when the wave passed. The eyes fluttered open. "*Vie gehts meine kinde?*" the voice asked. *How is my child?*

The wandering mind, like the needle of a compass pulled by a moving lodestone, hovered for a moment in her reality. "She is...struggling."

His hand reached out and groped for her. It hung pawing in the air, then gripped the aluminum rail of the bed. "I want you to tell my daughter that I loved her. Always. Will you tell her that?"

"Yes," she said, "I will tell her that you loved her. Always." She kept all irony out of her voice.

"It is good that she survives. So many lost. So many Paulinchens. '*Es brennt das Kind sogar, Und Minz und Maunz, die shreien. Das Kind brennt lichterloh.*'" *The cats are screaming. The child is burning.*

The mind swung from true north. The blue eyes widened in a kind of alarm. "*Doch weh! Doch weh!*" A lamentation.

"Doctor, let me ring for..." She was reaching for the call button, but a waving hand batted her aside.

He struggled to rise---"*Zu Hilf! Zu Hilf! Das Kind brennt lichterloh---*" *Help! Help The child is burning up. The child is burning.*

Now the head tossed back and forth on the pillow as if to drive the words away. She saw the jaws clamp down hard. Then the eyes were open, staring at her, rimmed red. "*Die mutter und der vater...*" A shudder passed over the body under the sheet. "*Zu spat. Zu spat.*" *Too late. Too late.* And then a cry, "*Zu spaaaaat!*" The head rocked back and forth, veins stood out on the neck.

Vale started up in shock and struck the IV stand. It teetered. She grabbed at it as it tilted to fall. "*Meaowww! Meaowww!*" screamed the face contorted before her. "*Meeeeaowwww!*" The howl of the cats, child-like and inhuman at once, tore through the air; the scream of the cats helplessly watching the little girl burn.

The blind eyes were starting from the skull, the mouth wide. Wilhelm Alexander's face became a horrid mask.

Suddenly Claire was beside her, pushing her away with a flailing arm. "Get out of here!" she shrieked into the teeth of the screams that raked them all. "Get out! Get out of this room and get out of this house." Vale, groped her way to the door and caught a glance of apology from the little bald man who pursued Claire, a white handkerchief dabbing at his brow.

Her heart pounding, Vale found the stairs, the unrelenting screams followed her, though muffled by the thick oak door. She gripped the banister and swayed there for a moment, visited by a vivid image of Wilhelm Alexander falling into some inferno.

Then suddenly it was silent in the room behind her, though her ears seemed still to hold the last echo of the old man's cry. Below her she saw a woman looking up at her, a face white with alarm.

By the time Vale had descended to the rotunda below, the woman had disappeared. Vale crossed the hall and passed the open door of the living room. "Messenger," Biron said, calling out to her. She had forgotten he was here. She stopped, looked in, and saw he was seated now.

"What?" she asked, hearing the parched croak of her own voice.

Biron had something in his hands. "Take this out of here," he said, and he tossed her a small brown object which by mere reflex she caught in mid-air. "Take it. You will see why. It's for Parthia."

Her mind was still gripped by the raving face that had so startled her, by the howls that had filled her ears. She could not think. Dumbly, with the little book in her hand, she let herself out into the disorienting heat and brightness of the summer morning. She went to her car and without a backward glance drove down the shaded drive and through the gates. She half expected the house behind her to fall into sudden ruin or to catch fire, ignited by the madness in a dying man's mind.

CHAPTER THIRTY-EIGHT

Vale watched Dean Venables spread the pictures across his desk. She was seated on the far side of the room in one of the aluminum frame leather chairs. It was half past three Friday afternoon, the first moment he was available, and almost the last before he left work to be home for the Sabbath.

She could see the thinning hair on the crown of his head as he bent over the spoils Biron had thrust upon her. Dean looked for a very long time without saying a word, the pipe left to go out in the ashtray at his elbow.

She had no regrets at having taken the little book. Knowing Claire as she did, Vale did not doubt that the woman intended the album as a kind of show-piece for her husband's work, a memorial of sorts, on a par with the record of the reconstruction of her own face years earlier.

Had the pictures been sexual in content, they could not have been more shocking. Indeed consensual pornography seemed innocent compared to the images of a girl so obviously terrified, exploited, shamed and alone. Vale could almost hear the pleading cries of the girl who was revealed in the pictures. She was not sure what was more heart-rending, Paula in the early ones, who seemed to flinch from the camera's eye and allowed herself to be exposed--- mutilated hands, fat belly, mottled face, defeated posture---or Parthia in the later frames, who seemed to declare herself to the camera with a fierce, triumphant pride. Which was worse the cowed victim or the arrogant showpiece? If pictures were worth a thousand words, these were worth ten thousand. She could imagine nothing that could so eloquently tell the story of the subjection of one will to another. It had been a kind of possession.

And Claire's complicity---her ignorance, her terrible, compelling ego-tism--- was perhaps the most horrible part of it all. In that house Parthia had no advocate, no protection. What chance did her small protesting will have against the alliance of those huge forces? "Two against one," Vale had offered Parthia, to which the small voice had replied, "I was always less than one."

There was no way to survive except through surrender, and in time that surrender was complete. The very choice of a name, "Parthia," finally revealed its full and tragic truth: This *Parthia*, born the virgin goddess from the mind of the father.

Dean Venables slowly turned the pages of the album.

Vale had come straight to the hospital from the Alexander house and strug-gled through her morning both exhausted and pre-occupied.

Julia, who had sat with Parthia all morning long, told Vale how the young woman had started up at one point in a kind of delirium. "He is going," she said, "he is going. I see fires, Julia. I see flames." Vale did not know what to make of that co-incidence. "She was weeping, Ms. Messenger, and then she slept. She rested."

Later Vale had looked in on Parthia and found that she was awake, but weak as if she were coming out of a long high fever. She did not wish to stimu-late or disturb her, but Parthia saw her at the door.

"You went?' Parthia asked.

"I did," said Vale, coming into the room and looking down at the wan face, gold curls plastered to the forehead, but the eyes steady.

"And?"

"He was in pain, disoriented, and..." Vale paused.

"Yes? Tell me."

She would spare her the images of her father raving. "He wanted you to know he loved you. Always. He wanted me to be sure to tell you that."

"I see," Parthia said in a voice without emotion.

"Biron was there."

"Really," she said. "Claire has quite a hold on him."

"Perhaps, but I actually thought he was there for me, or for you, if you had come."

Parthia considered this. Then Vale told her of Biron's strange gesture, toss-ing the Moroccan wallet to her as she fled the scene. "Have you looked at it," Parthia asked.

"Yes."

"Then you know. And the pictures Biron took, look at them also."

Then, as if that was all she had to say on the subject of her father, she spoke of Julia. "She was here. All morning. Whenever I woke up, she was here. She read to me." Parthia paused as if to gather her strength. "You know, Ms. Messenger, I feel you have cared about me, cared for me so very much, but I have never been able to get out of my mind that it is your job to do this. You are paid to care for your patients." Vale nodded; this was true, though not the reason. "But Julia, Julia did not have to come here to be with me. I have been beastly to her, yet she came to sit with me. I can't tell you how much that matters. I am not sure I ever felt someone care for me in this way."

It was a miracle, the survival of goodness in a life of loss and abuse such as Julia had suffered. "Yes," Vale said, "it's powerful. Love with no strings attached."

"Yes," Parthia said, "exactly. No strings attached. I'll never forget that she came to be with me." Parthia closed her eyes. Then, her voice drowsing, she asked, "Did you ever finish the story about the Princess who thought she was a chicken?"

"No, I didn't."

"Tell it to me now."

Vale came and sat by the bedside. To her astonishment, Parthia put out her hand, and Vale took it. It was warm and frail. "Where was I? What do you remember?"

"That the crone was under the table with the Princess, and the queen was getting ansty."

"Yes, and the crone said to the queen…"

"'These things take time, yes, I remember that.'" The frail hand stirred in hers, but was not withdrawn.

"So after many days of this, one dinner the Princess came to the table, and as usual slid underneath it, and to her dismay, the other chicken was not there. She missed her, and wanted to ask her mother where she had gone, and as she peeked her head above the table, she saw, seated among the usual guests, the crone, the old lady. And she was eating. At the table. With a knife and fork.

"The Princess hid back under the table and crawled down to where the old woman was sitting and tugged at the hem of her skirt.

"The crone leaned over and look down at the Princess. 'What are you doing up there?' whispered the Princess. 'Come down here. You are a chicken.'

"The crone slipped under the table and whispered back. 'I know I am a chicken; I know you are a chicken. But I can pretend that I am not.' The Princess' eyes went wide. 'You can pretend, too.' The Princess thought and then she nodded. 'So, come up and sit beside me, let's pretend together.'

"And so she did."

The hand in hers lay still. Parthia had drifted off to sleep; there was the ghost of a smile on her lips. "The end."

Vale sat for awhile in the quiet room and found that she was strangely hopeful. She believed she knew enough now to help Parthia construct an accurate portrait of her past. They would find Paula, the lost face, the lost child. Vale knew they would without knowing how. The pictures in the Moroccan album gave her the referents she needed to understand behavior that until now had seemed bizarre and impenetrably private. The hash marks, for example, that Parthia had drawn on the bathroom wall; the obsessive behaviors, the picking and tearing at her nails. Vale recalled with revulsion the two photographs---before and after---of Paula's hands. She wondered what discipline Dr. Alexander had contrived to get the girl to stop, and then she remembered the saucer of cuticles. If she didn't know this monstrosity to be true, she could not have imagined it.

Also, she believed she had seen the face of the one who would be her ally, the other Eva, the mother-stock from which Paula had come. She was sure that Paula had been loved, and however cruelly her mother had been torn away from her, there was, at some stratum of the girl's soul, a mother's voice waiting to be heard. Vale now understood that in the mime she and Parthia had been playing out, the girl and her therapist had been summoning up the lost mother, evoking her from her psychic exile.

No sooner had that thought formed than Vale felt a burning urge to see her own daughter, to enfold her in her protection, to reassure herself that Melanie had not yet been tainted by the world. It was all she could do to quell her trembling. Tears came. Until that moment Vale was not aware that she had absorbed so much sorrow.

•◆•

When she returned to her office a little after five to gather her bag, her papers, there was a message on her answering machine: "Mrs. Messenger, this is Dr.

Adenauer. If it is not too much trouble, could you call me at your earliest convenience?" A number followed.

Couldn't it wait until Monday? she wondered, but she was already dialing the exchange.

"Hello," a woman's voice. Not Claire's.

"Yes, this is Vale Messenger, I have a message from…"

"Yes, just a minute please. He was hoping you would call."

Presently she heard the voice of Claus Adenauer. She recalled her glimpse of him as he had come into the sickroom, the sweating brow, the dabbing handkerchief.

Wilhelm Alexander was dead, he was telling her, and his obligations to physician-patient confidentiality were loosened. He thought he had some information that Vale Messenger might find useful in her treatment of Parthia. But it was for her ears only. Did Mrs. Messenger understand that? A professional commitment. Yes, she said. She understood.

"But this is not something you would like to tell Parthia yourself?" she asked.

"Oh, no," said Dr. Adenauer, "I leave it to your discretion how or whether to make use of the information I have."

"I see." Vale kicked off her shoes and put her feet up on the edge of her desk. "You have my attention, Dr. Adenauer."

"First may I ask how your patient is?"

"She is resting. She never could have come to see her father. I tell you in confidence these past days have been an exceptional ordeal for her."

"I am not surprised."

"Did you know about her history? What her father did to her?"

"I knew, yes, but not till much later. In the years after Claire arrived I did not see Wilhelm very much. His relationship with Claire, first as his patient then as his new wife, took him into another world. We would gather, as we usually did, in the winter on a little island in the Caribbean. We had a kind of colony there, but we all conspired to talk only about the present."

"How did Parthia's mother die?"

"She had a congenital heart condition, rheumatic fever. She always had to be careful. She died of heart failure. No particular exertion. She was actually doing the laundry and Paula---I can never quite get used to the name Parthia---was at school. First grade I believe. She was seven. There was a funeral in the home. Candles, an open casket. Friends. Paula was bewildered, of course. She goes off to school one morning and comes home in the afternoon, and her mother is dead. Wilhelm asked her to be very strong. Paula was afraid to go to school, but Wilhelm helped her overcome her fears. All this I learned later."

"And you knew about his reconstructive work on his daughter?"

"There was a period of six or seven years when I did not see Paula or her father. I went back to Munich after my wife and I divorced. This was in 1970. I had a lectureship at the university, and I thought I would remain in Germany. It was my homeland. I was approaching my sixtieth birthday. It was appealing to think of returning to the place where I grew up. But then I met Ruth. She worked for British Airways. When they offered her a position in the New York office, she begged me to move back with her to the United States. We did. I resigned my lectureship, and we came to America. That was..." and here there was a pause ---"that was 1974. Yes, that's right. I became the senior physician at The South Shore Nursing Home. I renewed my friendship with Wilhelm. I introduced Ruth to Claire. We all enjoyed many of the same things together, cultural things. Paula was Parthia by then. She had become a striking looking girl. I never knew how and when her name was changed. Or why. I did not ask."

Vale thought this strange, but perhaps the tact of European friendships did not invite such questions and confidings.

"In the spring of 1976 Wilhelm and Claire made a party for Parthia. It was held at the Plaza Hotel. She was to be eighteen that June, and soon she was going away to college. It was a kind of coming out party, you might say. I suppose it was Claire's idea. Of course, Ruth and I went. Late in the evening, after most of the guests had left, I was in the hotel bar with Wilhelm. We had both had a good deal of champagne, and we lapsed into our old ways of talking to one another, and I remarked to him about how beautiful Paula looked. I remember he leaned forward and gripped my forearm, 'My friend,' he said to me, 'you must call her Parthia. That is her name.'

"I apologized. I said that she had turned out to be a beautiful child. I made some comment about nature, as I recall, something like 'Nature is a remarkable physician.' There is a phrase in German for it. Wilhelm said that nature had nothing to do with it. At first I did not understand. Perhaps I did not want to understand, but in a moment from the look in his eye, I realized what he meant to say. I accused him of taking life into his own hands, of playing God. He countered by calling me an old fool. More words were exchanged, and I did not see him again for a year. Ruth and Claire patched things up, and though I had never forgiven Wilhelm---I thought what he did was wrong---there was no doubt that Paula, that Parthia, was a very happy and very successful young woman."

From outside her window, Vale heard the two-stroke call of a bird.

"So yes, I knew what Wilhelm had done, and it was not until very recently--- when I learned that Parthia was at North Forks ---that I realized his experiment had----what is the word in English?--- backfired. But now that Wilhelm is dead I wish to..." and here Claus Adenauer paused.

Yes? Vale thought, what is it you wish to do?

"Mrs. Messenger I must ask you now to take what I am telling you in the utmost confidence. Wilhelm had the choice to tell this to his daughter. He could have left a letter. He could have told this to Claire." Again there was a silence on the line, and Vale pictured the elderly physician mopping his brow. "Go on, please, Dr. Adenauer."

"On this past Tuesday," Claus began, "Wilhelm sent his wife away for the morning. He spoke with me. He was lucid and relatively free of pain. We talked about the timing of his demise. I will spare you the details. He asked me if I thought Parthia would come. I told him I did not think it likely. He grew very quiet. 'All I wanted,' he said 'was to bring beauty into the world. It was all I ever wanted.'"

Vale pictured the two men together in that sickroom.

Claus was continuing. "I had never understood before. This was what his whole career had been about, and then I saw that, yes, his choice of a specialty, his work with Claire, his dedication not just to reconstructive but to cosmetic surgery, and his work with and on his daughter were all of a piece. It was not merely a successful medical practice, but a kind of mission for him, something fed by a deeper motive. 'I wanted to bring beauty into the world,' he said to me. And then he told me the story I am about to tell you." There was a pause. "Excuse me, for a moment, Mrs. Messenger. I wish to close the door to my study."

Vale stood up, carrying the phone to the window. The afternoon sun was slanting across the lawn. Catherine and Earl Andrews were at their eternal Frisbee game. Amanda and her girls had their heads together under the shade of the beach tree. And yes, she saw that Julia was down in the Glass House. She would be going on pass again tomorrow. Soon enough, Vale thought, they would all be gone. And others would come. And go.

"Are you still there?" the doctor's voice inquired.

"Yes," she said, "I'm here."

"So," the old man cleared his throat, "Wilhelm worked with his father during the war. I must tell you Mrs. Messenger that one thing we never spoke of---in all our years of friendship---was the war, of what we had done in the war. No one did. For him to speak thus was like the breaking of some taboo. It was not easy for him.

"His father was an eminent physician and persuaded his son to take up medicine, and Wilhelm began his medical studies. When the war came, his father summoned his son to work with him at an experimental medical faculty. It was designed to treat burn victims: officers, senior SS people. The firebombing in Germany was dreadful at that time---Dresden, Hamburg. You cannot imagine, Mrs. Messenger. Burn victims were everywhere. Wilhelm's father was working on skin grafts. He was experimenting with taking skin from one body and grafting it on to another. At the time no one understood the mechanics of tissue rejection. There was a great deal of trial and error."

Vale heard Dr. Adenauer hesitate.

"This is not easy for me to relate, Mrs. Messenger. I am ashamed of what it is I have to tell you. I am sorry."

"Go on, Doctor." Vale found she was gripping the receiver tight in her right hand.

"Wilhelm explained that for many months he and his father's medical team worked only on Jews. They had to..." Again a silence. "They had to replicate the appropriate conditions in order to experiment with grafting."

"You mean they burned Jews so they could understand how to successfully graft skin?"

"Mrs. Messenger. It was war." These feeble words explained nothing and it seemed that Claus Adenauer knew that they did not. "I am sorry. It was horrible. There is no excuse." Pause. "Are you there? Mrs. Messenger, are you..."

"Yes."

"He was not telling me this to relieve his conscience. He was telling me to explain his actions, his work, the work he came to this country to do. His devotion to beauty and restoration. You see his daughter was..." Vale's eye was held by the lazy spin of the blue disk that sailed between Catherine and Earl Andrews. Back and forth it went, hand to hand. "Her face meant everything to him. She was a kind of angel for him. Can you understand?"

Suddenly she was tired, so very tired. "Can you understand?" the voice repeated in her ear. "Mrs. Messenger? Can you..."

But Vale had heard enough. She settled the receiver in its cradle.

EPILOGUE

On the following afternoon, Vale was aboard the *Requiem.*

The sails were raised, and they were heading east. The bow wave curled along the boat's sides and flattened behind them. But though she was there in body, her spirit was still caught among the specters of the previous day. Her dreams had been thick with fire and the cries of the dying.

"You're very quiet today," he said.

She was settled on the cushions against the cabin and was looking up at him where he stood behind the wheel, feet planted against the heel of the boat, "Things happened I need to talk about before I can get here."

"Vale, you *are* here. You've just brought some gear aboard. Talk."

"Melanie comes home tomorrow, and I am pretty sure she will go to live with her father." Win turned to see her face; she was staring out across the Sound as if into the future. "I know her father is a good, loving man. I know how important a father is." She looked now at Win; it was not easy to speak to him about fathers. "I will not fight Robert; we will work things out for her best. I don't want her to bend to my needs. I have seen enough of that."

"Wait till she comes aboard the *Requiem* and sails with us." And for a long while, nothing further was said.

Then he asked, "And what about Parthia?"

Vale told him about her encounter with the dying man, about the Moroccan book and its contents, and then about her conversation with Adenauer and the final disclosures he had made about Wilhelm Alexander.

"So Parthia's father was trying to make up for the torment he was part of, that he had inflicted on others?"

"So Claus believes."

"But he went to the other extreme, didn't he? Parthia was his experiment; he used her for his own needs. He tormented her."

"But now I know he was tormented also."

"Does that make it all right?"

"No, Not all right. Just more difficult to judge him."

"Ah, yes, I understand that." He was quiet for a while. "I have Biron to thank for this."

"For what?"

"Just one of many things that came up that night. Hate. And judgment." Win took a moment, recalling. "The people who blew up my wife and daughter---Biron asked me, 'Who were they if you give them a face?' And I realized that I had never given them faces. They were blanks. Biron said, 'See what happens if you let one of them be a father, a husband, a brother.'" Win looked down at Vale. "It broke me," he said. "It was the thing of all the things Biron did that night that broke me. No one, not even Dean, had ever asked me to do that."

"Maybe you weren't ready until then."

"Maybe I wasn't." The sound of the wind snapping in the Genoa caught his attention. He turned the wheel a few degrees, and the foresail stiffened "Evil is a kind of mask," he went on. "For years those people---Hasballoah, Syrian extremists, Palestinian terrorists, whoever they were---were faceless men to me, evil men, and I would gladly and personally have torn them limb from limb with my bare hands. But suddenly I saw that they were men who had been driven to extremity in their hate, their fear, and as a response to their own suffering."

"And did that make your own pain any the less?"

"The pain, no. The loss, no. But the hate. The hate lessened. Hate is a horrible thing, Vale. It makes life so simple, and yet it oversimplifies."

"And in its place what?"

"I don't know." And here with one hand on the wheel he leaned over and very gently kissed her on the top of her head and drew her up to him. "But something is different."

She came behind him and wrapped her arms around him and laid her cheek against his back. It was quiet here, out of the wind, warmer. That Wilhelm Alexander's acts were wrong, were terrible, there was no disputing that. But what he had suffered, his father, that time... well, that too mattered. And out of all this, for her, there was Win.

"Parthia's father never met you, Vale."

"What do you mean?"

"It's what you do," he said, "you interrupt the chain of reaction. Parthia will not do to her child, if she ever has one, what was done to her because of you."

"Oh, Win, surely you..." but he was not finished.

"You, Dean, Willa, Ben Farmer, Pamela. What are you trying to do if not to keep suffering from perpetuating itself. You break the chain. Someone has to do it. Maybe once the priests did it, though I'm not so sure about that. Maybe you all can only be partially successful. But, still, you try. Parthia, Julia, Arthur, Liza-Jane---yes, I know their names---all of them. Isn't that what North Forks is about in the end? A fork in the road. Choice. I'm here to tell you, Vale, I think it's possible. It was for me. Another chance."

Suddenly she was here on this boat, with this man, on this wide blue water. The swirl of thought and feeling settled as she stood in the lee of his body and felt the tilt of the deck under their feet and the gentle lunge of the boat through the water. It was all past figuring; it had become too complicated.

"Win, can you do the stop-the-boat thing? I'd like another chance with you." She was stepping around him now and was on the first stair to the cabin below and the big forward berth. She looked back at him, and he saw the mischief in her glance. A turn of the wheel, a knot in the line, and he followed Vale where she led.

THE END

*This charcoal rendering, done by Susan Pitzele, is based off the
image of the angel in Leonardo da Vinci's "Madonna of the
Rocks" in the Louvre.*